# TREASON

*The Erinnan Legacy*

*Treason and Truth*
*Book 1 of 12*

J.A. Cauldwell

## <u>Dedication</u>
For Chris

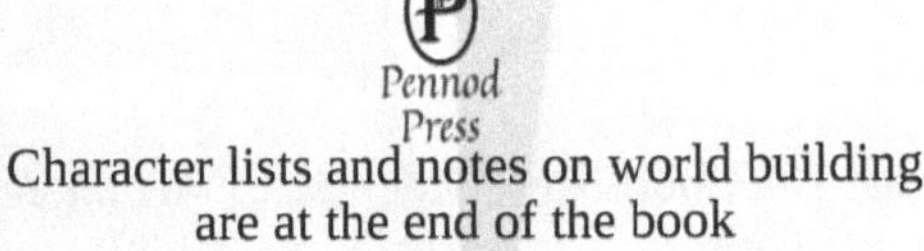

Pennod
Press

Character lists and notes on world building
are at the end of the book

# The Erinnan Legacy

## Treason and Truth

FROM THE PAST COMES MAGIC, FROM THE PRESENT, DANGER, GRADUALLY COLLIDING

| | | | | |
|---|---|---|---|---|
| <u>1</u> | TREASON | | <u>5</u> | THROWN |
| <u>2</u> | TERA | | | |
| <u>3</u> | TRAPPED | | | |
| <u>4</u> | TRAGEDY | | | |

## Stories From Erinna

EVERYBODY HAS A STORY AND SOMEBODY KNOWS IT

Standalone stories that may link to characters from other series.

<u>TIES</u>

# MAPS

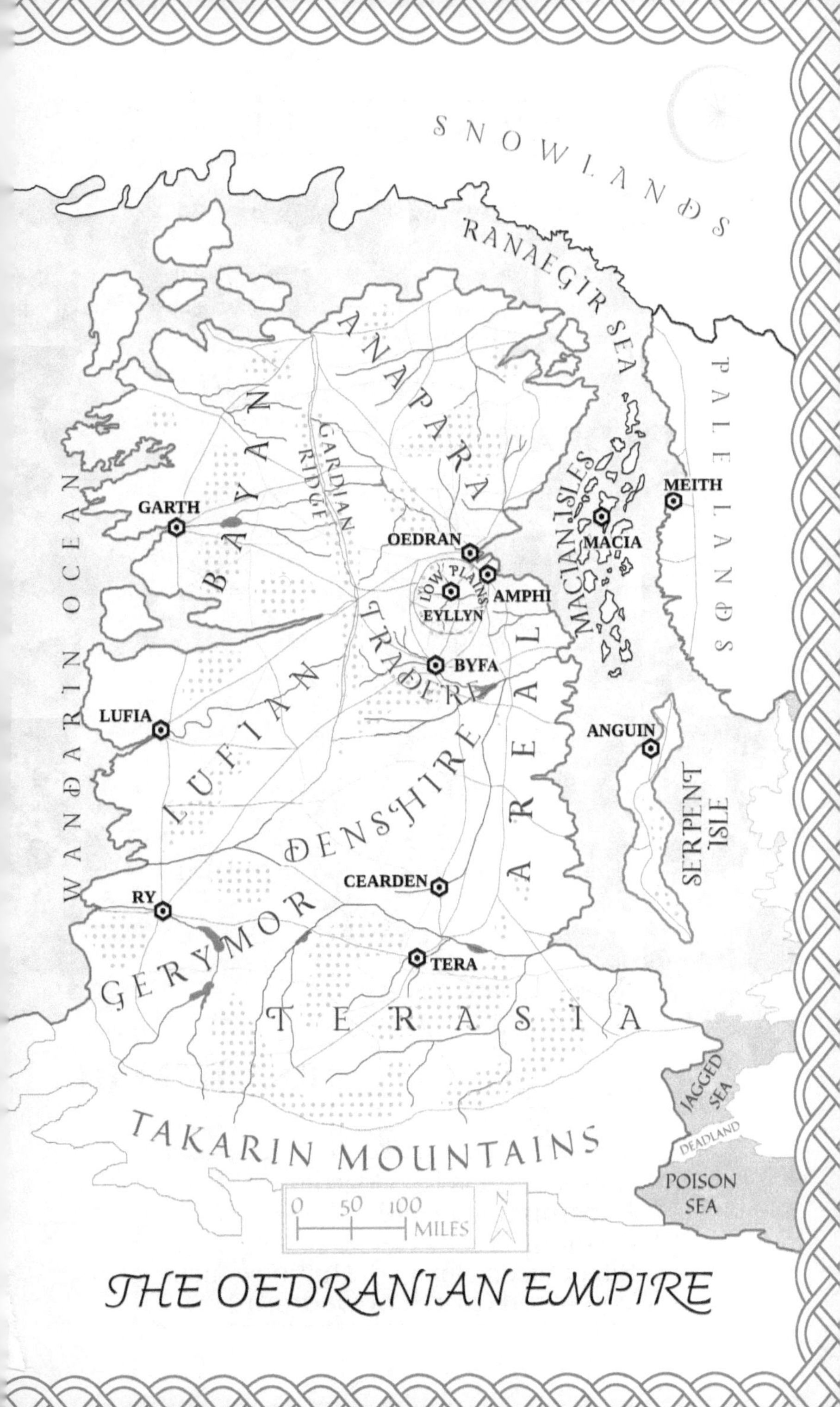


# THE OEDRANIAN EMPIRE

ENVIRONS OF OEDRAN
Paras Road
Torport Road
Carregshore Road
River Edra
River Edra
EDRA FERRY
WHARF REACH
Port Road
TWO WAYS
Garth Road
OEDRAN
CRABTREE
River Carn
CILFORD
Dallin Road
DELLWOOD
Hill Beck
River Enal
REX DALLIN
1: Pillars of Alcis | 2: Ceardlann
3: Encampment Field
4: Wishing Tree
5: Silversley's Farm | 6: Hillbeck Farm
7: Wynwood (North of Oedran)
N
0    1 mi

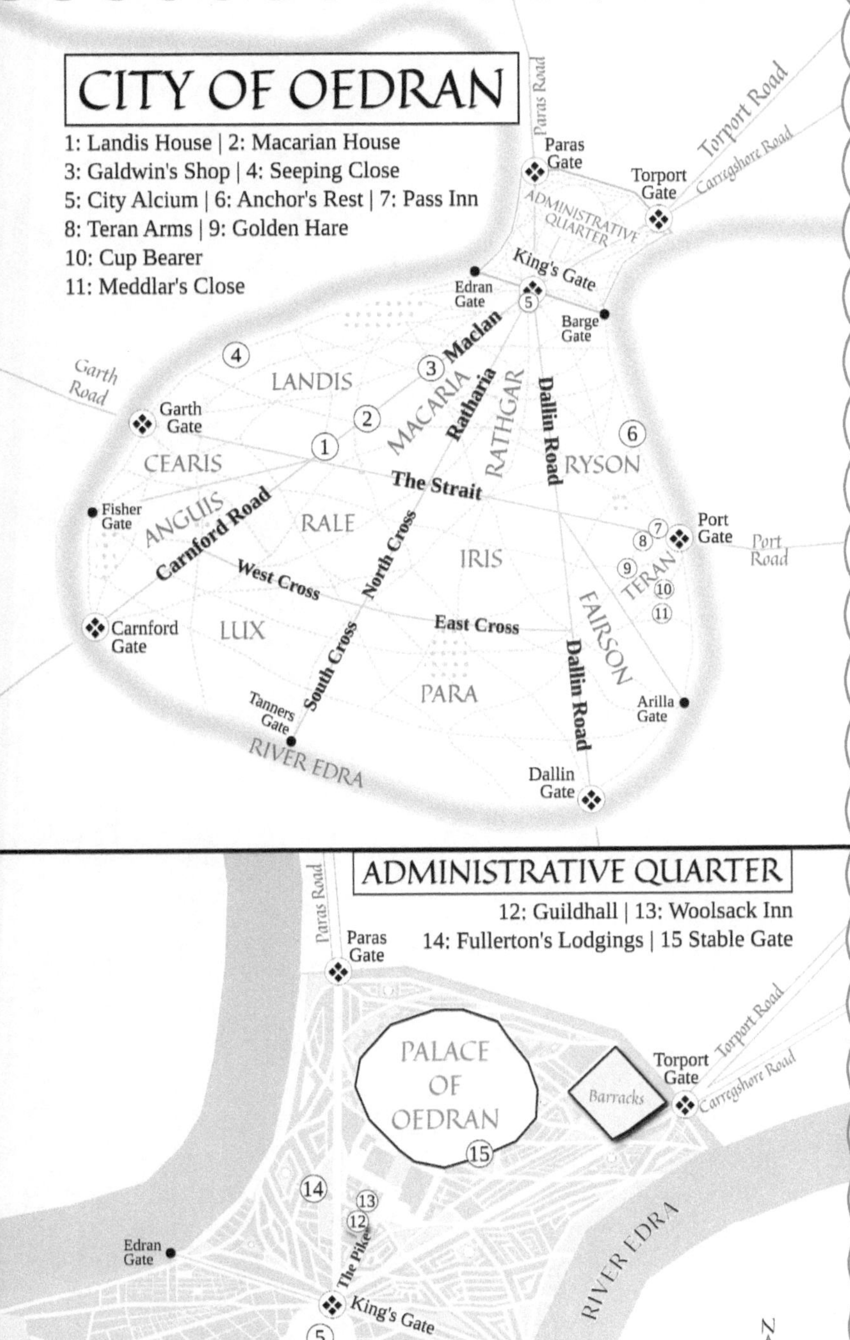

CITY OF OEDRAN
1: Landis House | 2: Macarian House
3: Galdwin's Shop | 4: Seeping Close
5: City Alcium | 6: Anchor's Rest | 7: Pass Inn
8: Teran Arms | 9: Golden Hare
10: Cup Bearer
11: Meddlar's Close
Paras Road
Torport Road
Carregshore Road
Paras Gate
Torport Gate
ADMINISTRATIVE QUARTER
King's Gate
Edran Gate
Maclan
Barge Gate
Garth Road
Landis
Macaria
Ratharia
Rathgar
Dallin Road
Garth Gate
Cearis
Angliis
Carnford Road
The Strait
Ryson
Fisher Gate
Rale
North Cross
Iris
Port Gate
Port Road
Teran
West Cross
East Cross
Fairson
Carnford Gate
Lux
South Cross
Para
Dallin Road
Arilla Gate
Tanners Gate
River Edra
Dallin Gate
ADMINISTRATIVE QUARTER
12: Guildhall | 13: Woolsack Inn
14: Fullerton's Lodgings | 15 Stable Gate
Paras Road
Paras Gate
Palace of Oedran
Torport Gate
Barracks
Torport Road
Carregshore Road
Edran Gate
The Pike
Guildhall
Woolsack Inn
Fullerton's Lodgings
King's Gate
River Edra
Barge Gate
N

# ARCHIVE

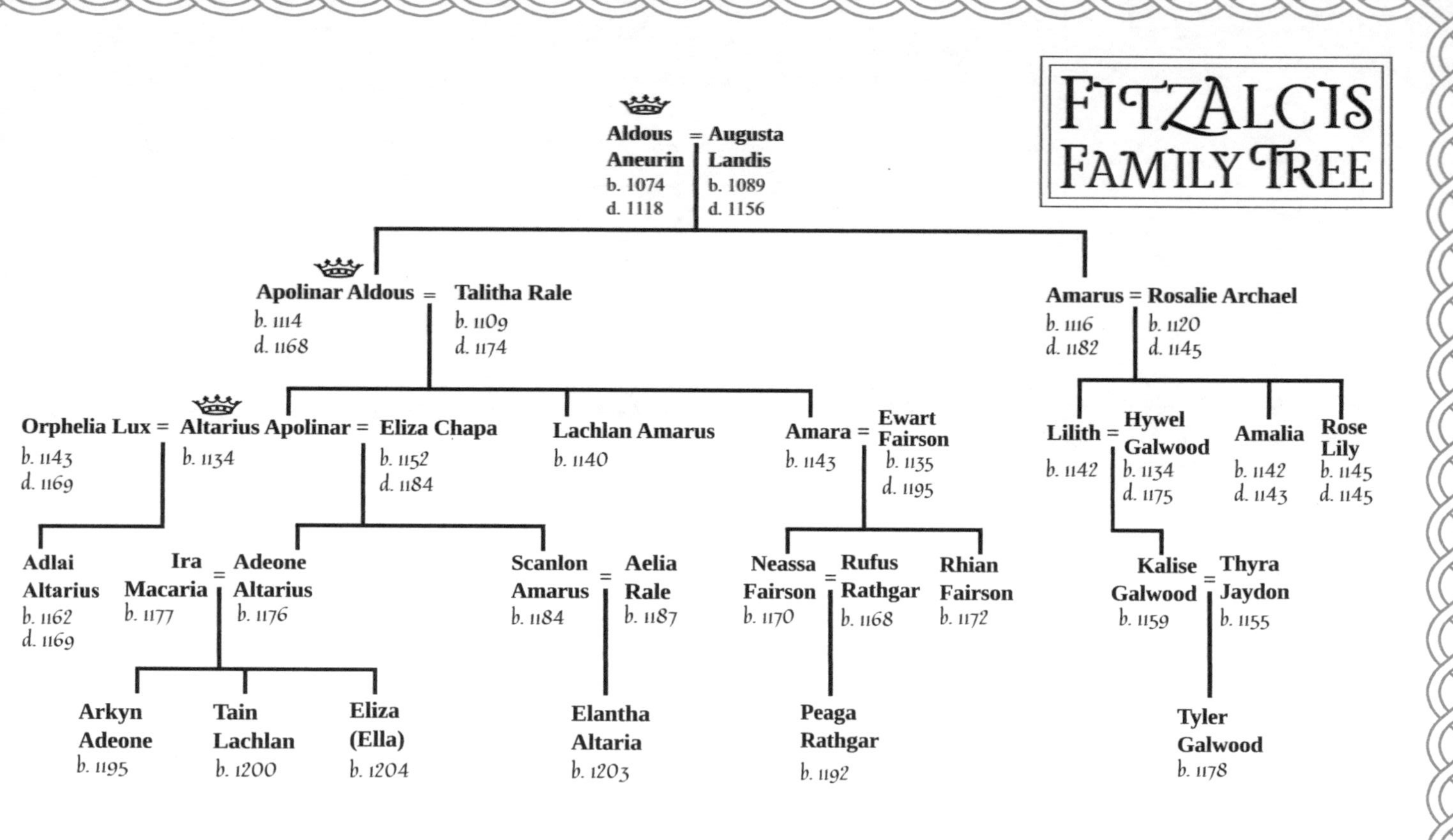

FITZALCIS FAMILY TREE
Aldous Aneurin = Augusta Landis
b. 1074
d. 1118
b. 1089
d. 1156
Apolinar Aldous = Talitha Rale
b. 1114
d. 1168
b. 1109
d. 1174
Amarus = Rosalie Archael
b. 1116
d. 1182
b. 1120
d. 1145
Orphelia Lux = Altarius Apolinar = Eliza Chapa
b. 1143
d. 1169
b. 1134
b. 1152
d. 1184
Lachlan Amarus
b. 1140
Amara = Ewart Fairson
b. 1143
b. 1135
d. 1195
Lilith = Hywel Galwood
b. 1142
b. 1134
d. 1175
Amalia
b. 1142
d. 1143
Rose Lily
b. 1145
d. 1145
Adlai Altarius
b. 1162
d. 1169
Ira Macaria = Adeone Altarius
b. 1177
b. 1176
Scanlon Amarus = Aelia Rale
b. 1184
b. 1187
Neassa Fairson = Rufus Rathgar
b. 1170
b. 1168
Rhian Fairson
b. 1172
Kalise Galwood = Thyra Jaydon
b. 1159
b. 1155
Arkyn Adeone
b. 1195
Tain Lachlan
b. 1200
Eliza (Ella)
b. 1204
Elantha Altaria
b. 1203
Peaga Rathgar
b. 1192
Tyler Galwood
b. 1178

# CHRONICLE

1168
Accession of
King Altarius

1169
Bayan
Rebellion

1175
Altarius marries
Eliza Chapa

1176
Birth of
Adeone

1184
Birth of Scanlon
Death of Queen Eliza

1203
Scanlon marries Aelia
Rale, Birth of Elantha

1200
Birth of
Tain

1195
Birth of
Arkyn

1193
Adeone marries
Ira Macaria

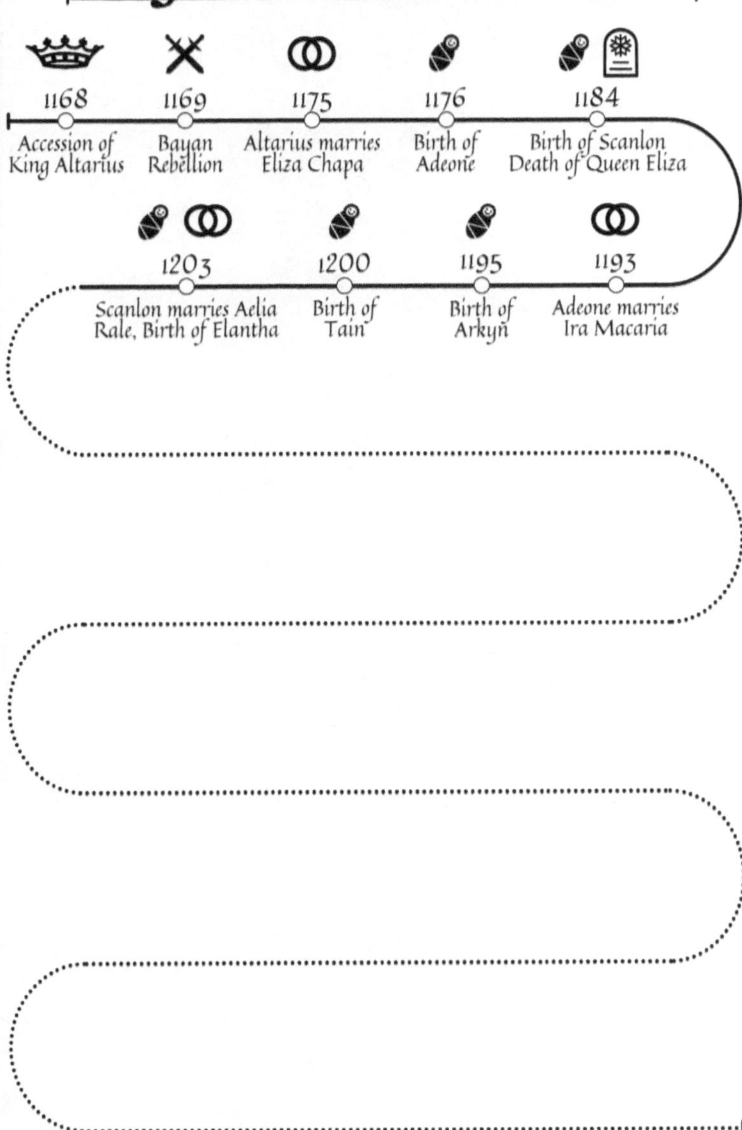

# TREASON

## PART 1

# Chapter 1
## CHANGING TIMES
### Imperadai, Week 31 – 18th Anapal, 4th Anapcis 1204
### Oedran

RUMOUR OF DEATH stalked the corridors of power, the streets of cities and the rooms of men. It dispersed on the winds of winter bringing the chill of the unknown. Death claimed even the strongest, not just the weak; it claimed the rich, not just the poor; it claimed adult and child alike, men and women, paupers and kings.

It drew close to King Altarius Apolinar FitzAlcis, holding out its hand, sapping the strength from his battle-hardened bones. He didn't want to fight; he had fought rebels, outwitted traitors, raised and lost family and now the hand that had snatched them reached out to him. Soon he would take it, following the path to his ancestors, reuniting with all those he had lost. It wouldn't be today, it wouldn't be tomorrow but it would be soon. He had people he loved still to protect.

"You've got to persuade Scanlon to come home," remonstrated Princess Ira. "Your father is—"

"Don't say it!" snapped her husband. "We're family but it's still treason."

"Your father needs both his sons with him."

"If you can talk sense into my brother, you're more than welcome to try. He says he isn't going to make the journey to Tera twice because I'm panicking."

"You're not panicking. Well, not without cause…"

Prince Adeone grimaced. "Father *might* rally." He cursed as a knock at their sitting room door interrupted their time alone. "Come in! Yes, what is it, Jacobs?"

His father's secretary bowed. "His Majesty has asked to see Her Elegance, Your Highness."

"We'll be there shortly," replied Adeone dismissively.

"Forgive me, sir, but His Majesty only sent for Princess Ira."

Adeone gave a curt nod, waiting for the door to close on the hapless man. "What have you done?" he teased.

"No idea. Should I be worried? He's never asked to see me alone."

"You'll be fine. I should get to Military Counsel. Advisor Rayburn's joining us and leaving him to the General may be a little unfair."

As the door clicked shut behind him, she turned to the windows, drinking in the view over the formal gardens towards the palace wall then over it to Palace Walk with its grand houses, and beyond those to where the buildings dropped away to the River Edra, circling the City of Oedran, capital of her wed-family's empire.

Checking her appearance in a mirror, she contemplated that city, the busy streets teeming with life; a hurried life of survival; a varied life of the poor, of traders and merchants, of lords and ladies; the very difference of position, of what made the city so contradictory. It hummed with the wind-blown rumour, whispered in the dark spaces: King Altarius was dying and change was coming. The rumour was true, but she shouldn't speak of it. To talk of the death of kings *was* treason, as her husband had reminded her. She tried to ignore her qualms about that and her appearance. Ella's birth wasn't that long ago. The changes were to be expected.

She hurried along the loop of the King's Corridor to the Audience Chamber doors, where the guards snapped to attention. Entering the opulent, gilded and polished room, she took in the familiar sight of arched panels painted with vistas of the empire: hills, forests, cascading rivers, rough seas, calm lakes and dry deserts; views of mountains and cities, of roads leading the eye to distant places or tantalisingly disappearing around corners.

As the dais guards snapped to attention; she inclined her head slightly – in acknowledgement to them and the throne they were guarding. Her skin tingled; soon her husband would sit there accepting the fealties of his lords. She wasn't sure she was ready for the change.

Turning right, she entered the more restrained Outer Office. The secretaries stood and she glanced at the elderly King's Administrator. He gave a slight bow before wordlessly showing her through the Inner Office to the King's Bedchamber where her wed-father's long-serving manservant opened the door and stood aside.

Rising from her curtsy, Ira met her wed-father's steely brown-eyed gaze. She shivered, even in the warm room with its fire-borne scents of apple and cinnamon. Adeone's hopes he would recover were for nothing. As the manservant left through the cleverly concealed servants' door, she turned to her wed-father.

Loose skin folded into deep wrinkles beneath her cool fingers as she took his scarred hand. Perching on the edge of the four-poster, a tenderness welled within her that few would have believed.

Quietly he said, "You'll soon be queen."

"You'll recover, sir."

"No, I won't. One can't recover from age." He squeezed her hand. "I'll join my ancestors quite happily. I'm *tired*, Ira, tired of the fight. It's time for my son's reign."

"Sire—"

"Don't deny the future, please – not here, not now. The day will come soon, but it won't be easy. Adeone will be a very different king."

"There's no doubt he is your son, though, Your Majesty."

"Physically speaking maybe not, but he's more like his mother was, which is why I've always found it hard to show him how much I love him. Too many memories, Ira, too many…"

Tears coursed slowly down his face. Without disturbing the silence, Ira pressed her handkerchief into his hand and glanced away as he wiped his eyes. Of everything she had seen in her years of marriage, her wed-father's frailty was the least expected.

He took a slow breath to steady his voice. "Keep loving him. He needs your love so very much."

"I don't think I could ever stop, Sire."

He searched her face. Hunting for any shadow of a lie or deception, or just for reassurance, she wasn't sure. Haunted eyes reminded her of his losses, of his loneliness since Queen Eliza's death.

"Good, but… Don't let him get so immersed in work that he misses the children growing. It's all too easy to do. I missed all their lives. I thought there were more pressing things, more important things, and I was never more wrong. Don't let him live with the same regret. Take care of the children – Elantha included."

"Surely, Scanlon and Aelia are able to—"

His hand twitched. "I don't doubt it but, promise me, if anything happens, to protect her as you would your own, and any siblings she may have in the coming years."

"Of course I will, Sire. You have my word."

Altarius sagged into his pillows. "Good. You can never tell what shocks the future brings. When you're a monarch, you must suspect *everyone*. Beware of trusting people. Don't let Adeone trust too many. No matter who they are. Just promise me that. Promise me that my son's heart shan't be his downfall. I trust your word, your care, your compassion as no other's."

Tilting her head slightly, she said, "You have my promise, Sire."

He studied her face once more. "You know, you've done him a lot of good. He couldn't have chosen better."

She blushed and studied their clasped hands. "I don't know about that, Your Majesty."

"I do and I'm still King." He squeezed her hand gently and whispered, as much to himself as to her, "Smoke and mirrors; that's all it is. Now, you'd better go. Let this old man get some rest. Give my love to the children."

"I will, Sire. They keep asking how you are. Arkyn especially."

"He's a good lad, that one. Keep him close whilst you can."

She replaced his hand on the coverlet and left in a thoughtful mood. Walking through the palace corridors, she didn't see the carvings, the gilding or the paint. She considered her wed-father and hoped, against evidence, that he wasn't dying. There had been a different side to him that day, a softer side, and she realised that maybe Adeone and Scanlon should have glimpsed it more often. She wanted to see more of it herself.

After dinner, Ira dismissed the servants before turning to her husband. He appeared drawn, but they were running out of time. "Your father looked pale earlier."

"Yes. I saw him after counsel. The doc says he's getting weaker."

"You need to get Scanlon home, Ad. It's time."

Despair washed over him. "He doesn't have to do what I say! He's the Justiciar of the Empire and I'm not Regent. I'm the King's Representative and heir, but that doesn't mean Scanlon can't do what he thinks is best for the Terasian Law Review, and that's what he's quoting at me every time I try. As brothers I outrank him, socially in Oedran I outrank him, for his official duties I don't. Father could order him home, but won't. By the time I can order the Justiciar around, it'll be too late. Aelia's tried and failed. I've even asked Uncle Lachlan to try but he's not got anywhere. Scanlon is as stubborn as a mule and the more we try, the worse he becomes. There's nothing I can do. There's just nothing…"

Ira cursed in the privacy of her head. The fact her wed-brother was being so intractable upset her more than she expected. He would surely regret not being in Oedran if Altarius died but Adeone was right: as Justiciar, only the King, or his Regent, could order Scanlon around and Altarius hadn't named Adeone as Regent simply because it would exacerbate the rumours that he was dying.

A week later, the message came from Doctor Chapa: Adeone and Ira were needed in the King's Chambers. They entered them quietly. Seconds later, Adeone sat by his father, holding his wasted hand. Ira moved around the bed and took Altarius' other hand, cursing Scanlon's absence.

With many pauses, Altarius murmured faintly, "Trust no-one, son. Love your wife and your children, but *trust* no-one. Implement my requests and bequests without fault. Give me your *word* that you'll do it."

"You have my word and my promise, sir."

"Ira… Keep him sensible."

Struggling to keep her emotions in check, she chided him to save his strength.

He held her gaze for a long moment. "My strength has gone. Don't… don't weep for me, Ira."

The door opened and his siblings and second wed-daughter entered. Ira moved away from the bed to stand with Aelia, but Adeone didn't want to leave his father's side; he wanted to have what time was left with him.

Altarius regarded his brother and sister. "The past is over… I'll give your greetings to them all."

"Thank you, sir. Make your presence known," replied Prince Lachlan.

Lady Amara sat where Ira had, her brother's hand in hers. "He always does, Lachy. Always keeps people waiting as well."

Altarius looked at her. With the last of his rapidly fading strength, he said, "Wish me luck, little sister."

"All the luck I can, Alt. Don't stand for any nonsense up there."

Altarius never heard the last words. His eyes glazed over whilst he turned to his son. Adeone reached over and with a shaking hand closed his father's eyes. The room was still. No-one moved for several moments; then Adeone jumped as Lachlan's consoling hand rested on his shoulder. Glad of the support it implied, Adeone didn't want to move, didn't want to recognise what had happened, but there were things to do. He drew a deep breath. The deepest he ever had. He rose and carefully put his father's hand down. Leaning forward, he kissed his father's brow in parting.

"Rest in peace at last," he whispered.

As he turned away from his father's body, everyone but his aunt knelt or curtsied; she sat watching her brother's motionless face; her own a mixture of contemplation and grief.

"No. Not now. All are equal in grief…" murmured Adeone.

"Just not in life, Sire," observed Lachlan. "You'll get used to it."

Adeone shook his head, amused in spite of himself and oddly grateful to his uncle for the moment of levity. "In that case, ruin your knees. Get up everyone, please."

Ira crossed over to him as he held out his hand, wrapping him in a hug as they gathered themselves. Silently she resolved to keep her promises to her wed-father, whatever the future brought. Lady Amara seemed unsettled – a stark reminder that times had changed and the reign of King Altarius Apolinar was already history.

# Chapter 2
## RETURN


THE POUNDING OF HOOVES on the road behind them made King Adeone turn in the saddle. He had almost returned to Oedran the previous evening but had told himself he was being a fool. He was away for two days, one night, that was all. Heart racing, he spotted the livery of a palace courier. His hands slipped on the reins. Taking a breath, he turned Pursuit and rode to greet the man.

He took the letter without a word. Doctor Chapa's seal did nothing to allay his fears. The brief missive merely told him Queen Ira had taken a turn for the worse and Chapa thought he would like to know, but Ira had insisted on him sending a note as opposed to contacting him via magical messenger. He didn't hesitate. Spurring Pursuit into a gallop, he headed for Oedran.

By the time he saw the city clearly, his heart pounded, his back ached and he had no escort. Gradually, the city dominated his view as he urged Pursuit on. Arkyn had chosen the name well and the horse, a true Anaparian Swiftfoot, revelled in a sustained gallop.

He was within hailing distance of the city walls now and could see the mosaic of stones, the areas under repair and those already finished. He should wait for his guards. Ignoring the nagging necessity, he slowed as he crossed the bridge, weaving around people, reining into a walk as he passed under the scaffolded arch. As he ducked low, he spotted a familiar figure and his heart plummeted further. His manservant wouldn't be waiting if it were good news. Nor would he be telling the city guards to keep people back as he was doing. He hardly noticed the army sergeant pushing himself away from the wall.

"Simkins, why are you here?"

"I thought it best, Sire. Her Grace is at Macarian House." His manservant's calm voice turned serious as he enquired where the King's guards were.

"Catching up. I should give them better mounts. Remind me, at some point. I'll meet you—"

A shout rang through the air; quick as lightning, the sergeant grabbed Pursuit's bridle as a pot crashed on the flagstones and shards went flying.

"What was that?" demanded Adeone.

"A pot, Your Majesty," replied the sergeant matter-of-factly. "It was knocked off the walk atop the gatehouse."

"Accident?" enquired Adeone, studying the man's face for it tugged at a memory.

"Yes, sir. A long piece of wood caught it."

"Then, thank you; that could have been nasty."

"Sire, if Pursuit had reared, you could have been killed," said Simkins.

"Yes, quite. Sergeant, your face is familiar, but I can't place you."

"I worked for Lord Macaria when Lady Ira was young… Sorry, Sire, I should, of course, have said Her Grace."

"If you worked for the family, Lady Ira will do," replied Adeone distantly. "Although it's now fifteen years since she carried that title. Where have they gone?"

"Into history, Sire. I was troubled to hear that she was so ill. I came to Oedran to hear news of her."

Adeone pulled himself out of the past. "Then I think we can do better than that for you. Any link with her past is dear to her now. Come and see her."

"It would not be right, Sire."

"Sergeant, I'm the one asking; how can it 'not be right'?"

The two men looked at each other. Adeone sensed a battle happening in the sergeant's head: what he wanted to do against what he should do, what his superiors would say if they found out and what he would face if he accepted the offer.

"If you will not come, at least tell me your name so I can tell her of your concern."

"It's Wynfeld, Sire, but I would like, very much, to see her again."

"Then meet me at Macarian House. You too, Simkins." Without giving his manservant the chance to object, Adeone spurred Pursuit on and moved at a trot down the street.

"He'll be heartbroken if the Queen dies," said Simkins sadly and later wondered at his rare confidence.

"I don't think he'll be the only one, Master Simkins." Wynfeld strode off through the crowds and momentarily wondered why the manservant didn't join him.

* * *

A short while later, Simkins entered the entrance hall of Landis House via the front door, enquiring of the new doorkeeper if Lord Landis was at home.

The footman's glance took in Simkins from his slightly disordered hair to his crisp white tunic, scarlet belt, loose white trousers and well-made leather shoes. He asked rather too pointedly who wanted to know.

Simkins told him, rather intrigued the footman hadn't at least recognised his uniform: scarlet was the colour of kings, white the colour of menservants. It wasn't difficult to deduce, that was the point.

Completely unabashed, Backery said that His Lordship was in the study. Simkins crossed the polished entrance hall and made his way to the old part of the house.

"Simkins? I thought you had a few days off. What's happened?" asked Landis.

"Her Grace is at Macarian House, my lord, and the doc isn't hopeful. The King's returned but alone, without his guards. I thought you'd want to know."

"Do you think it would help if I had Their Highnesses here for a couple of days?" enquired Landis, privately cursing his friend's stupidity with the guards.

"No, sir. I think the King needs them near him."

Landis nodded. "Lord Iris is presiding at Court for me today, just in case. I won't come and disrupt things but, if you think I'm needed, please let me know. Also, send Jenner this way. Marsh will now be duty sergeant."

"I understand, my lord. I'll keep you informed. Oh, you should know that one Sergeant *Wynfeld* of the army saved the King's life..." Simkins explained quickly and easily.

Landis raised an eyebrow. "Interesting. Thank you. I presume Fitz has decided he's needed at Macarian House in the circumstances?"

"Yes, my lord. He arrived as I did this morning."

Landis snorted. "There are days I wonder why His Majesty keeps Fitz as Captain of Intelligence when it's clear he would rather be at their side."

Simkins chuckled. "Privilege of being an Officer of the FitzAlcis, my lord. He delegates, the General can't object and His Majesty trusts him."

"That's why he's an Officer of the FitzAlcis," observed Landis dryly. "All right, Simkins. You've given me plenty of work to do. You'd better go and make sure His Majesty has all he needs."

Watching the manservant leave, Landis frowned to himself. Macarian House and Landis House were close but it was telling that the manservant had come to see him.

# Chapter 3
## A QUEEN'S PASSING
### Early Afternoon
### Oedran

**W**YNFELD STROLLED THROUGH OEDRAN, completely unaware he was a person of interest. He'd never intended to return, but events and his conscience had overtaken him. Claiming all the leave he could, he'd made the long journey to Oedran from Garth in Bayan. He'd saved leave in the hopes of retiring early when his time in the army ended; however, this was more important than those extra few weeks in a few years' time.

He hadn't expected to see his King, or to be invited to see Queen Ira again. He'd been leaning on the wall of the gatehouse to prolong the time until he had to face the past. Surveying the diverse and bustling city had helped calm his troubled mind. Oedran had survived battles and fire, famine and feasting, fevers and festivals. Limestone walls sparkled in the sun or glinted in the light of the two Erinnan moons. The wide cobbled streets with their smooth pavements invited the traveller in. Magnificent and domineering, crafted throughout centuries, Oedran's alluring and terrifying character overawed visitors. It was the living, breathing heart of the FitzAlcis' empire, which stretched from the northern coast to the southern mountains and from the western seas to beyond the eastern isles.

As he walked to Macarian House, the familiar sights and smells of home assailed his senses, bringing nostalgia with them: cookshops sold foods from all over the empire; spices from Serpent Isle vied with herbs from Lufian; roasting lamb from the Low Plains fought with pies from north Anapara; Bayan stews with large floury dumplings faced off against Macian seafood; the long slow-cooked meats of Denshire sold next to the sausages of Terasia and the fresh vegetable dishes of Gerymor; Pale Landian soups of all varieties complimented new-baked bread, made with Traderian and Arealian grains. As he passed a butcher's shop, he caught the metallic scent of blood before passing a cheesemonger where the earthy, ripe and musty tones were less disturbing, but he preferred the redolence of herbs and spices. The aromas mixed, providing a patchwork of variety for the senses marred by the pervading stink of humanity.

The buildings hadn't changed and people still moved with purpose or idled along the street, stopping to examine trinkets or essentials, to pass the time of day with friends or dodge aside to avoid others. Apprentices watched the wares at the front of the shops as their masters served within. Amongst the bakers and butchers, the cookshops and cobblers were the cloth traders and leather workers, chandlers and facilitators; there were the smiths and farriers, saddlers and tailors, inns and taverns, brothels and schools, all entwined together.

He passed a mail lodge with riders bringing news and despatching it to all places in the empire. Around the gates, people gossiped, trying to pick up the latest information; some would sell it on, others merely wanted to hear it to liven up their day. Wynfeld caught the eye of a boy who pretended he hadn't been about to slice a pouch from a distracted merchant.

Truly, the city never changed. Reassuringly, it was still the boiling pot it had always been. The words of an old man from his youth came to mind: be watchful, be careful but, above all, be alive for the city lives.

His feet found their own way to the servants' entrance of Macarian House and a friendly word to the guards saw him through into the yard, though he was aware they watched him as he knocked at the kitchen door.

A rosy-faced lady opened it. Hands on her hips, she said, "You've got a cheek, young man!"

Instinctively stepping back, Wynfeld shrank inwardly. "Aunt Maria, you're looking well."

"Humph. Never wrote, did you! What you turned up now for, like a bad talence?"

"Our King invited me. I—"

"He asked *you* to come *here? Now?*"

"It sounds unbelievable, but I assure you it's true," replied Wynfeld, placatingly.

"I've heard *that* before! You never were much good at sweet-talking. Wait there." With that – and all the family feeling she could muster – she shut the door abruptly and firmly in his face.

Wynfeld, his back against the doorpost, surveyed the kitchen yard. A grin slowly suffused his features; this was his childhood home and haunt, the flagged yard with the wall separating it from the stables, the outer wall to the street with its wrought-iron gate and the troughs of herbs against the house wall for easy picking. Chewing on a leaf of mint, as he had as a child, he grinned, glad he'd returned. Even his aunt berating him was worth it. Had he really been gone so long? It felt like no time at all.

Running feet and a spontaneous burst of laughter from the stable entrance heralded two boys with the familiar looks of their parents. They stopped abruptly when they spotted him. The elder took half a step forward, shielding his brother.

"Has father found out we come into the kitchens this way?" asked Prince Arkyn with an odd strain in his voice.

Wynfeld considered standing straighter but they probably had enough formality in their lives. "No, Your Highness. I am merely waiting for my Aunt Maria to verify some information."

"She made you wait outside?" enquired the bright-eyed, black-haired, nine-year-old incredulously.

"I'm afraid so, Prince Tain. Women can be so hard-hearted." He got no further before the door reopened and Maria said,

"You're to go to them in the gardens."

He pushed himself away from the wall. "Thank you. Now, is there *any* love left in that cold heart? Can you find a resting place for my kit bag? I also think Their Highnesses were on the scrounge for something."

Saluting smartly, he left, ruining the impression with a broad wink. He didn't see the way his grinning Princes watched him go or the way that his aunt shepherded them into the kitchen, but he did feel her suspicious glare and chuckled to himself. He'd pay for not having kept in contact, but he was glad to see her.

He idled through the grounds, lost in thought. Near the steps onto the lawn was a daybed with his King sitting on the bench beside it. Stopping a couple of steps up, he once more saluted and waited. His heart beat quickly against his ribs and he was sure his King would see it and wonder why.

Adeone glanced up, oblivious of Wynfeld's nerves. "Ah, you're here. My dear..." Adeone turned to Queen Ira. "Sergeant Wynfeld just saved my life. He used to work for your family, apparently. I thought you might like to see him."

Ira gasped. "Wynfeld? But... Truly... is it... you? I thought... No... matter..." There was so much light in her wan voice that both Adeone and the sergeant knew they had done the right thing.

"Yes, my lady, I've changed a bit though." His voice betrayed none of his angst as he stepped forward and saw how starkly her ashen skin contrasted with her black hair.

"No, you never could... Are you still... as skilled with horses?"

"I should say he is," remarked Adeone. "Calmed Pursuit down with a couple of words. Wynfeld, sit down; don't stand on ceremony, not today."

They spent the afternoon happily reminiscing, bringing up numerous anecdotes that kept Adeone chuckling. Halfway through the afternoon, the Princes joined them, listening to the stories. As the evening drew ever closer, Wynfeld contemplated how to excuse himself before he'd outstayed his welcome.

Ira said, "I'm tired; I think... I'll go in... for a while."

Adeone got up. "I'll find your chair."

"No, my dear... I'll walk. I'll be fine if Wynfeld and you... support me. I'm sick... of the chair."

"I'd much rather carry you – less chance of an accident."

Wynfeld caught the King's eye but kept quiet. They both knew Ira wasn't going to be walking anywhere.

"You can't ..." chided Ira, tiredness catching her words. "The doc has... said you must watch... watch your back, and I'm guessing... you rode recklessly... and harmed... more... than helped."

"My dear..."

"Why can't Sergeant Wynfeld carry mother?" asked Tain.

"Because, my prince, it would be inappropriate," replied Wynfeld quietly.

"Nonsense! Please do, if you can," requested Adeone.

Wynfeld smiled as he lifted Ira. Her head rested on his shoulder and he was surprised at just how light she was. As he carried her up the steps, he glanced at her.

She was watching his face. "Just like… that… last… day," she murmured with a wry smile.

"But no sprained ankle, my lady."

So quietly that Wynfeld thought it was only he who'd heard, she whispered, "No, just… a… sprained… heart… Look… after… them, Lex. I'm… so… so… tired."

Her eyes closed as she left them.


Entering the house, Wynfeld glanced at King Adeone to see tears in his eyes. He knew.

"Arkyn, which room has the Queen been using?" asked Adeone, hiding behind formality.

"Her childhood one, sir," whispered Arkyn, not wanting to disturb her.

Once they reached the room, Wynfeld laid Ira gently down and would have left if Adeone hadn't stopped him with a hand on his arm.

"Thank you. It has been the ending she would have wanted: laughter, family and friends."

"I am truly sorry, my king." He glanced at his Princes' pale faces, took a breath but words failed him; he left the family together, making his way to the kitchens where Maria snapped at the potboy to get a tankard of beer for him.

"You've been privileged, haven't you?"

"Aunt Maria, not now," replied Wynfeld, drained of emotion.

She quietly retreated from recrimination and moved with him to one side of the busy kitchen.

"Lady Ira died in my arms. I'm so sorry, aunt."

"No!" Maria's anguished cry silenced the kitchen.

Wynfeld held her close as her eyes filled with tears and her face drained of colour.

"Nice to see you, young Wynfeld, but what's happened?" asked one of the cooks.

Wynfeld swallowed. It wasn't his place to tell them, but he had little choice. "Queen Ira has started her journey to the ancestors."

Gasps and sobs shattered the stillness.

"May they greet her kindly and protect those she loved," intoned the cook.

"Come on, we've still got a job to do. You sit yourselves there. No, Maria, take time whilst you can. The Princes won't need anything for a while."

Wynfeld persuaded his aunt to sit down and accepted a replenishing tankard of ale. A plate of food appeared next to it and someone squeezed his shoulder in mute support. The business of the kitchen carried on around them: the staff silent. There were tears in eyes and hands that shook as they prepared the evening's meals.

Long after dinner was served and cleared, Maria said, "Come on, I've made you a bed up. I ought to see that—"

"Aunt, have I ever told you what a *wonderful* woman you are?"

"No, but with the amount you've drunk I'm sure I'll be hearing it a lot." When they got to the privacy of a bedroom, she chided gently, "Why *did* you come home, lad? Your heart will just break again."

Wynfeld murmured something so softly that Maria couldn't hear it. When she did catch anything, it was impossible to decipher.

She whispered, "Drown your sorrows in sleep, lad; it's better for your liver."

# Chapter 4
## REACTION
Evening
Landis House

TAKING THE LETTER his manservant held out, Landis ran his thumb over the plain seal. The lack of a cachet spoke a thousand words that Adeone's hand alone could not.

"Who delivered this, William?"

"My son, sir."

Dreading the contents, Landis broke the red wax. Moments later he was staring at the page, unseeingly. Ira had been his friend as much as his cousin, more than his Queen. Folding the letter carefully, he went to find his wife.

His face must have told a thousand stories, for as soon as she and their eldest children saw him, she asked,

"Ira?" When he nodded, she said, "May our ancestors welcome her."

Glancing between her parents, Julia let out a small sob. Landis simply hugged her tightly. Julius blinked back his tears. Men didn't cry. His mother held out an arm and he shook his head.

"It's fine to be upset. We are."

Julius hesitated but crossed to her. Realising she really was distressed, he returned her enveloping hug. The silence lasted for many minutes before Julia dried her eyes.

"How's Uncle Adeone?"

Landis said, "I didn't speak with him, but I expect he's emotionally shattered."

"Can we see him?"

"It may be better to wait for a time. Let him and your nearcousins adjust."

"Can you tell them we're thinking of them?" asked Julia.

"Of course. He's never in doubt about that."

"Can we write?" suggested Julius.

"If you want to. Just give them a couple of days."

A few minutes later, Cornelia persuaded the twins to go to bed. When she returned, she found her husband pale and drawn.

"How's His Majesty really?"

"I don't know. Honestly, Cornelia, I don't. He wrote, his hand wasn't steady and he didn't seal the letter properly. So, I can guess that he's not good. I saw her yesterday. I knew she was weak but I didn't think it would be today."

Cornelia sat on the arm of his chair and held him. He pulled her onto his lap, hugging her tightly as he let the realisation of loss wash over him.

"She's with Ella now."

Cornelia swallowed. "Yes, but the boys will miss her so much."

"She'll see Aelia as well."

Cornelia stilled. Her sister had taken her own life. It wasn't something she wanted to talk about or even acknowledge. Her wed-brother, Lord Scanlon, hadn't invited them to Aelia's funeral. He'd seen to everything before he informed them and used Princess Ella's death, which had occurred around the same time, to excuse his actions. So, to her, Aelia was forever elsewhere in the empire, not with their ancestors.

Landis realised he'd said the wrong thing. "I'm sorry. I'm so sorry. I'm not myself."

"I know. We've got to be there for our nearsons now, Festus, like never before."

"I asked Simkins if it would help if we had them to stay for a couple of days, but he thought not. He was right, I think. Adeone *will* need them close now."

"I wasn't meaning that," clarified Cornelia. "We need to be available to them if they want to talk. Arkyn's a year older than the twins and will soon be starting to take up duties. It'll only be a couple of years before he'll be touring the empire doing provincial reviews. He and Ira were close, Festus."

"He's close to Adeone as well."

"Yes, but not in the same way," explained Cornelia. "He feels the expectations more with Adeone. He doesn't want to disappoint him. Ira told me he fears the future. He'll do what he has to without complaint but he will need someone to talk to."

"I know. As will Tain and Adeone, for that matter." He whispered, "I don't know what I'd do if I lost you, Cornelia."

"You'd cope for our children, as Adeone will cope for his."

"How many have we got again?"

"Five, as you well know."

"Hmm. I might like a couple more."

She gave him a well-practised look, leaned down and kissed him gently. He responded immediately, then stopped just as suddenly. Carefully, Cornelia pushed his dark hair away from his forehead. Fourteen years of marriage and she knew him better than almost anyone else. He needed to acknowledge his emotion before he could work through it.

After a moment, she disentangled herself and poured him a whiskey. Turning back, she noticed his glazed eyes and smiled sadly to herself. It wasn't an evening for laughter or conversation. She put the drink on the table next to his hand and sat at a small desk, pulling out a sheet of paper. As she was sealing the letter, Landis asked who she was writing to.

"Feronia."

"It won't get to her before the news. Ifor will tell her…"

"I know, but I like writing to my wed-sister. Don't worry, I obviously sent your love."

Landis grimaced. He loved his sister and wished she lived closer than the Low Plains, but there was a difference between that and admitting it.

"I don't have to send the letter."

"Yes, you do. I should contact her myself. She and Ira were close as girls." He swallowed. "Why do I feel so ripped apart by this?"

"Because you loved your cousin and know what her family must be going through. You'll be better when you've seen Adeone at least." Changing the subject, she asked, "What was that with Sergeant Jenner earlier?"

"Oh, I was sacking him. The King arrived in Oedran without guards and there were none waiting for him. Pursuit is a quick mount and Adeone an excellent horseman, but they shouldn't have been as far behind as Simkins said. At the very least, if Jenner had realised that His Majesty was outstripping them to such a degree, he should have alerted Marsh to get guards to him at the Garth Gate, but, apparently, he didn't think about that. He left the King exposed. I can't allow that as Defender."

"Good. Who will you promote?" enquired Cornelia.

"No-one for the moment. I'll need to talk over the options with His Majesty and there will be less pressure on the King's Guard now, so it can wait a short time. They'll all know there's a vacancy and will be vying for my attention. I'll get the contenders thoroughly checked. It should keep Fitz quiet. Though he's at Macarian House, so it'll be his sergeants doing the work."

"I'm glad he's there. It'll be a weight off Adeone. You know he doesn't trust any other guard the same way."

"Neither do I," admitted Landis. "I'm not going to interfere. Though at some point, in the not-too-distant future, Fitz will have to retire. He's been with them since 1169."

"Maybe don't say that to His Majesty."

"Would you mind if I invited the King for dinner soon?"

"I'd prefer it if you invited *Adeone*. Make sure he realises he's always welcome, that we can make it private and that I still don't need warning."

# Chapter 5
## PROMOTION
Tretaldai, Week 12 – 24th Lowal, 17th Lowis 1209
Oedran – Macarian House

THE FOLLOWING MORNING, Wynfeld awoke to a thumping headache and heart. The subdued atmosphere of the kitchen suited his mood as he sat peeling potatoes, losing himself in memories. He'd see his aunt when he could and then start the lonely march to Garth and his regiment. He'd helped clear lunch away when Simkins informed him the King wanted to see him.

Again, he walked through the house in a dream; memories assailing him at every turn. Beside him, Simkins tried to lay out the rules for an audience with their King: answer all questions honestly, agree when required, never disagree, don't answer back or ask questions, stick to the subjects raised and don't comment on personal matters, however tempting. Their King would direct the conversation. All Wynfeld had to do was follow the path.

He entered the study to another jolt of the familiar: the desk in front of the square-paned window to his right, the comfortable chairs around the fireplace to his left. The last time he'd been in this room, Lord Macaria had been sacking him and for a moment he felt like that young groom again, not the seasoned sergeant he'd become.

His King exclaimed, "By Alcis you look rough!" as a greeting.

"Sorry, sir; got slightly drunk last night."

"Wish I could have joined you," remarked Adeone when they were alone.

"Now, after everything that happened, I'd like to offer you a commission in Oedran. I've spoken to your captain already."

Wynfeld blinked. "What does Captain Sharparu say, sir?" Even after the events of the previous day, he hadn't expected a promotion.

"If you really want to know, Wynfeld, he said he'd be sorry to see you leave but he always had the feeling that *you* would end up being *his* commanding officer. Something about every good sergeant he's ever had ending up promoted. For some strange reason, he normally finds out when they're on leave and have come to Oedran. I told him to take it as a compliment. Now, I can understand that you might like some time to think about it. So, tell me, Prince Tain mentioned they'd bumped into you before you reached the gardens. What was the little rascal up to?"

Wynfeld tried to form the correct words. "It wasn't anything nefarious, Sire."

He could feel his King taking the measure of him in a way he hadn't done the day before. There was a look in his eye, a certain set to his head, a stillness that was difficult to pinpoint.

After a couple of moments, his King observed, "I don't believe you'd tell me if it were. Do you mind explaining why?"

"Not at all, Sire. I don't think harmless fun should be used against lads who have the kind of responsibility my Princes do."

Adeone gave a short nod of approval. It was a pleasant change to find someone who *wouldn't* tell him what his sons were up to. The more he *knew*, the more he had to do something about. They had to be boys before they were men.

Wynfeld, who'd tried not to see the telltale worry lines on his King's face, made up his mind; Simkins could keep his rules. He took his future career well and truly in both hands. "Do you mind if I mention something, Sire?"

"I'll know when I hear it."

"Prince Arkyn is looking too highly strung, sir."

For several moments, Adeone considered Wynfeld gravely. The sergeant had literally marched from one side of the empire to the other for Ira because he'd heard she was ill; he'd not expected to see her, to become embroiled as he had in the events of the moment.

With that in mind, the King said, "Will you accept the commission?"

Remembering Ira's last request, Wynfeld saw he had no choice. If the commission was in Oedran, he'd be able to keep an eye on her family more easily. "Yes, Sire. I would like to, very much."

"Right. Please kneel." Adeone took Wynfeld's oath before saying, "Sit down. Everything I am about to tell you will go no further than this room. To answer your comment about His Highness, I'll shortly be sending your Princes to the Rex Dallin for their health and their safety. Their mother's death changed more than they can possibly understand. Their lives are in greater danger now than ever before."

"Sir, I don't mean to disagree or question you, but the idea that anyone could wish to harm Their Highnesses must be wrong."

"Is it? Maybe you have been out of Oedran for too long. I'm going to take your mind back to 1204; the year my father died. My brother turned alunan-age – taking over the full duties of the Justiciar of the Empire – and declared that he was dropping the title 'Prince'. Shortly after my coronation, he made a couple of comments. They were nothing in themselves, but the look in his eye and the way he said them worried me. It has since come to my attention that he is planning to kill me. More importantly, though, he is planning to kill your Princes as well. I think, however, he'll dispose of me first."

Half incredulous, the new Captain Wynfeld protested, "Sire—"

"I assure you, this is all true. Lord Scanlon may only be twenty-four, but he wants absolute power. To get that, he must murder my family and myself. I can't see him allowing Prince Tain to take over as Justiciar of the Empire; he, himself, would lose too much power." Adeone paused to collect his thoughts. "I, this will sound odd but I had a dream the other night…" He explained two dreams, saw Wynfeld's confusion and continued hurriedly, "However, Captain, the fact remains that Lord Scanlon wants us dead and our ashes cast to the winds. He has become more dictatorial recently. He doesn't notice his daughter or care for her. The Queen brought Lady Elantha into our nursery because of that." Adeone paused. "That's by the by though. The officer you are replacing is going with Their Highnesses. He's overseen your new regiment for years, but there's no-one I trust more with my sons' safety."

"It's not a new commission then, Sire?"

Adeone smiled to himself. "No. You've become my chief spy. You'll be overseeing the intelligence regiment, in charge of making sure that plots don't succeed and that I know what's happening in the empire; *especially* if people don't want me to know it. Tangentially, you'll be protecting Their Highnesses and Lady Elantha, though guarding is carried out by my guard or the Palace Guard. You will never be off duty. If you're in the city, keep your eyes and ears open. I understand you are on leave for another week and a half. Report to General Paturn, at the barracks, when your leave ends… and, Captain… Thank you for all you did yesterday. I will never forget it."

The two men looked at each other, somehow acknowledging shared grief in the glance, before Wynfeld saluted and left.

* * *

Once outside the study, he took a deep breath but never got as far as letting it out before a small hand grabbed his sleeve and started pulling him along the landing.

"Where are we going, my prince?"

"The nursery."

As they reached the door, a well-worn officer stepped out and barred their way.

"Fitz, let him pass!" wailed Prince Tain.

"Your Highness, I'm sorry, but the King's orders are to let no-one in today, especially if they have any bladed weapons and this gentleman has quite a few."

Tain sighed but he'd learnt to respect Fitz. "He's just been with father."

"Then I'll let him pass, but he must leave the weapons here."

Wynfeld turned to Tain. "If those are your father's orders, we must abide by them, sir." With a swift movement, he drew his sword and passed it over, took out the two daggers from the back of his tunic and the one from the front, before removing a knife from his boot. As he handed it over, Fitz, with raised eyebrows, asked,

"Any more? Wrist knives, maybe? How about a sheathed blade hidden between your shoulder blades, just in case?"

Tain was smiling; laughing at the rituals of an adult world.

To keep the smile, Wynfeld theatrically patted himself down all over before turning to Fitz. "Nope, that's it, sir. I should try the shoulder blade idea."

"What is your name?"

"Wynfeld, sir."

"What does it matter?" groused Tain. "Come on."

As Tain dragged Wynfeld past Fitz, he raised his eyebrows, amused.

Once in the privacy of the nursery, Tain asked, "What did you tell father we were doing in the grounds?"

"I didn't tell him anything, Your Highness."

"You *didn't*?" cried Tain, incredulously.

"No. Whatever you and Prince Arkyn were doing was your own business; it wasn't harming anything other than, possibly, your appetite for dinner."

Tain let out a whoop of joy.

"Tain, have some propriety. Think what it looks like!" snapped Arkyn entering.

Tain's face fell as though he'd been hit, his eyes filled with tears and he ran from the room. As he left, he choked, "Don't you ever feel anything?"

Arkyn let him go, dispassionately, it seemed. "I'm sorry about that, Sergeant, but my brother has to learn that there are modes of behaviour that people expect from us."

"Forgive me, sir, but if they expect anything other than the normal highs and lows of grief, then they are inconsiderate fools. If you can't act naturally at home, in the privacy of your rooms, then the world has turned very harsh."

"The world is always harsh to us."

"Not as harsh as you are to yourself, I think." The words were out before Wynfeld could stop them.

"You'd better explain that comment," ordered Arkyn, turning into a figure of authority.

Wynfeld realised once again that times had changed. When he'd last been in the house, Prince Arkyn hadn't been born. Oedran had altered from the city of his youth, but he recognised the tone of authority easily. Prince Arkyn would become a senior officer in the army, above even the General, within a year and had a steadiness of gaze unusual in a fourteen-year-old.

"Very good, sir. Since I saw you yesterday, I've thought you are on a tightrope. All your nerves are strung out trying to contain your feelings. In the last two years, you have lost a sister and now your mother. You are trying to be the one who doesn't fall to pieces, bottling up everything you feel to get through the day; thinking your father isn't, therefore, having to worry about you as well. Sir, forgive me, but he is worried, exceedingly worried. You are looking strained, and that will never go unnoticed in a warm and loving family. By hiding your feelings, you are storing up trouble. If you're not careful, soon you will break." Wynfeld had been watching Prince Arkyn's face change from hard determination into apprehension. "I'm being too presumptuous, I'm afraid."

"No, I asked you to explain. Is he really worried?"

"Yes. I remember His Majesty as a young man. He has lost more joy of life than age and grief can account for."

"Everyone expects me to cry but I can't," admitted Arkyn, almost whispering; he had become a child once more.

"Then what do you need to do?" Wynfeld matched his voice.

"Talk to mother…"

"Ah." Wynfeld considered for a moment. Being careful didn't have to mean being remote. His Prince was glancing into the corners of the room, as though he wanted somewhere to hide, somewhere to retreat from expectation. For a brief moment, he considered fetching his aunt, but instinctively realised his Prince wouldn't confide in her and he clearly needed to talk to someone.

"I am more than willing to listen. I can never presume to fill her place… but I would like to listen, not only for your sake, but for hers as well."

Arkyn could never explain why, in that moment, he trusted Wynfeld so completely. He stood realising that everyone left in his life would expect him to fulfil his role, not be himself. His father never showed any expectation but they both knew it was there. Arkyn had to become a man who could be king, Tain a man who could be justiciar; it was written in their lineage and in their birth. Their mother had made the weight of that fade away and Arkyn would miss that even though he couldn't explain the realisation. It was a nugget of understanding, ephemeral and fleeting, the shape of an idea. Maria would have listened but he was getting too old to run to her. He felt brittle, fragile, friable, as though the slightest thing would make him shatter. After a moment of contemplation, he poured two glasses of water. Holding something would help. He glanced around the cluttered room for somewhere to sit. Oddly, he didn't want to sit in a comfortable chair; he wanted the presence of something solid, so he settled himself with his back against a trunk and motioned to Wynfeld to find himself somewhere to sit as well.

Wynfeld considered carefully and decided it might be easier for Arkyn to talk if he didn't have to look at anyone; he settled himself beside his Prince and waited for a few moments before saying,

"Your mother and I used to play in here as children."

Arkyn rolled the glass in his hands. "I wish we were anywhere else."

"Why?"

"Because then she would be with us still… I know that's stupid but… How did you get to know her?"

"I grew up here as well. Your grandfather was very forbearing. My parents couldn't afford to raise me, so Aunt Maria took me in. Your mother and I were the only children in the house. It was easier for my aunt to keep an eye on us together. That dwindled when I started working. Then I was outside in the stables mainly and it was just when out riding that we talked."

"She liked to ride. Always said it reminded her of old friends… It must have been of you, thinking about it."

"No, sir. She used to ride with other ladies often. Lady Leila Ryson, the Rale sisters and others. They liked the Wynwood best."

"She used to take us to the meadows beyond the Wynwood when we couldn't get away to Ceardlann easily. I'll miss that."

"There's nothing wrong in missing what has made us happy."

Arkyn took a sip of water. "Isn't there? We're taught to avoid feelings."

"So are soldiers, but it doesn't always mean you shouldn't feel."

"What does it mean then?" asked Arkyn, perplexed.

"Well, it means not letting them rule you all the time, picking the moments to let yourself feel carefully. You can still feel. You must still let yourself feel, otherwise everything becomes twisted up inside and that is destructive. That's why I didn't think anything of Prince Tain's enthusiasm. Grief comes in waves. There isn't a time for it to be over. There isn't a moment you can say 'enough'. There isn't even a moment when you can say 'I should be feeling this'. It is normal to be numb, to be angry but it's also normal to forget in fleeting moments."

Arkyn considered that. "When Ella died mother didn't smile for months. When grandfather died, father was quiet and distant for so long. I tried to help but... Well, Uncle Lachlan told me just before he died that people must work things out before they can be themselves again."

"In many ways, he was right," replied Wynfeld carefully. "It takes everyone a different amount of time. There's nothing wrong with that, my prince."

Arkyn swallowed. "Father..." he trailed off before saying, "I wish I could turn back time to when I was eight. Grandfather, Uncle Lachlan... they were both alive... We were happy."

Wynfeld's heart went out to Arkyn. "It's been a tough few years for your family."

"It feels like it won't end and I can't say that to father. I feel like... Well, like everyone I love dies."

"I can understand why, but it's not your fault, any of it. Your grandfather was elderly and had lived a hard life, sir. Your great-uncle, well, sometimes deaths are sudden. Your sister's death was an accident, a tragic accident from what I heard and when I heard, even I wept for her. Your mother—"

"Did you weep for her?" asked Arkyn bitterly.

"Yes, and then I got very drunk," answered Wynfeld honestly. "My aunt had to put me to bed last night and she'll not let me forget it for years, I think."

"How is she?"

Wynfeld looked sideways at him. "Very emotional in her own way. She loved your mother dearly."

Arkyn blinked hard. "I know. When Ella died, Maria was the only one my mother would let near her."

"That must have been difficult," said Wynfeld.

"She didn't want me, us, to see her distressed but we heard her. Father wasn't here, Uncle Festus couldn't calm her, only Maria could and I felt so useless. I always feel useless. I can't... I want to hide. I want to run away and hide and never come back."

"Facing what you are, I can understand that," admitted Wynfeld without thinking.

"I can't though, can I?"

"Probably not. Someone would find you. It doesn't mean that you shouldn't be able to get time to yourself if you want it."

"With Tain around, that's easier said than done."

"His Highness does seem to love life."

"Yes. It's not that I don't…"

As Arkyn continued talking, Wynfeld felt the stress slowly ebbing away. He simply listened and answered, prompted and let silences mature. They didn't notice when Maria put her head around the door, didn't know that she kept Tain and Elantha busy elsewhere. Three hours later, long-held-back tears pricked at Arkyn's eyelids. Slowly, they began to flow. By the time evening arrived, the tears had dried and Arkyn had curled up asleep. Wynfeld left the room to find Maria.

Between them, they got Arkyn into bed without waking him. As they left, Adeone was coming along the landing.

"Maria, how are they?"

"As well as can be expected, Sire."

Adeone nodded. "Captain, what are you doing here?"

Before Wynfeld could reply, Tain appeared.

"I asked him here, father."

"Why?" queried Adeone suspiciously.

"To see what he'd told you, sir."

"Being inquisitive isn't always a good trait."

Tain's face dropped. "No, sir."

"Moreover, I doubt, having experienced Wynfeld's honesty, one that will get you very far. Did it get you anywhere?"

"No, sir." Tain grinned. "Arkyn might have had more luck though."

Adeone's brow creased. "We'll see. Captain, I'd like a word."

* * *

Wynfeld followed his King to the study with some trepidation. Had he pushed the chance acquaintance too far, presumed too much? If it had been the Palace, would he have made the same offer to Prince Arkyn? *Should* he have left the talking to other people? Whether he had been right or not, it now didn't matter. He couldn't change what had been and, as they entered the study and the door closed behind them, he remembered the ease with which people could confide in virtual strangers and yet not tell their nearest and dearest their thoughts.

"Captain, what did Prince Tain mean?" demanded Adeone.

"I sat with Prince Arkyn and listened to him talk for the afternoon, Sire. He needed to get things off his chest."

"Anything I should know about?"

"Sire, it was in confidence."

"Captain!" Adeone's tone lost all hint of reasonableness and tolerance.

Wynfeld's gaze fixed forward. "No, Sire, nothing that could be harmful."

"Thank Alcis for that." Relief poured off the King in waves and he sank onto a chair, obviously exhausted.

A knock at the door heralded the arrival of a sleep-tousled Arkyn, who'd been woken by Tain fretting that he'd got Wynfeld into trouble. He glanced at the captain before saying, "Sire, Wynfeld was listening to me. I needed to talk so badly."

Adeone studied his son. The youth had returned to his face. He turned to Wynfeld but the captain had gone. Somehow, Adeone reflected, he was pleased. His new captain apparently had tact and understanding. Crossing to Arkyn, he pulled his son into a hug before sitting with him for the evening, just the two of them.

* * *

Wynfeld entered the kitchens in search of sustenance. By the time he'd polished off a plateful of food his aunt had arrived. She clipped him around the head, as though he was still eleven.

"So then, *Captain*..."

"I was going to tell you, Aunt Maria," said Wynfeld hastily.

"Hmm. Well, congratulations. Where's your commission?"

"Oedran, so I'll be calling round to see you more often."

"That won't be hard, *will it*? This is the first time I've seen you in *fifteen years*."

"Isn't absence meant to make the heart grow fonder? ... Ow!" Wynfeld winced, reflecting that his aunt could give the army lessons on inflicting pain.

<h1 style="text-align:center">Chapter 6</h1>
<h2 style="text-align:center">ADEONE</h2>
Late Evening<br>Macarian House – Study

HAVING TUCKED ARKYN UP IN BED, Adeone returned to the study. An unfinished letter to an old friend in Terasia lay on his desk. Instead of finishing it, he sank into a comfortable chair by the fire, watching the flames without seeing them, watching them burn down until the dying embers of the fire represented his heart; the warmth was there but there was no spark to give it meaning, no flame burning brightly to give him drive and direction, nothing to make him feel alive. Even the evening drew to a close outside the windows. He didn't know what time it was and didn't care. The world had changed the previous day; there was a hole in his heart and grief strangled his other senses. He heard the distant sounds of the house – the tread of feet, a voice talking softly, another answering – but he couldn't connect to them. The aromas of his study pervaded his senses – the worn leather of chairs, the wood's polish, the wax from candles burned away – yet they were distant, not part of him.

He'd stayed awake all through the previous night. He didn't want to sleep; as soon as he did, he'd forget; sleep would take him to the darkest reaches, where memory and dreaming had no place. He'd driven himself too hard, fighting the knowledge that Ira wouldn't recover. He couldn't fight it now; it was proven beyond doubt. For the moment, he had nothing left to challenge, nothing to match himself against. Even as his mind denied it, his body knew it and was waiting for him to accept it. It would reclaim what he'd been denying it for months: rest. In rest was time to think, to remember, to despair. He couldn't give in to his body's demands. He had to get through the days ahead, the years ahead. He needed to survive until Arkyn was twenty and could claim the empire, else Scanlon would try to take it under the title of Protector, and he was unlikely to protect anything, certainly not his nephew's life.

Adeone recalled the talk with his elder son that evening. Arkyn had been shocked when Adeone had told him that he was sending him to the Rex Dallin. Then, when Adeone had explained why and had finally told his son that his uncle wanted him dead, the shock was replaced by understanding, more quickly than he expected. He realised Arkyn had grown considerably in the last two years – height and personality had become defined – and he wanted to tell Ira how proud he was of their son. Crushing reality hit him. He'd never tell Ira. She had gone. She had left him, left their sons. Curled into the chair, foetal like, he succumbed to his grief.

Half an hour later, the embers of the fire lit his face where tears washed his cheeks. Dimly, he registered someone had entered the room. Paralyzed by grief, he didn't care if they saw a broken man.


Retreating from the study with felted house shoes muffling his tread, Kadeem was glad he hadn't clomped his way into the King's grief; as a footman, his evening duties included checking the study was tidy, candles replaced, hearth swept and laid ready again. With no reply to his quiet knock, he hadn't expected the King to be sitting by the dying fire. It wasn't up to him to break into such a moment of loss. Closing the door softly behind him, he entered the adjacent room. A few moments later, satisfied he should have prevented anyone else blundering in, he hurried through the candlelit house to find Simkins in the King's bedchamber.

"Sir, His Majesty may need you. He is in a bad way."

"Thank you, Kadeem. Where is the King?"

"In the study, staring into the embers of the fire and crying, silently; just crying."

"You didn't see that. Is that understood?" ordered Simkins sharply but muted.

"It was understood, sir, as soon as I didn't see it. I've put a notice on the door so His Majesty isn't interrupted. I hope that was right."

Adeone's drawn face, sunken cheeks and dull eyes revealed the depth of his grief; dark rings hollowed his eyes and drew them back into their sockets. Simkins cursed. He should never have let Adeone get himself into such a state. Some of it was inevitable – the King would always push himself too far – but he was meant to prevent a collapse like this.

"Sire…"

Adeone stared at the embers, but there had been a flicker deep in the hollowed eyes.

"You should be in bed, sir," whispered Simkins.

Adeone shook his head.

Simkins left the study and closed the door gently behind him. A couple of minutes would make little difference. Seeing Kadeem standing nervously a short way down the landing, he crooked an eyebrow.

"I thought you might need a runner, sir."

"Which you are not." Simkins enunciated each word, most of his mind working out what to do.

"No, sir, but I thought it might be better if I were not, if you see what I mean."

"Discreetly fetch the King's Physician."

Finding the medical man reading in the library, Kadeem murmured, "Doctor, can you go to the study, please?"

Chapa looked up, worried by the tone. "What's happened, lad?"

"Simkins just asked me to fetch you, sir. I'm too lowly to know anything else."

Chapa chortled to himself; Kadeem might be the newest member of the King's household but had already proved himself more than a match for seasoned servants.

Kadeem likewise considered the doctor. He had a reputation for being a bit of a character. He had once been described as a smile so well wrapped up you only saw the smirk as he watched the world go by. Written across his face was the laughter of the years, his hair was never neat: it was fine, wispy, and unkempt – simply enhancing his eccentric attitude to his serious job. His blue eyes seemed to make a mockery out of everything but the most serious of situations. It sometimes fooled people into thinking he didn't care; he did very deeply, just not soberly. He always maintained, if you couldn't laugh at yourself, there were plenty of other people all too willing to laugh at you.

"I'd better go and see what he wants, hadn't I?"

"Who, Doctor?"

"Oh, himself, the King." The doctor chuckled in appreciation of the look of shock on Kadeem's young face. He modified his words to console the young man. "I should, of course, have said 'himself and the King'. Forgive me, lad, the mind at my age wanders and if it doesn't wander, it leaves completely. Are you to escort me?"

"I don't know, sir. Is it normal?"

"What is normality but a state in other peoples' minds? You'd better come; just in case. I might get lost."


"What can I do for the lad, Simkins?" asked Chapa as they reached the study door.

Simkins sighed. "He is the King."

"Yes, I know. I was at his accession and coronation – birth too, come to that. After all that, it's a bit hard to miss." His voice turned from jovial to serious. "How is he?"

"Not good, and he won't retire."

"Of course he won't! Never did know what was good for him. He got that trait off his mother. Tain will be the same, as I dare say will Arkyn, given half a chance and I hope I live to see it."

"Doc, you're not yet sixty and fit as a fiddle."

"Really? Oh, it feels like more. Must be my job."

"Just come on in. Thank you, Kadeem. Wait here, please."

Once in the study, Simkins muttered, "Will you please *not* shock new members of staff *quite* so soon, Chapa? Whatever their background."

"He'll be fine. William's taught him well."

"I know." Simkins motioned to where Adeone was sitting. The tears had ceased, but the dull, blank staring had not.

Chapa shook his head and slipped a vial carefully into his belt pouch, before passing the rest of his kit to Simkins. Moving over so he was in front of Adeone, he knelt, examining his wayward patient – concern splayed across his kindly features.

"Sire, you need to retire. See, Simkins is so worried about you, he fetched me."

"No need," replied Adeone so quietly the doctor almost missed it.

"I dare say there wasn't. It would be just like Simkins to get me out of your nice, cosy library for nothing. Did you know you even have a book on beetles in there?"

"Yes."

Which was more than the doctor did. He tried another tack. "If you're not careful, sir, I'll send for Lady Amara."

"Below the belt, doc."

"What else did you expect? Seriously though, you're worrying everybody."

"Am I?" enquired Adeone, beginning to take notice.

"Everyone who knows, aye. You need to sleep."

"I'm afraid to, cousin." The King's reply was so low that Simkins standing a couple of feet away couldn't hear it.

Chapa murmured, "Forcing yourself to keep awake will make the bill heavier. Please, go to bed, Adeone. Make my life easy for a change."

In a fit of pique, Adeone shook his head.

"Then I'll get a drink for both of us. It might stop people worrying; if they know I'm here, should you need me." Getting to his feet, Chapa retrieved the vial. It contained a potent sleeping draught, which he stirred into Adeone's goblet unseen.

It took a few minutes to work, but, once it had, the doctor, Simkins and Kadeem carried him to his room and made him comfortable.

When the three were alone, Simkins turned to Chapa. "He'll have your guts for that little trick."

"Let him try. They are quite happily attached to the rest of me. Anyway, his health is my concern and he isn't too healthy."

Simkins remembered Kadeem was there. "Off you go. Say anything about this and I'll have your guts, attached to you or not. Worse still, I'll have a word with your father."

Kadeem inclined his head slightly. "He always likes seeing you, sir. Goodnight."

# Chapter 7
## MORNING
Imperadai, Week 12 – 25th Lowal, 18th Lowis 1209
Macarian House – King's Bedchamber

THE BLACKNESS STIRRED; light filtering behind Adeone's eyelids. He'd been talking to the doctor; how had he got to bed? He struggled against the light, but the day wanted acknowledgement. He blinked awake. His eyes met Simkins' as his manservant turned from arranging the curtains into neat drapes. Adeone groaned as realisation dawned.

"Please tell me I didn't fall for the sleeping draught in the wine trick."

Simkins weighed up all possible answers. "Yes, Sire, you did: quite spectacularly. Would you like to talk to Doctor Chapa today?"

"I'll have a word with him, to keep up appearances."

"Now, sir? He's been outside all night," added Simkins without emphasis, but his eyes held a glint of anticipation, if not amusement.

"I'm honoured. You'd better ask the rogue to come in," replied Adeone, pushing himself out of bed and shrugging on his dressing gown.

Simkins busied himself at one end of the room whilst Adeone and Chapa eyed each other.

Trying to keep a straight face, Adeone said, "*Never* try that trick again."

Chapa's lips twitched. "If you promise to never again give me cause to, Sire."

"I'll try my hardest not to," responded Adeone dryly.

"Then I promise to try my hardest not to *try* to trick you again, sir," replied Chapa, leaving himself a loophole out of habit and necessity.

Adeone stepped onto a raised section below the windows, admiring the view. He slumped onto the window seat. "Thank you for saving me from myself once again, cousin. Alcis only knows how long I'd have sat there."

"Probably the rest of the evening if Kadeem hadn't found you, sir, and alerted me." Simkins had turned and answered before the doctor could formulate his reply. The King might be looking healthier, but Chapa's droll observations were probably better avoided.

"It was Kadeem who fetched me as well," added Chapa.

Adeone hesitated. Even his innermost circle shouldn't have witnessed his state, let alone a stranger. "Who is he?" he asked.

"A new footman in your household, Sire," answered Simkins.

Chapa tried to ease his mind. "He's a good lad. He was beyond discreet in fetching me. You really needn't worry, sir."

"The doc's right, Your Majesty. Kadeem is one of the best."

Adeone didn't reply. The footman had done the right thing in fetching Simkins and Chapa. It wasn't fair to blame him for something he couldn't avoid seeing.

"Sire, professionally, I'd like to request you take the morning off," remarked Chapa, interrupting his thoughts. "You've not given yourself a break since the Queen passed away, nor for many weeks before."

Adeone flashed him a glance. There was only concern on Chapa's face but the idea of having nothing to do unsettled him. He caught the tail end of a shared look between his doctor and manservant.

"Simkins, how many appointments have you cancelled?"

"All of them, Sire, on the doc's advice."

"There's a word for that," muttered Chapa levelly.

Adeone knew defeat when he saw it. "Very well, gentlemen. I will take the morning off. Are there any more conspiracies?"

"No, Sire. Not yet anyway. I'm sure, given time, we will come up with a few," replied Chapa with a wink.

"I have no doubt you will, cousin. Thank you. Go and get some sleep yourself." Once the doc had gone, Adeone eyed his nervous manservant. "Thank you. It's nice to know… Well, thank you."

As Simkins left, Adeone's gaze returned to the gardens. The warm morning sunlight tugged at something within him, yet it wasn't the distraction he needed. He looked around. The papers that had been on the table by the window were gone. That meant that the ones in the study would all be with his administrator, who could be just as determined as the doc and Simkins. Should he do anything about the determination? A knock interrupted his thoughts and he granted admittance.

"Your breakfast, Sire," announced a footman in his late teens with compassionate brown eyes and features that were familiar to the King.

With a hint of long sufferance, Adeone said, "Thank you. What's become of Simkins? He's not plotting something else with the doc, is he?"

The youth inclined his head. "I really wouldn't know, sir. He merely asked me to bring in the tray. I'm Kadeem."

"Very well. I believe I owe you thanks." He realised the neat way in which Simkins was trying to prove Kadeem's merits.

Having laid the table, Kadeem stood to one side. "There is nothing to thank me for, Your Majesty."

"Why?" enquired Adeone, sitting down.

"I only did what anyone would have done, sir."

Adeone regarded him; Kadeem's eyes showed anticipation but there was no hint of fear. "Hmm. Maybe or maybe not, young Will Kadeem. Yes, I've realised William is your father. You've done a variety of jobs for His Lordship, haven't you?"

"From the age of seven, Sire, but one cannot progress by standing still."

"Quite. How long have I been employing you?" enquired Adeone.

"An aluna-month exactly, sir."

"I'm sorry I didn't know. The last four weeks have been a bit of a blur," he added sadly.

"You have more than enough on your plate, Sire."

"Yes, and it's not getting eaten. Thank you, Kadeem." When the footman had left, Adeone lingered over breakfast, contemplating him.

Quarter of an hour later, Simkins entered to find Adeone again perusing the view. Unobtrusive as ever, he started to clear away.

Adeone turned to him. "I'd like to see Landis. Tell him ten o'clock."

"Would this be work, sir?"

"Don't push it," said Adeone tolerantly. "It is, in a way, a family matter. Neat trick with my papers and Kadeem, by the way."

"I can't imagine what you mean, Sire."

Adeone simply raised his eyebrows.

Adeone wandered along the landings of Macarian House. He'd come here often before his marriage – trying to get to know someone who had already captured his heart. There'd been no option of denying he was in love with Ira. Just a slow acceptance of how much he felt it. She'd been quiet, not believing it. There'd been early love in this house. He almost heard it seeping from the walls. Boys' laughter brought him back to the present. There it was again, a pure sound unadulterated by memory. His feet turned down a landing towards the nursery. He entered to find Tain sitting chatting animatedly with a lad Adeone didn't know. The fair-haired boy spotted him before Tain did and jumped up, clumsily bowing, the colour draining from his face.

"Tain, won't you introduce us?"

Apprehensively, Tain did so. "Father, this is Cal… Calumiel Galdwin, I mean."

"I'm pleased to meet you, Master Calumiel."

"And I you, Sire."

The well-spoken, traditional reply pleasantly surprised Adeone. From Cal's attire, he was the son of a merchant. His linen shirt, velvet doublet, knee-length breeches and hose were a contrast to Tain's cotton undertunic, knee-length silk outer tunic and hose. He had good manners, but his inherited name was one Adeone didn't recall; yet he seemed slightly familiar, as though he'd seen his face before. He put the puzzle aside; he saw many faces without knowing the names. Turning to Tain, he asked what his son's immediate plans were.

"I have none, sir. Why?"

"It's about time we found a horse for you and Old Jack told me they were breaking some in. Do you want to come and pick one?"

"Aren't you busy, father?"

Adeone felt the sting of guilt at his son's question. Making light of it, he said, "No, the doc has ordered me to take the morning off."

"Ordered you, sir?" asked Tain, encouraged by the amusement in his father's features.

"Yes, it's apparently for my own good. I never argue with him. It makes life so much easier. Master Calumiel, would you like to accompany us?"

"Thank you, Sire, but I should be getting home."

Adeone glanced at Tain; there was the shadow of disappointment on his face. "I'm sure word can be sent that you have been unavoidably detained here for the day. Who is your father?"

"Master Galdwin, sir. He's a cloth merchant on the Maclan."

A prestigious address but it only added to the mystery. Having attended many of the annual guild banquets, and with many guild members at Court, Adeone thought he'd heard of all the great merchant families. It was possible that Cal's father wasn't a member of the guild, but that would be rare for someone trading on the Maclan.

"What brought you here?" he asked.

"Delivering a letter, sir."

Adeone considered Calumiel; where Tain seemed to bounce continually this lad was more reserved but, other than understandable nerves, he was confident and Tain visibly enjoyed his company. Adeone was thankful for anything that made his son smile, for smiles brought healing.

"I'm sure we can return the favour. That is, if you would like to come with us?"

Cal looked at Tain, who glanced at his father. Adeone's face clearly said that the offer was genuine and that it was up to the boys. Tain nodded eagerly and Cal accepted. Adeone had word sent to Master Galdwin.

Turning to Tain once more, he asked, "Where's your brother?"

With all the affection his nine years could muster for his older sibling, Tain said, "Still asleep. He's being lazy."

"Really? Maybe he just doesn't have your energy. Shall we go?" enquired Adeone, glad to have found something to do that his staff couldn't interfere in, however well-intentioned they meant it.

# Chapter 8
# HORSES, HACKLES AND HECKLING
### Morning
### Oedran

THEY WALKED from Macarian House to the Palace, enjoying the warm, blustery morning. Adeone glad of the chance to stretch his legs. The way his son and Cal chatted animatedly warmed his heart and some anxiety left him. Given time, Tain would be fine: he lived in the moment. It would be quiet times when it would hit him or sudden moments when he'd forget and then remember; chance comments would bring the loss to mind, to reality. For Arkyn it was a constant burning loss, embers that depressed his mood all day. In time, they would burn lower, but Adeone feared that his eldest would never truly be at ease with his young mother's death.

As they ambled up the Maclan, the sombre atmosphere became almost tangible. It was busy, but there was a distinct lack of colour in people's clothes. There was muted conversation rather than laughter and jostling. The proclamation of Ira's death had been read the day before and although his Court was in mourning the proclamation hadn't required it of anyone else, yet here was their own offering and it touched his heart in the way official mourning never could.

He glanced to see if the atmosphere had affected Tain. The young boy was more subdued than he'd been in the privacy of Macarian House, but he was still talking with Cal and Adeone could see that the two were already firm friends. Walking through the city with the King and young Prince didn't seem to faze the lad and that was important if the friendship was to survive.

By the time they reached Alcium Plaza, word they were coming had spread before them, even without a herald crying it out. Sergeant Marsh's posture changed as he became even more watchful. The wide square with the City Alcium in its centre was almost silent. Ira's funeral would take place there and Adeone tried hard not to think about that. He longed for the privacy of his private alcium, for time just to contemplate, to order his thoughts and send them to ancestors, but the time wasn't right. He was too emotional.

Tain stopped talking and Cal appeared disconcerted for the first time. The guards walked a step closer as they crossed the plaza and circled the Alcium. The yeomen on the King's Gate saluted smartly as they passed into the Administrative Quarter and walked up the road towards the Palace. They entered Palace Plaza and Adeone led the way around to the right to enter the Palace at Stable Gate. The guards saluted crisply, grooms leading horses stepped hurriedly aside and there was an easily recognisable three-note whistle. It made Adeone want to groan. The chief groom broke off his conversation and glanced between the path to the Palace and the gate. He relaxed and crossed over to Adeone, bowing rheumatically.

"Sire, my condolences."

"Likewise, Jack, and thank you. Where are the foals?" he enquired, putting an arm around Tain's shoulders.

"They are in the paddock, Your Majesty. I think I know just the one as well, sir."

"If you don't, I'm rather surprised." As they made their way to the paddock, Adeone continued, "I met an under-groom of yours, from years ago, the other day: Wynfeld."

"I always wondered why he left. He was good with horses and enjoyed the work."

"Misunderstanding with Lord Macaria, I believe."

"His Lordship was notorious for them, Sire," murmured Jack. "How was young Wynfeld?"

"In himself, well, I believe. He's accepted a commission in Oedran. Here we are, Tain. Go and choose."

Adeone flicked his eyes at a guard, an instruction to go with Tain and Cal who had hared off. Two minutes later Adeone, who'd been watching Tain, said, "It seems we have a decision. Always quick that one. Not like Prince Arkyn, who takes his time."

"Both of them do you proud though, sir."

"Thank you. They're good lads; I just hope they grow into good men."

"Can't see how they could fail to, Sire."

They wandered over to Tain, who pointed at a jet-black foal: a Swiftfoot like Pursuit, bred for speed and endurance.

Adeone turned to Jack. "What's his temperament?"

"Good. He's the one I thought of for His Highness. He's got a bit of a mischievous, independent streak that I thought exactly right for my Prince."

Adeone hid his amusement. "Then, Tain, he's yours."

"His coat matches Prince Tain's hair as well, Sire," said Calumiel easily.

Adeone glanced from the bright-eyed lad to his son, "It does indeed, Master Calumiel. What will you call him, Tain?"

"I don't know, sir," replied Tain, downcast, but then he grinned and turned to the chief groom. "What did you call him, Jack?"

"Bandit, Your Highness."

"It hardly seems fair to him to change it. Will 'Bandit' do, father?"

"Very nicely I should think. Jack, when he has been broken in by your best ambler, please send him to wherever His Highness is and I really mustn't keep you from your work any longer."

Jack bowed and left. Adeone leant on a fence whilst Tain and Calumiel chatted amicably. A slender, blond-haired figure appeared on the opposite side of the paddock. Adeone's brows began to knit. Hackles rising, his eyes tracked the man as he strutted towards them.

"Uncle Scanlon, see the horse father has given me," said Tain excitedly.

"Very nice, Tain. You must be sure not to fall. It could be fatal."

Tain's face fell.

"Lord Scanlon, a word," snapped the King.

"Adeone?" Lord Scanlon's voice was silky.

"Are we in public? Why, yes, I believe we *are*!" Adeone's wasn't.

"Sorry, *Sire*! I came to offer my condolences on the death of the Queen."

"Offer them and go away if all you intend to do is scare my son," snarled Adeone.

"I *obviously* didn't mean to, Sire. How are you?"

"How do you think I am?" hissed Adeone.

"Dying of a broken heart?" enquired Scanlon confidently.

"No need to get your hopes up. Do you require anything else?"

"Not really. The justice system seems to run itself."

"I'm glad something does."

Scanlon finally took heed of the tone in Adeone's voice and left with an exaggerated bow.

Not long afterwards, the party returned to Macarian House. For ease, they entered by the servants' entrance. Cal blanched at the sight of his father at the kitchen door. Master Galdwin saw Cal but failed to consider his companions.

"What the blazes do you think you're doing?"

"I'm sorry, Pa..."

Adeone touched Cal's shoulder lightly. "I delayed your son's return. I believe a runner was sent to explain that."

Master Galdwin gave a curt bow. "Yes. I just assumed it to be a game."

"Next time, I'll send a sealed note. Do you require Master Calumiel at home? I wouldn't like to inconvenience your family, but Prince Tain has been enjoying his company."

"I... er... no, Sire."

"I'll see he's seen safely home later then," said Adeone, watching Master Galdwin hastily leave. The King eyed the boys. "What did he mean by '*a game*'?" Seeing Tain biting at his lip, he continued, "Prince Tain, please answer me."

"I've sent a runner before so Cal could stay and talk. I'm sorry, father."

"Ah. I thought you two knew each other well for a chance encounter. Why haven't you mentioned anything to me?"

"Because you were busy, sir."

"And because we thought you might disapprove, sir," said Cal, trying to help Tain out. "Although I'm born alunan, my father is cisan born."

"That, to me, is immaterial. Though I am guessing in your house it is not. There are prejudices, I assume."

"Prejudices?" Cal's tongue found its way around the new word.

"Inherent mistrusts. An opinion held without the foundation for it to be built on."

"Yes, Sire, you could say that."

"Right, well, promise me, both of you, no more *games* and I'll see if

I can reason with Master Galdwin." They agreed with alacrity. "Go on with you both. Enjoy your day. I think I've been spotted. All right, Simkins, I'm coming. It can't be ten yet."

"It is a quarter past, sir. Lord Landis is in the study."

"Must be such a novelty for him. It seems that, whenever I am with my sons, my life turns into one of apologies. Talking of which, how are yours? I've never apologised for cutting your leave short. Do give my regards to your wife."

# Chapter 9
# LANDIS
### Mid-Morning
### Macarian House – Study

ON REACHING THE STUDY, Adeone's eyes flicked to his desk. He'd been right: there wasn't a paper in sight. It was oddly disorientating – like being lost in a well-known place. As the door closed on the house and empire, he relaxed.

"Sorry, Festus. It's your nearson's fault."

"It's not a problem, Your Majesty," replied Landis, evaluating his friend's state and concluding it was better than expected. "What can I do for you?"

"Nothing serious. Apparently, I've acquired young Will Kadeem as a footman. Do you think he would cope as Arkyn's manservant?"

"Yes. William's trained him, but he has no experience of managing other servants."

"Understood. I'll have another talk with him and one with Arkyn. Thank you."

"Is that all, Sire?" Formality was all very well to hide behind but it never fooled him.

Adeone noticed his friend's concern. "Fancy setting the world to rights? I'm in need of a fellow reprobate because if Simkins finds out this was even vaguely work related, he'll *accidentally* let the doc know."

"Then I am, as always, yours to command." When Adeone frowned, he took a mental step back. "Sorry. It's not the time for levity."

The King passed his friend a drink and they relaxed into comfortable chairs; Adeone glanced at Landis. It was how he always thought of him, a complete enigma sitting with a glass of mellow whiskey. Well versed in the art of wielding a sword and equally well versed in portraying himself as a man of leisure.

Landis studied Adeone with shrewd grey eyes. "How are you coping? If there's anything I or Cornelia can do, you have only to ask. We'll miss my cousin."

Adeone swallowed. Formal and traditional outpourings would have been wrong from Landis. The simple statement that they were there was worth all the other condolences he had received.

"Thank you, Festus. I spoke to the Steward yesterday. Ira had planned everything but the date of the funeral for me." Tears sprang in his eyes and he took a sip of wine to cover the moment.

Listening as Adeone talked about his life with Ira, Landis knew it would take a long time for him to find healing. Eventually, the King fell silent, drained and contemplative once again.

After several moments, Landis said, "Simkins told me one Sergeant Wynfeld saved your life. He has an interesting background."

Adeone crooked an eyebrow. "You checked him too? General Paturn must have been busy. What did you think?"

"Reliable man. Unambitious. Discreet – Sharparu didn't realise he'd worked for Uncle Macaria. Just gets on with the job. If anything, he's probably underutilised because Sharparu doesn't want to lose him."

Adeone pulled a face. "He's not now. I've given him the intelligence regiment to oversee when his leave's up."

"What about Fitz?" asked Landis, astounded.

"He's going to the Rex Dallin with your nearsons and can guard them in relative peace and quiet. Whenever they return to Oedran, at least I'll know there's a guard I trust with them."

"Return…? How long are they going to be there for, Sire?"

Adeone swallowed. "At least until they start their duties in earnest. I can't risk them being in Oedran and they will be safe behind the protections there. Don't tell me it's a bad idea."

"It's an excellent idea, but I didn't think you'd do it."

Adeone glanced at him, then away. "I don't want to. I'd prefer them here, but I can't let them or Ira down now."

"It's not just your fight, Adeone. I know you think it is but it isn't. I'm right beside you, always have been."

"I know and I appreciate it, but I can't rely on anyone else—"

"Sicla, death and damnation, Sire, didn't I swear to protect your life with my own?"

Adeone snorted. "Not quite what I meant, though I do recall the oath and, you know, you're not meant to curse in my hearing."

"Traditions can be changed. So, please tell me if I, as your Chief Advisor and Defender, can't support you and make sure you're not killed, who can?"

"Traditions can be changed," suggested Adeone, with the first spark of mischief that he'd felt in days.

"Oh, very amusing, Sire. That's one way of avoiding answering."

"I know. I got it off you, my friend." A moment later, he enquired mildly, "Why isn't Marsh on leave? He said you pulled him back."

Landis considered what to say. Although Adeone seemed better than he expected, he hadn't anticipated having to address Jenner's sacking for a few days. "When I heard about Wynfeld, Sire, I also heard about your entry into Oedran. Jenner has chosen to retire due to the circumstances." Seeing scepticism, he added, "Fine. I gave him the options of redeployment, retirement or court martial, sir. He clearly didn't wish for demotion or to be court-martialled."

Adeone's eyes narrowed. "You dismissed him."

"Yes," admitted Landis. "If you think I'm going to sit by and watch you be left exposed then you're mistaken, *Sire*. Jenner's actions weren't acceptable."

"I left him behind, Landis! I didn't care—"

"Which is why I didn't pursue the option of trying him for dereliction of duty, sir, though, as your Defender, I could still have done so as Jenner didn't ensure guards were waiting for Your Majesty at the city gates. Simkins actually came to see me. It's not just assassins that worry us, it's accidents as well. If Pursuit had stumbled and you'd been thrown, who knows how long it would have been before you were tended. Threats don't have to be intentional either, as Wynfeld's actions proved. You need to be far more careful."

Adeone examined the goblet in his hand. "I need some freedom, Festus."

Landis pursed his lips. "I know and that's not at issue, but rides like the one you made aren't wise. Arkyn and Tain could have lost you as well as Ira that day. Next time there won't be an excuse; I'm having all your stables, including the mail routes, scoured for Swiftfoots for your guards."

Adeone, who didn't know whether to be angry, amused or thankful, said, "That at least saves me a job. Has Jenner enough security to not be bribed?"

Landis snorted. "He has. I did check, especially as he *voluntarily* resigned."

"There's an expression about being caught between magic and the explosion that might be apt here." Adeone let out a long breath. "Do you have any other observations about my ride and return to Oedran or have you finished berating me for the time being?"

Landis saw the mixed emotions and dullness that had returned to his friend's eyes. "I think that's all for now, sir. I wasn't going to raise it at all for a time."

"So, it's my fault for asking?"

"Never that. A king can never be at fault."

Adeone's eyes narrowed again. "There are days, Landis, when I could quite cheerfully throttle you."

Landis chuckled. "That would rather ruin the illusion of complete trust we've been building."

Adeone snorted. "I can still trust you as I throttle you. I'll consider what you've said, I promise. Just give me time. It wasn't a normal day."

"No, it certainly wasn't. I saw Ira that morning. She specifically asked to see me."

"Why?" enquired Adeone carefully. "I know you were close but..."

"To make sure I'd still have your back, no matter what came. I did my best to reassure her. Do you want to know what her reply was?"

"Go on."

"Traditions can be changed," said Landis, lips twitching.

"I'm glad she never lost her sense of humour. I've decided her funeral will be on Septadai. Arkyn and Tain will be there. If you think any of my nearchildren will cope with it, they are welcome to come."

"Thank you, sir. I'll discuss it with Cornelia. I've letters from the twins for all of you."

"Give it a few days and they can see each other, certainly before the move to the Rex Dallin," said Adeone. "Though Tain's formed a friendship with one Calumiel Galdwin. His father's one of your tenants."

"Are you worried about it?"

"Not at all," replied Adeone. "Quite pleased, in a way. It'll be good for the boys to have different friends. The nearcousins are all close, but I can see Tain needs someone else and Arkyn certainly needs respite occasionally. He's always kept an eye on Tain, as he did on Ella, but he shouldn't have to."

"Won't it be awkward with the boys living in the Rex Dallin?"

"I've been thinking of seeing if Master Galdwin will let Cal join them. From my one encounter with him, I can't imagine it'll be easy but there could be advantages."

"You're asking a father to give up his son, Adeone..." pointed out Landis, troubled.

"I know and I don't do it lightly, but I think the friendship is strong. It feels like ours did in the early days. Mutual without fear."

"I must have been a talented actor," said Landis pointedly.

"You faced down my father," retorted Adeone. "That took guts."

"Or stupidity. Just because father and he didn't get on, didn't mean we couldn't."

Adeone snorted. "Traditions can be changed. If young Master Calumiel can't adjust, I wouldn't force him to stay. He could visit home..." He hesitated. "I can't see Tain suffer the loneliness I did. I know Arkyn's there, but I don't want their relationship to be soured by the fact they only have each other. Tain and El aren't as close as I hoped they might be. Arkyn's duties will start in the next couple of years..."

Landis sighed. "All right. I'll see what I can do as well. I wouldn't mind if you wanted the twins to be there for a short time to help them adjust."

"Would you think me rude if I said I dread to think what state Ceardlann would be left in?"

Landis chuckled. "No, I'd think you know your nearchildren. I won't be offended if you'd prefer them not to be there. I can understand it if you'd rather the valley remained private."

Adeone shook his head. "It's not that, Festus. You're all dear to me and, although I joke, I know the twins wouldn't destroy the house. Tain will be a justiciar one day and I can't help thinking that he needs to mix with a wider range of people. Also, I watched him and Cal closely today. I think he's good for Tain in a way that the twins can't be because of our friendship and the relationships between the FitzAlcis and lords."

Landis began to understand what Adeone was trying to say. That in Cal, Tain could have a friend that had nothing to do with the world of privilege and that, for someone who would later dispense justice, would be invaluable.

"Well, if you ever want Ceardlann's peace overrun with mayhem and practical jokes, let me know and I'll send the twins along, whilst enjoying a breather."

Adeone crooked an eyebrow. "I don't know why you sound so long-suffering, Festus. They're your children in every way."

"I find I have more sympathy with my father these days," admitted Landis with a quirky grin, turning the conversation onto their own past antics.

# Chapter 10
## LADY AMARA
Pentadai, Week 12 – 26th Lowal, 19th Lowis 1209
Macarian House – King's Bedchamber

THE FOLLOWING MORNING, Adeone looked up as his administrator knocked and entered. Having heard the commotion of an arrival, the King took in his administrator's appearance.

"Should I be worried, Richardson?"

"Lady Amara wonders if Your Majesty has a moment."

That explained the harassed look.

"Of course. Do show her in."

"I'm in already," replied Amara. "Thank you, Richardson. I'm sure you've much administrating to do."

Adeone waited until his administrator had left before pushing himself to his feet. "You shouldn't do it, you know."

Amara snorted. "Does them good, Sire. Come here…"

He accepted the hug she gave him with a lump in his throat.

"Simkins said you collapsed a couple of nights ago. Why didn't you send for me?"

"Talking to anyone was beyond me by the time I realised how bad I was, aunt. I wasn't thinking about anything that didn't require immediate attention. I'm sorry. I know how much you care."

She accepted a drink from him and sat down, arranging her skirts with a precision he knew to be wary of.

Eventually she said, "The boys?"

"Coping as well as you might expect. No, that's wrong. Better than you might expect. Tain's found distraction in a new friend and Arkyn… Well, he's finally talked out some of his worries. He's devastated but coping."

"And you?"

He eyed her sideways. "Much as you might expect, aunt. I'll miss her every day."

"Yes, it gets you like that."

He studied her. "I wish you'd had more time with Uncle Ewart."

"There's never enough time when you love people as we do, little Adeone." After a moment, she said, "That's enough sentiment for now. We need to talk."

"There was me thinking I'd escaped remonstration for now," observed Adeone dryly.

"I didn't say anything about remonstration, nephew. Her Grace's passing has changed things—"

"I—"

"Don't interrupt. It's changed things. Are you going to marry again?"

Adeone was momentarily speechless. "Lady Amara, my wife's funeral hasn't even happened yet!"

"No, it hasn't. Unfortunately, the Court, your Court is already speculating, so get used to being asked and think about your reply. Marrying for love, as we did, is a luxury and you may not be able to afford it."

Controlling his temper, Adeone said, "I'm not discussing this. No. I'm not. I know what you're saying but I'm not. Sicla."

Her gaze scorched him. "Ira's death put your life and your sons' lives in even more peril."

"So would remarrying. What's more, this hypothetical wife would be in peril also." He stopped, considered, ruminated and concluded, "In peril from whom, aunt?"

"Scanlon."

"How?" He watched her face, her worried face. "I didn't think *you* knew. I tried to keep you out of it."

She snorted. "Haven't you learned anything about me in all these years? That is never going to be successful. So, you can either tell me your troubles or I can discover them from others, who I must admit merely confirmed my suspicions."

"Others being?" He sighed at her withering look. "Fine. Can't blame me for trying to find out who is—"

"Protecting your back, *defending* you?"

"Landis. Of course, it would be. He's feared you for years."

She chuckled. "I do my best. Young Festus merely confirmed my suspicions. So, what are we going to do about it? Moving the youngsters to Ceardlann is sensible, but it doesn't protect you." As Adeone glanced at his desk, she frowned. "You're not escaping this conversation, nephew."

"I don't want to," he replied, quite truthfully. "A moment." He rang for Richardson, asking for privacy until he was alone again. Sitting back down, he said, "How much do you know about Scanlon's aims, aunt?"

"Just that he's working to remove you and your sons."

"I don't want you caught in the middle."

After a moment, she enquired, "Who said anything about the middle? I cannot sit by and let our family descend into anarchy. How do *you* see Scanlon now? You wouldn't be the first king to disown family."

Adeone hesitated. "I might not be able to forgive him his schemes, the fact he wasn't here when father died but he's my brother. He will always be my brother, aunt."

"Do you have any evidence he's trying to murder you?"

"Not direct evidence, but he's definitely plotting. Aelia told Ira she was worried that Scanlon had lost reason a few years ago but Chapa confirmed that he's sane. Scanlon won't see Chapa these days and has employed his own doctor."

"Yes, I heard about that. He's a fool. Chapa's good. So, what are you going to do about this little problem?"

"I've always admired your habit for understatement, aunt."

"Stop prevaricating."

"Fine." Adeone considered. "First, I'm going to make sure my sons are safe, and Elantha, for that matter. I won't have him use them as pawns. I've also appointed a new captain for the intelligence regiment. I've briefed him but will let him settle in before I see if I need to do more."

"Whom have you appointed?"

"One Wynfeld. Used to work here when Ira was young—"

"Doesn't mean he's loyal or right for the job."

Adeone snorted. "Shall I send him along for you to check? He cared very deeply for Ira; I could see it when they were talking. I think it will help keep him loyal to us."

"You really can be too trusting at times. That's your mother in you. Keep an eye on him until you're sure."

"Oh, I think Landis will do that. It saves a lot of awkward questions."

"Good. Now, why haven't you moved against Scanlon if you're so sure he's after your life?"

Adeone considered how to phrase it. Eventually, he said, "I do not want to plunge the empire into civil war and cause thousands of deaths. Scanlon is good at manipulating situations to his advantage. Always has been."

"There are other options: assassination, arrest and trial—"

"Are we really going to sit here and talk about my brother, your nephew, like this?"

"Better than doing it elsewhere," observed Amara.

"True. I won't have him murdered, aunt. I just can't do it. Any murder is morally outrageous and I won't be that sort of king. I will never take a life that way. It would make me as bad as him. What's the difference? Murder is still murder."

"Isn't execution murder?"

"In a manner of speaking, but generally we're removing dangerous persons, would-be assassins—"

"Or traitors," interrupted Amara softly. "He is plotting your overthrow, Sire. That is treason."

"Yes. I've been talking with Judge Tancred over recent years about the issue. He informs me I can arrest Scanlon but unless Scanlon confesses, which he is never likely to do, then the only person who could try him would be—"

"A Justiciar of the Empire," finished Amara. "Much as that might be true, the law states a peer *or higher*. You are higher, sir."

"I will never set that precedent, Lady Amara."

"You won't order his assassination because it's murder, you won't arrest him because you can't try him, at least for eleven years until Tain is twenty, and you won't challenge him and face civil war. Just what *are* you planning to do to safeguard your life?" she demanded, exasperated.

"I appointed Landis to do that," said Adeone flippantly. He saw his aunt's face. "I'll suffer years of uncertainty and probably die of my principles, aunt, but at least I'll know I can face myself in my mirror. I'm not exactly looking forward to the experience." His eyes became haunted.

"Will anything change your mind?" she whispered, squeezing his hand.

"No. I cannot let him destroy who I am."

"I understand that. All right. I'll accept your stance. I don't agree with it but, as you're so adamant, I will work with that in mind."

"Work—?"

She smiled. "Young Adeone, you may be King, but that doesn't mean you have to deal with everything—"

"That's arguable."

"But you're not going to argue with me, young man. I will endeavour to do what I can to make sure he fails."

He finally looked at her. "Don't... I can't believe I'm saying this but... don't *you* have him killed or start a civil war, aunt."

"I have other methods, nephew. Now, tell me about everything that's been happening."

# Chapter 11
## AUTUMN MOVE
Alunadai, Week 14 – 8th Macial, 8th Macis 1209
Anapara Province – Rex Dallin Road

**T**HE FORTNIGHT since Ira's death had been strange; Adeone hadn't known what he preferred: working until he had no strength left to feel with or, when the guilt of that overtook him, sitting remembering all the good times with Ira. The funeral had been a sombre affair, but his sons had impressed him with the way they coped with the ordeal. Their mother had gone to her ancestors on a blazing pyre, watched over by two full moons. It had been, in one sense, a beautiful sight for all its solemnity. Then there'd been the normal routine. He'd grasped that gratefully, but it seemed surreal – almost as though the world should have changed more, not merely his perception of it. Meetings took place, decisions had to be made, people to appoint, others to persuade. Life happened.

On the day of the move to Ceardlann, autumn might have officially arrived but the sun was trying to beat off the chills. The smell of bonfires wafted down the lanes and the leaves were beginning to look like the flames of those fires. Yellows and oranges fought against the green. Some early fallers littered the path, to be scattered by the hooves and wheels of the FitzAlcis cavalcade, coming to rest in the gently stirring grass on the verges. A breeze blew them towards Ceardlann, but the clouds above raced each other to an unknown destination.

They had collected Cal on their way through Oedran and Adeone left the boys to ride together. They didn't need him complicating everything.

Tain grinned as his new friend mounted the horse uncertainly. "Grip with your knees..."

"I've never ridden before, sir."

"You'll get it. Trick is not to fall off."

Cal swallowed. "Yes, sir."

Tain manoeuvred his horse onto the other side of Cal so his friend was in the middle. By the time they were through Oedran, Cal was more confident.

Tain grinned. "See. You can do it. We've five miles for you to practise before we get to the Rex Dallin..."

Cal hesitated, feeling oddly delicate as reality washed over him. He didn't know when he'd see his parents again, that hadn't been discussed, and after pestering his father to let him go, he hadn't wanted to ask.

Tain kept up a running commentary on their surroundings. This first village was Cilford, but in a couple of miles was Dellwood and a mile beyond that was the Rex Dallin.

"The Rex Dallin is the King's Valley," explained Arkyn.

"Yes, sir," replied Cal, not wanting to admit to his ignorance.

"You can ask questions, you know," said Tain, grinning.

Arkyn muttered, "Take your lead from my brother and you'll never stop."

"Well, I like to know things," retorted Tain, "and father says it's important to learn."

Arkyn crooked an eyebrow. "Is that the only excuse you can find?"

"It works." Tain turned back to Cal. "So, ask. It really is fine."

Cal hesitated. "The Rex Dallin is special, isn't it? But I don't know why. People don't talk about it."

Arkyn grinned. "It's very special. The story goes that a great lake was drained and that then became the Valley of Encilla. The ancient Cearcall later surrounded the valley with powerful magic so that no-one could enter without their permission unless born there. They built Ceardlann, which became the home of the Skifta, one of their number. Then the Kings of Anapara inherited it when the Cearcall disappeared in the year 600. It's been our retreat ever since."

Cal absorbed that. "How come I can enter the valley?"

"The True Dallin token you were given proves to the resident guards you have the King's permission to be there. Your name is also on a scroll His Majesty holds."

"Why do I need a token though if the magic keeps out people who shouldn't be there, sir?"

Tain grinned. "The magic isn't as strong as it once was. Apparently, the entrance was invisible unless you carried the token. Now it's not, but the token is still important."

"Why, sir?"

Arkyn said quietly, "Because there is an alert whenever anyone enters the valley. If you don't have your token on you, then guards are dispatched to the southern gate and the Pillars of Alcis. If you do have the token, the alert is different. It's different for members of the King's family as well. Never forget your token, you'll be arrested for treason if you do and the alerts can be made to sound throughout the valley, as well as at Ceardlann and the lodges. His Majesty can choose not to have them sound at all apparently, but he never has done that."

"Thank you, sir."

"Is that all the questions? You need to get practising if you're going to beat Tain."

Tain stuck his tongue out at his brother.

Cal chuckled; he was in awe of Arkyn but it was oddly reassuring to see Tain treated him as he treated his own brothers. After a moment, he said, "So what are the Pillars of Alcis, Your Highness? I've not heard of them."

Tain grinned. "They're two standing stones that mark the northern entrance to the valley. One is smaller than the other so, I guess, someone said they represent the moons or something like that. I hope you don't mind wet feet; the Pillars are in the river."

Arkyn sighed. "Tain's hopeless at explaining. The River Encil flows through the valley; when it reaches this northern entrance, it forms a shallow river pool with a ford for this road. The Pillars are in the middle of the pool, on either side of the road. Also, you don't have to get wet feet as we're riding, so Tain should stop teasing you."

Cal swallowed. "Thank you. Is there anything else that marks the valley, Your Highness?"

Tain shrugged. "Just massive cliffs. They start as outcrops at the Pillars."

"Some people find them imposing," said Arkyn lightly. "There's also a forest on the east side. You'll see it all soon."

"Of course, sir. Sorry."

Tain snorted. "Don't be sorry. If he's answering your questions, he's not telling me off."

They all laughed. Arkyn caught his father's eye and his expression changed to a smile.

They'd passed through Dellwood when they caught up with a tribe of the nomadic Wanda. Chief Laioril had received permission years before to camp within the Rex Dallin and Adeone sometimes wondered how the old rogue had managed to persuade his father or grandfather, but most of the time he enjoyed Laioril's company instead. He bent down and addressed one of the Wandamen.

"Sayre, whereabouts is the Chief?"

"Walking up front, Sire."

Adeone motioned for his party not to follow him and set off through the Wanda at a trot hunting for Laioril. When he found him, he dismounted, falling into step. "Still walking at your age? I'd have thought you'd be putting your feet up in one of the carts by now."

Laioril's bright, piercing and mischievous blue eyes watched the King. "Walking keeps me young, lad."

Impishly, Adeone mused, "How old are you now, Chief?"

"As old as my tongue and a little older than my teeth, as always. How are you?"

Adeone swallowed. "Coping."

"You have all our deepest condolences. I was sorry and troubled to hear that the lass had died so young."

Adeone was touched to see the glimmer of tears surrounding the bright eyes. Quietly he said, "Thank you, Chief. I truly value them, as she would have done."

"Has she gone onto the ancestors?"

"Yes, on the Alcis Day, it seemed appropriate somehow."

"Aye, it would. Two full moons to guard her and the season's change to wish her well." They strolled in silence for a few moments until Laioril said, "Alcis *Day* has always struck me as odd, though, as it's the *night* when both moons are full. So shouldn't it be Alcis Night?" He sighed gently. "Probably just an old man's folly."

"Or pedantry, which, knowing you, Chief, is more likely. It is odd though. Our ancestors did on occasion refer to it as the *'Grey Day'* and I suppose it was appropriate as it can be as bright as any day. So maybe it isn't such a misnomer." A few minutes later, Adeone broke the stillness. "Could you camp closer to Ceardlann than normal? I'm leaving the children there. I'd be happier knowing that you were around to keep an eye on them – use Encampment Field instead of the Great Meadow. It's named appropriately, there'll be good fishing and the forest's closer…"

Laioril glanced sideways at the King. "Aye, I know it well. I'll gladly do it, lad, but they'll have plenty of people watching them, won't they?"

"Yes, all of them far too obviously and being too careful. The boys need to be treated normally."

"Well, I can give it a go. Sure that you trust me?"

"After you helped me years ago, I think so. Just about, anyway. I can trust you to dissemble and poach that I do know."

"I've got to keep my hand in at my age. I'll teach the Princes. There's nothing quite like corrupting the FitzAlcis, even after all the practice I've had. They'll be all right, lad, dunna fret, we'll cope."

They walked in silence until they reached the entrance to the Rex Dallin. Adeone watched Laioril stand between the Pillars of Alcis as the Wanda crossed into the valley. The Chief had once told Adeone he did it to make sure that no-one who shouldn't be entering took advantage of the loose permission he and his tribe held. Adeone had replied it was probably to make sure his feet got a good wash.

Minutes later, having watched the drivers on the coach and carts change to men of the valley, Adeone led his party over the ford and relaxed. He loved the valley's rugged cliffs, forest and rolling landscape. Every time he entered, it was as though hands were held out to greet him and take his burdens from him, which in some ways they were, if legends of magic were true.

# Chapter 12
# CEARDLANN
### Late Morning
### Rex Dallin

As THEY CRESTED the small rise on the far side of the ford, pasture land opened out and the River Encil curved away to their right. Further up, a lone and ancient oak stood in the centre of a meadow and a stone bridge spanned the river. They had left all the mail-clad guards near the lodge but had hardly made it to the top of the riverbank before Cal saw others were waiting dressed in leather and a padded cloth tunic he thought was called a jupon.

"Did Laioril pass you with a sardonic comment, Fitz?" enquired Adeone.

"Apparently we shouldn't have bothered on his account."

Adeone laughed, waiting for Fitz to manoeuvre his horse into step.

In his mind, Cal ran over the protocols the Steward had sent to him. Wasn't there something about always using sir, Sire or Your Majesty to the King? True, Crispin had been interrupting him when he was reading, but he was sure it was there.

When Ceardlann came into sight, Cal liked the house immediately. Even from a distance, it appeared welcoming: diamond and square-paned windows glinted, drawing the eye. As they drew closer, centuries of architectural whims became clear – including a tower. Yet it was no pretentious palace, no great house of a lord wishing to stamp his authority on an area – it was a home of someone respectable. It might be larger than most, Cal wondered how large it would be, but it felt like a home, even from a distance.

They turned off the lane and followed a smaller well-kept track to the front of the house. Cal, following Tain's instructions, dismounted. He briefly glanced around before helping Elantha scramble out of the coach, taking her free hand to steady her as she sucked her thumb. He watched curiously as an elderly man stepped forward from the line of waiting staff. He must be the Comptroller – hereditary guardian and steward of Ceardlann.

"Your Majesty, welcome home. I hope you had a good ride. My Princes, Lady Elantha and… you must be Master Calumiel."

"Thank you," replied Adeone. "The ride was pleasantly uneventful."

He led the way into an airy hallway and the Comptroller motioned towards the large antechamber of the Great Hall. Cal stared around with interest. Wooden panelling and plastered walls were the only impressions he had before they were in the antechamber and a footman was passing him a glass of water and asking if he wanted anything to eat. He said he didn't but Tain simply thrust a plate containing cinnamon cake at him and he realised his stomach was rumbling. Taking a bite, he grinned: two layers sandwiched with an apple jam tantalised his tastebuds. He'd soon finished the slice and crumbs. He peered around the antechamber curiously. The scent of lavender and beeswax was homely and relaxing. Again, there was wooden panelling and plasterwork. The polished panelling covered the bottom half of the walls, carved with motifs of wild roses. Above it was a tapestry that stretched the length of one wall, showing some sort of journey. Windows high in the adjacent wall let in light, and Cal idly wondered why they were too high to see out of. Tain saw him looking.

"It's a lightwell. A small courtyard. The only thing to see out there is another wall. Or, at least, that's why father says they're so high. There's a well in the courtyard, but that's all. We're not allowed there."

"Thank you, sir. Who's that?" he asked, pointing at a portrait below the windows.

Tain shrugged. "Probably one of my ancestors."

Arkyn sighed audibly behind them. "That, little brother, is King Arlis."

Tain pulled a face. "Here comes the history lesson."

Cal enquired, "Wasn't he something to do with the Age of Tyranny, sir?"

"He ended it," replied Arkyn, glad Cal had asked. "Well, his half-brother the Bard helped to restore him to the throne, ending the Age of Tyranny.

His story is interesting."

"If you like dusty scrolls," said Tain pointedly. "Some of us prefer to have fun."

"Some of us can do both," retorted Arkyn.

Cal studied the portrait curiously again. Here was a major figure from history and his descendant didn't care for his story. That somehow felt wrong but he knew he shouldn't say it. He turned his attention from the painting and saw Arkyn was sitting with Lady Elantha and Tain was watching the King and Comptroller talking. He sat by Tain and started talking about the ride, noticing the Prince's pensive brooding disappeared in an instant. After half an hour, Arkyn asked the King if they could be excused and they left for the nursery.

* * *

The King and Comptroller moved from the large antechamber to the Comptroller's office, where Adeone glanced over the books.

"Show it all to Arkyn. I'm leaving him in charge. Good training for him. Just make sure he doesn't overdo it, please."

"Very well, Sire." Having inherited his post before Adeone had been born, very little fazed the Comptroller. "His Highness seems to have grown a lot since I last saw him."

"Yes, he has. I realised the same thing recently. I've appointed Kadeem as a manservant for him and would like you to keep an eye on things. He might just need a discreet nudge in the right direction occasionally. I have told him to come to you if he is unsure of anything."

"Right, Your Majesty. How old is he?"

"Kadeem? Nearly eighteen. I thought it would be better for Arkyn to have someone younger. He's William's son, so he should know his job. As for Tain, don't let him wear you down and don't stand for any nonsense. I can't see that you would, but he'll be growing up here more than in Oedran, so you won't get the long respites you've had. For all he has his mother's colouring, he is more like I was. So, feel free to groan in anticipation. I'm hoping Calumiel might temper some of his liveliness. Elantha is struggling a bit. She's staying for as long as I can persuade her father to let her. She is like a daughter to me now. The only other thing is, do not be surprised if I suddenly descend on you. Oedran is going to seem very quiet but they are safer here."

Involuntarily, the Comptroller reached out and squeezed the King's arm. "Don't worry, sir. They'll be fine here. Safe and sound and, more than likely, causing untold mischief."

"I'll apologise for the mischief in advance," said Adeone ruefully.

"No need. I wouldn't have it any other way. Your Majesty is staying for a time?"

"Yes. Richardson will be coming each day with a pile of work for me. They like to keep me in condition."

"Kind of them that. What about a rest though?"

"Oh, don't worry, Comptroller, they'll keep the rest for me for later." Their eyes met in shared amusement, tempered by serious contemplation. "Next, the alerts. I'd rather the children didn't always have warning that I'm coming. I'd like to catch them out."

"I'll stop them sounding through the house then, Sire. I, however, might need warning," said the Comptroller dryly.

"I'd like to catch you out as well – if that's even possible." Adeone leant back in his chair, studying the lined face of the Comptroller. "Scanlon's been threatening me again, obliquely, but also Tain with a veiled comment."

"Can't you work out of the Rex Dallin for more than a few days: a couple of years say?" asked the Comptroller, worried.

"No. I'd never do that to the place. Also, I'm not going to run and hide. Scanlon will succeed one day, but I'll not hide like a coward."

"I'm sorry, Sire, I didn't mean to imply—"

Adeone cut across him. "Comptroller, don't be a fool. I know your meaning well enough. I'm not going to let my brother think he is getting to me. My children are simply here to recuperate after the death of their mother, as I did after the death of mine; as far as the people of Oedran are concerned anyway. Over time, it will become obvious what Scanlon now is and why I only have the boys in Oedran occasionally. As soon as the Princes start taking up their responsibilities properly, I am going to try to make sure we are never all together as a family for too long at a time. It will be hard, but it will make it more difficult for Scanlon to kill us all without showing his hand. We can always come here though. My father had extraordinary foresight when he refused permission for Scanlon to visit Ceardlann in his requests and bequests."

The Comptroller, still serious, said, "King Altarius certainly had that. I wonder whether anything sparked it."

"Probably a lifetime of being paranoid. He knew we weren't close; there being such a big age gap. Scanlon was only nine when I married and I was travelling; overseeing the provincial reviews. You would have seen him growing up far more than I ever did."

"Do you ever regret that, Sire?"

"Sometimes I wonder if I'd been around more as a brother whether this enmity would have flourished in him. I suppose we'll never know. Trying to outwit him has become so much more pressing a matter."

"Do you think you'll succeed?" asked the Comptroller, deeply concerned.

"No. He'll kill me; I feel it in my bones. Alcis help me though; I need to survive until Arkyn turns twenty. I just hope he manages to stop Scanlon; he and Tain together. I hope they survive to have children of their own, but I'll not persuade them to marry early, as my father did me and Scanlon. Don't get me wrong, I loved Ira and feel like a knife has been plunged through my heart, but I married early to set my father's mind at rest more than anything else; though Ira was captivating after her return from Garth. The first time she caught my attention was on her birthday. She was laughing with Lady Leila and Cornelia; walking through the Macarian House gardens. It was such a fresh sound, and, caught in an unguarded moment, her face was full of unconscious beauty." He sighed. "She never let me down as I did her."

"Sire, don't torment yourself."

Adeone shook his head. "I should have been here when Ella fell. I should have been here to support her. I failed that day and I seem to have been running away from the failure ever since."

Torn between telling *Adeone* exactly what he thought but being diplomatic to *the King*, the Comptroller decided he could temper the former with the latter. "You aren't running away from failure, sir, because there was no failure. You were days away at the time." He studied Adeone's haunted face. "Ira would never have wanted you to be blaming yourself like this. You do everything you can for your family, always have done. Never have I known you shirk your responsibilities."

Adeone slumped forward, head in his hands, shaking slightly.

Reminded forcefully of Adeone's childhood depressions, the Comptroller squeezed his shoulder and left the office. A few moments to himself would help, but the tricks of previous years weren't going to be much use.

Adeone leant back in his chair, rubbing at his face, conscious again of how drained he felt. Was the Comptroller right? Was he berating himself over nothing? Some days he felt like he was; some he knew he wasn't. Lying on his conscience most heavily was the fact he'd never apologised to Ira for not being there when their daughter had died. Ira wouldn't want him to feel this way, but that didn't expiate the guilt. He watched the bustle of the stables, losing himself in the view of life continuing.

"Sire, get that down you."

He turned to find the Comptroller holding out a glass of amber liquid as though it were medicine. He drank the whiskey with a sad smile, blinking back tears. "Thank you."

The Comptroller simply nodded in return, one friend to another. Bringing the world back to normality, he said, "Cook suggested seven for dinner, Your Majesty."

"That sounds fine to me. Lady Elantha will be in bed, but the boys and Cal can join me. By the way, the Wanda arrived as I did. I asked them to use Encampment Field. Laioril will be keeping an eye on the boys as well. Probably he'll end up telling them stories the day through, but it should keep their minds off other things. Arkyn's especially. I've told him what his uncle is. I realised I needed to explain why I was really bringing them here."

"I'm sure we'll cope. If you'll excuse me, I'll just go and give orders about dinner."

Both men left the room in companionable silence to be almost mown down by two lads running down the passage. Tain grinned at his father and carried on; Cal stopped, bowed and waited for Adeone to pass before he ran off after his friend.

The Comptroller saw a grin light up the King's face. "They've certainly livened the place up, Sire."

Chapter 13
## NEW BEGINNING
Morning

Oedran – Barracks

IN OEDRAN, Wynfeld counted down the days until his leave ended. Being idle frustrated him, but he had little choice. The day he was due back on duty, he reported to the barracks unsure what to expect. The last time he'd been there, he'd been a raw recruit and the memories were lost in the haze of confusion and time.

His aspirations had never included promotion to captain. His stomach churned as he stood in front of General Paturn's critical gaze. It wasn't the moment to admit he didn't know what he should be doing.

He was handed over to the care of the Major whose curiosity about Wynfeld's commission was obvious. He asked which of the rumours were true: had he visited Queen Ira on her last day or had he saved their King's life? Wynfeld smiled but said his King's reasons were his own. He wasn't a fool. The last afternoon of Queen Ira's life should be private to her family. He had blundered in by accident and had done what he could to make her and her family smile. Saving his King's life had been unintended and he'd already been rewarded enough. To change the subject, he admitted he didn't know what he was doing. His commanding officer shrugged. It would be a steep learning curve, but Wynfeld had to either cope or resign.

The Major showed him to a large office with a desk and many shelves and cabinets, which did nothing to demystify his new job. Two waiting sergeants saluted as they entered. Having introduced Beaver and Jones, the Major left Wynfeld and his sergeants eyeing each other. Uncertainty radiating off him, Wynfeld listened as the sergeants gave a potted summation of their regiment's job before dismissing them with a word of thanks.

Once alone, he explored his desk and discovered a wad of notes from Fitz, explaining more about the regiment's activities. After reading them, he opened a drawer and read some reports on various members of the Court. Gradually, he built a picture of how the regiment operated. Fitz's records outlined his spies or information gatherers in the Palace and city.

A corporal entered and saluted. Wynfeld raised a querying eyebrow. Even if he didn't know what he was doing, he'd faced enough captains in his time to mimic them.

"Note from Lord Landis, sir."

"Leave it on my desk and I'll take a look at it."

The corporal did so, saluted and left. Out of curiosity, Wynfeld retrieved Fitz's file on Lord Landis: one sheet of paper with the words, *'Leave well alone and pass on information requested.'* Breaking the seal on Lord Landis' missive, he read the welcome message. It also contained an undercurrent that his King's Defender would be watching him.

'*Well...*' thought Wynfeld, '*...You're so close to our King, I'll return the compliment.*'

The letter made Wynfeld question why King Adeone had been willing to trust him with something vital when he had no experience of command; how had his King discovered enough about him to decide? After a time, he walked over to the drawers and pulled out W. Where *Wynfeld* would have resided was a note from the General: he had the file. Groaning, Wynfeld closed the drawer. Did it really matter? He had the commission and he'd do his best to never disappoint Queen Ira's memory.

He called for his corporal-clerk. "Are we informed of our King's itinerary, Drave?"

"Yes, sir. Copy's in the top drawer of the black cabinet. There's also information on which lords are currently granted travel leave and where Lord Scanlon should be. The King likes updating on a regular, daily, basis as to which lords are in Oedran. Regarding the Lords of Oedran, they don't need formal travel leave to visit their estates in Anapara, for up to a court-cycle including travel time but minus the day they must preside at Court – so that's eleven days, sir – but for anything else, they require the King's leave and the King likes them to notify him informally when they are to be absent from Oedran at other times. Other lords in their families have more freedom; they can visit elsewhere, but His Majesty expects to be consulted and to know where they are. Generally, therefore, they will also request travel leave, or their head of family will do so for them. His Majesty also likes to know the movements of any palace guests."

Wynfeld was intrigued. "Doesn't the Palace Guard deal with that?"

"Only at Court, once they leave the Palace, they are our responsibility, sir. We do a report each morning; each sergeant on duty writes a portion of it. You read it all and sign it off before it's delivered to Administrator Richardson. The King tends to read it first thing and highlight anything he wants investigating."

"Right, thank you, Drave. That's all."

Once the door had closed, Wynfeld found the itinerary. King Adeone would be at Ceardlann for a few days. That gave Wynfeld momentary respite to find out exactly what he had to be doing before his King could summon him to give an account of himself.

Two days later, his men dragged in a man who had been shouting that King Adeone had killed their Queen. The reports said everyone who had heard the rumours had laughed and told the man to shut up. He hadn't and had come to the attention of Wynfeld's men. The rumours, if people began to believe them, could be devastating and Wynfeld – telling his men to leave the man in a cell to sober up and calm down – realised the importance of his command.

Later that day, Landis sat down in Wynfeld's office and asked about the man in custody. Wynfeld crooked an eyebrow.

"None of your men keep me informed, Captain. I have ways of finding things out other than by bribing soldiers."

Wynfeld said, "Might I know them, my lord? They may come in handy."

"Nice try, Captain. My information comes from a source far above your head. Oh, and, stop openly questioning my servants about my movements – for one thing, most of them don't know anything useful. Secondly, those that do aren't foolish enough to tell anyone and, thirdly, if you'd asked, I'd have had my secretary give you my itinerary a week in advance. Would it be useful to you?"

Wynfeld eyed his guest. The Lord of Oedran had certainly become more serious since their youth. "Thank you, that might save my men valuable time. Will it be accurate?"

"When it is sent to you, it will be accurate. I cannot promise that it will stay such. I have a lot of appointments that simply appear with no warning; however, I will update it if any major changes occur. Does that satisfy you, Captain?"

"Yes, thank you, my lord," replied Wynfeld whilst thinking, *'What you would do if I said no?'*

"Good. Now you will please tell me why, when you were advised to leave me alone, you have gone your own way."

Wynfeld smiled gravely. "Because, my lord, I would be a fool to accept someone else's word as reliable in the job His Majesty has given me. Everyone has a different viewpoint on the world. I'm charged with protecting His Majesty and his family. If that means distrusting people then I must distrust them. I'm sure Your Lordship can appreciate that."

*'You do have a long way to go, don't you? Never give more than the necessary information.'* Landis stilled. "I can but remember that, sometimes, an appearance of trust is better than that of constant distrust; it can yield more useful information. Now, the man in your cells, do not put him on trial for treason; it will never get to court and you'll simply give Lord Scanlon another supporter when he lets him walk. Show him the error of his ways, point out the benefits of a job in the army, then, when he's accepted, post him to Bayan or Terasia." Landis' tone was half dismissive and half ordering compliance.

"You are sure he'll accept the job?" Wynfeld was sceptical. *'Credit me with knowing the men of my streets better than a silver-spooned Lord of Oedran.'*

"He is a homeless man. Offer him a home and he'll be yours. Your books sadly lack informants for those provinces. You need to learn to manipulate men into working for you before they realise what they are doing."

"Thank you for the advice, my lord. I'm sorry if I caused offence."

Landis regarded him steadily. *'I know better liars than you, Captain.'* He said, "No offence was given, Wynfeld. You have, at times, shown your naïvety. Your job is not one in which to show it. Don't let Lord Scanlon hear about it, he will find a way of using it against you. I am also charged with protecting the life of the King and the Princes. They are like my family. If any harm befalls them, I will cease to be a nice man." He rose. "Thank you for your time, Captain." *'Not that you had much choice.'*

Once he had left, Wynfeld considered everything Lord Landis had said. He began to appreciate why the note had said to leave the Defender well alone. How many informers were there in Oedran? Was everyone gathering information for someone? He would have to be more careful.

# Chapter 14
## SNEAKING OUT
Alunadai, Week 15 – 15th Macial, 15th Macis 1209
Ceardlann

CEARDLANN WAS A HOUSE OF STORIES speaking of lost rooms and secret areas, of magic and mundanity, of the everyday and the unexpected, of the future and the past. Entering any room for the first time, Cal thought what a strange place the house was. He expected it to be grander, but the pleasantly proportioned rooms were never too vast, their ceilings never too high. There was no lavish display of gold and silver, no unnecessary embellishment, but there were the finest of glass drinking vessels from Denshire, the most delicate pottery from Terasia, the best quality cloth from Lufian. Together everything gave off an air of tasteful wealth, of muted, refined opulence: craftsmen had excelled themselves to build and furnish this retreat. It *was* the home of a respectable man, but undoubtedly a rich one. In his father's mind, riches and respectability were opposites, and Cal had never considered they could occur together.

* * *

A week after arriving, a hand shook Cal's shoulder and he pulled himself out of sleep reluctantly.

"Come on, get up," said Tain, grinning. "I want to get outside before anyone can stop us."

Cal pushed himself up. It was barely light. "What about breakfast, sir?"

"We'll sneak something from the kitchen."

"Shouldn't we tell—?"

"Yes, but if we do that, we'll be caught with lessons."

They entered the kitchen to be met with, "Are you giving Maria the slip, sir?"

"What gave you that idea, Cook?" enquired Tain innocently.

"Experience. Where are you off to? And don't think about telling me a lie or I'll get the whole of the guards out hunting for you," threatened Cook, waving a wooden spoon at them menacingly.

Tain beamed. "Down to the Great Meadow. I want to show Cal the Wishing Tree."

"Right. Will you be here for breakfast? Or are you trying to avoid your lessons again?" When Tain swallowed, Cook added sagely, "You're avoiding your lessons. One of these days, your father will notice."

Tain shrugged. "He's too busy to. I just don't feel in the mood for them."

Cook's eyes narrowed. "Hmm. So, what do you want for this picnic?"

Tain's grin brightened. "What have you got?"

They ended up with pastries, apples, a skin of water and a bag for it all before Cook returned to his normal grumpy demeanour.

"That's it. Out you go. I've got breakfast to prepare for the FitzAlcis."

Tain chuckled. "Thanks, Cook."


As they reached the Great Meadow beside the River Encil, Tain pointed. "That's the Wishing Tree. People get married here, or wish for luck and happiness, that sort of thing."

The early morning mists gave the oak an ethereal quality, with its canopy above the swirling vapours. It was the tree Cal had seen when entering the valley.

"Isn't there an alcium here then?" asked Cal.

"No. Valley inhabitants have this instead. Or Welcome Field at the south of the valley. I love this meadow. In summer, you can almost hide in the grass. Come on. Let's have breakfast. I'm hungry."

They sat with their backs against the tree. After a few minutes of munching silence, homesickness washed over Cal. He blinked hard.

Tain said, "You know, it's not that bad."

"I know, sir. I just miss my ma."

Tain swallowed. "Me too."

Cal cursed himself. "I'm sorry, Your Highness."

"Don't be. We used to come here with her when father was out of Oedran. We'd bring a picnic and just run about." He paused, swallowing back his tears. "You can go home, if you want, you know."

Cal hesitated. "I know, sir, but it's not that. I… I don't know. At least here no-one is giving me chores to do. I don't miss those. My home is so noisy as well and Ceardlann isn't."

"We can change that," replied Tain with a grin. "I'm sure we can liven it up a bit."

Cal knew he shouldn't disagree with Tain. "Do you mind if we don't, sir? I mean… well, I don't want to get into trouble. Your… His Majesty's been so kind to me."

"He mightn't find out," pointed out Tain. "He's so busy still."

"I'm… I'd rather not, sir, that's all."

Tain sighed. "Fine, but we can still have fun." He bit his lip. "I wish he wasn't busy. We don't get to see him much anymore."

"I don't get to see my pa much. He's always in the shop and, unless he wants us to help with something, we're kept out of the way, Your Highness."

"Oh. So, can you swim?"

"Never tried, sir," replied Cal.

"I'll have to teach you. Though I guess it'll be too cold so they'll stop us for now. Oh well, I'll have to teach you to ride properly instead."

"Thank you, sir."

"You don't have to keep calling me 'sir'," said Tain.

Cal hesitated. "I'd rather not stop, Your Highness."

"Or *Your Highness*, for that matter," grouched Tain. "We're friends, aren't we?"

"I hope so, sir, but I think I should use it, for now at least. I don't want His Majesty to think I've forgotten myself."

"Fine. So, what do you think of Ceardlann?"

Cal considered. "It's smaller than I thought it would be. I mean, I thought it would be like the Palace… but it's nothing like as grand. I like it. Is Cook always so blunt with you though? I didn't think it was right."

Tain grinned. "No, it's not, but Ceardlann's home, whereas the Palace is where we live in Oedran. That's what father says, anyway. I'm glad you like it. Cook is Cook. Nothing changes him and we need to eat."

They were talking about heading to Ceardlann for lunch when Arkyn rode into the meadow. He dismounted, took off a laden saddlebag and left Ponder to roam.

"You know, sooner or later, you'll have to stop skipping lessons."

Tain grinned. "How are yours going with Advisor Spellen?"

Arkyn chuckled. "Apparently as well as yours with Ewall. Here, I persuaded Cook that you'd need something for lunch."

Tain and Cal grinned, unpacking their second picnic of the day.

"Father expects us there for dinner."

"You told him?" asked Tain, outraged.

"No, but I said I was going out for a ride and he saw the saddlebags."

Tain groaned. "There goes our freedom."

Arkyn shrugged. "I wouldn't be so sure, little brother. He didn't say I had to return to my lessons."

* * *

Scruffy and unkempt, they reached Ceardlann an hour before dinner. Maria stood Tain and Cal in front of her, trying to keep a straight face.

"You can face His Majesty like that. He wants to see you two in the study," she informed them, hands on hips.

Tain bit his lip. "Is he very annoyed with us?"

"Go and find out."

Adeone watched the two nervous boys enter and had to stop himself laughing. They'd plainly been playing at the water's edge, for their legs were covered in mud, the grime of which had made it to their faces.

In a sterner voice than the situation truly warranted, he said, "Where were you?"

Tain swallowed. "In the Great Meadow, sir. We were… We lost track of time."

"Tain Lachlan FitzAlcis, I don't believe that. Your stomach would have reminded you, for a start."

"We didn't mean to be so long, father, honestly…"

Adeone crooked an eyebrow. "*Honestly* is normally used when bending the truth. Do you have anything to say for yourself, Master Calumiel?"

In a small voice, Cal said, "No, sir. That is, I am sorry, sir. I didn't mean to cause any trouble when I suggested we went."

Tain stilled.

Adeone regarded both boys. "Hmm. Are you saying this was your idea, Cal Galdwin?"

"I guess so, Your Majesty. I'm truly sorry, sir."

"Go and get a bath, Tain; I want to see you presentable at dinner. Go on. I want to talk to Master Calumiel alone."

Tain opened and shut his mouth but reacted to the glare his father was giving him and left the room.

"Master Calumiel, what you did is called lying to your king and it's not acceptable," said Adeone.

Cal examined the floor: wide polished floorboards, swept clean.

The King's voice softened. "Apart from that, let him take his fair share of the blame. You are not here so he can do as he likes and get away with it. I wouldn't be doing either of you any favours if I let that happen. I respect what you were trying to do, but you don't have to do it."

Cal's gaze shot up.

Adeone smiled warmly. "Come and sit down. I'm trying to say you don't have to take the blame for my son. I guess the documents that the Steward sent you – which you seem to have read in detail – outlined that a prince can never be wrong and must always win, yes?"

"Yes, Sire, and that I should do as he wishes," admitted Cal.

*'No wonder history is littered with idiots in my family,'* thought Adeone. "How very correct *at Court*. This isn't Court. So, Cal Galdwin, I'd like you to make me a promise if you think it appropriate: you will not treat my sons any differently to any other friend you might have – Arkyn as well as Tain – that you will let them take the blame when it's their fault and that you will teach them how to lose and be wrong."

Cal swallowed. "What if Their Highnesses don't like it?"

"Then they're not who I thought they were," revealed Adeone. "You don't have to tell them about it if you don't want to."

Cal considered for a short time. "I'll do my best, sir."

"Thank you." Adeone chuckled. "Now, what *were* you and Tain doing to get so muddy?"

Cal laughed. "I don't know, sir. We were trying to catch fish at one point and then I tried to show him how to climb trees, but there's no good holds on the Wishing Tree and we couldn't catch Ponder and it just happened."

"I wish I could have joined you. Sounds much more enjoyable than my day has been. Go on. See if Maria can't help scrub you clean."

Cal was quickly getting dressed when Tain found him and sat on the bed, saying, "Did you get into a lot of trouble?"

"No. His Majesty was all right about it really."

"He didn't let me explain. I'm sorry, I should have taken the blame. It was my fault. I'll tell him the truth when I can, I promise."

Cal grinned. Suddenly, he felt better about things. "Can't have that, Your Highness. A prince can't take the blame..."

"This one can when it's my fault," admitted Tain. "Otherwise, it's not fair when it really is yours."

Cal chuckled. "So, tomorrow – any ideas?"

# Chapter 15
## CAL AND LAIORIL

Imperadai, Week 15 – 18th Macial, 18th Macis 1209
Ceardlann

OVER THE FOLLOWING DAYS, bouts of homesickness washed over Cal. He missed the noises he'd never heeded before – the shop bell tinkling, the clatter of pots in the kitchen, the squabbling of his siblings – and he missed his mother's cooking.

On Imperadai he dined alone, giving him too much time to dwell. Needing space until the gripping sadness loosened its hold, he passed through the kitchen, taking solace in the warmth and familiarity of the busy environment. He wandered out of Ceardlann and towards the forest, passing through the stables, along the rear lane past White Cottage, currently unused, and Oak Cottage, the house for the servants of Ceardlann. No-one stopped him, no-one interrupted him. He climbed the rise, heavy feet dragging him down. Walking wasn't the solace it had been. He sat on a flattish stone, hugging his knees, watching Ceardlann, the grooms hurrying back and forth; the carts moving off: the King was returning to

Oedran imminently. His own family was there. Everything that was familiar and normal was there. He swallowed, tears pricking his eyes. He didn't hate Ceardlann; it was fun, warm and welcoming but it wasn't home. His fingers traced marks in the stone, interlocking triangles; others had sat here before, others had watched Ceardlann. Was it home to them? His father's voice resounded in his head, don't get too comfortable, don't get close to the FitzAlcis, don't trust them, don't, don't, don't... His mother's voice came to him, telling him to enjoy himself, that they'd be there when he got home, whispering that she'd miss him.

He angrily wiped tears away.

An elderly voice said, "It'll ease. Let them flow, lad. It's the best thing you can do."

He glanced up to find a spry old man with piercing blue eyes looking at him kindly. He went to get up.

"Nay, lad, you sit still. If you don't mind, I'll join you."

Cal gave a small shrug.

"I've always liked this spot. It's the best place to see Ceardlann from. You must be Calumiel. I'm Laioril, part of that dreadful tribe of the Wanda who camp here and cause mayhem every year. I'm still trying to persuade the gamekeeper that we don't poach. For some reason, he never quite believes me – can't think why." He carefully placed two dead rabbits on the grass beside his walking staff. "What's brought you up here alone? I've only ever seen you with Tain."

Cal glanced at him askance; surprised that Laioril hadn't added the title on the front, as was normal.

"Never have had much time for titles," remarked Laioril, as though he could read Cal's mind. "I watched Adeone grow up as well. They're only people, same as the rest of us. Mind you, I can get away with it, old man's prerogative. I'll use 'em when I have to, but that's all."

Cal didn't know how to react, so he answered the question instead. "The King's leaving tonight..."

"Let me guess, you felt homesick and alone, thought you'd get a breath of fresh air so no-one could see your tears. Then some inconsiderate old buffoon goes and interrupts your solitude. Listen to me, I'm insulting myself. Who will ever take me seriously if I continue to do that? Mind you, not many people do anyway. I keep telling these weird and wonderful stories, you see. I can't help it if nobody believes in the old legends anymore. It's hard when you feel you're outside something. When you feel you're not the same as others. One reason I'll never use titles unless I must. They set people apart. It's as hard for those with 'em as without 'em."

"Father says I have to use the titles even if they ask me not to. He doesn't want me to be here. Thinks I'll get grand ideas. I know who I am and where I come from. I'm proud of it. Proud of the fact my father was born cisan and worked so hard that by the time I was born we could be counted amongst the alunan, proud that he did it without being a member of the guild. I'm not going to forget it in a while."

Laioril nodded; it explained a lot that he'd heard in the short time since they'd all arrived. People had commented that, for saying the boys were meant to be friends, Cal had never lessened the Court formalities.

"It's always good to know your roots. Mine are so deeply buried at some point marked X on the map that they've been lost. Mind you, I and the King get on well enough and I do *occasionally* use his title. Not too much. Dunna want him getting grand ideas either. I remember when he came here as a lad your age. He spent more time wandering through the valley on his own than was good for him. Got too caught up in grief. He pulled through though. Seems like yesterday to me. Just remember, a title is only another name. Rather like you shorten yours to Cal. Tain simply lengthens it. Don't let it bother you, lad."

"Is that true?" enquired Cal, perplexed and suspicious.

"Works for me," remarked Laioril. "Now, have you ever heard the Lay of Ull?"

Before he could answer, a voice called for Cal from Ceardlann.

Laioril glanced at the surprise on Calumiel's face. "Part of the magic of the valley, lad. They made it so you can't hide here. Can't possibly be because of the shape of the landscape; that's much too mundane. The story will wait. Go on with you, I ought to be getting these rabbits somewhere the gamekeeper can't find 'em. Otherwise, he'll go hopping mad."

Cal laughed as he wished Laioril goodnight and tore down the slope.

When he reached Ceardlann, Maria was watching for him.

She said, "The King is about to leave. Come and say goodbye." She noticed his surprise. "Come on, sooner you're there, sooner the King can be in Oedran. He's touched you left them to dine together but he does want to see you before he goes. He'll need to tell your parents that he saw you were whole, well and extremely grubby when he left."

Cal followed Maria down the passageways of Ceardlann to the Great Hall. He hung back, seeing the family taking leave of each other.

Adeone spotted him. "So, Master Calumiel, how do you like Ceardlann?"

"Very much, Sire."

"Is the homesickness easing?"

Cal blushed. "A bit, Sire."

"It will take time. I can pass your home on my way through Oedran;

do you have any message for your family?"

"Only that I love them, sir," replied Cal with faint embarrassment. He wanted to say, *'Can I go home, can I see them, then can I come back...?'* but didn't dare.

A couple of minutes later, Cal watched as Adeone hugged his sons and Elantha. A moment later Adeone wrapped him in a hug; the strength of it warmed him, a lump rose in his throat and he blinked back tears as the King whispered, *'Thank you,'* before ruffling his hair to cover the moment. As Cal watched him leave, he began to feel better, in a strange, unreal way.

* * *

The following day, the day was still; no breeze drawing the warmth from the autumn sun. Arkyn, Tain and Cal found their way to the Wanda camp, where a wry voice observed,

"I wondered how long it would take for you to find us. If I didn't know better, I'd think you had been too busy studying. Luckily, I do know better. Greetings, young Cal. Got time for that story now?"

Cal grinned at Laioril. "Might have. Depends how long it'll take. I've been warned."

"That's very unfair of them at the house. I'll just have to shorten it a bit, won't I?"

"I believe that when I hear it, Chief," remarked Arkyn, amused.

"It does everyone good to be proved wrong once in a way, lad. Come to my tent, for I won't prove you wrong standing here. Plus, we'll be out of the sun. Always good for an old man that. I've got some elderflower cordial stuff hiding somewhere around here. I'm sure you could find a spot for it."

Used to Laioril's ways, Arkyn and Tain followed him quite happily and Cal followed them. Various members of the Wanda shouted greetings. A middle-aged woman stood watching them, amused.

Laioril spotted her. "Miranda, any chance of some of your wonderful elderflower cordial? I've already promised the lads some, so don't disappoint me."

Miranda chuckled. "I'm sure I can find some somewhere, Chief. Are you hungry, Your Highnesses?" When Arkyn and Tain nodded, she winked. "I'll have to do something about that as well then."

Twelve minutes later, they were settled in the Chief's tent, tucking into an array of fruits as the Chief started to tell them the story of the Majistar Ull.

# Chapter 16
## THE LAY OF ULL



AT THE BEGINNING of the reckoning of the years – to be exact, one thousand two hundred and nine years ago – the lands we now know as the Oedranian Empire were split up into warring factions. There'd been fighting between different tribes and kingdoms from time immemorial. Now, though, the land suffered, crops were burnt; fighting was constant and unending; families were torn asunder, thousands died. Anarchy was heralded and the hearts of men bled.

Stories that became legend and myth say Ull appeared in a small village, in the loop of a river…but that isn't where his story truly begins… It is said it starts on another world.

Imagine a world where magic prevails, where men of might do not carry swords but control the substances around them by thought, by wish, by touch. Imagine a man, a man who wants not only to rule what he can through this power, this magic but wants to rule over men; who wants to control not just the inanimate but the living; who wants to cast aside those who have mocked him; who wants to be the power amongst those who were equals, the one who decides what is right and what is wrong. There have been many men who have desired what he did but none with the power, the magic he had. His name, the legends say, was Ull and he is the one who brought magic to this world. It is said he was nothing to look at – until he was. That he could pass you by in the lanes and not be known but then he would catch your eye and you'd know it was he.

He was known as a majistar and legends say he came from a world called Annire. The twin of Erinna but a very different place. On that world, the power resided with the Council of Maji, made up of majistars, who had completed years of gruelling training to wield magic. Ull was one such majistar but not a member of the council for all he wanted to be. He wanted to teach them that he was owed their respect without earning it. Wanted to show them that he was as powerful as they, more than they were. They had laughed at him for his height, his accent, his origins and even his dedication. He searched through the libraries of Mebyd, hunting for something, anything, that could help. His dedication should be rewarded, his determination should have its prize. He found, as though by accident, the book that he wanted. He'd been delving in the dusty shelves of Mebyd's Archive Library, which held a copy of all tomes considered important but this one didn't appear important, it didn't feel important, it seemed as nothing, a pamphlet between sagas. It was dog-eared and dusty, torn and tattered, worn and warped. He'd opened it more out of curiosity: surely something so damaged would have been recopied. There was no title he could see, just three instructions. The first to turn the moon dark – why that would be needed, he didn't know, but it was simple and he memorised it easily; the second to make others listen, which would be useful and again he memorised it easily. It wasn't a spell, as such, just a mental catechism; the third he couldn't believe: in green ink, mockingly clear against the age of the book, was a true spell – a set of instructions and items to make the one who could wield the magic the most powerful majistar in the world. Ull read it over and over but could not memorise it. It seemed to shift and change before his eyes. He decided to take the book, forbidden as it was, but as he was soon to become the majistar it described, he could pardon himself then.

Once in his quarters, he sat and opened the book again. The orange light of the dying day seemed to set it afire and it tingled to his touch. He smirked smugly to himself. Here was the answer he'd been searching for, here was the solution to his troubles, here was his reason, his prize. No-one would remember his roots were low born, no-one would care he was a head taller than the tallest of them, no-one would laugh and ask him to tell them when it started raining. He would simply be the first of the council, not the first amongst equals but the omnipotent and invincible leader. He would break the clique, the model that excluded rather than included, he would bring reform in his image.

The spell wasn't even difficult or expensive. It asked for twelve different coloured star stones, all of them with twelve points to the star and all the same size. That had surprised him slightly. Star stones were common enough on Annire. They were on streets, in fields and tumbling along river beds. Normally spells required something more valuable to be part of the process: a cart full of the most exotic wood to burn, a chest full of the most precious metals to melt. To perform a spell in the desert lands you'd need gallons of water. This spell only required twelve different coloured star stones. It seemed almost parsimonious and gave him pause for thought, but, if the spell didn't work, no-one would ever know.

The next council meeting he observed left him furious. They had voted once more to exclude on origins as well as skill. He could see his fellow majistars muttering, could feel their discontent but he knew they were weak, they wouldn't challenge the council; they would murmur and mutter and that would be all. He was seething when he returned to his room. With enraged thrusts of his palm, he forced the fire into life, the candles to light, the curtains to close. He retrieved the book, the star stones and his embroidered cloak. He inhaled. Soon the world would change and he would become the omnipotent majistar, the one who combined all the able spirits of magic, all subtle hues of skill. He would simply become.

He spoke the words of the spell, felt the change in the air – felt the change in himself – and strode to the door. He flung it open, then paused and glanced over his shoulder. His room was still there, all the rich trappings were in place; the tapestries that adorned all the rooms at the Academy of Annire were there, the gold thread catching the light of the fire. So where was the corridor? Why was there a village street? Why was a gaggle of children laughing at him? A stern glance later, they ran off, still laughing. He stepped out into the street and a young man clad in mail and girt with sword, asked,

"Is this one fancy dress then? Or have I missed the turning somewhere?"

Ull looked at him, up and down the street, turned on the spot and examined the spot before inspecting a small one-storey longhouse; such buildings were common enough on Annire – he'd been born in one though he seldom admitted it – but the plants here were as different as the fashions.

It's said, his altercation with the soldier was full of frustration and misunderstandings. He learned of the battle, of the struggle between the Battle-King, or Cary, Anaparus and his cousin, who considered burning crops and razing villages an acceptable way to take control. Imagine, if you can, what that must have been like for Ull. Stories tell Annire was peaceful; they worshipped the moon deity Cisluna bringing safety to the night, but on Erinna the moon is Aluna, with a whole different emphasis in the ancestors' blessing. Imagine learning that magic is not might but vanquishers wield weapons, that oratory is outlawed and slaying is standard. No-one knows what happened to the soldier Ull met, but as the tales speak of him, it's likely he survived.

Ull returned to the longhouse. Expecting his room at Annire, he was dismayed. There were no hangings, no rich furnishings, just beaten earth for the floor, cracked pots and crude-hewn furniture. His room had vanished, leaving nothing but a dying fire, candles burned out and glowing star stones. On the crude table lay the book, like new; the caking dust had gone and the title was discernible: *The Egotist's Downfall*. He collapsed onto a spindly three-legged stool and sat there, holding the book. His whole being crashed down around him as he read those words accusing and describing him in equal measure.

Ull was angry; what had gone wrong? What had happened? What on *Erinna* was going off? He opened *The Egotists Downfall* at random. He squinted at the page; twelve words were there. All described spirits, abilities of magic in different coloured inks; it took him a second to realise that most colours matched the star stones – but the white was in black ink.

He cursed the book, frustrated at the lack of help within its pages. He railed against the futility of his situation. The book in front of him snapped shut and then fell open again. Words began to scrawl across the blank pages:

*You wanted to be the greatest majistar in the world. You forgot to specify which world. This world had no magic until today. You are the greatest and only majistar on this world. You have brought something that should never have been here. Before you can return, you must find the people who can wield the power locked into these stones. You must stop the fighting. You must balance the world again - before it destructs. It is already fragile, go carefully. For if this world falls so will its twin Annire. You wanted to be great, be good instead. Stop the battle, find the twelve and rebuild the world.*

The book snapped shut again and Ull almost threw it into the dying fire in exasperation. Some instinct stopped him. He opened it again and there were the twelve colours and spirits. He scooped up the stones into a pouch and strode from the house with the book in his hand. He set off walking up the hill. Over the rise, the first things he discovered were the carts and tents, which always followed an army around. He sighed; the camp seemed to be full of toothless grannies, women of rather dubious occupations and children by the score. He set off through the throng until he found the biggest tent and strode in, saying,

"Who's in charge here?"

A dry, crackling voice replied, "Our cavalry, by the sounds of things. Though I think… yep, that's theirs joining in. I hope my son knows what he's doing."

It was told, through all the years that followed, that Ull simply strode out of the tent, having realised he'd never get a straight answer. Who can say what the truth is? He strode to the high point and, summoning all the magic within him, turned the weapons into air. He felt an enormous sense of satisfaction as men looked bewildered and scared. The satisfaction transformed swiftly to rage as man after man resorted to manual combat.

He yelled and cursed before spotting the standard of the Cary – an arrow in flight – caught in the streaming wind. The emblem caught at Ull's latent imagination. He flicked the book open and at the top of the list was the word Skifta; next to it was the description 'to shift.' Glimpsing the standard again, he made his way towards it. Every time a soldier went to attack him, he thrust out his palm and they were thrown backwards. By the time he reached the standard, the Cary had seen him coming. They faced each other; the Cary brown of hair and eye and tall; Ull fair-haired, blue-eyed and just that tad taller. The Cary stood there waiting for Ull to bow. Ull stood there waiting for the Cary to bow. The surrounding men watched the scene with confusion. None capable of interfering.

Ull broke the silence. "Are you the one responsible for this?" He motioned over his shoulder to the two fighting armies.

The Cary looked at him. He prided himself that he could appraise a man's character in seconds: the seconds normally prior to him killing the man. He stared into Ull's eyes and saw something in the depths he'd never seen before.

To the surprise of the surrounding men, he said, "It takes two to fight."

"But one may stop it. You are destroying this world. Hundreds are dying for you. It is *your* fight – not theirs. End the battle and I will show you another way to settle your differences."

The Cary looked again into the depths of Ull's eyes and knew what this man said was true. Something strange had happened; where were all the weapons? Was Aluna displeased with the fighting? Had she sent this man to tell him that? He turned to the trumpeter and gave the order to sound the retreat. The men below them stopped fighting, slowly; the Cary's soldiers made their way back to camp in some confusion. The opposing side, mystified, watched the retreat, cheering until the trumpet of their leader sounded and they went in the opposite direction.

The Cary and Ull made their way back to the tent Ull had earlier left. Ignoring the heralds waiting for him, the Cary entered to be greeted by the old woman.

"Not dead yet? Doing better than your pa then. Not sure how though because your cousin's the better fighter. They should never have split the kingdom up but that's men for you."

The Cary glared at her and she left, laughing to herself. He then faced Ull, who started to explain his day. The Cary thought the man was insane, a trick by his cousin, until Ull pulled out the star stones. Common they may have been on Annire but on Erinna they were unknown. The Cary became lost in the depth of the violet stone, which glowed when he picked it up. Ull curiously opened The Egotists Downfall again. The entry for Skifta had disappeared. He had found one of the twelve; maybe he wasn't going to be too long before he returned home.

Ull's prediction was sadly misplaced. He and the Cary worked out the power of the first stone. The Cary could think of a place he wanted to be and move there in the blink of an eye. The Cary pointed out that this might not end the war. So Ull told him to challenge his cousin to a race, specifying that whatever skills they had, they could use. The winner would rule over both kingdoms. The Cary's cousin laughed at the proposition but agreed – knowing he was the faster runner. His advisors warned him to be wary of a trick, but he was so certain of victory that he never listened. The day of the race came. The Cary's cousin started running and easily overtook the Cary. They rounded a bend and suddenly the Cary was in front of him again. The same thing happened all the way throughout the two-mile race. When the end came in sight, the Cary's cousin was perplexed to see the Cary still running in front of him. When he crossed the line, he began yelling about tricks. The Justice-King, or Justa, adjudicated. As the only stipulation had been that the competitors could use whatever skills they had at their disposal, the Justa decided that the Cary had won the race fairly. The Cary declared his cousin as his second-in-command and the fighting ceased. Both lands combined once more to form one kingdom. In time, they became peaceful.

Ull stayed within the Kingdom of Anapara: named after the founding Cary. It is said he performed many wonders whilst there, but soon one of the neighbouring tribes started to attack over the western ridge. Ull went with the Cary's troops to see if he could stop the fighting. He found the Chieftainess of the area. Her standard was a bird in flight. He talked with her and showed her the star stones; she took the orange stone and became lost in its colour. Ull opened the book again. The entry for Sundrian had disappeared, but the word *splitter* was still just legible. The Chieftainess and Ull sat outside to try to find a way to stop the fighting.

The Chieftainess spotted an eagle and sighed. "I wonder what the country looks like from up there. It must be so beautiful."

"Why don't you concentrate on the eagle? Concentrate on the mind of the bird. You might be surprised."

The Chieftainess considered that he had lost his senses, but something in his face made her try. She felt the strangest sensation in the world. She was soaring, scanning the land, watching herself watching the bird. She realised she could focus the thoughts into either the bird or herself.

Ull asked her what she could see. Was there anything to give her pride, hope, a future to believe in?

The Chieftainess concentrated; she was swooping free over a country that was… not beautiful; the fields were poor, the houses decrepit and the people worn down. She flew on until she reached the battlefield and all she saw was blood and men dying. She drew her consciousness into her body. Ignoring Ull, she got up and told her advisors to stop the fighting and wouldn't listen to arguments to the contrary. Ull gave her two minutes before following her into her tent. She rounded on him, upset by what she had seen, lashing out but realising her greater understanding was a power she had not had before.

Ull explained that the stone had chosen her, that the world needed to stop fighting. With the country around them recovering, Ull moved south.

The next altercation he found was fierce. In one camp he came across the Chief's disillusioned wife, tired of speaking reason to men who didn't listen. Feeling helpless and hopeless, she begged him to intervene. He said he could not, that she had to find the strength herself, for it was her world that was dying.

He offered her the star stones. She picked the blue, becoming entranced by the colour. Soon the fighting had stopped; the illusions the new Jeci had managed to create had stopped this battle and had shown her husband what it had done to the world.

* * *

Laioril looked at his audience. The youngsters were drooping, and Arkyn wasn't faring much better.

"Part two will be told whenever you find time to visit an old man. Now, if I'm not careful, I'll have Maria and Kadeem after me. So, go on with you all. Must be getting to your dinnertime. I'd hate to stop you eating."

The lads grinned and left. Arkyn considered ruefully that he'd only ever heard the first part of the story. Laioril always stopped there. This time, he was determined to hear the rest. The history he had been taught dealt mainly with the last four and a half centuries; since the Bard had helped to overthrow the Age of Tyranny in the year 777, but his interest in earlier times had definitely been piqued.

# Chapter 17
## THE STORIES CONTINUE
### Alunadai, Week 16 – 22nd Macial, 1st Easis 1209
### Wanda Camp – Laioril's Tent

THREE DAYS LATER, Arkyn, Tain and Cal eluded their tutors once more and made their way to the Wanda camp talking about the stories. Cal had never heard any of them. Tain was being infected by both his and Arkyn's enthusiasm and relished the chance to avoid more formal lessons. Laioril merely chuckled when he saw their excitement and settled down to finish the Lay of Ull.

* * *

Ull travelled the lands between the southern mountains and the northern seas. Each time he came across a battle he gifted a stone to an instigator and showed them how their actions were destroying their world. He became a legend in himself. In the southern tribes, he had found twins fighting and they had taken the black and white stones. They found they could manipulate magic together but only together. They would have to stop fighting to be able to explore their new powers and help their people. The siblings faced each other and agreed; they would make peace. The brother found that he bore the magic whilst his sister balanced it. He became the Beran and she the Rheol. Because all siblings will fight at some point, they divided their land and lived apart. Over time, they discovered they could communicate with each other through the stones. They didn't need to be together to use magic but the other participant still needed to be willing.

The next fight Ull came across was a small one, concerning two brothers in a deeply rooted dispute: the first had murdered their father. Ull showed the stones to the first brother, who took no interest in them. The depths of the brown stone captured the eye of the second brother. It glowed. He became the Wright. Forging a sword that couldn't fail, he avenged his father.

Ull left the surviving brother and travelled north. On the eve of another battle, he offered the stones to the commander, who picked the turquoise stone. Ull checked The Egotist's Downfall and found the word Amser followed by 'a timer.' The man concentrated and pulled his mind back in time. He saw his country as he remembered it: bountiful and beautiful. Then he saw it in the present: dying and decaying. He stopped the fighting.

Ull carried on north. In the border regions, he found a lady distressed at the state of her country. Stirred by her feelings, he showed her the stones. With the green stone, she could see into the furthest, unharmed, depths of her country. It gave her hope. All but one of the lands around had stopped fighting and she could help to rebuild her country by focussing and seeing the areas that needed help. She became the Sennachie or 'a seer'.

Ull travelled to the last mainland country to be still in conflict. He found the Queen beset by treachery; she didn't want civil war, but scheming factions meant she didn't know whom to trust, who would help her stop the fighting. He showed her the stones and she picked the grey one. Instantly, she could recall all the conversations she'd had with her advisors. She located two traitors, both of whom denied it. Ull whispered to her and she laid a hand on both. The Queen latched onto their thoughts and memories and proved the treachery. The fighting ceased. She had become the Memini or 'a memoriter.' Over time, the spirit of magic within her would become known as a memor.

Ull thought his work done, the destructive civil wars tearing the lands apart were ending, peace stole over those same lands and soon prosperity would burgeon in croft and town. Sitting in the Queen's Palace, watching the storm-ravaged sea, he drew out the remaining stones. They foretold unfinished work. He spoke to Queen Arelia and discovered that there were offshore islands. When the weather calmed, Ull travelled to them. The winds blew him south to a long island, split asunder by war and stupidity. Expelled from the first camp, Ull knew that the man or woman he was hunting for must be in the second. He crossed their lines, deliberately drawing attention to himself and was taken before the officer of the watch, who listened to his stories and laughed at him for a crackpot until one of his guards said he'd heard of Ull. He was passed up to the commander, a son of the northern Pasha. Time had taught this man to be distrustful and although he had heard rumours from the mainland, he asked to see the stones, to confirm Ull was who he claimed. Ull held them out, the yellow, the pink and the red. The man shunned the red, too blood like. The pink didn't speak to anything within him, too gentle a colour, too soft a calling. In the yellow he found neither unease nor weakness, but clarity and calling. Reaching out, he lifted the stone carefully, asking what it did. Ull, unsure if he liked the man, said it would be for him to find out.

The man managed to observe the proceedings at the treaty unnoticed; he managed to see the flaws and the double-dealings. He saw the treachery of the opposing side and saved his father's life. He showed the treaty for what it was and the sides came to a more amicable agreement. Over time, the island became united. The new Espier – an espien – saw to that.

The next country Ull arrived at was an archipelago of islands to the north of the first. Each island was at war with its neighbours. He found a man who bore a spider's web as his standard. He knew that to end these fights it would take someone of exceptional cunning and patience. He showed the man the last two stones and he picked the red. By this time, more than two years had elapsed since Ull's first appearance. People had felt the magic in the world and were beginning to wield it. The power gifted by the red stone was that of the Sentire. It gave the bearer the ability to sense the use of magic, moods and the elements. He soon found that the other lords on the islands were using and abusing magic. He tricked them in turn and brought an uneasy truce. He became the Guardian of the Isles and kept them peaceful until nobody wanted to fight. He encouraged trade with the mainland, found the richest farmland and fishing stocks, the minerals and resources they needed and soon the isles prospered.

Ull still had one stone left: there was a land he hadn't discovered. He asked the Sentire, who told him that to the east was a land which lived in perpetual predawn light. Ull made his way there. The fighting had ceased of its own accord, but the country seemed red with blood, stark against its northern snows. Ull was invited to a sanctuary of ladies who were trying to heal the wounds, both with prayers to Aluna and more practical herbs. He showed the stone to all the sisters, but none would take it, thinking it merely a bauble with no use. A novice was drawn to the gentle beauty of the pink hue. She hesitated – what the sisters had refused, she should not accept – but Ull held it out. Standing on the cliffs, she accepted the stone and a blinding white light streamed from it, shooting into the sky over the Ranaegir Sea where it joined others far off in the sky. They combined into one bright strand that then split and covered the lands in a dome of bright white threads of light. Somehow, Ull knew that all twelve stones were giving off the light. The light faded but, before it disappeared, it turned to gold. Strands of light bound themselves around the Meithrin's wrist for the briefest moment, before being absorbed. The novice glanced at Ull. Both faces showed surprise. Over the next few days, the novice learned to wield the healing power of the pink stone. She became the Meithrin. Time showed that the magic on Erinna had been bound within the stones. Few now could wield it outside the twelve bearers.

Ull relaxed; his long journey over. He had located those with the ability to wield the power in the stones. The star stones themselves protected their bearers. The bearers discovered they could communicate through the stones and, in certain cases, share their skills. They managed to keep the lands peaceful. Ull travelled to the mainland. He wandered for a while contemplating his home, longing to return. He found the Sennachie still trying to mend the hurts in her country. He stayed with her, helping. Then one day he opened the book and found there a spell. He went at night and stood in the light of the moon. He spoke the words of the spell and nothing happened. He was still on Erinna. In a rage, he summoned all the stone from the surrounding country and sent it at the moon, trying to block out the mocking light. The summoned stone missed and started revolving, forming the lesser-moon. In that rage, Ull lost his balance and fell to his death from the tall, thin outcrop of rock he had created. During the years he had been in the world, stories of his first appearance had spread. The lesser-moon was named Cisluna and collectively the moons became the Alcis. Soon, people prayed to both.

* * *

Laioril smiled at the boys. "And that, my princes and young Cal, is the story of the Majistar Ull, the founding of the Ring of Twelve – later to be known as the Cearcall – and the advent of the Ullian Spirits, or magical abilities, and the hues of those spirits. The story of the Cearcall and the spirits is, however, another matter – another story for another day.”

“What was the spell that Ull cast before he created Cisluna?” asked Tain.

“No-one is certain, lad. No-one knew at the time from what the legends tell us. Maybe it closed the link between Annire and Erinna. We will never know. Maybe it is better that we don’t. Only the fact he came from Annire made it possible for him to cast it at all. Some legends tell us that the magic he used came from his world and not ours. That the magic on Annire differs from that on this world. It may be true, it may not, but no-one has ever matched his magic, that much is certain.”

Arkyn took a peach from the stack of fruit. He was halfway through eating it – and listening to his brother and Laioril talking – when he realised something. “Chief, where do you get peaches from?”

“Oh, we find them; you know how it is, lad.”

“The only place they grow in this part of the empire is our gardens here. What would father say if he knew?”

Laioril winked. “I believe last time he was told by the head gardener he said, and I quote, ‘Good. We can’t eat them all. When we’re not here, send them a basket occasionally. Save them the trouble of having to climb in and pick them.’”

All three lads laughed.

“But we are here,” pointed out Arkyn.

“Yep, and you’re eating the fruit, lad. I don’t know how we get the reputation for poaching. I really don’t.”

The boys spent the walk to Ceardlann talking about Ull’s story and what each of them would do if they had one of the spirits. The Princes knew that the star stones existed for their mother had owned the blue one, though she had been unable to wield it.

When they reached the house, they were informed King Adeone was sitting on the lawn with the Comptroller and Lady Elantha. The boys ran out again and greeted their father. Cal following sat next to Elantha and started entertaining her. Adeone watched him unobtrusively. The more he saw of Cal, the better pleased he was that the lad was at Ceardlann. Elantha seemed to like him and his sons were somehow freer. He asked what they’d been doing.

“Talking to Laioril; he’s been telling us about Ull,” replied Tain.

“You don’t want to believe everything that old rogue tells you, but that story is one of his better ones. Where did he get to?”

Arkyn said shrewdly, “The creation of Cisluna. I’ve never heard him get so far. He usually stops with the Jeci.”

"Neither have I. That is unusual. You must all have been listening *very* hard. I'll have to ask him what his secret is so I can pass it on to your tutors. They, by the way, haven't seen much of you for a couple of days." Adeone grinned at the shifty appearance his charges now had. "You thought I wouldn't find out. Be warned, I might be further off but that doesn't mean I'm not getting updates from everyone here; messengers are very useful. Mind you, Tain, I'm a bit concerned; you've not destroyed anything yet."

The Comptroller who had remained silent since the boys had joined them said, "I appreciate the fact you added 'yet' onto that, Sire. I'm sure Prince Tain is finding his feet."

"Now, now, Comptroller, whatever gives you that idea?"

"Experience, sir."

# Chapter 18
# A PLEASANT RIDE
Late Afternoon
Palace – King's Chambers

ADEONE LEFT CEARDLANN MID-AFTERNOON, his straight-faced charges having assured him they would return to their studies. As he crossed the ford out of the valley, he slowed to give Sergeant Marsh and his guards time to get in position. Landis' actions over Jenner and his subsequent warnings had been clear, and Adeone didn't have any reason to tempt fate with this ride. He idled along the road not wanting to return to Oedran quickly. If he timed it right, he'd be able to ignore everything waiting for him. He rode through Dellwood thoughtfully. The small village boasted an inn, several houses and a fork in the road with the second path petering out into marsh. He glanced at the unkempt inn. Old Ezra did his best, but it appeared he might need a hand. Adeone decided to send someone along. The guards and residents of the Rex Dallin used the inn as much as the village.

The guards on the Dallin Gate saluted smartly as he passed. He inclined his head in thanks and slowed so his guards could reorganise. They'd been riding behind him on the road, but he had to be flanked in the city. Marsh caught his eye and inclined his head. Adeone merely winked. He had no good reason to make his sergeant's life more difficult.

They made good progress through the city and sooner than he wanted, Adeone was dismounting. He nodded to Jack – who came forward to take Pursuit's bridle – asking if all was well.

"Aye, well as ever, Sire."

"Pursuit enjoyed the ride. Let him into the paddock for a bit when you've rubbed him down."

"Will do, Sire. He isn't the only one to have enjoyed himself."

Adeone chuckled and crooked an eyebrow.

"Sergeant Marsh seems very relaxed, Sire."

Adeone snorted. "Very quick, Jack." He left for the Inner Office, contemplating that the old groom had sharp eyes and remarkably sound instincts.

He entered the Outer Office easier than he had been for days. His relaxed gaze swept around the room.

His hopes for a quiet afternoon and evening vanished.

His secretaries, Jacobs and Kenton, were missing. Richardson's face was graver than he'd ever seen it, a guard he didn't know saluted, and Landis' face was a warning.

Something had happened, something serious, something that would have repercussions. If it had been a rebellion, he'd have been contacted at Ceardlann. That meant something else, something in Oedran, something that threatened him. Everyone was now waiting for him to be told, for his reaction, for his orders. A tense atmosphere pervaded his rooms. Everyday jobs stopped; everyday routine paused. Silence instead of small everyday sounds. Adeone's skin crawled. There was only one thing that could cause this. His Defender's presence spoke volumes. With an unspoken agreement, he and Landis entered the Inner Office alone.

The King sat behind his desk, crooking an eyebrow. "How would I have died?"

PART 2

# Chapter 19
## HILLBECK'S STORY
### Late Afternoon
### Outer Office

**T**RAPPED IN THE OUTER OFFICE, Sergeant Hillbeck of the Palace Guard wondered if he would see the dawn. He had never intended to be party to a plot to poison the King. Never intended to do anything but investigate. Searching for truth had placed him in a precarious position and now that the King's life had been attacked it made his uncertain.

Standing around for hours wasn't what his dreams had promised when he'd left the Rex Dallin. The city was meant to be full of possibilities, not boredom and aching feet. The Teran Arms' dark, dank atmosphere had suited his mood the evening of Queen Ira's death; the beer wasn't worth the coin, but something drew him back day after day until the curious and judgemental stares stopped. Then came the fateful evening. Sitting in his usual dark corner in the small room, drinking the flavourless beer, frustrated by boredom, anticipating the hangover, trying to find something that would give him meaning, he'd overheard their conversation.

"No, it's got to be his private triniculum…"

"Why?"

He'd ignored them again. He wasn't interested in the whys and wherefores of his fellow drinkers. There was a marital dispute occurring in the opposite corner. The ruddy-faced wife wasn't having her scrawny husband's excuses.

"Ya're telling me ya expect me t' simply forgive ya for whoring 'n' gamblin' 'n' who knows what else—"

"It weren't like that, Becka—"

"Sounds remarkably like that t' me, ya bastard. 'Ow many others 'ave the' bin?"

He'd got the feeling that the couple argued in public most of the time and didn't care. He'd wanted to get up and shout at them both to shut up.

A lady whose profession was easily readable from her clothes' suggestive nature had sat down with a jug of ale and poured him a top-up, before trying to engage him in conversation and sell her services. In trying to get rid of her, he'd heard the conversation at the next table again.

"The easiest way is to use the triniculum; we don't have a choice."

"Yes, but all I'm saying is there might be complications."

*'Stuff your complications; I've got my own here,'* he thought.

The couple were still arguing loudly and the prostitute had sat on his knee, her legs folded on either side of him, breathing into his ear. She stank of cheap scent and sex. He'd wanted to hurl her from him but couldn't bring himself to. Her hands had loosened the belt of his off-duty breeches. When she'd slipped her hand into them, he'd had enough. Standing up, he'd tipped her off his lap and into the table, knocking it over. Her pimp had confronted him, but Hillbeck had caught his arm and tumbled him into the table too. Stepping over the collapsed mess of prostitute, pimp and broken table, ignoring the outraged innkeeper, he'd marched over to the arguing couple.

"For the love of Cisluna, SHUT UP! Take your argument elsewhere. Some of us were trying to get a drink in peace."

A cheer had erupted from the men who'd been at the table next to him. Ignoring them, Hillbeck had left. He'd stomped through the cool night air of Oedran until he reached another tavern, continuing his drinking, fuming about the idiosyncrasies of his fellow citizens. The scene played itself over and over in his head. When the room began to spin, he'd realised he needed to get home and sleep.

This time the cool night air sobered him up and – in that moment of clarity – the strangeness of the conversations he'd heard in the Teran Arms came back to him. He'd never seen the prostitute or her pimp before, yet the landlord had ignored them, and the married couple hadn't worn any rings. The landlord might have been a grouchy git all his life but he had tended to stop trouble. So, what had been different tonight? Why had so many disparate elements come together? He had shaken his head, trying to focus through his alcohol-saturated body. It was no good. The answers didn't present themselves, but the questions continued to niggle. He'd weaved his way home and dropped into bed, hoping he'd have forgotten the questions by morning. He hadn't, and they continued to bother him all through his shift the following day. Captain Haster had reprimanded him for being hungover and later that had seemed odd. Haster was normally subtler than an open reprimand.

The more he'd considered things, the more worried he became. Something was happening, something more than a knife in a dark alley, something that would impact all their lives. He'd wondered what to do and reasoned that his current lack of anything substantial would get him laughed out of Haster's office – especially as it was obvious that he'd been drinking heavily for days.

He hadn't known why he was so worried. Eventually, he'd realised it was the word 'triniculum'. The word was only in use at the Palace for describing the smaller formal dining rooms. There was a story about the word, something to do with a prince or king who hadn't been able to say triclinium and so the word had changed. The Pala of Lufia still had formal triclinium but in the Palace of Oedran the word was forever triniculum and the only 'private' one, currently, was the King's own.

He'd returned to the Teran Arms the following evening and the two men were there. He'd sat down close to them and managed to overhear something that they said; however, the men had realised that they were under observation. He'd played stupid and started agreeing with what they were saying, even when he thought they were wrong. At the end of the evening, the men apparently thought they'd found an ally. By the time he left the tavern the following evening, the men had confided most of their plan to him. They still wouldn't tell him their names or the date they'd planned.

As he'd left, he heard the taller man say, "Don't look like that. He's just a stupid sergeant. The overseer and his lackeys won't care."

He'd never given them his name or rank, though he had mentioned he was a guard. Exceptionally worried, with a tightness in his chest, he'd come to the Outer Office to try to warn the King.

Lord Landis and Richardson had seen the state he was in and believed his story. They'd summoned the Steward and a complete search of the kitchens and the King's Triniculum occurred. They'd found poisoned food in the latter, but no-one knew how it had got there. Lord Landis told him not to leave. So, he'd stayed, becoming increasingly anxious. A hunt for truth had brought him here, to the Outer Office, to the point of not knowing if the King would order his execution.

# Chapter 20
## INVESTIGATION
Late Afternoon
Inner Office

ADEONE SCRUTINISED HILLBECK as he told a succinct and sanitised story. As the story concluded, trying to keep his temper, he asked, "Why didn't you report the incidents sooner?"

"The men said something about Captain Haster being part of them, sir. Something about how easy it would be."

Adeone frowned. "Wait outside." When Sergeant Hillbeck had saluted and left, Adeone turned to a concerned Landis. "Other than the fact poison was found, do you trust Hillbeck?"

"I believed him before we started searching. He's valley-born."

"That saves a lot of questions. What do you think about the reference to Haster?"

"Nothing's impossible, Sire," remarked Landis impartially.

"If that's— Come in, Richardson."

The administrator entered, handed Landis a document and waited. Adeone raised a querying eyebrow. Landis passed over the document. It was a list, neatly inscribed, of everyone the guards had allowed through the service entrance to the King's rooms. The only unnamed person was a 'guard' with a message for Simkins.

"Get me Haster and Simkins," ordered Adeone.

A few moments later, Simkins entered. After reading the list, he said, "I wasn't given any message, sir. The rest is correct."

"Right, thank you. You didn't happen to see the guard?"

"No, sir. If I had, I'd have asked him what he was doing there."

With his fingers steepled against pursed lips, Adeone sat almost immobile as Haster entered the Inner Office. The captain had been in post since his father's reign and they usually had an easy relationship; however, if Hillbeck's story were true, then Haster had betrayed that relationship.

Adeone didn't miss the slight wince as Haster saluted. He didn't move to acknowledge the salute but mildly considered how crafty his ancestors had been in devising one that meant the person saluting couldn't possibly be holding a weapon, as both palms were brought up to opposing shoulders. It was a salute saved for the monarch, but the normal salute of the right hand brought up to the left shoulder meant that it was unlikely a weapon could be used. What it said about the paranoia of his ancestors was a question for another day.

He studied Haster's face as Landis asked him for his weapons. Watched the infinitesimal pause before he obeyed the request, which wasn't a request at all. Saw how the colour started to drain from the captain's face. It suggested Haster did have something to answer for – an innocent man would likely have asked why he was being disarmed, or would they in this office? Adeone didn't give time to the speculation. Landis and he hadn't discussed disarming Haster but he wasn't going to interfere. As his Defender, Landis was within his rights to do so, and he evidently wasn't taking chances. Landis moved away, putting the sword and dagger through his belt, which Adeone knew had loops specifically for such moments. He'd originally laughed when Landis had told him, but he wasn't laughing now. He was watching Haster as the captain became more disconcerted.

Eventually, with his fingers still steepled against his mouth, he enquired, "Are you aware of events today, Captain?"

Haster racked his brains but concluded that he wasn't. "No, Sire."

Adeone lowered his hands but never his gaze. "There has been an attempt on my life. The *interesting* thing is that the traitors were certain they would succeed because you are one of them. Why would that be?"

Captain Haster went whiter than any man the King had ever seen. Something was certainly wrong.

"Well?" he demanded.

Haster struggled to get the words out. "Sire… I…"

Anger surging, Adeone used all his willpower to remain calm. "Haster, you undoubtedly know something. What is it? I'd rather find out *before* I arrest you for treason than give orders for the secret to be discovered *when* I've arrested you; I will not hesitate to do so."

Haster took several steadying breaths. "Sire, I knew nothing about an attempt on your life. As the moons will bear me witness, I didn't. I… Two men cornered me a week ago, or more, saying that, if I didn't want the men, my wife and Your Majesty to discover my secret, I had to find them a guard's tabard. It seemed such a small thing but I didn't want… Anyway, I thought that was the end of it. Then two nights ago, they asked me about a guard. I recognised the description as Hillbeck and told them he was a sergeant. They started asking more questions, I stalled saying I'd need time to find out. I haven't seen them since. Oh, Sicla…" The captain ran a hand over his balding head.

"Remain at attention!" snapped Adeone, still grim-faced, his anger bubbling hotter. His willpower broke. "What is the secret?" he snapped, knowing Haster would be compelled to answer.

Haster straightened up, wincing slightly. "I once had a relationship with Lord Ryson."

Adeone's features set. "You are married."

"Yes, Sire, and I was then. I can't see my wife appreciating the fact."

"Wait outside." After, Haster saluted and left, Adeone said, "Your opinion, Landis?"

"I think he's telling the truth," replied his Defender. "I also don't think he gave in easily to the men. You could get Ryson here to check if the blackmail had any foundation."

Adeone called for his administrator. "Is Lord Ryson at Court today?"

"I believe, sir, he is rather *in* court," replied Richardson. "I'll find out which judge."

"I'll contact the Keeper myself. Just see Haster is lodged where he can't do a runner. Dragoris."

Adeone's messenger, a tiny dragon, appeared in a flash of green light and landed on his outstretched palm. He raised the dragon to eye level.

"Can you get me a private link with the Keeper of the Justice Hall, please, Dragoris?"

Seconds later, the link formed. For Landis, the air shimmered opaquely heat-haze-like around the King. For Adeone, he seemed to be at a comfortable speaking distance from the Keeper in a shimmering white corridor.

A couple of minutes later, in Court Six, Judge Tancred was intrigued to see Dragoris appear and advise him of the King's request to adjourn. He'd known King Adeone since he was born but had never known him ask for an adjournment. He noted the significance of the tiny dragon, as opposed to a runner or courier. Lord Scanlon would no doubt object to 'the King's interference in justice matters,' but Tancred would let him. It was not for him to refuse the King.

"This court is now adjourned until tomorrow. Jury, I will explain myself to you and the prosecuting counsel in a few moments."

Acting as counsel for the defence, Lord Ryson was perplexed: to end now seemed unwarranted. He was even more intrigued when Dragoris appeared and told him that the King wanted to speak with him. He left the Courthouse in some agitation, wracking his brains as to why he'd been summoned.

# Chapter 21
# INTERROGATION
### Early Evening
### Inner Office

**W**HILST WAITING FOR RYSON, Adeone brooded on events; his relaxing time at Ceardlann already a distant memory. Landis took Haster into the triniculum. Six minutes later, Adeone silently watched the captain pass back through the Inner Office. Once the door closed, he raised an eyebrow.

"The bruises are still livid," replied Landis.

Blackmail and a beating: Adeone would have been surprised by just one or the other, but the fact Haster had caved at all was alarming. At the very least, he should have informed someone, anyone that it had happened. There must have been time, opportunity; if he, himself, hadn't been available, Haster could have seen Landis, Paturn or Fitz, even Richardson. Someone. They could then have protected Haster. Instead, inaction had condemned him. Adeone cursed him for it. He considered Hillbeck's actions as well. Had he, in trying to get information, condemned himself? He was pretty certain that Hillbeck wasn't a traitor; it went against his instinct to disbelieve the old legends that said the valley-binding was life-binding. Hillbeck might need a few lessons about what to do when things appeared wrong but, in the end, he'd acted correctly, whereas Haster hadn't. Hillbeck had saved his life and Haster had jeopardised it. He was still ruminating when Richardson announced Lord Ryson clad in his pale-green lawyers' robes.

Adeone pulled himself out of his contemplations and, before Ryson had finished straightening up from his bow, snapped, "Have you ever had a relationship with Captain Haster of the Palace Guard, my lord?"

Surprise, shock and worry flickered across Ryson's face. He would be evaluating the ramifications of the question but, for Haster's sake, Adeone didn't want to give him chance to circumvent answering, even momentarily.

"It's quite simple, my lord, either you have or you have not! Take your pick and make sure it's the truth. Lawyer's questions will wait."

There was an edge to the King that Ryson had rarely seen and he knew he didn't want to feel the blade. Truth was the only option, even if it unleashed wrath. "Yes, Your Majesty, a few years ago."

"Has anyone ever approached you about this? Have you ever told anyone?" demanded the King.

Increasingly concerned, Ryson answered with a negative. Why was Landis still in the room? Had something occurred under the remit of a Defender of the King's Life? The unusual summons suggested treason. As he was here answering questions, it implicated him. He forced himself to focus, to answer the King's questions.

"I don't think anyone has, Sire, and I don't remember telling anyone about it. I knew he was married, you see."

"My lord, *somebody knew*," remarked Adeone. "Either you or he must have told someone. Or, of course, you were abysmally stupid and somebody found out and used it to compromise you both."

"My preferences aren't a secret – Lord Scanlon knows, for instance – but I don't know who could have known about Haster, Sire; I shall give it some thought." Ryson hesitated. "Your Majesty, may I ask if the captain is in difficulties?"

"That remains to be seen. He is in a predicament and he isn't the only one. There was an attempt on my life earlier; the captain is linked to it by name. He wasn't, however, responsible and, I believe, didn't know of the plot. He made a mistake. What, as a lawyer, would you suggest?"

"I'm hardly unbiased, Sire, but he has served your family loyally for many years. The mistake might well have had unthinkable results. If it had resulted in your death, then I have no doubt Haster would have ended his life. He still might. He will know he has failed you, Your Majesty. He will be in torment. Your good opinion means everything to him; it's why I ended our relationship. Our involvement could have compromised him and I never wanted that. I suppose it still did though."

"Would you send him to trial?" asked Adeone, filing the revelation away in his mind. He wasn't sure who it said more about.

"On that, Your Majesty, I am unable to advise you without the full information. I would say it is possible, on the information I have, that a jury would find him guilty."

"Thank you, my lord. I would be grateful if you would promise me, on your fealty, to say nothing of this to *anyone*. If I can settle it quietly, I would prefer it."

"You have my promise, Sire."

Ryson bowed out with his mind still awhirl with questions he had realised he had better *not* ask, including exactly how the King's life had been attacked and by whom. That sort of knowledge was dangerous.


Once the door had closed, Landis mused, "Could Ryson have told Lord Scanlon himself, as a planned entrapment? They were friends."

"Yes, Landis, many years ago. I hadn't overlooked the possibility, but I can't simply accept that, because he *was* friends with my traitorous brother, Elidir wants me dead. To my knowledge, they've not been on sociable terms since Ryson's sister refused to marry Scanlon and ran from Oedran. Not everyone is as fortunate in their childhood friends as we are."

"I know, but it's my duty to be suspicious. What are you going to do?"

"As my Defender, what is your advice?"

"Haster should have thought beyond himself. He *has* failed you, but if you truly believe he had no notion of the treason – and don't want to pursue the charge and broadcast what's happened – then I suggest you renew his oath and watch him carefully. When you can do so, replace him. If you let people know your life's been attacked, it could be seen as a call to arms. I think quietly replacing him may be best for now."

Adeone considered his friend gravely. It was a reasonable course of action and would make sense. No-one would ever need to know outside of the few who already did. He didn't want to force Scanlon into any action; for he had no doubt now that somehow Scanlon had watched his former friend and, with the unerring knack he had, used the information to get at him.

He reached his decision. "Get Haster and Richardson in here."

He pushed himself to his feet as they entered. Landis moved to stand behind his right shoulder. Richardson settled himself at the clerks' desk, leaving the captain, pale and alone, in front of him.

He started speaking softly, "Captain, you have allowed your personal preoccupations to endanger the stability of the Oedranian Empire, my life and that of my family. You have failed to take thought for how your actions might affect more than yourself. Because of this, there is little choice left to me. You have, over the years, done much to protect that which you have more recently endangered. These are my terms to your continued freedom: one, you tell your wife about any secret that might in the future be used to blackmail or pressurise you – likewise, you rid yourself of all other secrets that could be used against you to the appropriate person – two, your tenure as Captain of the Palace Guard is limited to the point at which I find a suitable officer to replace you and, thirdly, you swear a life-binding fealty."

Landis inhaled sharply. He had realised the attack had disturbed his friend and that such a close official to him had been an accomplice, but he hadn't suspected that Adeone would make an example of Haster. He recognised that his friend would never have been easy ordering Haster's execution as an unwitting accomplice but there was no way he could condone the captain's actions either; to do so would send out the wrong message, if the events became known. Adeone had therefore realised, more swiftly than Landis, that he had to take such action as could never constitute a pardon for Haster. Even so, the action astonished Landis. He'd sworn a truth-binding fealty at the King's coronation. If it were tested, he'd be compelled to speak the truth to the King; given the wrong circumstances, it could be life-changing. Honour-binding – usually reserved for new ennoblements – and speech-binding – which limited what a vassal could say – were rare. Life-binding terrified him; if the vassal ever broke the fealty, by thought or deed, then he would die where he stood. Some said there were other forms, the Rex Dallin was meant to have its own – valley-binding – but life-binding was the strictest and feared. From what he had gleaned as a boy, no-one had sworn it for over a hundred years.

The thoughts sped through Landis' mind in an instant, and he'd hardly had time to absorb all the consequences before Adeone's voice continued.

"Haster, do you accept these terms?"

The captain knelt, shaking slightly.

"No, Captain, this is sworn differently. You will need to stand. Ask Hillbeck to join us, please, Richardson." A moment later, he said, "You are here as a witness, Sergeant."

Hillbeck inclined his head and stood by the door. Inwardly, he began to unwind and even hope. If the King wanted a witness, he probably wasn't going to be sent for execution.

The King turned Haster's palms up as though in the first move of the salute before turning to his friend. "Defender, I'll need your dagger."

Landis knelt and drew his dagger, offering it hilt first to the King, before standing once more.

Adeone laid the weapon across the captain's palms, placing his own hands palm down on top. He ensured Haster kept eye contact. "Do you hereby bind your mind, body and soul to the promise that treachery and treason will never again be part of you?"

"I do so bind."

"Do you bind your very life itself to the promise?"

"I do so bind."

"Do you swear to answer the call for assistance and to uphold the values of the empire?"

"I do so swear."

"Do you swear to never, by word, thought or deed, plot harm to me, my immediate heirs and advocates?"

"I do so swear."

"Do you swear to never enter into agreement with any, for purposes that might be, are, or will be, detrimental to the empire?"

"I do so swear."

"Then your life is bound, your mind is held, your body will suffer torments and your soul will never be welcomed in the heavens if you are forsworn."

Adeone glanced at Landis, who, swallowing slightly, removed the dagger with a swift movement. He knew how sharp it was and, when it was clear, he saw the drops of blood on the end. It was how it should be, but he still glanced at the King in apology.

Adeone simply dismissed Haster. Once the door closed, he said, "There are times I wish you weren't so conscientious about keeping your weapons sharp, Festus. Hillbeck, stay where you are. Richardson, see if Simkins has a bandage, please. I'd rather not have to send for the doc."

Hands tended to, Adeone turned to Hillbeck. "There is a commission with your name on it, if you want it, Sergeant."

Hillbeck blinked, stunned. "I'm sorry but I don't really want it, Sire. I like being a sergeant. We find out things that the officers don't. I don't particularly want any more responsibility than I have. I suppose you could say I'm content." The involuntary words surprised him. He wasn't content but he didn't want to be a captain, so he failed to amend his statement.

Adeone considered him. He noted the slight surprise in Hillbeck's eyes and knew that the sergeant hadn't meant the last part. "Thank you for a straight answer. That's all for now." After Hillbeck had left, Adeone said, "Get him assigned to my guard, Richardson. I always have one duty sergeant, might as well make it one I can trust."

Once Richardson had gone, Landis said, "I'd like you to dine at Landis House, Sire, whilst we test everything in the kitchens here. I've also told

Simkins to stop having a selection of food in the triniculum. I know you like to help yourself when you're ready, but we can't take the risk anymore."

Adeone eyed him. "We're letting Scanlon win minor victories—"

"Better than him winning the ultimate one!"

"Quite. Fine. What's for dinner then?"

"I have no idea. They don't know you're coming."

Adeone chuckled. "Cornelia does say she doesn't need warning."

# Chapter 22
# TURNING POINT
Very Late Evening
Wynfeld's Office

**F**OR WYNFELD, still working at eleven that night, it had been a normal day, with its normal working pattern. All the men had reported for duty and nothing significant had occurred. Reports had been compiled and sent to the Palace. As he considered going to bed, his office door crashed open. Glancing up, he rose and saluted as the Major and Lord Landis entered.

The Major snapped, "Remind us what your job *is*, Wynfeld!"

"Collecting information with a view to the protection of our King and his heirs, sir," responded Wynfeld crisply.

"Correct. So where, in Sicla's Cavern, were you and your information when would-be assassins nearly poisoned the King earlier today?"

Aghast, Wynfeld swallowed before answering. "I suppose I must have been here, sir. Unfortunately, I can't be precise, as I don't know *when* they nearly poisoned our King. Is he unharmed, Lord Landis?"

Landis, keeping his temper, thought, *'Pedantry is no saviour, Wynfeld.'* In an uncompromising voice, he said, "Yes, but no thanks to you or your men. A palace guard foiled this attempt. Your regiment isn't doing its job. The men were talking about this quite openly in the Teran Arms. You're naïvety shows as you've not found out about it sooner. There is no room for mistakes! If you make another, you *will* be replaced. I am not allowing anyone in your post to fail, this spectacularly, more than once. You might be in Terasia for all the help you are!"

The Major weighed in, "And I shall not tolerate my subordinate officers making a mockery out of the militia. You are failing, Wynfeld. The King has requested that you remain in post or I'd have you out. He only gives people one second-chance. Sharpen up your act. The King appointed you but circumstances change quickly. You will get the men up to scratch or suffer the consequences. I want to see a marked improvement on the information coming in. What's more, get out on the bloody street yourself. Don't rely on your men to do all the work."

Wynfeld had barely taken a breath before Lord Landis said, "Maybe, Captain, you would like to consider the consequences of Lord Scanlon getting more power than he already holds, just as an incentive. That's all I have to say. Goodnight, Major."

Six minutes later, when his senior officer also left, Wynfeld collapsed onto his chair and thought for all he was worth. He started making notes. They didn't have enough people in the taverns. He went and counted the number of people from the Teran Lordship that were working for them. They might as well have had none. He'd have to have a good look at where they had men and where they didn't. The sergeants would also have to step up. He could only use the information he was given to compile the reports. He might stop the sergeants writing part of it, or start interrogating them on the report to make sure it contained all the information possible. Then the words 'palace guard' seeped into Wynfeld's brain. They needed to stop relying on Captain Haster and get informers inside the Palace. They had to tidy up the way they collected and collated information. Maybe he should engineer some time at Court. Even in the midst of his angst, he smiled. Queen Ira would have laughed at the thought of him there. Things were certainly going to change. He'd speak to his sergeants in the morning and discover where informants were lacking. He walked over to his quarters and told his batman to wake him at six o'clock. He needed an early start.

# Chapter 23
## KING'S GUARD

Cisadai, Week 16 – 23rd Macial, 2nd Easis 1209
Palace – Court

THE MORNING SUN streamed through a square-paned window onto Sergeant Hillbeck standing almost motionless by an entrance into the Court rooms. Every so often he glanced out of the windows, happy to be able to. The previous day, with its fears and freedom, felt like a dream. After leaving the Inner Office, he'd borrowed a horse and ridden home, glad to be within the Rex Dallin's embrace after fearing he'd never see the valley again. His brother and wed-sister hadn't asked what had prompted the sudden visit and he hadn't explained, he'd simply enjoyed being there. Now, he was just relieved to be back with the reassuring predictability and boredom of his days.

A fellow sergeant disturbed his ordered and predictable morning with a summons from Captain Haster: he was being relieved of his post. He didn't lie to himself; by reporting the captain he'd been on shifting ground but his upbringing, instinct and duty had guided his steps. He proceeded through the Palace and, other than a slight twinge of foreboding, his conscience didn't trouble him.

Walking along the Guards' Corridor, he nodded to a fellow sergeant whose eyes met his with a new wariness. Haster couldn't have broadcast the events of the previous day. His life-bind would have prevented it, unless the King had told people, but that was unlikely. He, himself, certainly hadn't told anyone. So why the wariness?

He entered the captain's office and saluted, trying to determine if their relationship had changed.

"Orders from the King's Office, Sergeant. You've been assigned to His Majesty's Guard with immediate effect. Report to Sergeant Marsh and be mindful of the honour." Haster paused. "You deserve the promotion, Hillbeck. You're an excellent guard and I hope you serve His Majesty with the same dedication as you showed recently. That's all."

Once out of the office, Hillbeck didn't know whether to curse or celebrate. The King had taken him at his word and left him a sergeant; however, the King's Guard answered to the King or his Defenders and there wasn't a captain. In comparison to other 'Guards', a sergeant in the King's Guard was a captain. He wasn't sure he appreciated the irony. He couldn't refuse the transfer. The method of the order, through the King's Office, meant that refusal was never an option. The day before, he'd faced King Adeone with a debt between them, which had been cleared in that room. This was the King's *whim*, one that couldn't be refused under any circumstances. The King had spoken and Hillbeck recognised the tone of voice.

He'd have to clean up his life but, for the first time in months, the day promised something new, something unknown. Even though he had decided to embrace the predictable the night before, he grinned and part of him wanted to whistle as he walked, but anyone who saw him whistling would be cutting in their remarks.

As he approached the doors to the Audience Chamber, he knew Sergeant Marsh was evaluating him. He'd heard enough about the senior sergeant of the King's Guard to be wary and respectful. Marsh wasn't yet thirty and headed the most prestigious guard in the empire. An excellent judge of character, a pragmatic attitude and a decent sword-arm had got him noticed. He'd become head of the King's Guards in 1207 after travelling with the King to Lord Faran's in Lufian. In the last two years, he'd gained a reputation as a disciplined, fair man who worked hard.

Marsh turned to his fellow guard. "Nip and get one of the lads, Smithers." Once the extra guard was there, he continued, "I shall be in the guardroom. Come with me, Hillbeck." Once in the guardroom, Marsh said, "Find somewhere else to sit and natter, lads. Me and your new sergeant need to talk." Once alone, he explained, "They'll end up in the antechamber and give anyone who enters pause for thought. Now, Lord Landis informed me of events yesterday and I've seen reports about you. I'm not concerned about your record as a guard, but I am by your off-duty record. If I find you hungover or drunk on duty, you'll be gone. Your predecessor blundered and there was no second chance. You're on duty this afternoon and evening. We mostly follow the Palace Guard shift pattern for actual guarding. His Majesty's not got anything planned elsewhere, currently, so you should have a nice quiet first shift. Administrator Richardson will inform you if that changes. I've put you with men who know the procedures, but I'll run you through things properly tomorrow morning because we have extra duty hours for training and the like. Your new room is ready for you and you're expected to be available at all times unless you've taken formal leave with His Majesty's permission. That doesn't mean you're on duty, but you can be called back to be on duty at any time. Is that understood? Good. Now…"

A couple of minutes later, they left the guardroom as Landis was passing. Both sergeants saluted, and Landis looked sharply at Marsh.

"Not at your post?"

"I was quickly explaining matters to Sergeant Hillbeck, Defender. The King has knowledge that I was meaning to do so."

"Thank you, Marsh. I won't keep you any longer." Landis turned his attention to Hillbeck and pointed to the guardroom. Once there, he continued, "Congratulations on your transfer. I want to thank you again for what you did yesterday, but there is the small matter that we can't seem to find the men responsible for the attack. Haster's admission is nothing in comparison to conspiring with the men. That is a rather dangerous position to be in. You need to help us find those men. So, in an hour and a half, I want you to report to my house ready to remember. Is that understood?"

"Yes, my lord," replied Hillbeck, swearing in the privacy of his head.

"Good, until then, Sergeant." With that, Landis went to update Adeone on what had occurred when he saw Wynfeld the previous evening.

Hillbeck used some of the time between leaving Landis and heading through the city to move his belongings from his billet to the small room on the ground floor of the Privy Wing that was his new home. It wasn't much: a bed, a small table, chair and nondescript wardrobe. He'd just put his off-duty clothes away when a knock at the door heralded a curious footman with his new living tokens. They were used to inform others what your place was and, more importantly, to get fed and watered.

After the footman left, he turned the tokens over in his hands, examining them. His previous ones had entitled him to use the Guards' Hall. These entitled him to use Upper Hall also, the most prestigious refectory in the Palace. He didn't know if he would ever use it. Sitting having dinner with the likes of the Steward and other heads of departments would probably give him indigestion.

He made sure his personal chest was locked and headed out into the city. The walk from the Palace to Landis House wasn't unpleasant. The day still retained crisp clear skies but, now he wasn't busy organising his new life, he was in too much turmoil to enjoy it. By the time he'd finished with Lord Landis, he might be the shortest-lived sergeant the King's Guard had ever had.

* * *

At Landis House, he presented himself at the tenants' door. It seemed the most appropriate. He had a strange look from the footman who answered, which was explained by Landis' manservant.

"King's senior staff come to the front door. His Lordship is particular about that. Don't worry, you'll get used to it, Sergeant. Lord Landis has not yet returned from the Palace. Please, just wait in here; I will collect you when His Lordship can see you."

*Here* turned out to be an empty room with a tiled floor and tiny window. Nothing else marked it out. Not a chair or painting. It had the feel of a cell and he idly wondered if it had been used as one in the past and whether it would be one again. He'd been waiting for around a quarter of an hour by his estimate when William collected him.

He stood in Lord Landis' study unnerved by the way the lord simply watched him as though he was taking him to pieces, one inch at a time. The grey eyes bored into him with a steeliness at odds with Landis' persona. For years, he'd heard people mention Lord Landis as a man you *didn't* cross; he suddenly understood why.

Eventually, Landis spoke. "What have you got for me?"

"I can't remember much, my lord. The Teran Arms isn't that well lit."

"Really!"

Hillbeck riled. "Yes, my lord. I can tell you one was roughly five-foot-eight and the other just under six feet. The shorter one was stocky, the other

109

more slimly built and taller. Both had middling brown hair and their eyes were dark rather than light. They didn't sound like they came from Oedran, but I wouldn't say they came from that far afield either – maybe a twenty-mile radius. They knew one another well enough to finish sentences for each other. Might even have been brothers or cousins. Same features if only slightly different through life experiences. Straight noses. Clothes were thin, well-worn calf-length breeches and loose tunics, but they were each wearing gloves and a cloak made to last. Thick, oiled material—"

"For saying you *'can't remember much,'* you've remembered a remarkable amount of detail," remarked Landis. "What were they drinking?"

Hillbeck snorted. "Probably the same gnat's pee the rest of us were, my lord. There was a prostitute and her pimp who might have noticed more."

Landis stilled. "You didn't mention them yesterday."

"I was considering His Majesty's presence. She was there the first evening I noticed the men. I think the landlord might have more knowledge of them all, although no-one seems to ask questions there."

"Talking about not being from Oedran, you're not either, are you?"

"Erm, no, my lord. About ten miles away. Small farm. Too many sons. Had to find myself a spot in the world and Oedran was close."

"Is that the answer you give to everyone?"

"Yes, my lord. It is the truth, after all." A shiver went down his spine as Landis studied him. This man was dangerous.

Landis said, "Yes. It is the truth. It is now even more imperative that you continue to give that answer. Is that understood? Good. We need you to keep an eye out for those men. I doubt anyone will see them at the Teran Arms again. They'll know their plan went wrong; however, we'll see that men are in place there just in case. Your information has been very useful. Don't return to the Teran Arms yourself. It will be dangerous for you. If, however, you see any of the other people who were in the bar with you that night, you don't show recognition, but you do tail them and then tell me where they are living. Just remember the person following who doesn't think *he* is being followed has a very short lifespan. Keep your eyes open for trouble, Hillbeck. You've helped to save the King's life. That puts yours in danger. You can go."

Hillbeck left, thinking that Landis had shown another side to his character. How on Erinna did he know the rules for tracking people? What sort of *lord* would ever need to know them?

# Chapter 24
# PROGRESS
### Morning
### Wynfeld's Office

WOKEN BY HIS BATMAN, Wynfeld realised that the knot of dread in his stomach hadn't disappeared as he dreamed. Not that he had been dreaming; his sleep had been unusually light, his mind trying to work out what to do.

His batman passed him his belt, adorned with scabbards. Donning it, he sheathed his sword and dagger.

"I've warned the mess you'll be wanting breakfast early, sir."

Wynfeld entered the officers' mess and glanced at the duty corporal. "What's for breakfast, Evans?"

"Cap'n says porridge is good."

Wynfeld chuckled. "Porridge it is then." When the corporal passed him his breakfast, Wynfeld eyed him balefully. "I thought you said porridge?"

"Well, we got a bit bored of that and, this early, porridge is still stewing. Hope you don't mind bacon and eggs, sir."

"It'll set me up nicely for the day. I'll have to start coming in early more often."

He watched the corporal's features struggle between the conventional *'it'll be a pleasure'* and the reality of *'please don't'*. He merely winked and tucked into the breakfast. His mind still turning over the events of the previous day.

When the Major entered, he rose and saluted. It was rare that the Major entered the mess and Wynfeld feared another dressing down.

He hesitantly resumed his seat at a nod from his commanding officer. He could see Evans taking a careful interest in what was happening.

"You're up early, Wynfeld," remarked the Major from the opposite chair.

"Have a few things to sort out, sir."

"Yes, you have, haven't you?" He glanced at the plate in front of him. "Don't get too used to officers' fare. Things change quickly. I'd recommend you go and start the day's work. Ah, Evans, I hope you've more bacon."

Wynfeld felt Evans watching him leave; cultivating that corporal might be an idea. The officers' mess was a hive of untapped information, especially with the men who bought Oedranian captaincies.

He unlocked his office, thinking about the structure of the army and how captaincies were usually bought, though some were arranged before being purchased, especially those in the great families. There was little point in giving up the freedoms of privilege if you were going to end up in the middle of nowhere, manning a secondary or tertiary fort. He'd served in some of those forts; rarely did lords end up in them.

He brought himself out of the contemplation to consider the bigger one: how to prevent a repeat of the previous day. How to ensure his regiment discovered the plots. He heard Drave arrive at his desk and heard the first of his sergeants hand over their section of the report for the Palace.

"Tell himself nothing of note."

He opened the door. "A word, Escott." The sergeant sauntered into the office with a swagger that Wynfeld disliked. "Nothing to report?"

"No, sir. Nothing happened yesterday that we got to hear about. Though, I did hear Landis came by last night, but he keeps odd hours, what with gallivanting at Court."

Wynfeld's lips pursed. "When you are talking about anyone other than your closest friends, you use their proper titles! It is *Lord* Landis and I am *not* 'himself', is that clear?"

Escott never turned a hair. "If that's what you want, sir."

"It is the normal convention, *Sergeant*. Now, nothing to report is rather too bland. What were you doing yesterday?"

"I managed to speak with Merchant Figgis' apprentice, sir, but then I was on duty when he's let off for the day. The merchant dined with Merchant Chapa the other day, but nothing was of note in that. The 'pren' asked me what a *heritor* is. Figgis is trading with one. Don't know myself, so I couldn't tell him."

Wynfeld sighed. "A heritor is a landowner in Bayan who doesn't owe fealty to a lord or king. King Altarius forbade use of the title after many were part of the rebellion. Those that kept faith with the empire got to keep their title, but there were precious few and their descendants can't use it. It was part of the Ramifications. Was there anything else?"

"Nah, nothing. I got a drink at the Golden Hare but didn't hear much. My normal girl was otherwise engaged, you might say."

"Anything else? Or are you telling me that you only have two informers, one of whom works in a brothel?"

Escott hesitated. "I always keep my ears open, sir, but there aren't that many willing to spy. 'Tis 'ard persuading 'em to when they can see what we are. We each have our network, but we can't get information if they're not there to talk to, and Jess won't go with just anyone, won't talk to just anyone either—"

"We are charged with protecting our King's life and the safety of the empire and you think that having two informers and spending your duty time in a brothel is acceptable?" enquired Wynfeld too mildly. "You should be producing a bit more than 'nothing to report'."

Escott coloured. "I ain't the only one, sir."

"No, and you're not the only one I'll be speaking with," remarked Wynfeld. "All right, dismissed."

Escott saluted and left, inwardly chuntering.

As each sergeant going off duty reported, Wynfeld called them in and went through similar questions and answers. He concentrated on getting the morning report to Richardson before interviewing the sergeants who were going on duty. Hearing much the same from them, he spent some time making notes of what he'd elicited. He was drawing his notes together to re-read them when Drave knocked.

"His Majesty, sir."

The corporal jumped at the speed at which he rose and saluted. He hadn't expected a personal visit.

Adeone dismissed the corporal with a glance before saying, "I believe you were informed of yesterday's events, Captain."

"Yes, Sire. I messed up." He remained at attention, trying not to shake.

His King was grim. "Yes. I'm glad you admit it. You're a bloody good soldier, Wynfeld; your record in the legions was a pleasure to read – make a good captain. I believe you can do it, but Lord Landis and the Major have insisted that they aren't happy with events yesterday and, therefore, you are currently on borrowed time. If you fail again, I shall have little option but to replace you. Get it sorted, or your future here is an uncertain thing. Sit down, you're looming. I had a report when Fitz left on the current number of people working for you in the provinces. I'd like an updated one every season, please. You need to make sure that people are still willing to pass you information. Go through everyone on your lists and recruit more. I realise it will take time but do it. From your service record, you are good at spotting what needs doing. Improve the regiment. Your subordinates won't like you for some time, but you need their respect, rather than their appreciation. You are not the only one who has been lax."

"The men won't know what's hit them, Your Majesty."

"Good. As I've given you more than enough work to keep you going for a couple of years, is there anything you need from me?"

Wynfeld realised there was. "I could do with an opening at Court, Sire, if Your Majesty doesn't mind my presence there."

His King was regarding him appraisingly. "You'll have it within the week. For now, please accompany me to the gates of the barracks."

* * *

When Wynfeld reached his office once more, he shut the door and began

113

to examine how the regiment worked. He'd been too accepting when he received his commission, he hadn't questioned what occurred and he'd let his sergeants direct him too much. He began to realise the regiment wasn't the right means for collecting information. They had people in the provinces, but it was on too friendly a footing. Someone knew someone who knew something. The men in the regiment worked Oedran in the same way. It was too makeshift, too clumsy. The events of the last couple of days proved it wasn't always going to work. They had to be smarter and rely less on chance. His King was right: he needed to make changes.

He drew out the current structure of his regiment. It was the same as every other one in the empire. One hundred and fifty-two men, including him and his corporal-clerk; ten sergeants, twenty corporals and a hundred and twenty unranked soldiers, forming ten units, consisting of a sergeant, two corporals and twelve soldiers. Three duty shifts a day, each with three units, the final unit on leave. Some did what he'd done and saved leave up, those who reported for duty were found a myriad of different jobs to do.

He sat back, examining the diagram. In the normal way of things, it worked. Why didn't it in this regiment? He re-read the brief history of the regiment in the notes Fitz had left. He had been its captain since its creation. King Altarius had wanted it to appear normal to any outsider. Wynfeld groaned as understanding erupted in his mind. King Altarius had handed intelligence duties to a normal regiment to hide its purpose. No-one had questioned its formation. Why was the pretence continued though? People had realised what they did. It served no purpose. Lord Scanlon had grown up knowing all about them and how they operated. Maybe it was time to change that. To change the way the regiment worked so the Justiciar couldn't use it against their King.

The more Wynfeld looked at the parchment in front of him, the more he realised the changes would have to happen. He called for his corporal. "Any of the people on leave reported for duty today?"

Drave was surprised; it was the first time Wynfeld had even acknowledged the practice. "Erm, yes, sir. Sergeant Jones and a couple of his men."

"If Jones isn't out collecting information, I want to see him, now."

When Drave had gone, Wynfeld pulled out Jones' file, scanning the front sheet and half wondered why he'd never read it before. It explained a lot. A knock at the door heralded the sergeant. Wynfeld regarded the now-familiar face with new understanding. Heavily built with deep-set eyes, Jones presented a hard, fixed gaze to the world of frustrated ambition and disenchantment. Maybe Oedran wasn't where he needed to be.

By the time an exasperated Jones left, Wynfeld realised they had a good basis for the network, but the men weren't in the right places. He wrote out his plans, fashioning them into a dossier and took it to the Palace. He asked Richardson, to see their King read it as soon as possible. The administrator added it to a pile, which left Wynfeld wondering if it would be read at all.

# Chapter 25
## A RATHER DIFFERENT REGIMENT
Tretaldai, Week 16 – 24th Macial, 3rd Easis 1209
Wynfeld's Office

DRAVE ENTERED Wynfeld's office the following morning and passed over a note. Seeing his King's seal, Wynfeld hastily broke it. He was needed in the Inner Office to discuss his report. He owed Richardson an apology.

Entering the Palace by the stables, he walked through the increasingly familiar corridors and courtyards. The Palace Guard and militia were separate bodies but the ranks were respected. So, salutes followed Wynfeld and he still felt uncomfortable acknowledging them.

He reached the King's Corridor. The duty sergeant on the Audience Chamber asked his name. Wynfeld gave it without rancour, noticing the way the sergeant's eyes evaluated the information. He crossed the Audience Chamber with an inclination of his head to the throne and entered the Outer Office.

Richardson pushed himself to his feet. "Good morning, Captain. I will see if His Majesty is ready for you. He has Lord Landis and Advisor Rayburn with him."

"Am I late?" asked Wynfeld with concern.

"Not at all."

Two moments later, he entered the Inner Office and saluted.

"Come in and sit down. I thought this would be easier," explained his King dryly. "Your report wasn't what we were expecting."

"It wasn't exactly what I was expecting to write, Sire," Wynfeld admitted, "but as I looked at everything following Your Majesty's visit yesterday, I came to those conclusions."

"Did you discuss them with the Major or General?" probed Landis.

"Not completely, my lord, because they can't make the decisions on this."

"There is a point there," observed Adeone. "However, they might be able to advise you as to when things may be said to be going too far."

Wynfeld swallowed. "Your Majesty, I meant no offence, but they are of the army. Their first thought is surely to protect what the army holds."

Landis coughed. "Their first thought is loyalty to the King's wishes."

"Yes, my lord," answered Wynfeld uncomfortably. "No-one should ever doubt it but—"

"Ripping a regiment to shreds might be beyond their comprehension?" enquired Rayburn. "I tend to agree. Paturn is an excellent General, Sire, but the power of the army lies in maintaining structure. Wynfeld's suggestion destroys it. The General may not be happy with him."

Wynfeld saw the amusement in his King's eyes. He'd always had a sense of humour. "I'm not exactly suggesting destroying it, Advisor. I'm suggesting creating an unofficial regiment of captains in the empire with a core unit left in Oedran overseeing civilian and military spies."

"Yes," said Landis gravely. "That's where it gets a bit unbelievable. You should explain how you came to your conclusions."

"It wasn't an immediate conclusion, sir," replied Wynfeld. "King Altarius' solution was a logical way to set up a network but that doesn't mean it's right with the current situation." He glanced sideways at Rayburn.

"Rayburn is aware of the 'current situation', Captain," revealed Adeone.

"Thank you, Sire. The way I reasoned it was that Lord Scanlon knows all about us, he knows how we work; so, if we want to be effective maybe we need to change that. There are other threats but even as a young man I'd heard about a regiment of spies in Oedran. It's not a secret organisation. It relies on people knowing people who may know something. Recent events have proved how disastrous that could be. I refuse to be complacent and continue with something just because that's how it's always been done. We need more informers, more men in the empire, more targeted strategies. We aren't going to get informers if our spies look like soldiers. We aren't going to get more men in the empire if all the spies are here and we aren't going to develop strategies without more information, which needs those informers and spies. We need more varied specialists: for example, there's no point sending a clerk's son to talk to a blacksmith; their language, their manner will just rouse suspicion; we'd need a blacksmith. We have a good start, but it currently isn't going to prevent Lord Scanlon's aims, or others who wish Your Majesty harm."

"Interesting points," remarked Adeone. "What do you need first?"

Wynfeld took a deep breath. "Clerks, sir, to help the sergeants compile reports and update our records—"

"And you can't find clerks in the army?" asked Landis. "You have clerks assigned to key officers. Surely a few more can be found."

"Yes, my lord, but they'd be part of other units, prone to redeployment. If they are assigned to my regiment, I lose ears on the street. It will also test how the militia and civilians can work together."

"I'm sure Richardson can find you three trustworthy clerks," said Adeone. "However, I meant what is stopping you from getting better information?"

Wynfeld considered. "The fact my men look like soldiers."

Landis snorted. "Well, they are soldiers."

"Yes, sir, but do your spies wear uniform and plod about the streets so obviously?"

"Wynfeld has a point, Lord Landis," remarked Adeone trying to ignore Rayburn's amusement. "Why *are* your men walking around the streets in uniform? Even I can see a problem there."

"Regulations, Sire," answered Wynfeld. "Jupons, breastplates or tabards must be worn when on duty."

Adeone snorted. "And no-one's considered this a problem before?"

"I honestly don't know, sir," said Wynfeld careful not to criticise Fitz. "Sometimes, it's only when things go wrong people question practices."

"You have a point. I agree it needs to change. I'll speak to the General; your regiment can be excused from the requirement to be in uniform at all times. Save it for appropriate occasions instead. What else? Make the most of my attention."

Wynfeld hesitated. "If you insist, Sire. I *do* want to scrap the duty times. The city doesn't work to the military clock, so I'd like the men to be active as needed. I'd also like to make sure that each informer has two handlers, so we don't lose them if we post a man somewhere else. Over the next year, I'd like to start moving men to regiments in the provinces. I'll then need reliable civilians to fill the gaps – hopefully, some of our regular informers to start with. As I said earlier, by the end of this I'd like a civilian organisation run by the militia. I think it will yield better intelligence."

Wynfeld watched his King and Lord Landis share a significant glance.

"Sire, Wynfeld apparently has the resolve to see this through," said Landis, "but I do think that it's ambitious and potentially destructive to what's already in place."

"It's not *potentially* destructive, Landis, it *is* destructive," observed Adeone, "but I certainly accept that times have changed. Fitz and I were discussing possible changes, but even his didn't go this far."

"Sire, I can understand the allure of this," remarked Landis carefully. "I agree change is needed but I have reservations about such wide-reaching change. Men of the militia answer to you. Their oath of allegiance is to you and no other. There are laws under which they operate. A civilian organisation has less discipline and fewer restraints. Treason laws help but Lord Scanlon controls the civilian courts."

"Noted," said Adeone, before glancing at a timepiece. "You'd better go, or Cornelia will never forgive me. I'll see you this evening." After

Landis left, Adeone laughed. "Do you think that gave my nearchildren time to ambush him, Rayburn?"

Advisor Rayburn chuckled. "I expect so, Your Majesty."

Wynfeld's brows knitted.

Adeone noticed. "It's His Lordship's birthday, Captain. My nearchildren asked me to keep him occupied whilst they decorated the house and, if I know anything about the twins, rig up a couple of practical jokes. Your report was exceptionally well-timed. So, Rayburn, you've been quiet. What do you think about it all?"

"I think Lord Landis might get suspicious next year, Sire."

"Rayburn!"

"Sorry. If anyone can carry off this change it's Wynfeld, sir. I understand Lord Landis' reservations, but I don't share them all. Your Majesty has admitted that you've had your misgivings, that Fitz thought the time was right for a change and it's clear Wynfeld has his concerns. I couldn't spot anything I think wouldn't work, but Lord Landis' comments regarding Lord Scanlon's control of civilian law is certainly pertinent."

Wynfeld simply waited as Adeone thought.

Eventually, his King said, "Wynfeld, with regard to scrapping uniforms and the duty rota, implement those as soon as possible; however, with regards to recruiting civilians, I am not averse but if traitors infiltrate the regiment, you'll be held personally responsible so be careful and sure. If you want to deviate from what we've discussed, talk to the General, but, in implementing what we have discussed, you have free rein. Allocate men where you need them in the empire and recruit more. For the most part, if you can justify why you want someone, they're yours. A new captain is often a new broom and you have a short period to use that fact, so use it. Just don't make too many personal enemies."

"Thank you, Sire. I shall try to get it all working within a year."

"Don't be too optimistic but thank you. That's all for now, gentlemen."

Once in the Outer Office, Rayburn said, "I'm impressed, Captain, and I don't mind admitting it. If you can spare the time, I'd like to talk several matters over with you. I think your talents could prove indispensable."

"Certainly, Advisor, though I can't speak for my talents."

Richardson, who'd been waiting patiently, said, "Captain, you'll need this seal to add to documents for the King's immediate attention. It is for your sole use; do not delegate its application."

# Chapter 26

# OF ADVISORS AND OFFICERS
### Late Morning
### Palace – Rayburn's Office

SILENTLY, Wynfeld accompanied Rayburn through the Palace, to the latter's office. When dealing with Adeone directly, Wynfeld knew what to expect. Dealing with Rayburn left him uncertain. The position of King's Military Advisor was one of the most senior and influential in the empire. Gaining Rayburn's good opinion was crucial.

Once seated in his modest office, overlooking the Palace Gardens, the advisor said, "I don't know much about you, Wynfeld. What's your history? Where have you served?"

"All over the empire, sir. I transferred a few times, so have seen a lot of places."

"Sounds like you had a past to leave behind," joked Rayburn.

"Maybe I did," sighed Wynfeld. "It found me again though."

"Oh, yes?" queried Rayburn, intrigued.

After a brief silence, Wynfeld admitted, "My Aunt Maria raised me at Macarian House."

"Curious. I thought nepotism was going out of fashion," said Rayburn.

Wynfeld chuckled. "I doubt my promotion was my aunt's handiwork. I tarnished her good opinion of me when I didn't write for fifteen years; I was surprised Lady Ira was pleased to see me, after that."

"Hmm. The Queen's favour will have done you the world of good. His Majesty isn't prone to giving men of his army second chances. Says it destroys discipline."

Wynfeld swallowed. "I did offer to resign, Advisor."

"Yes, I've heard. I've also heard that His Majesty paid you a rare visit, normally reserved only for long-standing officers. That has got you noticed more than the ineptitude. Now, you seem to have formed your intriguing ideas for your regiment's restructuring very swiftly."

"I had to do something. The regiment isn't effective and we need to be. We can't fail again."

"No, it would not be wise." Rayburn poured two drinks and put one by Wynfeld's hand. "Fitz came to see me before he left. Said he was worried some of the men might undermine you just because they didn't know you. He had a strong grasp on what motivates men. Was he right?"

Wynfeld picked up his drink. "Why do you wish to know?"

"I'm an advisor. Advice is what I do."

"Advice for whom?" enquired Wynfeld.

"Ah, you think I will run to the King. I do not habitually do so. I am a man who collects information so that I am better able to advise the King. I do not, however, tell His Majesty everything I discover. If you're undermined, your reforms will be less successful, which weakens His Majesty's position; therefore, if you wish to talk things over with someone who is not your commanding officer, I am willing to listen for you also should not be talking them over with any of the men and as to your fellow captains, shall we say there are several I wouldn't trust to walk in a straight line when sober?"

Wynfeld snorted. "There are certainly those, sir."

Rayburn let the silence mature.

Eventually, Wynfeld said, "I've threatened to post Jones elsewhere."

"Yes, that was one name that came up."

Wynfeld sighed. "I tried to talk things through with him, to get some sort of order. Not everything, but trying to determine where we went wrong. He blocked every suggestion, every option. He certainly doesn't like people from the provinces and he didn't get much better when I pointed out that I grew up here."

Rayburn snorted. "Fitz did say that he would make a good captain if he could learn to take orders."

Wynfeld chuckled. "Ah, well, maybe that's where I go wrong."

"You take orders, Captain. You just bypass your traditional commanding officers. General Paturn may want a word with you. He is traditional and won't have liked the fact you circumvented his command, but he won't interfere now you have the King's word. He will, however, remember. You said you've threatened to post Jones elsewhere. Did you mean it?"

"Yes. If you don't mean it, there's no point making a threat."

Rayburn snorted. "I agree. You should always be prepared to carry through. In fact, I would take the earliest opportunity you can. For one thing, he will stop undermining you; for another, you'll have an informant elsewhere in the empire to start a new network but don't post him, second him. It gives you more options. Once Jones is gone, the other men may start conforming. Not only because he's gone but because you'll have proved you're up to the job and will take difficult decisions. Leading is about being fair but firm."

"Aye, I know. I've had my fair share of poor captains to explain how not to do it."

"Yes, I can imagine you have. His Majesty has been far more open to promoting men from the ranks than any monarch in centuries but that hasn't stopped the purchase of commissions. It's dangerous. Not only can idiots buy them but so can traitors."

"Most traitors are idiots," said Wynfeld without thinking.

Rayburn laughed. "There is that." He considered Wynfeld for a few moments before saying, "You'll be fine, Captain. More than a match for idiots of all varieties. Do you have a couple of hours now?"

Wynfeld shrugged. "If I can help with anything, of course. I was only going to depress my sergeants."

"I'm sure they'll be glad of the respite. I'd like to introduce you to a few of my colleagues and the Court. There's ample opportunity there for finding idiots, but the contacts might help you. I'm not sure who's presiding, but I'm sure they can't object."

Lord Ryson looked quizzically at Rayburn as he introduced Wynfeld before glancing at the captain. "Welcome to Court, Captain Wynfeld. Advisor Rayburn can explain the rules if you don't know them. I'm sure you're not going to cause any trouble so please don't prove me wrong."

"I'd need orders before causing trouble, my lord," replied Wynfeld.

Ryson snorted with amusement, glanced at Rayburn and left.

Rayburn was chortling to himself. "You're going to be fine. Who is here? Ah, Advisor Vanval, might I introduce Captain Wynfeld. It's his first time here. I'm sure you've plenty you can tell him." He turned to Wynfeld, "Vanval is the King's Court Advisor. I'm sure he's here to keep an eye on everything rather than just enjoy the wine."

A grey-haired man in his late fifties, nodded to Wynfeld. "Pleasure to meet you, Captain. Rayburn will have his jokes."

Wynfeld returned the pleasantry, adding, "I'm sure to be on the receiving end of them as well, sir. Is the wine worth the joke?"

"Oh, definitely," said Vanval pleasantly. "The King's vineyards are rightly well-renowned. What brings you to Court?"

"Advisor Rayburn," replied Wynfeld seriously.

Vanval chuckled. "Yes, but other than that?"

Rayburn who'd waved over a server, passed Wynfeld a goblet, smirking. "He's stepped into Fitz's shoes at the barracks, Vanval."

"Ah," said the older gentleman sagely. "That explains everything. Let's see how I can help."

# Chapter 27

# SERGEANTS' BRIEFING
### Afternoon
### Wynfeld's Office

THE WALK BACK TO BARRACKS had been refreshing. On entering his office, Wynfeld sent for the duty sergeants. There was no point wasting time now he had permission to start. Sergeants Escott, Beaver and Jones, along with three others, reported, if not promptly, at least quickly. He outlined the plans regarding duty time and civilian dress, adding it was to be implemented immediately.

Predictably, Jones interrupted. "Hang on, sir, 'with immediate effect'?"

"Yes, Jones. Our King wants to see this in place as soon as possible."

Jones didn't hold back. "The King, or you, sir?"

"Does it matter? Either bloody way, it is an order from an officer."

Escott spoke up, "We recognise that. We'd just like to have been consulted. We've worked fine for the last few decades—"

"Really? Is it *'fine'* that there has been an attack on our King's life that not one of you has found out about? No, it's not. It's not *'working fine'* when that is the case. Now, if you don't want to find that we're all posted to the far-flung corners of the empire, start listening. This regiment is the laughing stock of His Majesty's closest advisors and rightly so. I'd rather not continue to be that and have promised His Majesty that we shall no longer collect information in the cack-handed manner which seems to have *'worked fine… for the last few decades.'* Any objections?" (A couple of the sergeants opened their mouths.) "No? Good. Now, you've all volunteered to be the first units to change to the new regime. Talk to the men under your command. I want a list of their informers and I want them to pass you as much information on those men as possible and the last pieces of information gleaned from them—"

"Would that be another report, sir?" sniped Jones.

"*Let me finish!* You'll be collecting the information in the morning when there will be a clerk apiece to help. So, don't worry, you won't have to wonder about the spelling of 'Oedran' or 'street' anymore, Jones."

"Right, sir. How do you spell tyrant?"

"Get out!" As Jones left with a defiant stare, Wynfeld asked, "What is his issue?" for appearance's sake.

"He was tipped as the next captain, sir," replied Escott.

"Then, here's a tip for you all – of slightly better premonition – I'm Captain of Intelligence and I will be getting this regiment up to scratch. Have you got that?"

There was a sensible chorus of '*Yes, sir!*'

"Good. I am sorry people were passed over when our King gave me this commission but I received it for a reason. Now, I am not going to have to inform His Majesty that my sergeants are in mutiny over the proposed changes, am I?"

"I hope you're not, sir, but it wouldn't necessarily be us you understand. The men like their traditions."

"I know that, Escott, but I'm trying to ensure we regain our reputation."

Sergeant Beaver said, "Sir, I'm not opposed to the change, I'm truly not. I think it could be good for us all, but what do you ultimately envisage this regiment to become? I think you've got some plan in your mind; might we know it?"

"I plan for us to be effective. The next part is to increase our informers. I want every man in this regiment to run *at least* five and to partner with another man in the regiment. So, the men will be working in pairs and have ten informers, minimum. For five, one man leads; for the other five, the other man leads, but it should mean that if we lose a man, we don't lose the informers. Any questions?"

"Even the sergeants, sir?" queried Beaver.

"Yes. You'll partner up with one of the men though, not each other. Now, talk about this only amongst yourselves for now. I'll inform the other sergeants as and when they come on duty. That's all."

The remaining sergeants saluted and left. Wynfeld thought for a moment. Jones had played straight into his hands. He waited for a minute, yelled for Drave, and two moments later Jones was standing at attention in front of his desk.

"Sergeant Jones, your insubordination isn't helping your career. I have a transfer form to hand."

"Really, sir? I can't see you signing it. Men wouldn't be happy."

"Let me make this clear to you, Jones, neither *you* nor *the men* run this regiment." With that, Wynfeld pulled a transfer slip from a drawer and filled it out before silently signing it. He called for the corporal. "See that gets to the General today, Drave. It's at Sergeant Jones' request."

The corporal took the proffered form and left.

Rather red, Jones growled, "I didn't request it!"

"Yes, you did, by being insubordinate. I was kind, I posted you to Garth. Bayan's city isn't so different from Oedran. I shall, however, be speaking to your new commanding officer and making him aware of why you've been posted. You can go."

Jones went to say something, then his features set and he left. He tried to see the General who happened to be too busy. When Paturn saw the form, he signed it and sent Jones his marching orders. The sergeant was out of the barracks by the following morning and, despite his prediction, the men didn't mutiny.

By the time Jones left, three clerks had reported for duty, all unnerved to be working with the militia under Wynfeld's direction. Normally civilians and the army stayed separate.

Wynfeld had decided to treat them much as he would anyone else, but by asking and explaining rather than ordering. Part of the agreement had included him moving offices to allow the clerks access to the records. A unit from a different regiment emptied a storeroom on one side of his office to provide him with an office.

The speed of the changes intrigued the clerks; used to working in a highly bureaucratic environment – where it took weeks for anything promised to be talked about again – it came as a pleasant surprise.

By the end of the morning, they were all ensconced in their new rooms. Wynfeld had a doorway made between his old office and his new one but the carpenters couldn't fit a door for another day. He listened as the men started giving the clerks up-to-date information. Some forgot the door wasn't there and discussed the new arrangements. A couple even admitted they'd spotted loopholes. Working silently in his office, Wynfeld smiled to himself. He'd left those loopholes to help the transition. He'd close them gradually if necessary.

He promoted one corporal to sergeant to help morale but didn't promote anyone to corporal. He'd keep an eye out throughout the barracks. In the officers' mess that evening, it was clear his fellow captains weren't sure what to make of him anymore. Ignoring the unease, he entered into a conversation with the training captain.

# Chapter 28
# JONES IN GARTH

Imperadai, Week 19 – 18th Meithal, 4th Meithis 1209
Bayan – Garth

Marching through Anapara and Bayan, Jones cursed Wynfeld with every step. The woods, fields and rivers of the rolling countryside didn't distract him; he was a city boy. The wide expanses of countryside and sky made him bilious. He muttered to himself that *Wynfeld* had had the gumption to post him, *him* to the other side of the empire. Grouching over events, he cursed that he had to babysit raw recruits with another sergeant. He should have been a captain. Why the King had promoted Wynfeld, he would never understand. Eventually, his companions gave up trying to make conversation, which was fine by him. It was a shame that his fellow sergeant was so conscientious about their stops being in guarded locations: forts or major mail lodges. Disappearing into the morass of the empire at night wasn't an option.

When they reached Garth, the capital of Bayan, shock ran through him. The towers, minarets and spires of the city certainly *looked* very different from Oedran. Evidence of empire was non-existent and Jones began to wish he'd deserted on the march. Terrace after terrace of buildings reached up to the Citadel; their multi-coloured spires and minarets twisting and turning as they sought the sky; high above the streets sky-bridges, their undersides painted in many colours crossed from one building to another.

Wrapped up in the injustices of his posting, the beauty and splendour of the proud city completely escaped Jones' attention.

He reported to the fort in a bad temper, which only got worse when his new commanding officer said,

"I hear you've been annoying Wynfeld, Jones. My old sergeant certainly knows how to return the favour, I must say. Seems he did learn something."

Jones swore, not audibly, but well and truly cursing. His grievance had been silenced before it had been heard.

Two days later, Sharparu pulled him once more into the office saying, grimly, "I've received orders concerning you. Seems you're not here to help me. You're to be allowed time in the city and access to the highest in Garth society. Any idea *why*, Jones?"

His mind raced. It could only mean he was needed to spy. "Not really, sir. I'm sure everything will become clear in time."

"Oh, most likely. When you have remembered what your orders from Wynfeld were, let me know. I'll have something to say about them as your commanding officer."

He took a split-second decision on how to play the situation. "Yes, sir. I'll take my off-duty time same as the other men. I think Captain Wynfeld might be having a joke at my expense, sir."

From a dim corner by the door, a man said, "Really? My information is that Wynfeld rarely jokes. Captain, that is all for now."

Sharparu saluted and left without a word. The man walked over and seated himself. His tunic's blue stripes indicated an important lord, the narrow red band on his clothes marked him as a King's Representative.

This had to be the Exarch – Governor of Bayan – Lord Tyler Galwood, a distant cousin of the King.

"Why did you just lie?"

"I'm sorry?" asked Jones, unnerved by the scrutinising gaze.

"You know who I am, please address me correctly or I'll have you posted to a *really* remote fort."

Jones modified his tone, the Exarch commanded respect by his very posture. "I didn't exactly lie to Captain Sharparu, Your Excellency. I don't *know*, sir. Captain Wynfeld ordered me to leave Oedran. I *suspect* he means me to carry on with the work of the intelligence regiment."

"Yes. He only seconded you to this regiment, not transferred you. He could recall you to Oedran or move you on with no notice; therefore, do not annoy anyone here. Your work is, or could be, too valuable. Find a couple of trustworthy men here and get them collecting information. *You* must appear to be a regular sergeant. That is imperative. One last thing, keep on the right side of the law and be discreet. No-one can protect you if you are arrested. Lord Scanlon mustn't get to know of your work. One of my agents will be in contact with you. Password will be *minarets of Oedran*. He will put you in contact with others who might be of help. I have my own informants; You may work for Oedran but do not tread on their toes. Goodbye, Jones."

"Sir." He held the door open for the Exarch and stayed holding it open as Captain Sharparu re-entered.

"What did His Excellency say to you?" enquired the captain.

"Nothing much, sir. Asked after Oedran mainly."

"If I lose another good sergeant because of your arrival, I will *not* be happy, Jones! Is that understood? There is a ban on all leave that gives you time enough to reach Oedran. I hope that's also clear."

"Crystal, sir," replied Jones, unnerved again.

"Good, because if I have another morning when the King gets in touch to tell me I've lost a sergeant, I shall have to take it out on someone. Now, I believe you have recruits to get up to scratch. Bugger off."

He snapped to attention, saluted and left, wondering what Captain Sharparu had been talking about. It didn't take much digging for him to find out it was Wynfeld's commission. He suddenly wished he knew *how* Wynfeld had got his commission; the captain had obviously been liked and respected here, taking aggravation from Sharparu to save others. That hole still needed filling. No-one here knew of his aspirations and disappointments. He could start again.

* * *

For all it was part of the empire, the province of Bayan chose to believe it was independent. The country of the chieftainess who had become the first Sundrian, its people had been fighting Anapara for centuries, eventually bowing to the pressures of an empire but with a knife hidden in their boot. Oedran was rarely mentioned.

Garth's towers and minarets inspired the city to be reaching ever upward, but after the 1169 Bayan Rebellion, King Altarius had disbanded Garth's City Guard, leaving law enforcement to the militia.

For all he admired the spirit, Jones watched the inhabitants of Garth carefully. For his first few weeks, he walked the streets half-dazed, his eyes more often watching the sky than the ground, the spires drew the eye. Along the steep, winding streets were brightly draped market stalls, between them ran alleys crammed with shops or houses. They wended their way, narrow and steep, to hidden courtyards or great squares until he became disorientated but he began to understand why Wynfeld had said that it wasn't so different from Oedran. The pride of the inhabitants might be more noticeable but the same motives drove them; their lives had the same markers of their passing. Violence and poverty lived side by side here with love and riches.

His new regiment had responsibility for guarding the Exarch. It meant he was constantly at the Citadel and Trades Hall and, whilst there, Jones overheard many different conversations. Some he reported directly to Oedran, some to the Exarch's agent. Occasionally he waited to see if rumours were substantiated. Always, though, he kept in mind the fact that he was trying to protect the FitzAlcis.

After the first few weeks, his annoyance at Wynfeld had all but disappeared. It still rankled occasionally but there was no fire behind it. The challenge of something new helped and he was benefiting from it. The recruits yielded three trustworthy spies. Being raw recruits, no-one thought twice when they seemed to be listening keenly. It was assumed they were trying to learn how things worked. One man mastered the art without anyone ever realising he was listening. In the sergeants' mess, Jones heard about more than the doings of the Garth Lawhouse and Citadel Court. Guarding the Exarch meant he got to hear the conversations at the top of society but missed the small tell-tale everyday gossip that was sometimes more illuminating. He became good friends with one sergeant from a different regiment which patrolled the city and they were often seen sitting chatting the night away over a tankard of ale. They would discuss the day's happenings and the antics of their regiments without an obvious thought for anything else, but Jones learned much.

# Chapter 29
## ELIZA'S STORY
Imperadai, Week 19 – 18th Meithal, 4th Meithis 1209
Ceardlann

AROUND THE SAME TIME as Jones arrived in Garth, Prince Arkyn was poring over a plan in the Comptroller's office at Ceardlann. Suddenly, he rubbed the bridge of his nose between his thumb and forefinger, sighing. The Comptroller glanced at him in concern but, noticing determination, didn't comment.

Six minutes later, Prince Tain burst in through the door with his normal verve, saying excitedly, "Arkyn, come and see this."

Arkyn laughed seeing Tain covered in mud up to his knees. "Can it wait a bit?" he asked half wistfully.

"Suppose," said Tain, deflated.

The Comptroller seized his opportunity. "Your Highness, if you want to go and see what Prince Tain has been doing, I can finish off here."

"No, thank you. Father is expecting me to do this."

"I think he is also expecting that you learn how to delegate, sir. We've been at this for well over two hours. Go and get some fresh air."

"Comptroller…"

"No, sir. If you want to, come back later and carry on, but you need a break and, to tell you the truth, so do I. Your father won't be too pleased with either of us if—"

Arkyn faced the Comptroller and the Comptroller faced Arkyn.

Tain resolved the matter. "Arkyn, stop being a fool. Come outside."

Arkyn again saw Tain muddied up to the eyeballs and with a face blown into smiles. "Am I being a fool?"

"Yes, but if you weren't, I'd wonder if you were ailing for something," observed the Comptroller without any hint of deference.

Arkyn and Tain grinned. Suddenly, both of them were boys.

The Comptroller smiled. "Now, what time would you like dinner?"

Arkyn glanced at Tain. "What do you reckon?"

"Ten!"

"Past your bedtime," pointed out Arkyn with brotherly directness. "We'll go with eight, Comptroller."

"But that *is* my bedtime," cried Tain.

"Yes, and you won't be up quite so late as though it were ten, will you?"


Tain dragged his brother to the trout stream that fed the River Encil. They found Fitz there, trout rod in hand.

Feeling better, Arkyn said, "What *have* you been up to?"

"Trout fishing, without a rod. See? I caught those." Tain pointed to a couple of smaller trout.

Fitz merely chuckled to himself as Tain pulled Arkyn over to the stream whilst explaining, his enthusiasm obvious.

Quarter of an hour after they left Ceardlann, the Comptroller was intrigued to see Adeone dismounting looking frazzled. He walked to the stables to greet the King.

"Sorry for the unannounced visit, Comptroller; I needed to get away for a time. Where are the terrors?"

"With Fitz, sir, fishing in the trout stream above the bridge. Prince Arkyn has only just gone."

"I shall go and find them. What time did they order dinner for? I'll probably stay for it."

"Eight, Sire. Prince Tain did try his luck for ten, but Prince Arkyn is learning compromise more effectively than I could try reason."

Adeone clapped the Comptroller on the shoulder and left.

When he reached the trout stream, Arkyn and Tain were both kneeling on the bank, one arm up to the elbow in the water.

Adeone grinned, recognising the posture and found himself relaxing properly. He turned to Fitz. "Are you teaching your Princes poachers' skills?"

"Looks like I might be, Sire, and not for the first time. Why don't you have a go? See if you remember how."

Adeone's lips twitched. "Well, as you *did* teach me, I shouldn't complain. How are things?"

"All quiet, sir. Truly, there's nothing for you to worry over. They're doing all right. Prince Tain does remind me of you at his age."

Adeone watched for a moment. "A bundle of trouble, you mean? It's nice to see him happy, thank you. Have the afternoon off properly. You deserve it."

"Shall I send up a guard?"

"No, not today. We'll be all right." Adeone walked up behind his sons and whispered, "Nice you notice when I arrive."

Arkyn almost lost his balance with the speed at which he turned. Tain caught him with brotherly exasperation. Two seconds later, both boys received bone-crushing hugs before Tain dragged his father to examine their catch.

"We should let Cook have those. He does a good pan-fried trout."

"I must tell mother…" Tain trailed off as tears welled. He tried to pull away, but his father pulled him close. He struggled, trying to free himself, trying to run from memories and himself.

Adeone knew that battle as he knew himself. He held his son tightly pouring all his love and support into their embrace. Tears ran down his face. His sons shouldn't be suffering this loss.

Arkyn collapsed onto the grass, knees drawn up and his head resting on them. He stared into the distance fighting for control. Seeing his father was also crying, he let go, tears washing his face.

Tain finally stopped struggling and collapsed onto the ground, sitting like Arkyn. Adeone settled himself in the middle of his sons, an arm round each of them.

Finally, with the tears all shed, Tain started to apologise.

"There is no need to apologise," chided Adeone gently. "We need to acknowledge our loss when we can. I was about your age when my mother died. I know the loss."

"What was Queen Eliza like?" murmured Tain.

Adeone lay gazing at the clouds. "She was beautiful and always laughing. I remember that most of all – always laughing. It's why my father married her. He always said she brought merriment to his life."

Overcome with curiosity, listening to the wistful note in his father's voice, Arkyn enquired, "When did he meet her?"

"It is an odd story; I'm surprised I've never told you it. Father was riding through Oedran and badly cut his leg somehow. His guards noticed the sign for a doctor up one of the side streets and knocked the poor man up. They carried father into the man's front room and he was made comfortable whilst the doctor tended to his wound. Suddenly, not knowing what the commotion had been, a lady walked into the room carrying a fresh stock of bandages. The doctor asked her to give him a hand and introduced her as his cousin, who kept house for him. She was about twenty-three and vivacious. Halfway through seeing to the cuts and bruises, the doctor commented that they'd have to find a husband for her as her skills shouldn't be wasted on him. She readily agreed, saying that the last thing she wanted to do in life was to take care of a layabout cousin. They carried on wrangling for six minutes, completely forgetting, it seemed, just who the patient was. They were all chuckling by the time the doctor had finished dressing father's leg. They carried on talking and laughing for some time. So long that father forgot he'd hurt his leg and when he got up to leave, he put his weight on it and almost crumpled to the ground again. The doctor's cousin was quick and supported him. Father left the house feeling younger than he had for years. He went through the next couple of days in a dream and the next time he was passing, he called unannounced on the doctor, who took the visit with his normal eccentric affability. Father offered him a job and the doctor, not quite believing it, did the unthinkable and asked for time to consider it. Father agreed, saying the doctor would have to talk it over with his cousin. The doctor grimaced, revealing that his uncle had effectively ordered her home, stating it would be easier to find a husband for her there. Intrigued by the doctor's frankness, father was more disturbed by the idea of his bright cousin marrying. He made up his mind then and there. At that point, the door opened and the doctor's cousin entered. Not noticing father, she said something like, *'As I can't trust you to feed yourself on Millie's half-day, I've brought you dinner.'* It was only then that she saw my father; she beamed, dropped into a curtsy and excused herself. Doctor Chapa has always said that from that moment on, whenever she was in the room, my father had eyes for no-one but Eliza, his cousin. Father approached her father and then asked Eliza to marry him. She never quite believed it. I've been told her last words were, *'I'll wake up in a minute. It'll be ten years ago and this will all have been a dream.'* She never woke. The doc also accepted my father's offer of a job and we've been lumbered with him ever since. Mind you, we've also been laughing ever since," finished Adeone tolerantly.

Grief had unlocked memories; family history that Adeone had never told his sons flowed from him in waves. He told them stories about his father and grandfather. He'd never met his grandfather, but there had been enough lords when Adeone had been young, who had talked to him about King Apolinar Aldous. He spoke of his father's first wife, who had died from a fever – along with their son – whilst King Altarius dealt with the Bayan Rebellion. Their deaths kept secret until he was home. Intrigued, Tain asked why King Altarius' siblings hadn't informed him. Lachlan had been with Altarius, whilst Amara had been in Tradere. Neither of them had been advised their wed-sister had died.

Enraged, King Altarius had executed his nearfather as a traitor for keeping the news from him and ordering others to. He dismissed the then doctor and never believed anyone when they told him it had been natural causes. After that, Altarius hadn't trusted anyone for years. Adeone wryly thought to himself that Scanlon was showing some of those traits that resided in the FitzAlcis blood.

* * *

Lord Scanlon was concentrating his thoughts on his contemporaries. His plans were failing, and Wynfeld's endeavours certainly needed curtailing. He'd heard the captain had saved Adeone's life, but that had been a mere fluke. He was interested to hear that he had spent the afternoon of the Queen's death talking with her and Adeone, but that didn't concern him.

He knew the history of that meeting. With the last bit of compassion that he'd ever feel for his family, he was pleased Ira was comforted when she died. She'd tried to reach out to him when she'd married Adeone and he'd been nine years old. Scanlon pulled himself out of the past as his advisor remarked,

"What about Prince Tain? Surely, he's a threat, Greatness?"

"Do not presume to instruct me. Tain is too young to die. If he dies now, the King will get a lot of sympathy and *questions* will be asked. He is too full of life to have a fatal illness, too nimble to have an accident. Give it a few years and his mischievous side will get him into trouble, one way or another. He is like the King was. People won't stand for a practical joker as a justiciar; they will turn against him because of it. He will engineer his downfall. I'll not let him reach twenty, but he must live for a bit longer. The longer he lives, the less chance there is of the King remarrying to get more heirs. He will be security for my plans for a couple more years yet."

"Very well, sir. I've heard that one of the younger Traderian lords is upset with the King. He's cursing him in private and is planning an accident for him."

Scanlon considered his advisor steadily, "Deal with him. I don't want people getting ideas. I want to know my plans are settled when the King dies. I will be the one who succeeds in saving this empire from his influence, no-one else. Make sure the lord realises who he's upset before he greets his ancestors."

Bantling said gravely, "Very well, Greatness. I shall attend to it directly."

"Do so. Have you heard the rumours about the intelligence system?"

Knowing the Justiciar's temper, Bantling opted for the truth. "I have, sir, but I think Wynfeld might be finding his days numbered. He's a sergeant with no experience of command, promoted beyond his capabilities. He's already disgraced after the Triniculum Plan. One more mistake and he'll find himself demoted. At least, that is my information, sir."

"Arrange a mistake then. You can go."

# Chapter 30
## LANDIS' SECRET
Afternoon
Oedran – Landis House Study

LORD LANDIS WAS OSTENSIBLY staring into a gold bowl of clear, steaming water. What he saw though was the steam, twisting and parting into the shapes of clouds, and he forced his mind's eye past them down into the streets of Oedran. Searching. Somewhere in the city were the would-be assassins. The Teran Sector had yielded nothing. The men might be in the buildings but entering them was dangerous for him. Ullian seers and espiens, scryers and mediums could know he was scrying. In a confined space it was more likely that they'd sense him; therefore, he kept out of houses.

The ethereal silence of scrying didn't help him find two men who didn't sound Oedranian and Hillbeck's description could fit a hundred men in any sector of the city. It was a hopeless case, but determination drove him on.

Rubbing his face, he pulled himself from the mists, wondering for the thousandth time whether he should tell Adeone that Ull's Legacy affected him. He'd kept his scrying secret for years, telling himself over and over that Adeone didn't need to know, that the skill could only adversely affect their friendship. Adeone might try to get him to use the power granted by the hue too much, and he might come to rely on it. Landis wasn't worried about the motives, merely the strains it could place on their relationship – the frustrations and attached blame when it didn't work. No, it was better Adeone didn't know. Better that he lived in ignorance and ruled the empire without drawing on magical spirits and hues. It had been thus since the Fall of the Cearcall and should continue to be. Even the Bard, when he overthrew the Age of Tyranny, had only used the magical spirits as a last resort, or so the stories told them. It was a better world without the magic that Ull had brought onto Erinna. Magic shouldn't be used to rule – of that, Landis was certain.


A knock at the door preceded one of the two people now alive who knew about his hue.

"Any luck, my lord?" enquired William, closing the door.

"No. Not today. I don't think we're going to find them by this method. I'm reconciling myself to giving up on it for now. What time is it?"

"About half-past three, sir." The manservant walked over to the bowl of water and emptied it into a jug, before placing the obsidian-lined gold scrying bowl, covered with a black cloth, in a secure cupboard.

"Can you get them to saddle Skit, please? I'll go up to the Palace."

"Certainly, sir. The King has ridden to Ceardlann. Richardson informed me half an hour ago. I didn't like to disturb Your Lordship."

"I'll do my social duty and see who I can annoy at Court then. Thank you." Landis stared out of the window for several minutes, his thoughts in a jumble. Had anything other than a wish to see his sons taken Adeone to Ceardlann? Had he been more sensible about guards? Idly, he wondered how Hillbeck was getting on. The newly appointed Captain Pixney of the Palace Guard seemed to be doing a good job, and Haster had decided that Terasia was probably the safest place for him. There would be little chance of becoming an unwilling traitor there, and it also meant he escaped his wife's remonstrations.

* * *

On entering the Palace Stables, Landis glanced around. He dismounted, passing Skit's bridle to a groom and would have walked away but a voice hailed him. He met the chief groom halfway.

"Somewhere more private, m'lord?"

"Of course. Shall we go and take a walk in the paddock?" suggested Landis, knowing Jack hated being inside. Once they were pleasantly leaning on the fencing, Landis raised a querying eyebrow.

"It's a small thing, Lord Festus, but Her Grace's horses… Tradition dictates that they can't be ridden, but they're still here. I don't want to trouble the King but—"

"You're right not to, Jack. Traditions can be changed but they shouldn't be cooped up here. I'll have a think and possibly have a word with the King myself one evening when he's in a mellow mood. Was that all?"

"Nearly, m'lord. I was just wondering what you and the King have done to young Wynfeld. My old under-groom's becoming the talk of the guards and soldiers based in Oedran."

Landis laughed. "We've done nothing; the potential was always there."

"Oh, aye, just I heard there's an accident planned for him. The young 'un will want him out the way. That's what I've heard."

Landis glanced at the chief groom thoughtfully. There was no doubt that by *'young 'un'* he meant Scanlon. "I see. What else have you heard?"

"That my old groom is on borrowed time. That's all over the place. If I were the young 'un I'd be looking for the lad to have some kind of failure. The King would have no choice but to replace him and Her Grace isn't around these days to temper the sentence, if you follows me."

"I follow you all right, Jack. I've taken note as well. I suppose the rumours told you who it was put Wynfeld on borrowed time?"

"Aye, m'lord. You and the Major was what I'd heard," replied Jack.

134

"It's fair enough; you've both got your jobs to do. Just don't blame the lad if the young 'un gets clever."

"Don't worry, we're wary of his tricks. I don't suppose the rumour machine has told you why I considered Wynfeld on borrowed time?"

"Nah, m'lord. Too tight-lipped about that one, it is. There's been a bit of speculation, though, one way or another. Whatever it was, would have been deserved. You're a fair one, when all's said and done."

"You'll make me blush one of these days."

Jack laughed. "Doubt that, m'Lord Festus. You've never been the blushing type. Never since you were a wee lad."

"Yes, well, I'm no longer, as you used to put it, 'scrumping' apples from the hayloft."

"Never did you or us any damage though, m'lord. Seems years ago, now."

"That's because it was. Before I knew the King, and well before my cousin married him. Jack, will you do me a favour?" Landis explained about the two men and the attempt on Adeone's life, asking the groom to keep an eye out for the men. He came to the end of the description.

"I'll keep my eyes peeled. I'm guessing they were of the Palace anyway. That much knowledge of the layout and structure of the King's rooms certainly suggests it. They knew what they needed to do to fit in inside the walls. Wouldn't have thought they were inners. No, if they were, they'd have a servant's badge anyway. No, they're outers right enough. We'll track 'em down, my lord. Don't fret. I'll let you know when I've found 'em."

"You seem certain about their credentials, Jack," commented Landis.

"From where I'm standing, it's obvious. Had the thought not occurred to Your Lordship?"

"My conclusions are my own. Thank you, though, for your help."

"My pleasure, m'lord. Now, get yourself where you should be."

Landis left him still leaning on the fence and walked through the Palace to Court, considering his conclusions. They were ones he had initially dismissed. The men had been plotting in the city, which suggested they lived there. He was a fool. They could live anywhere. They could have quarters in the Palace. Why had he never given the idea proper consideration? He'd become too wrapped up in trying to scry out the men in the city! If Jack was proved right, he wouldn't forget the lesson in a hurry.

Court was the normal roundabout of duty, politeness and gossip. Wynfeld was there, and Landis was pleased to see it. They exchanged greetings in passing but that was all. He bore in mind what Jack had said about Scanlon wanting Wynfeld demoted. Ironically, it was a vote of confidence. If Scanlon wanted someone out of the way it meant they were a threat to his plans. He wouldn't let Scanlon get what he wanted. Wynfeld had transformed the regiment. He wondered whether to warn the captain or not and then decided not to. If nothing happened, it would draw Wynfeld's mind away from protecting the King.

# Chapter 31
## OF TRAITORS AND POSSIBILITIES
Septadai, Week 25 – 7th Ralal, 7th Ralis 1209
Palace – Gardens

AT THE END OF the first week of winter, Landis took an early morning walk through the Palace grounds. He fell into step with the chief groom on one of the paths.

"This is where you hide early in the morning!"

Jack turned. "Only on occasion, m'Lord Festus."

"That's a shame. None of the gardeners will have a natter with me."

"Aye, the head keeps 'em all in their place. Just been talking with him about our manure and his roses."

"So, what's the gossip?" enquired Landis without subterfuge.

"Well, m'lord, only that George Adson and his cousin Eric Adson, known as Gad and Adson respectively, have been out on the town once too often. Other than that, the gardeners seemed as happy as ever. Our head gardener was his normal mixed self. Not quite sure whether he's simply irritable by nature or by choice."

"Is anyone? What's the talk on the rest of the situation?"

"Bit mixed. Winter's ne'er a good time for a gossiper. People stay inside too much. Though my old groom, Wynfeld, still seems to be causing some. Not as much as you might 'ave thought but some. Things are quieting down nicely."

"Still think there's something planned for him, Jack?"

"Aye, m'Lord Festus, I do. I'd watch some of the men coming to Court if I were you. There were a couple I distinctly disliked the look of the other day. Couple of the new advisors, for a start, had something more than usually evaluating in their gaze. They also seemed to be hiding uncertainty, if you catch my drift. Trying to act like they knew what they were doing, I thought. How's the King?"

Landis glanced at Jack shrewdly. "As well as ever. Why?"

"It's none of my business, m'lord."

Landis made sure they were alone. "No, but you are obviously concerned."

"I thought he looked a bit drawn last I saw him. As I said, none o' my business. Well, I think this is where I leaves Your Lordship," stated Jack turning down the stable path.

Landis watched him for a moment before gazing back along the path they'd ambled along. There was no-one there, so why did he have a nagging itch in his mind that someone was following him?

Trying to rid himself of paranoia, he moved off down the path. Entering the building by a little-used door, he strode along corridors. The few people he did meet moved out of his way pleasantly enough. He went to find the Steward, a man with the physical appearance of rich living but a harassed air. Landis knocked at his office door to be met with the words,

"Unless it's important, I'm busy."

"Do my enquiries class as important, Steward?" enquired Landis, entering.

"Depends how long they're likely to take, my lord."

"I wondered who was new at Court in the last couple of weeks..."

"List's in the top drawer over there."

"Thank you. I also wondered if I could have sight of the list of staff for the Palace."

The Steward frowned. "Never one thing, is it? Can you narrow down the search for me? There are quite a lot of staff, you see."

Landis smiled. "Of course. Then I'll see the list of outside workers first."

"Right, my lord. I'll get one of the clerks to copy it out for you today. First though, I've got to deal with Advisor Meyer who thinks he can say and do what he pleases. Graduated from the school in Lufia. Thinks Oedran is right for his talents, whatever they may be. One of these days, I'd love my job to be easy. Was that all, Lord Landis?"

As he reached the door, Landis said, "For now."

"I wish!" muttered the Steward as the door closed behind Landis.

Landis walked to the Rolls Library, not far from the Steward's office, which contained books on lineages, and graduates of Advisor Schools around the empire.

When the perplexed librarian asked if he needed help, Landis declined and gazed around, apparently disinterestedly. Two scriveners had their heads bent over their work. He sat down, placed the scroll in a holder and unrolled it. There, in a neat hand, was the information on all the new faces at the Court that year. He ran his eye and finger down the lists. Most were visitors who had left again, a couple were young lords and ladies who had turned fifteen and so could now attend. He read the next entry:

*Advisors Adrian Meyer and Henry Blunt: Age 24: Separate Interviews concur:*

Had the Steward checked the story? They'd travelled across half the empire on a vague hope of being allowed to attend based solely on their Lufian credentials; that was intriguing.

He called the librarian over, asking for sight of the Lufian Advisors' School scrolls for the last six years.

"Is there any name Your Lordship is interested in? I have a cross-reference system which might help."

"If it saves me time, I'd be grateful." He gave the two names.

The librarian left, noting the names disinterestedly on his wax tablet.

Whilst he waited for him to return, Landis glanced incuriously around the library and at the obscured windows; the libraries and archives of the Palace were mostly kept dimmed to protect the scrolls and books. Suddenly, he had the feeling he was being watched again but when he turned around nobody was observing him. He tried to shake off the preoccupation but couldn't. He was irrationally glad when the librarian reappeared.

"I'm sorry, Lord Landis, but neither of those names appears on the lists. I've checked and indexed them for the last ten years."

"Right, thank you. That's all for now."

Landis returned to the Steward's office with the scroll, contemplating whether to tell the Steward there was a problem. The men weren't what they claimed to be, which raised a lot of questions about who they were. With the hunt still underway for the two men who had attacked the King's life, strangers from outside Oedran who weren't what they claimed, or didn't appear on the correct scroll, were of interest. Who Meyer and Blunt were and why they were at Court would need investigating.

He decided not to alert Wynfeld; the regiment still had a long way to go before it was an effective body of men and a case involving the Court wasn't technically their expertise anyway. It would burden Wynfeld too much whilst he was reforming the regiment. It would also be interesting to see if Jack's summation of the situation was correct. The old groom had seen and heard much over many years and tended to feel which way the wind was blowing whilst it was still the susurration of a breeze, which was why Landis had confided in him. He'd convinced himself that Wynfeld didn't need to know by the time he reached the Steward's office.

He knocked on the Steward's door to be greeted this time by,

"I'm still busy!"

Landis opened the door. "What gave me away?"

"The simple force of your knock, my lord. Welard knows to leave me in peace at this time, as do the rest of my clerks."

"I shall endeavour to remember that, Steward. I'm simply returning your scroll. Thank you for the loan of it. I shall leave you in peace."

"I'm sure Your Lordship can see yourself out."

Landis' tolerance snapped. "I can and you might do well to remember to moderate your tone, Steward. Or at least to pretend you can bear to be interrupted. We might have a history, but there is no reason for that attitude."

The Steward looked over, discomfited. "Sorry, my lord."

"So am I for disturbing you twice in one morning. Goodbye for now."

Lord Landis left, inwardly muttering. Glancing out of the window, he reckoned it must be about half-past nine and he still had to see the King before he went to Court.

* * *

He ambled through the corridors to the King's Chambers. Richardson, busy as ever, greeted him with a pleasant 'good morning', asking if he wanted announcing. Landis didn't. He entered the Inner Office as normal – without fuss or herald.

"Morning, Festus." Adeone saw tell-tale signs in the set of Landis' head and slight worry lines that usually weren't there. "What's bothering you?"

Landis tried to avoid the question. "Anything I should know for Court today, Sire?"

Adeone crooked an eyebrow. "Nothing new. Does whatever is bothering you endanger me?"

Landis hesitated. Refusing to answer twice wasn't acceptable in the Inner Office. "I keep getting the feeling I'm being watched when it's absolutely impossible for me to be being observed."

"That's technically known as paranoia. What are you doing when these fits come on you? Planning something dubious?"

"No, Sire. Normal everyday things. Walking through the gardens here, for example, talking to old Jack."

"How is he?" asked Adeone with a grin.

"Well enough. Still going strong."

"Actually, thinking about Court, there is one thing you can do for me. Discreetly, make sure Wynfeld's coping. I think he is, but you never know."

"Right, Sire. I'll see if I can manage that." He went to leave and caught sight of a mirror above the sideboard. He blanched.

A sixth sense alerting him, Adeone saw his friend's reflection. "You've gone somewhat pale, Festus. What is it?"

"Have I, Sire? It's nothing."

"You're not leaving until you stop lying to me, Landis," ordered Adeone.

Landis knew if he left there would be repercussions. Adeone wouldn't

139

be able to let it pass. They might be alone, but there were unwritten rules he needed to obey.

"It's the mirror, sir. For some stupid reason, I suddenly remembered the stories Laioril used to tell. I'm wondering if I'm being followed by a scryer." That was as close to the truth as he'd be telling Adeone at that point.

"You've let your concern get the better of you, Festus, you would only be able to sense a scryer if you were of Ullian predisposition…"

Landis was thinking that was exactly the point. Should he tell his friend the truth here, now, whilst the opportunity presented itself? No, it was the wrong atmosphere. Admitting he'd kept secrets when he'd just annoyed the King wouldn't be wise.

"…You're probably just getting paranoid. One thing: don't stop watching your back because suspicion is getting the better of you. There's something brewing. I can feel it. You'd better go and make sure people are behaving themselves. Give my regards to Cornelia."

* * *

Fretting, Landis walked to Court. Could it be a scryer watching him? If so, he had a problem. He couldn't stop them; there was nothing he could do. He was as vulnerable as a baby.

He spoke to the sergeant allocated to the rooms that day. The gentleman had nothing to report but, as normal, Landis asked him to keep a careful eye out. The sergeant enquired if they should watch anyone in particular. It tended to keep the guards alert if they had specific people to watch for. Landis thought for a moment before saying he'd like the advisors observed: how many attended Court and who they were and who they spoke to. The sergeant inwardly groaned. Lord Landis was notorious for coming up with complicated requests. As he walked away, Landis knew what the sergeant was thinking, but he gave them such broad challenges to mask who he was interested in and to check the clerks were recording people correctly.

The Chief Merchant of Oedran crossed his path.

"Come to remind us all who runs the city, Merchant Chapa?"

"Would I presume, my lord?"

"Yes. Definitely. How's trade?"

"Good enough. How are you and Her Ladyship?"

Lord Landis had to smile. "Well enough. Are you alone today?"

"For now. I'm sure others will turn up soon." Merchant Chapa discreetly looked around. Noting no-one was close, he said, "The King was looking careworn when I last saw him."

"He must have had a good night's sleep since then," said Landis dismissively. "He was perfectly well when I spoke to him earlier."

140

"I'm glad, my lord. I should allow you to continue."

When the Chief Merchant had gone, Landis frowned. Two people had said the same thing to him in the space of a few hours. Yet he hadn't thought the King looked strained.

* * *

In the Inner Office, the King was talking to Wynfeld. "...For the next thing, I need your discretion to be absolute. I believe Lord Landis is a scryer, but I don't wish to ask him myself. If I'm right, there will be reasons why he's never told me. I wish to respect those reasons but I need to know the truth. He knows you're watching him and he wouldn't concern himself with that – it would be a simple annoyance to him – but he's convinced he's being followed. Someone is targeting him. I have no doubt that Lord Scanlon is ultimately responsible but I need you to check it out. Firstly, Lord Landis' safety is paramount but, secondly, I need to know if he's a scryer. I realise you'll need your men's help, but I don't want a whisper, not even a thought, that I have doubts that Lord Landis is telling me everything. I dislike the idea myself. It has crept up on me over many moons."

"Very good, Sire. I'll do my best. When would you like to know by?"

"Whenever you can be certain, but hopefully not more than a couple of seasons."

Wynfeld rose, saluted and left, wondering how common such challenges were going to be. Finding out a secret a Lord of Oedran didn't want known by his closest friend was going to be difficult when he couldn't openly enquire about it. The best he could hope for was circumstantial proof.

Once alone, Adeone tried to dismiss the surging feeling he'd just betrayed Landis' friendship. It wasn't just the events of the morning that had sowed the seed. He'd called round to Landis House unexpectedly one day. Instead of being shown straight to the study, William had informed him Landis was seeing to business and would the King mind waiting in the library? That hadn't been odd, but Landis had been unfocused when he appeared. Adeone had also sensed a different edge to his friend, something that could be described as a high metallic note – something unnatural. Over the next year, whenever he thought about it, it had seemed strange. One night, on the edge of sleep, he recalled Laioril's stories and the metallic note made sense. It was the note, the colour of *magic*. Some, it was said, would see a gold outline to a person who had recently been utilising the magical energy and some would hear a golden note. It was the latter that Adeone had sensed in watching his friend that day. Landis had, when younger, had his signet ring specially made from obsidian. Adeone had accepted the eccentricity at face value. Now he fretted that there was more to it. He tried to picture the ring. Did it contain a polished surface? If it did, Landis was being dangerously negligent wearing it in the Inner Office, but Adeone didn't like to think he'd be that careless.

# Chapter 32
# BLACK-SCRYERS
Alunadai, Week 28 – 22nd Ralal, 1st Noris 1209
Oedran

GHOSTLY FIGURES moved in an intricate dance of unknown destinations; mocking the decay of humanity, the inanimate world around them was in sharp focus. Landis' mind's eye strolled amongst them: hunting, searching. No-one came into focus: he didn't know any of them, hadn't heard descriptions. He passed through throngs and along streets and into alleys, some barely more than unroofed rooms in size. Houses squeezed together, caking river mud - or what he hoped was mud – stuck to ancient cobbles and cracked paving stones. Two child-sized shadows raced around, pushing past adults. The uncanny silence filled his mind. He stilled. Gradually, people slid into focus. Women talking in a doorway, no, arguing; the older with hands on hips clearly telling the other to take a long hike over a short cliff, the other, with arms flailing, explaining exactly what she thought to that idea. Men, leaning on the wall, taking bets on who would win. Children mimicking them all. He focused on the details, the alley nameplate, the front steps, brushed clean, the door posts needing care, the symbols denoting their occupants' professions scratched into doorposts or painted on the walls.

Even in the spectral state, he blanched. Above the door with the arguing women was a symbol he feared. As he noticed it, he noticed the older lady's eyes scanning the alley, her arguments falling silent. He pulled back quickly to his study, draping a cloth hurriedly over the scrying bowl. He emptied the water from it and stowed it away.

Shaking, he collapsed onto a chair. She'd sensed him, she'd known he was there watching. Who was she? Had the ancient scrying bowl he'd borrowed from Ceardlann magnified his presence as it magnified his skill? Maybe Ira had been right when she lent it to him, maybe there was something unknown about it still. His heart caught in his throat. He wished she was present to talk to, to confide in. She'd kept his secrets so well he feared he didn't know how to keep them himself any longer.

The mark he'd seen in Seeping Close haunted his mind. What was an unscrupulous scryer, a so-called black-scryer, doing in his lordship? Why would any scryer sell their services? Legends said there were never more than a handful of people alive with each of the Ullian Spirits but hues were more numerous. Scryers were probably the most abundant of the hues, but Landis was willing to bet there were no more than fifteen in any province with one. He'd always believed there would be, at the most, three in Oedran: himself, the intelligence regiment's and one other. Had he just found them?

Reaching for pencil and paper, he tried to sketch to clear his mind, but he was sketching the alley, the symbol, a black six-pointed star in an eye. Cursing, he threw his pencil down. He'd have to discover why she was in his lordship. Could she be the one who'd been following him?

He had to deal with the situation. His bylawman could terminate the tenancy agreement on some pretext; however, that would appear highly suspicious. He had to be subtler and plan for the longer term. He debated with himself for twelve minutes or so, completely failed to hear a knock at the door and was surprised when William entered unbidden. Landis made up his mind.

* * *

Six minutes later, in response to a summons, the warden knocked and entered the study to find Landis writing letters. He inclined his head slightly. "You wished for a word, my lord?"

Landis looked up. "I did, Sandbine. Nothing to worry about. Can you let Gibb know I want a word when he gets back from his rounds? I'd also like to see the tenancy lists, please."

Sandbine hesitated. "Of course, my lord."

Landis chuckled to himself as the man left. He was from a Denshirian merchant family and had started work within the Landis staff as a scrivener. Landis could remember Sandbine helping him with his lessons, so that meant the man had worked for them for over thirty years. He really should be used to their eccentricities but he never quite managed equanimity over them.

A few minutes later, the warden returned with a clerk loaded down with the lists and a footman carrying an extra table to put them on. When Landis had waved them to set everything down at the side of his desk and the footman and clerk had left, Sandbine hesitated.

"Is there anything I can do to help, sir? Some of these are cumbersome."

Brightly, Landis said, "No, thank you, Sandbine. I am more than capable of managing cumbersome things."

Only uncertainty and concern met the wry observation. "If you're sure, my lord. Is there anything else I can help with?"

"No, thank you. That's all. Don't look so worried. What's the worst I can do?"

The warden merely inclined his head before leaving, his silence speaking volumes.

Waiting until he was sure that the warden wasn't returning on the pretext of having forgotten to mention something, Landis turned to Seeping Close. Unsurprisingly, no-one had declared themselves as any type of scryer. The occupations helped to determine his tenants' rent. He never wanted to charge more than a family could reasonably afford, and had been understanding if an accident had meant the breadwinner couldn't work for weeks. He'd waive their rent but he might call in the debt in other ways.

He studied the names of the other occupants of the alley but recognised none of them. Tapping his fingers on the desk, he idly drew other symbols and the black-scryer one. Trying to think, he looked out of the window. The twins were getting on each other's nerves in the garden. They were certainly growing up quickly. They spotted him and waved, as though they had just been talking pleasantly together. He simply shook his head at them and turned back to his desk. He wasn't fooled.


A couple of minutes later, running feet stopped outside his study and whispering ensued.

Welcoming the distraction, he said, loud enough to carry to their ears, "You know, you might as well come in and discuss whatever is so important on this side of the door."

Tentatively, the door opened; Julius put his head around it and then Julia's appeared. Landis motioned them inside. Normally kept well away from the study, they entered hesitantly.

"What mayhem are you two up to then?" asked Landis.

"Nothing, father," replied Julius innocently.

"I used to try that line on your grandfather. He never believed me, so why should I believe you?"

"Because, for once, it is the truth, father."

"I like the fact you added 'for once'. Shouldn't you both be studying?"

The twins looked at each other. "We've finished for the day, father," they replied in unison.

"Shall I check?"

Julius shook his head. "No, sir."

"Finish off properly later and I might forgive you for so blatantly lying."

Julia smiled a sweet, deceptive, smile. "Thank you, father. What are you doing?"

"Checking the tenancy lists over. It's not the most exciting job."

She walked over to him and draped her arms around his neck. "Are you hunting for anything?"

"No, just checking that they're in order."

Her gaze fell on the lists on her father's desk and she suddenly asked, "I wonder if Becka Tolse realises that her name is an anagram of 'to see black'? It would be funnier if it were 'to see red' but, then again, her name wouldn't be Becka Tolse in that instance, would it?"

Mercifully, there was a knock on the door, so Landis didn't have to reply to his daughter's musings that had just provided him with the answer he needed. Instead, he said, "I think that knock will be our chief bailiff. Run along and tell your mother you're dining with us when the King visits later this week."

It hadn't been the chief bailiff; it had been William delivering a letter from the Palace. Once he'd left, Landis studied the lists for the Seeping Close again. This time, the name did jump out at him. Becka Tolse: a widow from South Anapara. He stared at the name and smiled slightly. Julia was quick.

The next mystery was why Becka Tolse was in his lordship. The list said she'd been a tenant for five years. Long enough for Scanlon or his agents to have found her. Whatever she was up to, she was up to it in his lordship because scrying close to home was easier. Her name could be an unfortunate coincidence, but Landis had an inner certainty it wasn't. It was far too dangerous for him to investigate further by scrying.

The bailiff arrived half an hour later. "You needed a word, m'lord?"

"I did, Gibb. How often are these lists updated?"

"Every season, m'lord."

"How do you check people's professions?"

"Ain't easy to, m'lord. We tend to find out over time when they've lied. Their rent's backdated for as far as we can prove."

Landis inwardly noted the information. "Right. When was the last update of this list made?"

"Beginning o' winter, m'lord. They're as accurate now as they can be? Why? Is there summat wrong?" If there was, the bailiff wanted to get his hands on whoever had informed Lord Landis before informing him.

Landis smiled. "I'm merely curious."

That didn't reassure the chief bailiff. No lord was ever *that* curious. "Right, sir."

Landis decided to ignore the disbelief. "Next question, have you ever seen any of these?" He tossed the sketch of the symbols over.

"I've seen them all in me time. The eye's rare, sir. Never 'ave found out what it meant. The anchor's pretty common, 'specially down by the river."

"Yes, I thought that might be the case. I found the eye in an old book once. It means a black-scryer. I expected it would be non-existent, but you tell me you have seen it?"

"Aye, sir, but I've been walking the streets o' the city for o'er thirty years now."

"True. I wonder what other signs there are. I know there are signs for most of the magical hues and spirits. From what I recall, the book is fragile, but I'll have the relevant portion copied for you. Now, you will please document and record every sign you come across in my lordship – on a map, if it will make your lives easier. I'm curious about the different trades that use them and the number of people who advertise their professions in such a way. Basically, I want to know of *any* symbols you find. Don't worry about sparing my blushes."

"Very well, m'lord." He had long ago ceased to ask any but the necessary questions. The fewer enquiries he made, the more likely he was to find out something, eventually.

Landis obliged. "I wish to stop non-declarers and rogue traders but don't let that get out. Just pass it off as another of my eccentricities."

"Very good, m'lord. I'll let the lads know. We're all on a different beat."

Landis noticed that his chief bailiff hadn't asked what eccentricities. "Thank you. For curiosity's sake again, I'd like a map with the men's routes on them when you hand me the information a week before the Munlumen."

The bailiff relaxed. A week before the beginning of spring gave him more time than he'd been expecting.

# Chapter 33
## OF SPIES AND GOVERNORS' GUARDS
### Cisadai, Week 31 – 16th Anapal, 2nd Anapcis 1209
### Wynfeld's Office

THREE WEEKS LATER, Wynfeld broke the red seal, telling himself it was a coincidence but not believing it. There, in Richardson's careful hand, was a summons to see his King. Stomach churning, he folded the letter and put it carefully away. With his commission in his breastplate, in case he had to rescind it, he made his way to the Palace, going over the events of the previous day.

The thronged streets didn't calm him, nor the quiet corridors. Should he admit he'd failed immediately? Or should he let his King lead? He knew which Simkins thought best, but there were days he wasn't so certain.

The Outer Office fell silent as he entered, which did nothing for his nerves as he waited. Richardson gave nothing away, Jacobs and Kenton busied themselves with their tasks. The only sound was the scratching of quills and the soft breathing of those wielding them.

When Richardson asked him to wait in the Audience Chamber until the King was free, he was only too pleased to do so. The cloying atmosphere made it hard to breathe.

Six minutes later, he watched the Steward leave with a frustrated gait. Something had rattled him. Was their King in a bad mood? Richardson crooked a finger at him.

Once in the Inner Office, Wynfeld blurted out, "Sire, I think, first and foremost, I'm going to have to tell you that I've failed. The men won't accept the changes I'm proposing and, given the delicate nature of their work, I didn't feel it was right to force the change."

Adeone rose, crossing to a window. He surveyed the scene: the lawns and gardens below invited him to take a walk. He ignored the invitation.

"That's unfortunate and disappointing. Landis thought this might happen. What is your summation of the consequences if we were to force it through?"

"Basically, Sire, gathering intelligence would stop. I'm to blame. I said that it would be accepted."

Adeone simply raised an eyebrow. "Not just you. Tell me what happened."

Wynfeld did. However trustworthy Beaver had become, telling him that his unit would remain in Oedran, but others would be moved elsewhere had been risky. Telling the other sergeants even less had probably been stupid. Somehow – an *unintended* utterance, no doubt – the corporals had discovered his plans, or guessed enough. Their visit, polite though it had been, clearly said they didn't want splitting across the empire.

Adeone listened carefully. Wynfeld's agitation was clear but nothing was broken irreparably. As the captain finished, Adeone said, "We just need to take a fresh look at the situation. What are your immediate thoughts?"

"Leave the men as they are, promote or transfer those who wish to take that route, then fill their places. There isn't anything else I can see. Sergeant Jones has proved if we get good men elsewhere, we get good information here. The Exarch wants to keep him in Garth when his regiment moves."

"Yes, that's why I asked to see you. Can you keep him in Garth?"

Wynfeld started. It *hadn't* been about the semi-mutiny in his regiment. The King didn't know what was happening there. He let out a breath and then tried to cover his relief. "Your Majesty, technically, Jones is still my subordinate. I only seconded him." After a moment's consideration, he continued, "Are there any free captaincies in Garth, Sire? He was tipped as the next captain for my regiment. I posted him for insubordination, but he has made a fresh start."

"I'm sure a captaincy can be manipulated between now and the beginning of Geryal – when his regiment is set to march to Lufian."

Wynfeld paused for the briefest second. "Sir, does the Exarch have a guard? Could Jones be moved under his direct eye?"

Adeone resumed his seat. "Interesting. You are saying there is the possibility of setting a guard up for the Exarch and having Jones in charge?"

"Yes, Sire, or at least as a captain to liaise with the militia at Garth more permanently. I know from experience how frustrating it is when a new regiment has to learn the ropes of protecting someone of high standing. It isn't quite like anything else the militia undertakes. There is also the fact that the Exarch is a descendant of your great-grandfather. With Princess Lilith still alive, it would look better."

"Are you trying to tell me how best to protect my governors and family?"

Wynfeld was about to apologise when he saw a spark of amusement in Adeone's eye. "Does it not come under my remit, Your Majesty?"

"In a roundabout way. It would also open up eleven or twelve more captaincies for your men; would it not?"

"The thought had not occurred to me, Sire."

"Stop twisting the truth in front of your King, Captain Wynfeld. It isn't the wisest of ideas. Look for more men to promote and ask Richardson to arrange a meeting for me with General Paturn. I want you and the Major there as well. In the next week would be best. Was that all?"

"I think so for now, Your Majesty."

"Probably best to save the rest for later. I've got a meeting with the Chief Merchant coming up. I'll need all my strength for that."

* * *

Wynfeld reached his office and closed the door on Drave's curiosity. Over the course of the day, he found four sergeants happy to be promoted, had their files copied and distributed to the General, Major and his King – all of whom were privately impressed with the detail Wynfeld had collated over the winter of 1209.

He studied the pedigrees of the twelve King's Representatives the following day: eleven of them governors of provinces, the twelfth overseeing much of Anapara, from the original capital city of Paras in the north, but not technically a governor. All were lords, but only Tyler Galwood at present had the FitzAlcis connection so closely.

Wynfeld studied the family tree of the FitzAlcis and realised how fragile its branches were. The laws of kinship for the FitzAlcis, drawn up after the Age of Tyranny – ironically to protect distant relations – meant only descendants to great-grandchildren of a king would be considered FitzAlcis. True, it included children in the female lines, but tradition debarred them from the crown itself.

Only three men, therefore, had any claim on the crown: the Princes and Lord Scanlon. All others were descended from female lines and therefore debarred. A shock ran through him as he saw plainly for the first time how dire the situation was. If Scanlon usurped the crown, there was no-one left to challenge him.

Female descent widened it to two more men. The Exarch's father, who was the great-grandson of King Aldous Aneurin through his mother Princess Lilith. The King's acknowledgement of the Exarch as kin didn't make his claim certain, though it might keep lawyers in drink.

Peaga Rathgar was the last man. The only grandchild of Lady Amara – who had been born Princess Amara and then, on her marriage, had declared she would take her husband's rank. Wynfeld wondered what arguments there had been about that behind closed doors. She was someone you didn't mess with and she had to have started somewhere.

Speculation had been rife when Scanlon had dropped the title Prince. Was there a trend? Precedents being set? Now, considering the family tree, Wynfeld wondered if Scanlon had been planning to takeover even then. Was the Justiciar trying to draw attention away from himself? If their King and Princes were to die, his friends amongst the Lords of Oedran would be seen to persuade him, just a simple lord, to accept elevation. Scanlon would appear to be saving the empire. If that was his plan, it was certainly a dangerous game and one that could easily go wrong. He'd have to be sure that the Lords of Oedran would push him to accept the crown and not fight for it themselves.

The regiment already kept a watching brief on the Lords of Oedran, but it might be worth observing them more closely and remembering that plans had probably been put in place a long time ago.

Wynfeld mentally extended the range of his protection to the Galwoods and Peaga Rathgar. At some point Scanlon would try to harm them, he was sure.

* * *

A few days later, Wynfeld was again sitting in the Inner Office discussing plans for his regiment and the sergeants to promote.

His King opened proceedings in a rather unorthodox manner, "Go on then, Wynfeld, what have I got to do this time?"

Wynfeld said, "My ideas are merely recommendations, Your Majesty."

"Yes, recommendations I find myself agreeing with and following. Remind me to research the old hues. I can't remember if *smooth-talker* was amongst them but, maybe, you're an aeromancer instead…"

"Sire?" Wynfeld was truly confused. Why on Erinna was he like a weather forecaster?

"You seem to be able to tell which way the wind is blowing. Now, the four men wishing to accept promotion… I am not proposing to promote all of them at once. The General said to me earlier that it would appear highly suspicious and I agree. It is unheard of for four sergeants to be promoted from the same regiment at once."

"I had been thinking the same thing, Sire," admitted Wynfeld. "Two could ask for transfer because they 'dislike my method of command', Sire. That should allay suspicions about them. We tell them privately that their promotion is going ahead, but deception is needed. We post them to the provinces where they will obtain their captaincy. The other two promotions we could handle traditionally."

Unaware of the numerical pun, General Paturn remarked, "Someone will still put two and two together, Wynfeld."

"Most likely, sir," admitted Wynfeld; "however, if they are convincing actors and do a good job, then people won't question it for quite some time, and then only after enough time has passed for the men from my regiment to have set up good networks."

"It's still not believable, Wynfeld. I don't want to lose good men because of decisions made rashly or quickly without thought for appearances from an outsider's perspective. Lord Scanlon is perceptive. As soon as men start moving from your regiment, he'll have them followed and watched."

"What do you suggest, General?" enquired Adeone mildly.

"I suggest the men request transferring properly, one at a time and months apart, Sire. They are not sent directly to their intended province but rather to regiments that will reach them later. Send one, for example, to Garth to reach Lufia. One to the Macian Isles to reach the Pale Lands and so on. Even make them move a couple of times. It must seem accidental that they end up where they do. Anything else and there will be questions. The men must be out of Oedran long enough for people to forget that they were ever here and served under Wynfeld. We can alter some records but not men's memories. The army is an oddity. It's so large that you constantly bump into the same people, even when that should be impossible."

"Major?" requested Adeone.

"I agree with the General, Your Majesty. Especially on the last point. The assumption that men will never meet again could lead to problems."

"Wynfeld?"

"Everything that's been raised is valid, sir. The men transferred could be the second or third incumbent to act as a liaison captain. It would give us time to get their record in Oedran changed. That is, if the posts are going ahead, Sire."

"There will certainly be one for Tyler Galwood. General, you've had a couple of days to consider that proposition; might I now have your honest thoughts on it?"

The General said seriously, "I wish it had been my idea, Sire. It is a stroke of genius. We eliminate risks to your Representatives at the same time as getting spies in every palace, residence and citadel in the empire's cities."

Adeone smiled. "Then you must congratulate Captain Wynfeld – for the idea was his, not mine. Then, gentlemen, if the new captains aren't all to be from Wynfeld's regiment straight away, I suggest we find more sergeants to promote or current captains to move. Might I suggest those men close to retirement? Or, perhaps, heirs who are merely working in the army until they can laze about all day?"

Wynfeld caught his King's eye, amused; both knew the men in the final category simply lazed about all day anyway.

Paturn didn't miss the spark pass between the two men and he had the odd feeling that the afternoon of the Queen's death had drawn these two men together when every convention should have put them miles apart. He realised that the King hadn't had a reply to his questions. "Yes, Sire, they would seem obvious men to go for. I shall look at the files directly I get back to barracks."

"Thank you, General. The sooner you can, the sooner we can make a start promoting people and moving them round the empire again. Thank you, gentlemen. Wynfeld, stay a moment, please."

After the General and Major had left, Adeone said, "I will say this for the General, he'll accept change, eventually." He idly twisted a filigree ring on his right hand. "Queen Ira would be proud of what you're achieving."

Wynfeld saw a brief flicker of grief pass over his King's face. "I'm sure she'd have forgotten I existed again, Sire."

"I thought you knew the late Queen better than that, Wynfeld. She never forgot anyone."

Wynfeld smiled and Adeone saw the truth of the deprecating comment. Wynfeld had known it but hadn't wanted to admit to it or the praise.

"You're right, Sire. I hear Her Grace found work for all the household of her youth when her father died."

"She always said it was the least she could do. That you'd all cared for her so well, it was now time to return the favour. Some have moved on again, but some, like Jack, have stayed. He was asking after you as soon as I said I'd met you."

"I was like a nasty cough he couldn't shake off when I was a lad."

"I think all children are like that to adults,' said Adeone thoughtfully.

"You should visit him at some point. I'm sure he'd be pleased to see you."

"I might just do that, Sire. See if he's got a more successful cough linctus."

"If nothing else, you might well find yourself roped into helping him in the stables in your spare time. What little you have."

Wynfeld noted the unspoken thanks for the hard work he was putting in. "Nothing changes by sitting back and accepting what's there, Sire. Sooner or later all conscientious people work too hard."

"I know that, Wynfeld. Don't exhaust yourself though."

"Nor you, Sire." Wynfeld had said the words before he knew they were out. "I'm sorry, Your Majesty. That was out of line."

Adeone regarded him. "Yes, it was. I thank you for your concern though. Oh, you might be interested to know that Lord Scanlon has informed me that he'll be in Garth for the law review at the beginning of next year. That means he'll be sitting on their courts. I thought your ever-efficient Jones might like warning."

"Thank you, Sire, I shall certainly pass on the information. I'm sorry for the remark."

"One apology is enough, Wynfeld, at least for these circumstances. Now, I should get back to my desk. I shall be in contact. I'd like to know if you're having any luck locating the men who attacked my life, but it can wait for another day."

Closing the door as he left, Wynfeld realised that the King hadn't moved towards his desk. It seemed he was still taking Ira's death harder than he would admit.

# Chapter 34
## CHATTER
Tretaldai, Week 32 – 24th Anapal, 10th Anapcis 1209
Inner Office

MEMORIES PIERCED ADEONE, sharp and cutting as they had the day Ira died. He balled his fist, but they played across his mind's eye. Laughter rang in his ears. Her laughter, her eyes bright through the years. That last day with Wynfeld knowing how to coax that laughter, the laughter that had died with Ella, the laughter of a younger woman with her heart full of life, not knowing death waited. He should have done more, should have helped, should have, should have, should have… He bit his lip hard, closed his eyes, fighting the overwhelming sense of failure.

Entering, Richardson saw Adeone's state and went to find Simkins.

The manservant said, "Cancel everything the King has on this afternoon. I think he might need some time away from his duties. He's not let up at all since the beginning of winter. Who was he meant to be seeing this afternoon?"

"Nothing and no-one who can't wait. The Chief Merchant and Aulnager, the Herald about—"

"Put off the Aulnager and Herald but have a quiet word in Merchant Chapa's ever-willing ear. The King might need someone to talk to. If he's coming here anyway—"

Richardson frowned. "Surely, Lord Landis would be better."

Simkins snorted. "Yes but Merchant Chapa knows when to back off. Lord Landis doesn't always do so."


Simkins silently entered the Inner Office. He watched Adeone for a time before saying, "Sir, come and have a break, away from your office."

Adeone never even glanced at him. "How long have you been there?"

"Long enough to see Your Majesty needs a break."

"How long, Simkins?"

"Only about a minute, Sire."

"That had better be true. Who told you?" demanded Adeone.

"Sire?"

"Don't mess around!"

Defeated, Simkins admitted, "Richardson, Your Majesty. He's very concerned. I've asked him to clear your afternoon."

Adeone finally looked at his manservant. "Very well. What have you arranged for me?"

"Erm, Richardson did say Merchant Chapa was due for a meeting. I, well, I wondered if…"

Dry tears poured from Adeone's eyes. "I… All right, Simkins, you win. I'll talk to Merchant Chapa. Promise me one thing… Don't tell *Doctor* Chapa anything about this!"

"Of course not, Your Majesty. Would you like refreshments bringing?"

Adeone pulled himself up and walked over to his desk. "Not here. Take them into my sitting room, please. I'll just…" He sat down and simply stared at the desk.

"Sir, Richardson is more than capable of sorting out the detritus."

"Then you'd better get him to."

Within moments Adeone was ensconced in his sitting room. He accepted the drink Simkins passed him and, with atypical action, simply downed it, passing the glass back. The glass, Adeone was half-amused to see, wasn't refilled and handed back but was put on the side with the decanters. A couple of minutes later, Richardson announced Merchant Chapa. Once the door had closed behind the administrator, Simkins passed both the Chief Merchant and the King a drink before leaving.

Adeone, who'd barely greeted his mother's cousin, asked, "What have you been told?"

"Only that you're taking the afternoon off, sir. Your administrator must be the most discreet man in the empire. What's caught your thoughts, Sire?"

"Memories. Everyone I'm close to dies. The only way I can keep my sons alive is by distancing myself from them. I sometimes wonder what mother would have made of what's happening. Then I tell myself that, if she'd lived, Scanlon would never be what he is now. She made me who I am. I miss her laughter every day."

"Mostly, Sire. My cousin was always warm and loving. Which, given her childhood, is something of a surprise."

Adeone frowned. "She never got a chance to tell me her early story – one of the many losses of her dying young."

"It wasn't spectacular, sir," explained Merchant Chapa. "Her mother left her father. Left her behind as well. Her father remarried. My new aunt wasn't someone who wanted to bring up another woman's daughter. She didn't want to do any work, either. As soon as Eliza was old enough, she ran the house and servants. Her father didn't care about her. She became drab and the laughter gradually died. We all became concerned and then our cousin qualified as a doctor. He kept a close eye on her and, one day, told her father that Eliza needed caring for properly and moved her to his house. She thrived there. That laughter we all loved returned. It didn't take long; a few months. Then your father cut his leg and her father got to hear of the visit. He seemed to realise that she was an asset, or that she was ripe to be married off. He insisted on her returning home. Your father proposed. One night, before they married, she told him her story. It was the first time she'd seen him irate. Your grandfather was excluded from all the official engagements and your mother, much to her relief I believe, never saw him again."

Adeone said, "I've sometimes wondered why no-one ever mentioned my mother's family, her immediate family. You and the doc get enough mention, though, that I never pursued it. By the time I was old enough to concern myself, my maternal grandfather had died."

"Aye, sir. I think this is where I say good riddance as well. I never liked my uncle. I was pleased when you favoured your mother. She lived life to the full when she could but when..." he trailed off, cursing himself.

"Go on."

The merchant hesitated. "When the depression took hold, it was hard to move, sir. She became a different person."

"Rather like I do as well?"

"Yes, sir. I'm not too good at this, am I?"

Adeone managed a smile. "No, cousin, but who is? You've still told me something of my family history I didn't know. It all takes my mind off other things, which will keep everyone else happy."

"Aye, problem is, Sire, you're the King. If you're unhappy, what business has everyone else with smiling?"

"A sensible one. There is little point the whole world living in misery."

"Look, can I make a suggestion?" (The King nodded.) "Take some time away from here. Go to Ceardlann. See the Princes. For a few days at least. Even a week. Name a Representative here."

Adeone said, "You are as bad as the rest of them. You do know that? You never let go of an idea. Can you imagine what would happen to that Representative?"

"Yes, sir. He'd be given all the headaches you are currently experiencing."

"Very funny. You're certainly my mother's cousin!"

"Might I suggest Lord Landis?" asked Merchant Chapa innocently.

"*Very* funny! Can you imagine what would happen if I let Landis loose on Oedran?"

"Yes, sir. Everyone would be glad to see you return in full health and it would be a hundred times better than any other option I can envisage."

"If I tell you to stop envisaging, what would you do?"

"I would obey my King, sir."

There was a note to the merchant's voice that made Adeone groan. "Go on. I'm not going to like this, am I?"

"I'd then visit our mutual cousin to unburden my mind."

"Ah. By *mutual cousin* you mean the doc, don't you?"

Merchant Chapa's lips twitched. "Yes, sir. Mind you, you could now tell me not to and I would have to obey that." The merchant paused. "Sir, it is your decision, of course, but I think a few days at Ceardlann would—"

"Leave it there. I follow your thoughts. Let me come, as you put it, to my decision. Will you stay and dine here this evening? For one thing, it will prevent my household from conspiring to create other diversions for me. Sometimes I just need to be left to feel and come to terms with those feelings. I know why they do what they do, but I wish they wouldn't occasionally."

"Why don't you tell them, Sire?" enquired Merchant Chapa.

"They do it for good reasons. They know when to back off properly."

"I can imagine they do, sir. For all you are your mother's son, you are also your father's."

"No-one crossed my father. That is certain. Though time and heartbreak made him that man. I'm convinced of it. I fear that I will become like that some days."

"No, sir, those days are elsewhere. Your Majesty is more your mother's son than your father's and you took the best from both."

Adeone got up to refill their glasses. With his back to Merchant Chapa, he said, "Would anyone tell me if I hadn't?"

"There'd always be one, Sire. There always is."

"Yes." He turned to Merchant Chapa. "You know, cousin, Simkins thinks you are only ever respectful. I doubt he'd leave us alone if he was ever disillusioned."

Merchant Chapa smiled. "I'll be careful not to do so then, sir. I promised your mother that I'd be honest with you and that I'd look out for you whatever happened."

"Really?"

The merchant laughed. "Yes. It's been an interesting job, one way or another. Especially the Guild Banquets. Your unique representation of your father there has provided the merchants with many stories over the years."

Adeone smiled a true smile, but it was the smile of a mischievous boy. Then the illusion broke. "I find that you're full of surprises. My father never told me."

"He didn't know, sir. I think your mother didn't want your father to find out that she wished you could grow up unpretentious, level-headed and as normal as possible."

"That makes sense. My father was ever conscious of the degrees of society. I must be as well, but I'm certainly more relaxed about it. I'd say you've done a good job over the years. Just one thing, why do you keep making me so much work if you promised mother to watch out for me?"

"No-one's perfect, Sire."

Adeone chuckled at that. With a crooked eyebrow, he said, "I think, if what you say is true, then it is time that you called me Adeone. Isn't it?"

"Possibly, sir. Though, if it's all the same to you, I'll continue as normal. I'm getting to be an old man, am feeling my age. I would get confused and you wouldn't want to do that to an old man, now would you?"

Adeone regarded him through narrowed eyes. "You're still as sharp as ever. I'd pit you against Aunt Amara, and I wouldn't be certain that my aunt would win. Unlike on most occasions when I would be certain everyone else would lose."

The Chief Merchant laughed. "I shall take that as a compliment."

"A wise move; however, I believe I made a request and your excuses so far don't pass muster."

Amusement sparked between them.

Merchant Chapa said, "I am sorry, *sir*, but I am too old fashioned to feel comfortable, cousin or no, to call you by your name."

"Oh, I give up – for now. So how goes trade?"

"As ever. There are some nice things coming out of Bayan. The Exarch has relaxed the bylaws for the traders from Garth. Though there's rumours that Heritor Fullerton is ill and so is his son. It's affecting some decisions at the Garth Guild as he's their Chief Merchant. Whatever the illness is, it may well kill them. Doctors are flummoxed, which doesn't always take much to be fair. I expect it's some sort of ague. Hopefully, the son will pull through, but I think it's the end of the Heritors of Bayan by that name."

Adeone said, "I curse the fact that so many were traitors in 1169. Father had little choice but – much as I'm of Landis' ilk in some ways, that some traditions can be changed – changing the inheritance of titles is one thing I shy away from. Within them is so much of a province's identity."

"Aye, but on the other hand, some die out naturally anyway. Look at Areal. There's not a thane left and hasn't been for a long time. They married up or died off. There weren't masses of heritors left. The loyal families still have their land, if not their title. Maybe it will rankle less as that's the case – well, after fifty or so more years."

Adeone chuckled. "True. So what other news is there? You've normally given me lots of issues by now. I'm almost feeling cheated."

Merchant Chapa considered. "We can't have that, sir. The only issue is that there are rumours of bandits again in the woods of the Gardian Ridge."

"Yes, the General told me that. He's increasing the men at the forts before attempting to find them. Lord Scanlon might then have the pleasure of trying them during the Bayan Law Review. He seems to prefer doing the reviews to being in Oedran dispensing justice here. Ira always said he had wandering feet, but I'm not too certain. I think he likes knowing he's the most powerful man in a city. I'm not upset he's elsewhere."

"Nor, I think, is most of Oedran. How are the Princes, Your Majesty?"

Adeone beamed. "Oh, they're turning the Comptroller grey. At least, Tain is. Arkyn is working hard from what I can gather. I wish Ira could see it. She'd have been proud of him."

"Just because Her Grace isn't here watching doesn't mean she isn't observing her family from the heavens, Sire. She'll be watching her sons and protecting them. I have no doubt about that."

"I wish she was here in the flesh though. I still expect her to greet me when I stop working for the day. It's completely daft, I know, but I can't help it. Still expect her to tell me what madcap scheme Tain has come up with this time and listen to the reasoning of why it's my fault."

"Your fault, sir?" Merchant Chapa didn't know what else to say.

"Most things I've found are my fault sooner or later and Tain is said to take after me. I might let him loose on the Guild Banquet one of these days."

"He'd always be welcome, Sire."

By the time his cousin left, Adeone had reconciled his mind to a week at Ceardlann. He could manage it so his Representative didn't have much to do. The only problem would come when Scanlon realised that he'd been deliberately passed over.

# Chapter 35
## COURT SURPRISES
Cisadai, Week 34 – 9th Bayal, 2nd Bayis 1209
Palace – Court

THE KING'S COURT OF OEDRAN could refer either to its members or the area of the Palace of Oedran where they gathered. Sumptuous rooms, glittering and glorious, epitomised Oedranian Society. The beautiful FitzAlcis Chamber at its centre with its domed stained-glass ceiling – of the twelve-pointed star of the empire – sending shards of coloured light dancing into the room below. It was here that people waited to be presented to the King. The Court applicants could admire the beautifully carved fireplaces where symbols taken from the empire and nature wound their way from hearth to mantle: Anaparian horses galloped to unknown destinations with quivers of arrows at their saddles. Bayan birds flew over a Denshirian desert with the twelve-pointed mystic rose used to represent a blazing sun. Flowers of Lufian bloomed amongst falling snowflakes and vipers of Serpent Isle snaked towards Macian ships with triskele-marked sails. An Arealian key opened a chest of Gerymorian gems with scales to weigh them. The Low Plainers, with their eye-marked tabards, sold their weapons next to the hourglasses of Tradere, and a Terasian bear galumphed its way through a forest watched by a snow fox of the Pale Lands with a vial hung around its neck.

Surrounding the fireplaces were murals for each province depicting fictional scenes that captured the essence of the lands. Doors led to large rooms named for those provinces, whilst other smaller private rooms snuggled at the edges. Guards in pristine tabards stood with halberds next to some doors and servers, ushers and pages stood around the sides of the rooms waiting to be called for. Elsewhere, court valets and maids would be on hand should anyone need them. At great feasts, lords could bring their own servers but at other times the men and women of the Court household would serve them.

On each side of the Court were great halls. The Queen's Hall on the east side was used for dancing, whilst, on the west side, it was said that hundreds could be seated at the laden tables in the King's Hall, which had survived hundreds of years of changing fortunes. The Palace had developed around its time-tested walls. A dais dominated the head of a flight of steps, with the great doors behind, barred and closed on the world – they were used only by the FitzAlcis for coronation feasts, marriages and great gatherings. At each end of the dais were smaller doors, one leading into the Court, the other into the Privy Wing. The side walls in the main hall held two sets of doors each. Facing into the hall from the dais, those on the right led to the Court, those on the left to a corridor that ran the length of the hall, off which were other corridors containing the rooms of the King's household.

Opposite the dais were doors leading out into the Court Gardens, above them on the right was a musicians' gallery, on the left with its carved screen was the Viewing Gallery whose entrance had been purposefully lost after the assassination of King Alvern and the Age of Tyranny. A great fireplace opposite the dais heated the hall. It was so large it could roast whole stags, though normally a more modest blaze was known.

Rails ran along all the walls, from which tapestries could be hung at feasts. Great candlestands held dozens of tapers with specific candle wardens to watch over them. Tables against the walls held jugs of wine and water, juices and ales. The great oak tables would groan under pies and pastries, roasts and stews, fruits and confections. It was said that the only difference between the Court Supper and the great feasts was the amount of food, but the feasts held to mark special occasions would include dishes and drinks from around the empire and sugar sculptures that took days to prepare.

The opulence of the Court wasn't a mask. Wherever one looked there was gold and silver, fine glasses and abundance. Wine was free-flowing; the Court Supper served every evening was plentiful and rich. The King's hospitality was known to be unstinting and generous. It created an atmosphere of ease. Courtiers dressed in the finest silks, velvets and satins. They showed off fine goldsmithing, leatherwork and gems. Ladies wore the worth of whole cities without a second thought. All trying to vie for attention, to catch the attention of those who could further their standing, whether that was a lord or the FitzAlcis.

The Court had a mythology all of its own and many faces: the superficial where loyalty and adherence to the King's wishes were all that mattered, to the shadier where patrons and protégés bargained and favours became debts, to the dangerous where the wrong word at the wrong moment could start a plot that would destabilise the entire empire. If you wanted to know what was happening in Oedranian Society, you needed entry to Court and you only got entry to Court by introduction, being of the lordships or certain professions. Unless FitzAlcis, every member of the Court had to be presented to the King at Court, no matter if they knew each other beyond its bounds, and so the first evening when Adeone and Wynfeld were both there, the General presented Wynfeld very simply.

"Sire, Captain Wynfeld of Your Majesty's army."

"Thank you, General. You may get up, Wynfeld. Walk with me."

Wynfeld pushed himself to his feet and fell into step, confused by the request. Surely his King had more important people to talk to.

Adeone looked sideways at him. "Do you need any introductions?"

"No, sir. Thank you. Advisor Rayburn is very diligent."

"Good," replied Adeone. "I hope— Excuse me."

Wynfeld stepped back as Adeone strode over to a man just entering; dusty from the road, he hadn't even bothered to take his cloak off. He spotted Adeone striding towards him, grinned and bowed with an ease Wynfeld had only noticed from a few.

Smiling from ear to ear, Adeone said, "Faran! I didn't expect you!"

"Landis seemed to think the time was right for me to visit, Your Majesty. I hope you don't mind the surprise."

"Mind? Not at all. You're always welcome but at least make it look like you're staying. You'll sit next to me at the Court Supper, I hope."

Faran chuckled. "An honour, Sire. If you'll excuse me for a short time?"

"Certainly." Adeone turned slightly. "Simkins, see His Lordship has all he needs."

A voice beside Wynfeld said, "Lord Faran of Lufian, Captain. A confidant of His Majesty. Once a ward of the FitzAlcis. He lived in Oedran when studying at the Advisors' School."

Wynfeld thought to himself that he knew that already, though it had been years since he'd seen Lord Faran in person. "Thank you, Advisor Rayburn. The King seems pleased to see him."

"The King isn't the only one. Excuse me."


Wynfeld watched Adeone working the different rooms with interest. His King was always polite, but he managed to convey by subtle changes in body language whether someone was favoured. Wynfeld watched a master of manipulation at work. He watched as Landis greeted his friend with more formality than he'd ever seen him use before. Then the illusion broke as Adeone asked him whom the show was for. Laughing, Landis said he'd thought he'd act the courtier. Adeone asked him why he was breaking the habit of a lifetime. Wynfeld shook his head slightly. Others were watching the two friends with interest and someone by Wynfeld's shoulder said,

"Makes you wonder if they ever seriously disagree."

Wynfeld turned round. "Surely all friends must at some point, Advisor."

The advisor moved away. Wynfeld continued to watch Lord Landis unobtrusively. Turning slightly to answer a passing comment, Landis caught Wynfeld's eye. He raised a discreet eyebrow and Wynfeld turned away.

Wynfeld watched Lord Landis from the corner of his eye, trying to fathom him out at Court. He was surprised when the Lord of Oedran crossed to him next, having excused himself from a conversation with Lord Fairson.

"Captain Wynfeld. How are you finding the humdrum world of Court?"

"It's certainly different from anything else I've experienced, my lord."

Landis laughed. "Hardly surprising. You've been busy since your return." Realising they were momentarily alone, he added, "So busy that there are whispers about you. Be careful."

"You too, Lord Landis," replied Wynfeld.

"There's been whispers about me since I was fifteen and I became friends with a twelve-year-old prince."

Wynfeld smiled. "Believe it or not, my lord, I do remember you when you were young."

"Really?" asked Landis, thinking, *Damn! I should have made that connection before.'*

"Yes, sir. I was, after all, a groom of Lord Macaria's. Too humble to be noticed by you, but I do remember that you and Lady Ira were close."

Before Landis could reply, Adeone and Lord Faran disturbed them.

"Are you monopolising Wynfeld, Landis?"

"Certainly not, Sire. I've just discovered that he has the dubious pleasure of remembering me when I was a youngster."

Adeone chuckled. "That probably means you remember me as well."

"I do, sir. An impeccable prince," admitted Wynfeld.

"Your memory is playing tricks on you, Captain. I was only ever a nuisance as a prince."

"I'm sure that's not true, Your Majesty."

Faran laughed. "It seems, Sire, that the world is in disagreement on that point."

"We are at Court, Faran: apparently, you can only flatter me here. Have you met Captain Wynfeld? He took over from Fitz earlier this year."

"If I can ever be of assistance, do let me know, Captain," said Faran.

"Thank you, my lord," replied Wynfeld determined to accept the offer.

"Captain Wynfeld, I must borrow Lord Landis' company," concluded

Adeone, drawing the lords away with him.

The same advisor as before remarked, "The King seems to favour you."

"I'm sure it is an illusion caused by the fact he needed Lord Landis," responded Wynfeld, suspecting the advisor was causing trouble.

Turning up a contemptuous lip, the advisor moved away.

Having witnessed the exchange, Advisor Rayburn asked, "What did Meyer want?"

"The opportunity for another snide observation."

"I don't know that much about him, but he's only been at Court a few months and he's already disliked."

"I expect you know more than I do currently, Advisor," said Wynfeld.

Feeling he'd been in the same room for long enough, Wynfeld moved on. Several people greeted him warmly and, for a couple of hours, he talked with various courtiers, watching how people reacted when ushers announced King Adeone each time he entered a room. Some bowed then continued the conversations they had been having previously, others changed their conversations slightly. Once Adeone left a room a more relaxed atmosphere swept over it. He wondered at that. He knew and had experienced Adeone's highly official side, respected it and knew what that side could be but still found it hard to fear his King. Then he realised that most people at Court only ever saw their King there. They didn't work for him directly. They only saw the ceremonial side of him. They didn't see him working hard to keep an empire together. Didn't understand why he had to do what he did in handing out favours or showing displeasure.

Wynfeld was in the Lufian Room when Adeone was next announced. Saluting, his eyes tracked his King's path. Landis and Faran were still with him and he thought Landis was guiding his King slightly. Advisor Meyer realised too late that his amble was crossing Adeone's path. He stopped and bowed.

Wynfeld couldn't hear the exchange, but he could see every action. Landis had obviously made a remark, an introduction, an observation that made Faran perplexed. Whilst Meyer's attention was on Faran, Landis rested his hand ever so lightly on his sword hilt. Wynfeld noticed the guards stiffen. Landis had put them on alert with a simple glance. Their King's hand rested idly on his dagger. Either he was mimicking Landis or he'd also become suspicious.

The hair on Wynfeld's neck stood on end. Everyone around him was talking as though nothing was happening.

"Guards!" Adeone's voice rang out.

The room fell silent. Meyer stepped back and into the guards' embrace.

A short exchange between Adeone and Faran – clarification? An order from Adeone and Meyer was led out. Another quiet discussion, this time between Landis and his King before Landis left with a glance at Wynfeld.

Wynfeld cursed. Had he just failed again? His companions had moved away, leaving him alone in a sea of uncertainty. Rayburn was now speaking with their King, glancing at him. He wanted to cross to them but Court protocol demanded he waited for his King to summon him. Lord Faran looked increasingly troubled as the sound of a commotion in another room reached their ears. Landis re-entered and gave their frowning King a nod. Adeone turned, crooked a finger at Wynfeld and moved away. The captain followed, his heart in his mouth.

As soon as the door of the private room closed on the retreating server, Adeone demanded, "What did Meyer say to you?"

"One comment was to the effect that you were favouring me, sir, and the other, well, he was wondering if Your Majesty and Lord Landis ever had a serious disagreement."

"What did you say to the latter?"

"That I assumed that all friends must at some point, Sire."

His King's face hardened. "You utter bloody fool! Landis and I spend years perfecting the idea that we never disagree and you ruin it with one unguarded comment. Meyer spread a rumour that you are being favoured for not saying anything about a disagreement you witnessed. He was damaging many reputations. Just be thankful that it was noticed."

Wynfeld swallowed. "I am, Sire. When I could leave unnoticed, I was going to check his history. I didn't like his attitude and my information is neither did anyone else here. He might have been a spy of Lord Scanlon's."

"Would you have found the evidence to support that supposition in time? To save you some delving, he wasn't an advisor at all. If he had studied in Lufia, as he claimed, Faran would have taught him. There are a few reasons why he might impersonate an advisor, but the most common one for gaining false entry into Court, at the moment, is to harm me. He and his companion had already been here for too long."

"Would you like my resignation, Sire?"

"What I'd like, is your network to do its job!"

Wynfeld's gaze fixed straight ahead. "Lord Landis and the Major of Oedran might see things differently, Sire, as regards my resignation."

"For your damned information, Wynfeld, Lord Landis is now sticking up for you," revealed Adeone, still displeased. "He likes the work you've been doing and can see the merits of you staying on. Just get this part of your act sorted, Captain!"

Wynfeld stood at attention as the door closed behind his King. Then, legs giving out, he slumped into a chair.

Six minutes later, the door opened and Landis entered.

Wynfeld rose. "My lord?"

"Don't sit back down," replied Landis, apparently relaxed.

Wynfeld appreciated the acting as soon as Landis began speaking. He was soon wondering if the King was right in saying the lord supported his captaincy; therefore, it came as something of a shock to find Landis saying,

"I discovered what Meyer was and engineered the event today. I'm to blame for you not knowing. That is why I am supporting you this time. I viewed your network as I always have; something separate, something that doesn't work; however, you're endeavouring to change that. I'll start passing you the information my more informal network provides. We both want to see the King survive and it's in our power to make sure he does. Pay the men in the cells a visit and take your best information gatherers with you. You know the ones I mean. Remember, it would be better if they aren't put on trial."

Wynfeld felt sick. "But that would mean they'd have to admit their guilt in front of the King or die under questioning."

"Putting them on trial isn't an option. The only person to benefit would be Lord Scanlon. Now, we'll leave this room together and restore some of your standing at Court."

Wynfeld eventually parted from Landis with a smile before the Court Supper. He didn't need to attend that, to be watched by all, speculated over and judged. The smile would keep them all guessing anyway.

He returned to the barracks, collected the men Landis had suggested and discovered his complete distaste for the methods. It was hopeless. Meyer and Blunt weren't going to talk. They'd been imitating advisors with the aim of entering the Court; that was illegal. By not admitting their true identity when introduced to the King it was treachery. Lord Landis' research, which he passed Wynfeld, went a long way to proving treason. Needing to know if they were the men involved in the Triniculum Plan, Wynfeld asked which guard had saved the King's life. Hillbeck was sent along the next morning and gave Wynfeld the bad news. The men weren't those from the Teran Arms. So Wynfeld carried on asking the men questions, trying to discover as much about them and their paymaster as he could. They didn't answer and didn't survive.

Wynfeld then talked to Hillbeck about the evenings he'd been in the Teran Arms. He filed the statement alongside everything else they had gleaned on that attack. It wasn't an impressive file, and most of it was from Hillbeck and Haster.

That evening, he sat in the officers' mess and resolved, once again, that the ineptitude of his regiment would be fixed.

# Chapter 36
# LURKING DOUBTS


WINTER – with its flurries of snow and icy mornings – invaded Oedran with stealthy predictability. All through the long weeks and shorter days, Landis continued with his regularly irregular duties travelling between Landis House and the Palace by coach or, if the crowds weren't bad, riding. With increasing frequency, the feeling of being watched would leach into his bones. At Court it was a foregone conclusion but there was the niggle, an irritation in his mind that told him it was different. Feeling observed when alone was more concerning and if he was in either his office or study, he would put away whatever it was he was working on, however inconvenient it was, and find something else to do that wasn't going to endanger anything. He went for so many walks that the scryer pursuing him must have thought him a man of leisure. He stopped scrying over winter. It was too risky. He would rather Adeone didn't know of his hue and he *certainly* didn't want Scanlon to. He was thankful that he hadn't had the feeling in the Inner Office. That could get very tricky.

Although he was certain a scryer was following him it didn't mean that people weren't as well; therefore, Landis kept his eyes and ears open.

The day after Meyer and Blunt's arrest, he rode home, using the curved bay windows of shops as mirrors to glance behind him. He thought he saw the same face a little too often to be a coincidence.

He rode into his stableyard and dismounted swiftly. Handing over the reins to one of his grooms, he walked parallel to the wall marking the curtilage of his house before sidling along the wall and peering through a spyhole. He cursed under his breath. Looking back to the stables he noticed the grooms were watching, intrigued. He chuckled to himself. Their faces clearly asked, '*What's he up to* this *time?*' He motioned his chief groom over.

"Clodach, see the lurker opposite…"

Clodach peeped through the spyhole. "Aye, m'lord. What o' 'im?"

"He's been following me." They shared a significant glance before Landis said, "Would you and my grooms like a few hot pies as a thank you for all your hard work? Especially as it's so cold today."

Clodach grinned. "Oh, I'm sure we could find a 'ome for 'em, m'lord. We'll sort it out."

Landis entered his house and made his way swiftly to a room where he could see the busy street, the new cookshop opposite and his stables. The lurker looked like he'd received the best Munewid present of his life when Clodach asked him to help. His chief groom had been a rare find, a tenant in difficulty who had brains, brawn, a way with horses and loyalty. Landis had offered him a job when his father's chief groom had retired. Four years on, he had no regrets and a stable staff with many hidden talents.

Landis watched as Clodach and the lurker entered the stableyard and put the pies down on a mounting block. The grooms surrounded him.

Minutes later, when Landis entered the storage room, his grooms had done their best at doing their worst. The lurker was bruised, one black eye swelling, blood from a split lip running down his chin. Backed into a corner, he was crouching, trying to ward off the blows. His cloak wrapped protectively around him, his free arm raised to protect his face, his gloved hand fisted in defiance.

Landis gave a small cough.

Clodach stood with arms folded, overseeing the grooms. He glanced at Landis. "Enough for now, lads. 'is Lordship's 'ere."

The grooms grabbed the lurker and tossed him at Landis' feet before standing back, mirroring Clodach's stance.

Landis watched impassively for a moment before asking, "Why were you following me?"

"I... I don't know what you mean..." the voice was contorted but there was an edge that told Landis that he hadn't been wrong.

"Don't lie. Who are you working for?" When the man didn't answer, Landis snapped, "On your feet!"

The man winced as he pushed himself up.

Landis watched his darting eyes assessing escape possibilities. "Don't bother," he said placidly. "You were following a Defender of the King's Life. What makes you think you're leaving until you tell us what I want to know?"

The man swallowed and went to push past the grooms. They laughed and tossed him against the wall. Landis exchanged a glance with Clodach and then strode over to the lurker, forcing his head back by his hair.

"What's your name?" When there was no answer, Landis landed a blow in the man's stomach that made him double over. "Your name and your paymaster's name. Now!"

The man stayed silent. Landis had just grabbed him by the throat when a polite cough heralded his manservant.

"Her Ladyship wonders if you're dining with your guest, my lord?"

Landis could bet what Cornelia had probably said was, *'See where he's got to this time.'* He turned to Clodach. "I want those names and when you know who his paymaster is, truss him up and leave him on their doorstep. I like to return gifts."

The grooms all laughed as Landis and William left.

When they were clear of the stables, Landis said, "I don't like doing it."

"I know, my lord, but it has to be done. There's more than your safety at stake." He held the kitchen door open.

They entered the warm bustle to be met with, "Blood again! What do you do to yourself, m'lord?"

Landis chuckled. "This time it isn't mine, Cookie. Apologies for delaying your wonderful dinner."

"Thank you, m'lord. We're coping, but it'll be overdone in six minutes and Lord Faran doesn't deserve that."

"Start serving, William, and I'll be down when I've put a fresh tunic on. I don't want to upset this lot." He slipped up the backstairs to general chuckles from the kitchen staff.

* * *

Clodach asked to see him after dinner. The names he gave meant little to Landis. The lurker was Alf Harbottle, and the paymaster was Merchant Haynal of the Iris Lordship, a name that had never been linked with the underworld of Oedran. Landis would be privately surprised if it was correct, but Alf had begged them not to leave him trussed up on the man's doorstep, as it would mean his death. He'd offered to work for Landis instead.

"Hmm. What do you think, Clodach?"

"You've a few of the city lowlife already on your books, m'lord. 'e might prove useful 'aving been on the other side. Might not, but what can you lose by trying?"

Landis considered for several minutes. "All right. Accept his offer but watch him. Put him with your cousin. He can give him a few lessons in observing without being observed."

# Chapter 37
## REPRESENTATIVE?
Alunadai, Week 36 – 22nd Bayal, 15th Bayis 1209
Landis House Study

LANDIS' CHIEF BAILIFF had handed him the information requested on the day of the deadline. It was illuminating, but not in a good way. He sent for the gentleman.

"Gibb, why are these plans incomplete? I have reliable information that a black-scryer is advertising their services in my lordship and yet these maps do not show me where."

"Maybe they aren't using a mark, m'lord."

Landis eyed him. "I said *reliable* information. Accompany the bailiffs on their rounds. When you do find the black-scryer, tell me their location. I'll take things from there."

"Very good, m'lord. I'll give the men a roasting."

"No, you won't. That would give the game away. Simply thank them for their hard work and then tell them I've asked you to accompany each of them to check all's well."

"Very good, m'lord."

Once the man had gone, Landis swore. He'd wanted to get to the woman sooner than this and had a fear that time was running out for him.

* * *

He went to the Palace for a meeting to be greeted with the news that the King was taking a week's break during the first days of spring.

"It's a good idea, Sire."

"For me," replied Adeone. "I'm leaving you in charge of Oedran as my Representative."

"Can I just change my mind about it being a good idea, sir?"

"You could refuse the honour," observed Adeone. "But you wouldn't want to do that to me, would you? I promise you, Festus, I've been making sure you won't have much to do. The declaration will be read at dawn on the first day of spring. I'll be leaving Oedran around about mid-morning. If that seems sensible?"

"Sensible as ever, sir," replied Landis, his lips twitching.

"Jesting and jousting aside, will you do it?"

"Of course I will, Sire. I'm not promising Oedran will be in one piece when you return though."

"Is it now? Thanks, Festus. I think I need the break. Now, this meeting…"

Returning home in a contemplative frame of mind, he passed through the King's Gate into the lower city and dismounted. The crowds were making Skit jittery again. He patted his horse's neck, talking softly to calm him and then had the now familiar itch in his mind. He glanced around but no-one was staring at him, or suddenly avoiding his eye. He used the moments of calming Skit to concentrate on the feeling – after all, he didn't need to put anything away, didn't need to divert the watcher's attention. He was in full view of a hundred people: guards, merchants and traders, customers, pickpockets and thieves, the old, the young and the nondescript. Even were the watcher physically present, they'd be a fool to try something by the gate. Concentrating on the feeling, it formed into something more identifiable, rather like a page of text coming into focus, but now it was a feeling morphing into a memory of two women arguing.

Patting Skit's neck for a final time, he led the horse across Alcium Plaza and onto the Maclan, keeping his eyes out for threats. Skit shielded his right side as much as he provided reassurance for the horse. He passed the shops without considering their wares, glanced automatically at Master Galdwin's – he seemed to be doing a good trade – and carried on until he was home. Entering by the stables again, he passed Skit's reins over to Clodach.

"He's been a bit spooked today."

"Right, you are, m'lord. Do you want to take one of the others later?"

"No, thank you. Skit and I will cope, won't we, lad?"

Skit nudged him affectionately and Clodach smiled to himself. No matter how many times Landis had to walk home, he never wanted a different horse and Clodach suspected it was more than the fact that Skit had been a present from King Adeone. There was a loyalty between man and beast that was rare in the lords.

Having seen Skit stabled, Landis wanted to know for certain who it was observing him. He entered the house by the kitchen taking his gloves off and not paying attention to much else.

An exasperated, "Watch where you're going, m'lord," reached his ears.

He started. "Sorry, Cookie. Things on my mind."

"Well, if you're not careful it'll be this evening's soup down your tunic," she replied. "Anything we can help with?"

He glanced around the amused kitchen. "Stranger things have been known but I don't think so with this puzzle."

"Well, how about a cup of tea and biscuits to help your thinking along?"

"What sort of biscuits?" he asked, ready to negotiate.

"Oat, or fruit shortbread, even ginger if your brood has left you any."

Landis chuckled. "A couple of each would go down a treat."

She smiled back. "Your old nurse would say you'd spoil your dinner."

"You gave me biscuits then, as well," said Landis cheerfully. "Anyway, nothing could spoil your dinners, Cookie."

She gave him a withering glance. "Sweet-talking me—"

"Normally gets me more biscuits," observed Landis with a grin, to general amusement. He was still chuckling to himself when he entered the entrance hall.

William crossed to take his cloak and gloves. "All well, my lord?"

"Well enough, William. Cookie's putting me some refreshments together. I'll be in the library."

"Very good, my lord. Her Ladyship is visiting Lady Fairson."

"The terrors?"

"Attending to their lessons, my lord. Well, in the schoolroom anyway."

Landis chuckled. "I appreciate the distinction."

He crossed to the library, fiddling with his signet ring, spinning the seal around on its connecting pin, first the seal uppermost then the polished underside. Slipping the ring on his finger, so he could open the library door, he knew the polished surface was face up. He let it reflect in the gold of an ornament and, without seeming to, glanced at the picture reflected back at him. Becka Tolse's face flashed before his eyes. Rubbing at his finger, he took off the ring and put it back on, seal uppermost. Retrieving a random book he settled into a chair. He wondered what Becka could deduce from his walk home, banter with his servants and by watching him drink tea, eat biscuits and read a book on the history of Lufian.

# Chapter 38
## RESPITE
### Alunadai, Week 37 – 1st Teral, 1st Teris 1209
### Outer Office

**A**DEONE AWOKE on the first morning of spring already considering Ceardlann. He felt as though he was being unleashed. He couldn't remember the last time he'd taken more than a day for himself. Even more than half a day or a few hours was rare. When he left the Inner Office, he found Landis chatting with Richardson, and it was just chatting. They'd known each other a long time and, although there was a professional note, they were relaxed.

Adeone's eyes narrowed at his friend. "What are you plotting?"

"Me, nothing, Sire."

His administrator smiled. "His Lordship was persuading me that a party of the type from a few years ago was a good idea, Sire."

Adeone chuckled. "It wouldn't be the same without Finn but, now you've mentioned it, save it for when I return. Just make sure he doesn't mix his drinks. As far as I recall, after last time, Lady Landis said that if I ever returned him home in such a state again, FitzAlcis or not, she'd have something to say to me."

Both Richardson and Landis laughed whilst the other secretaries tried not to appear intrigued.

"So, Richardson," said Landis, "obviously, the running of the empire can wait—"

Adeone snorted. "You're not getting away with that, Festus Landis. There's a list on my desk. It should keep you out of trouble." He gave his friend a warning look. "Watch your back."

"Of course, Sire. Give my regards to Their Highnesses."

"Will do." Adeone turned to Richardson. "Thank you. Keep him busy."

"Certainly, Sire. I hope all's well at Ceardlann," replied his administrator.

* * *

The ride was pleasant and uneventful. Having asked the Comptroller to do away with a formal welcome, Adeone rode round to the stableyard and dismounted. Handing his bridle to the chief groom, he said lightly, "I don't suppose you know where any of the children are, do you, Alfred?"

"The Princes are out riding, Your Majesty. Lady Elantha and Master Calumiel, I think, were in the gardens."

Adeone set off for the gardens where he discovered Cal and Elantha had found a spot out of the wind.

"Come on then, squit, let me see…"

"I'm not a squit," wailed Elantha.

"You're younger than me, my lady, so you're a squit."

"I'm not!"

"I call all my siblings squits; it's a term of affection."

"Uncle Adeone, what's a sibling?" asked Elantha, spotting him.

Blushing, Cal jumped up and bowed.

Adeone answered his niece, "A sibling is a brother or sister."

"Then I can't be a squit because Cal isn't my brother."

The flush of colour reached Cal's ears. Adeone perched on the walled edge of a raised flowerbed and sat Elantha on his knee. He realised she was getting a bit big for it. He looked at Cal with an unfathomable expression.

"Are you calling my niece a squit, young Calumiel?"

"It would seem so, Your Majesty. I'm sorry, sir."

"I don't think it's me you should be apologising to."

"I'm sorry, Lady Elantha. I take it back, you're not a squit."

Elantha wore the expression of a child who had got what she wanted, then realised somewhere along the line she'd missed out on something. "I don't have any siblings, do I, Uncle Adeone?"

"No. It's a lot less hassle without them."

Cal grinned at that. He couldn't have agreed more.

Elantha was pensive. "Yes but it must be nice. I'd like a sister."

Adeone hugged her tighter. Lady Aelia hadn't wanted Scanlon to have a son but he had forced her back into his bed. When she had found out she was pregnant again, she'd taken the only way out she could see. There'd been an 'accident' and months of trying to reassure the motherless child.

She snuggled into her uncle's shoulder, sucking her thumb.

"Your thumb will shrink if you suck it."

"Won't," replied Elantha through the thumb.


Half an hour later, Tain and Arkyn tore around the corner, Tain leading by a head. They ground to a halt and bowed, beaming at their father.

He gave them both a bone-crushing hug. "I'd have thought you'd have been here to welcome me…"

"It's Arkyn's fault. He said we had time for a ride—" started Tain.

"You hared off towards the woods—"

"Yes, but you were meant to be keeping an eye on the time—"

"How?" enquired Arkyn.

Adeone simply laughed. "There's no need to fall out over it. I can cope, despite my wounded feelings."

Elantha sat back down on his lap, hugging him. "I was here."

"Creep!" muttered Tain under his breath.

Adeone chuckled. "Yes, but true all the same. Now, what have you got planned for this afternoon? I was going to suggest we took a ride, but you won't want to do that now."

Arkyn shrugged. "We still could, father."


The Rex Dallin was beguiling countryside with its woods and forests, cliffs and caverns – farmland and meadows met streams that fed the River Encil and ponds and pools the children would swim in. There were the hillocks known as The Warrens, a quarry and a small cavern mine. It was beautiful, bewitching and peaceful. A breeze brought the first warmth of spring along the tracks and the hedgerows seemed hungry for the new life it heralded whilst birdsong brought harmony to the day. They met few people but those they did meet greeted them with open and honest smiles. For the first time in weeks, Adeone felt truly at ease. He was happy to be alive and content with that life. He simply listened to the boys chattering away, telling him what they'd been doing.

Dismounting in the stableyard, on their return, Adeone didn't want to go back inside and feel enclosed; he started to teach Tain and Cal how to care for their horses. He'd always insisted on a low level of formality at Ceardlann, so the grooms continued as normal, whistling and calling to each other, even cursing as, after being outside for hours, the last cold of winter froze their hands and caused them to drop saddles and stirrups.

Half an hour after they returned, Adeone glimpsed the Comptroller grinning and leaning on a stable door.

He said, "We won't be long, Comptroller."

"That's all right, Sire. I simply came to say there're refreshments in the snug, when you're ready for them."

"Thank you. We'll be glad of them. Could you get some sent out to the grooms as well and add something to spice it up a bit for them? There's a nip in the air again."

"Will do, Sire: whiskey all right?"

"Sounds admirable to me. Ask Alfred though. He might prefer brandy and I'd hate to get it wrong."


They entered the snug six minutes later to find a fire keeping the chill off the room and a steaming pot of tea steeped with dried berries and spices; both brought warmth to the senses and relaxation to the mind. Arkyn sank onto a chair, removed his boots with a sigh and curled up, cradling a beaker of tea, drinking in the scents as much as the flavour.

Without letting his smile get the better of him, Adeone said, "Hardly the way a prince should sit, Arkyn." He lay on the couch to ease his back.

"Should I follow the example of my King then, Sire?" enquired his elder son, innocently.

Adeone grinned. "I wouldn't. He's a dreadful influence. Follow the example of your brother…"

Tain was lying on his front on the floor, watching the flames of the fire and trying to stifle a yawn.

Arkyn laughed. "No stamina, has he?"

"None at all. What's up, Tain? You're normally full of energy…"

Tain grinned. "I thought I'd follow your example, father…"

Adeone, just finishing his yawn, leant over and tickled his younger son until Tain rolled out of reach.


Elantha hadn't accompanied them on the ride, but she soon joined them in the snug. Adeone held her off long enough to swing his legs onto the floor so she could snuggle up to him, chatting about what she'd been doing. She had so much love to give, yet Scanlon couldn't see it or didn't care about it and that made him angry. He was just glad she was at Ceardlann, where her father's disinterest and disapproval couldn't easily reach.

A quarter of an hour later, they were talking when the Comptroller entered to see if they needed anything and to tell Adeone that dinner would be ready at half past eight. Immediately, Tain and Elantha started pestering him to let them stay up. He pretended to consider for a couple of moments, and the Comptroller suppressed a chortle. Tain realised before Elantha did that they were being teased and that they'd be allowed a later bedtime.

After the Comptroller had gone, Adeone said lightly, "Oh, the dinner will be formal this evening. Something about the King being here. He's an inconsiderate man or so I'm told..."

"If I ever see him here, I'll pass on the message, father," replied Arkyn.

"I'm sure he'll thank you for it. Now, Tain, Cal, Elantha maybe you'd like to tell Maria what a dreadful influence I'm being in your lives by letting you stay up later than normal." Grinning, the younger children left. Adeone turned to his elder son. "How are things here?"

"Good enough, father. Nothing seems to have happened over winter, yet I've still been busy."

"It gets you like that. There's always more to do, no matter how much you are already doing. How is young Master Calumiel coping?"

"Fine. Or at least he seems to be. Tain and he are getting on well enough. Can't stop them talking to get a word in sometimes."

"I'd noticed. I used to be as bad some days. What's that smile for?"

Feeling slightly mischievous Arkyn replied, "You still are, father."

"Should you cheek me like that?" enquired Adeone.

"The mood overtook me and there was nothing I could do about it."

Adeone finally laughed. "You know, there are some days when I think you and Tain aren't so very different after all." He sighed. "I'm pleased to be here. Half eight did the Comptroller say? I might go and get cleaned up and then find something to interfere in. Give Cook a chance to throw me out of the kitchen, maybe. Oh, how is Kadeem shaping up?"

Together they made their way out of the snug and up the stairs whilst Arkyn replied. "He's a philosophical marvel, father, who copes more than competently with everything I've thrown at him, which has included some rather hectic days."

"That's something then..."

# Chapter 39
## DISTURBING DISTURBANCE
Tretaldai, Week 37 – 3rd Teral, 3rd Teris 1209
Ceardlann – Great Hall

THE NEXT COUPLE OF DAYS PASSED with a well-balanced medley of laughter, rest, mayhem and calm. Adeone spent time with all of his charges individually and together, he sat and chatted with the Comptroller, reminiscing and relaxing. He sat in the kitchen talking with Cook and making *helpful* suggestions, which ultimately led to Cook threatening to throw him out as he always did. He took a solitary walk, enjoying being truly alone and resolved to do more of them, for he could feel himself healing from hurts he didn't know he had.

They were all tucking into a dinner of roasted belly pork when Landis' messenger appeared, asking for a private link. He nodded to Cassion with a feeling of trepidation; Landis had promised to deal with whatever occurred.

As the link formed, Adeone's heart plummeted seeing his friend's wan face. "What's happened?"

"Bit of blood loss—" started Landis flippantly.

"Festus!"

"I was attacked. Chapa said if I didn't tell you, he would and he meant it. You know how he gets when he's determined. I'm sorry."

"How bad? You, not Chapa."

"I'm confined to bed. He even threatened to tie me down. Can he do that as I'm your Representative?"

Adeone ignored the question. "Where are you?"

"At home. I can manage…"

Adeone shook his head. "I'm coming back. We'll discuss it later. Thank you, Cassion." When the link closed, he quickly got to his feet. "I've got to return to Oedran, I'm sorry." He tried to ignore the confusion on their faces. "Simkins, I'll need Ponder and the guards. Contact Marsh, he's to meet me at the Dallin Gate. Inform Richardson also. I'll just see the Comptroller." He hurried out of the hall.

Arkyn followed him. "Father, what is it?"

Adeone looked at his elder son. There was little point in keeping it from him. He was nearly cisan-age. With a deep breath, he said, "There has been a failed attempt on your nearfather's life. He's wounded. I must return."

"You don't think it's a trap?"

"No. Put that thought clean out of your head. This was aimed at Festus; aimed at him because I was foolish enough to name him my Representative. Arkyn, keep the rest from worrying. I'll send word."

Adeone galloped as much of the way as possible; luckily the road between Oedran and the Rex Dallin wasn't a busy one. He sped across the city and entered Landis House in a flurry. Entering the old drawing room unannounced, he found Lady Landis remarkably calm. She curtsied.

Adeone shook his head gently. "Not now, Cornelia. Where is he?"

"In bed, sir. Doctor Chapa has given him some pain relief. He won't tell me what happened."

"Then he's a fool." He strode up the stairs two at a time and made his way to his friend's bedchamber in the old house. He walked into the room saying, "You really shouldn't throw parties, Festus – especially after I asked you to wait for me." His friend's face was no less wan than it had been. "What happened?"

"I was coming home, there were crowds; I dismounted. Then there was a sharp pain in my side. The man came at me again. Let's just say, he hadn't the balls for the job, especially after I finished with him. He's dead. An off-duty corporal saw what happened. I think he saw to everything because I came round here with Doctor Chapa bending over me. That was scarier than the attack."

"What was Chapa's prognosis?" enquired Adeone, fighting down nausea and guilt at what could have happened.

"I'll live long and prosper. He did say that, if you didn't wish to hear that, give him time and he'd come up with something else... I'm sorry you had to come back."

Adeone shook his head. "I'm not. You've been there for me, Festus. The terrors are safe enough. I'm not going to name you my Representative again. Not if this is what happens. No, don't argue. He can't get both of us; that would be too catastrophic for words."

A knock at the door heralded Cornelia saying, "Would you care to join me for dinner in half an hour, Sire? Simkins said the news disturbed yours."

"Thank you, but I'm fine, truly. I really ought to leave you all to it."

"There's no rush, sir. Stay a while yet. Richardson knows that you're here. I'm sure Festus would be glad of your company. Doctor Chapa also wonders if you want a word with him."

"Might as well." When Chapa entered a couple of moments later, Adeone asked, "What was the damage?"

"The man was extraordinarily kind, Sire; he missed all the major organs and then passed away through blood loss himself. His Lordship will be up and about within a fortnight, sir, though *not* before, and movement should be kept to a minimum in the meantime... So, no wild rides."

"I did that earlier. Yes, yes, berate me later. Who alerted you?"

"He was here anyway," explained Landis. "Cornelia is carrying."

Adeone stared at him, before relaxing into a smile. "Congratulations to you both. Then, Chapa, you'd better make sure he recovers, hadn't you?"

"I'll do my best, Sire," said Chapa dryly before leaving.

"When did you find out?" asked Adeone.

"It was confirmed after you left for Ceardlann. Then this happened. I just hope it's not had an adverse effect."

"Cornelia was calm when I arrived, so stop worrying. You'll need all your strength to recover. How much of that list I left did you get done?"

"Oh, you know me and paperwork, sir. I seemed to misplace it… can't think how these things happen. Richardson has all the details."

"He'll probably have found the list as well to cheer me up. I wonder if I could lose it again for a time. As an aside, I realised yesterday that I need to find Arkyn an administrator – I spent some time with him going over the books at Ceardlann – but he needs younger people around him. I'll see what Richardson suggests. I wish it could be as easy as finding Kadeem. He appeared at just the right time. If I didn't know you better, I'd think you planted him in my household."

"Lucky you do know me better then, isn't it, sir?"

"Yes, I know I'll never be certain whether I've been manipulated because you'll never tell me. Now, I ought to leave you to rest. You're dropping to sleep as it is I'll come and see you soon. I wouldn't want you to be bored."

Landis stopped stifling his yawns. "I think Chapa laced my medicine."

"Good. I'm sorry they attacked you, Festus."

"Better me than you, Sire. Go carefully and don't argue with my last statement."

* * *

The ride from Landis House to the Palace did nothing to dull the guilt and responsibility burning within Adeone. He entered at the Privy Gate, the nearest to his chambers, ignored everyone he met and strode into the Outer Office in a flurry of frustration. A courier bowed.

"You are?" demanded Adeone.

"Edward, Sire. I'm watching the office for Richardson for a moment."

Entering the Inner Office no less vexed, he sat making notes until his administrator entered. Laying down his pen, he steepled his fingers against his mouth.

"A secretary should man the Outer Office until I have finished for the day. With the attack on Lord Landis, it is even more imperative that you wait for my return. Luckily for both of you, the courier wasn't reading any documents when I entered."

"I understand, sir, but Edward *is* trustworthy, Sire, and wasted as a

177

courier. He should have trained for a clerk, secretary or archivist."

"Why didn't he then?" enquired Adeone, his mind racing.

"As an orphan, he took the jobs that were going, sir. He's quick and helpful. When Your Majesty was in the Rex Dallin, after Her Grace's passing, he came in with a message one evening. He saw how chaotic the office was and offered to help. He had everything organised before I knew it. I must admit that I borrowed him for a couple of weeks to sort out the office archives for us. We'd wanted to get that done for years."

Astounded, Adeone scrutinised Richardson's face. "What made you think he was dependable enough for that?"

"He's as open as the day, sir. I've had him investigated and carefully watched. He's never talked about anything I entrusted to him. If his colleagues teased or asked him what he'd been doing he replied the mundane stuff that no-one else would, that he was so bored he'd happily swap. He wasn't bored; he was having the time of his life. You could see that. He's not a plant of Lord Scanlon's, Sire. I will stake my life on that. Give me six months with him and I could make him the best clerk there is. Better than I am now, probably."

"Very well. I'll hold you to all of that. You have your six months, which would you prefer, aluna or cisluna?"

Richardson stared at the King dumbfounded. "Sire?"

Lips twitching, Adeone reiterated, "Would you prefer six aluna-months or six cisluna-months? Do you want to opt for safety or do you like a challenge? One hundred and twenty-six days or one hundred and sixty-eight days? Your choice."

Richardson swallowed. "Call me a coward, Sire, I think I'll take the aluna-months."

"You're a coward. Get Edward in here and we'll see if he accepts the proposition." When the apprehensive courier was in front of him, Adeone regarded him solemnly. "Richardson tells me you're wasted in the couriers, that you'd make a better clerk. Is that true?"

"I suppose it is, Sire, yes."

"Then, if you wish to accept Richardson's tutelage, I'm sure we can make you into a passable clerk. Richardson reckons he can do it by autumn. Are you willing to try?"

Edward beamed; as though he had just received all the birthday presents that he'd never had at once.

Adeone chuckled. "I take it that is a 'yes' then. Thank you, Edward. I hope you find your new career enjoyable." As the door clicked shut behind Edward, the King said, "Let me know in an aluna-month whether you think he's any good, Richardson. If he is, I'll take his oath and you can carry on training him as Prince Arkyn's *administrator*. If he isn't, put your mind to the task of finding a young clerk who is. Expect tomorrow to be chaos. That will be all for this evening."

Once Richardson had left, Adeone remained at his desk, turning the events over in his mind. King's Representatives in Oedran were rare and sent out a message to the empire both about the standing of the Representative and the King's intentions. It had been dangerous naming Landis one. No-one doubted that he was high in favour, but Scanlon wouldn't have seen it as inevitable. Landis had stolen something that traditionally stayed within the FitzAlcis family, something that could be seen as Scanlon's right. Power in Oedran was power throughout the empire; being excluded from that would be noted. Easily roused to jealousy, Scanlon would act on the feeling, but the attack on Landis lacked finesse. It still sent him a message though: no-one was safe if they took power that should be Scanlon's. His brother would just have to get used to it; for although Adeone wouldn't willingly put his friends in danger, he wasn't going to retreat either. His little brother's tantrum wouldn't stop him from ruling the empire.

His mind made up, he took a piece of paper and started making notes for the morning: questions he'd wanted answers to first thing, questions that would take longer and then ones that might never be answered for they mostly involved Scanlon himself.

# Chapter 40
# FRIENDSHIP AND FARMING
### Late Evening
### Ceardlann – Nursery

ONCE THEY'D FINISHED DINNER, Arkyn shepherded his brother, Cal and Elantha to the nursery. Once there, Tain rounded on him, demanding to know what had happened.

"Uncle Festus has been attacked."

Tain whitened and Elantha looked at Arkyn with easily read distress. He gently hugged her, saying quietly,

"He's not dead. Father had to be in Oedran to deal with it."

She nodded, trying to be brave. Arkyn kept his arm around her.

"He'll be fine—"

"You don't know that!" snapped Tain. "You don't know that. Mother wasn't and you said she would be..." He ran out of the room.

"I thought she would be," whispered Arkyn with a note of inward despair.

"Are *you* all right, sir?" murmured Cal.

Arkyn sighed. "I will be."

Elantha gave him a spontaneous hug. "Tain's a prat." She started sucking her thumb.

Arkyn said quietly, "You're tired, El. Shouldn't you be in bed?"

She shook her head, leaning into him.

Cal found himself smiling. Having found Arkyn slightly intimidating for the first few weeks, Elantha's trust reassured him. The elder Prince cared about people but had learned not to show it.

Cal sat in the window seat, watching the darkening gardens. He hadn't expected to find a family life at Ceardlann, not really, but he was beginning to realise that he'd been welcomed into a close-knit family and it was helping him adjust. He was so deep in thought he missed the fact that Arkyn had persuaded Elantha to go to bed. He jumped when Arkyn asked if he was all right.

"Yes, sir." Cal hesitated for the briefest moment. "Are you, really?"

Arkyn considered. "I've been better." He caught Cal's eye. "I just want to know Uncle Festus will be all right."

"I'm sure His Majesty would have said if it was bad, sir."

"I'm not," admitted Arkyn unthinkingly. "He doesn't like to worry us, and Uncle Festus is strong and an excellent swordsman. I'm sure Uncle Festus is wounded. I just wish I knew more."

"I expect you'll find out tomorrow, sir. Is there anything I can do?"

"You're doing it. I've found talking helps," replied Arkyn with a small smile. He watched Cal for a moment. "Have you settled in?"

"Mostly, sir. I... Do you know how long I'll be here for?"

"I think as long as you want to be. Father's not said. Do you want to go home?"

Cal shrugged. "I don't know. I like it here, but I miss my family a bit, sir. I don't miss Hal but the rest I do, a bit, anyway."

Arkyn chuckled. "I can understand that. You should write to them at least... I mean, I'm sorry, but I assume they can read and write."

"Yes. Pa's made sure we all can. I went to school a couple of days a week... I don't miss that, well, maybe a couple of my friends—"

"Write to them as well."

Cal hesitated. "Won't someone mind, sir? I'll be using a lot of paper if I write to everyone."

"We'll cope. You shouldn't lose touch with people. None of us wants that. We like having you here but keep in touch with people you care about."

"Thank you, sir. Though I'm not sure what His Highness will think."

Arkyn snorted. "Can he think?"

Cal chuckled. "If he has to, sir."

"He'll be fine, Cal. Does him good not to be the centre of attention. You're not our servant, you're our friend. The rules are different."

Cal wasn't sure how but didn't like to say.

After a moment, Arkyn said, "You're looking tired."

"I won't sleep at the moment, sir. Do you want me to go to bed?"

Arkyn snorted. "No, I just think I shouldn't be keeping you up."

"I'll cope, sir. Perfect excuse and all that."

They both chuckled and settled down to talk about life generally. Maria peered around the door after half an hour and simply left them alone. Cal was tired but some things were more important than sleep, and she recognised a friendship was forming between them. Arkyn needed someone to talk to as much as Tain did, but he was far less open about it.

* * *

The following morning, she left Cal sleeping and chivvied Tain and Elantha into their day. Tain pouted slightly when he realised Cal was getting a lie in, but Maria simply pointed out that he'd been up late.

Tain wandered into the Comptroller's office after breakfast and sat down, brooding.

The Comptroller watched him shrewdly for a couple of moments. "Your nearfather is recovering, Your Highness."

Tain swallowed. "What happened?"

"A dagger wound, sir, but the doc's confined him to bed."

Tain picked at the hem of his tunic. "I wish… Father was meant to be here for longer."

"Yes, he was, but I've not had instruction that you're to be back at your books, sir. So, enjoy skipping lessons with a clear conscience."

Tain didn't smile. "I wanted to see father more."

"We all did. I've got to go to Silversley's for a chat with young Carlon. I'd be glad of your company. Let the day blow the cares away."

Six minutes later, they left Ceardlann to walk the mile to Silversley's farm. The early spring breeze had lost the bite of winter but hadn't found the warmth of the coming season yet. The slight frost was melting before their eyes and the hedges were greening. Tain drank in the clear air letting it lift his spirits.

They reached the farm to be greeted with, "Spring's blowing in trouble."

The Comptroller chuckled. "That must be referring to me, Silversley. You can't possibly be talking about His Highness."

"Can't I? Oh. Take after His Majesty, do you, Your Highness?"

"People say so," said Tain, confused.

"Hmm. Spring's blowing in double trouble, Comptroller. Come on in.

There's a pot on the fire and my wed-daughter has a cake with your names on it, I've no doubt. Can you find a spot for a slice, Your Highness?"

"Always," replied Tain with a grin. "There's always room for cake."

"Aye, there is that." He led the way into a warm kitchen. "That looks good, Martha. You know the Comptroller. This is Prince Tain. Now, Your Highness, this is my wed-daughter Martha. That ruffian is Carlon and this bundle of trouble is Perry. Sit yourselves down. What can I do for you?"

"I came to talk with Carlon actually, but after we've had a brew is fine," replied the Comptroller. "Are you sowing?"

"Aye. Well, preparing to. We've finished the ploughing. If you were a couple of days earlier, you could have helped, princeling."

"I'm not sure what father would have said to that," observed Tain.

Silversley snorted. "I taught him to plough so I hope he'd 'ave helped. Now, know much about farming, do you, sir?"

The Comptroller chuckled to himself as Silversley quite successfully drew Tain's mind away from the events in Oedran. He winked at Martha, picked up his mug of tea and jerked his head at Carlon. They walked out into the yard together.

"I was due to come to Ceardlann, sir. Is there a problem?"

The Comptroller shook his head. "Quite the reverse. No, Lord Landis was attacked yesterday and His Highness needed distracting. If you still want to join the guards, Fitz will have you quite happily. I need to check what you expect to do longer term. Your grandfather will be slowing down soon – well, there's a chance he might."

Carlon chuckled. "He's well enough, sir. Father's here to help and Perry. I can't see that I'll be needed for the twelve years that I'll serve in the guards, but, if I am, what'll happen?"

"We'll assess it then. There are several possibilities. Not least that we have a tenant here from a different family for a time. Just like you could have been asked to mind someone else's farm. If it's closer to the end of your indenture with the guards, then His Majesty could release you but, as you say, your father is here and your younger brothers."

"Well, I'm not sure Iestyn is old enough to help yet. When should I report to Captain Fitz?"

The Comptroller snorted. "If I know your family, it won't take long until Iestyn's toddling about helping. I'll tell Fitz to expect you on Alunadai. There'll be three of you starting. I'll send one of the men with the details. Now, I should find out what your grandfather is talking His Highness into."

As soon as the Comptroller entered the kitchen once more, Tain said, "Farmer Silversley says I can stay and help, Comptroller. May I?"

"If you want to, sir, I can't see any harm in it. Though I should perhaps ask 'help with what'?"

"This and that, Comptroller," replied Silversley with a twinkle. "I'll teach him to plough when he's a bit bigger but we've animals to tend, and crops to sow. The princeling might as well help with that as he'll be eating the produce. Here, Perry, show His Highness your jobs. He can help with those."

The Comptroller watched his charge leave with Perry and crooked an eyebrow at his friend.

Silversley chuckled. "They'll be fine together. Carlon'll see him safe to Ceardlann later – unless you want to stay and help as well."

"It's my back these days, Arthur, plays me up something rotten."

"You tried that one in our twenties."

The Comptroller chuckled. "Aye, well, it's a self-fulfilling prophecy. Thanks for the tea, Martha. Don't let His Highness play you around. His Majesty wouldn't want that."

"He'll be fine. I know how to handle his mischief. He is like his father was," said Silversley.

Walking into the yard, the Comptroller admitted, "They're similar in their ways. He's still hurting after the loss of his mother."

"Which he?" asked Silversley dryly. "How's His Majesty anyway?"

"Coping. He planned to pop by but got called back to Oedran before he could. Carlon's coming to us on Alunadai. Do you really not mind?"

"Nah. It'll do the lad good. He wants to stretch his wings a bit and it's better here than Oedran. Talking of which, you might want to drop by Hill Beck Farm at some point. I'm not sure Radley's well. We've not seen young Caswal as much as we normally do, and when we have, he's been tired. Not admitting anything's wrong, you know that family, but I think his pa might be ill. May need a bit of a hand."

"Thank you. I'll check on them."

# Chapter 41
## PROTECTION OR DEFENCE?
Imperadai, Week 37 – 4th Teral, 4th Teris 1209
Inner Office

IN OEDRAN, Adeone had risen before dawn. He entered the Outer Office, asked to see the Chief Yeoman, Doctor Chapa, General Paturn and Captain Wynfeld, completely ignoring any plans that might have existed for his day.

Just over quarter of an hour later, Richardson announced Doctor Chapa.

"Does he need announcing?" enquired Adeone mildly.

"Told you so!" muttered the doctor.

"He might have forgotten who he was at his age, Sire." Richardson inclined his head and left before the doctor could retort.

Chapa ignored the comment. "You wished to see me, Sire."

"What happened to the body of the would-be assassin?"

"The yeomen took care of it, sir. Corporal Leech alerted them."

"Why was the corporal there?"

"He was obviously off duty," remarked Chapa. "Professionally, his liver won't stand up to drinking that amount of alcohol for long. He was still coherent and able to walk in a straight line though. So maybe he'd merely spilt some."

"Well, he wouldn't still be in the militia if he's drunk on duty. Is there anything you need to tell me about Landis' health you couldn't before?"

"No, sir. He's perfectly well – apart from the dagger wound."

"Good and Lady Landis?"

"She should be fine, Sire. This won't have affected her or the babe. All your nearchildren are likewise a picture of health. Some are also taking after Lord Landis, so I must warn you that there is still no known cure for mischief making."

"Otherwise you'd have used it years ago on me and Festus, I know. Right, I think, for now, that's all, doc, but thank you for everything you did yesterday."

Once in the Outer Office, Chapa said, "Don't work him too hard, Richardson; the days at Ceardlann have had a positive effect."

"I'd noticed. What will you do when he works himself too hard?"

"Pick up the pieces. Who's the lad? He seems familiar."

Richardson followed Chapa's gaze. "Edward? He was a courier. The King thought he might like to be trained as a clerk."

"Good luck. I have to go and see if Lord Landis is behaving himself. I very much doubt he is on past experience."

Richardson raised his eyebrows in amusement as the doc left. He idly wondered if he was ever truly respectful to or about anyone.

The Chief Yeoman of Oedran entered the Outer Office to find quiet endeavour. Richardson wasn't giving anything away and Aldhouse cursed the administrator's professionalism. He would have liked warning about the King's mood given the previous day's event. As he was announced, Aldhouse realised that the King's mood was focused, potentially a mixed blessing: anger would cool, focus spoke of longer-term upheaval.

The King said, "Correct me if I'm wrong, Aldhouse, but I pay you to keep the city peaceful, do I not? Therefore, knife-wielding, would-be assassins shouldn't be roaming the streets."

Aldhouse tried to be honest. "They shouldn't, sir, but it seems they are."

"Yes. Where were your yeomen yesterday?"

"Close by, sir. They were on the scene in less than two minutes."

"How fortunate for Lord Landis that Corporal Leech was closer. I thought I'd been precise about the Maclan needing a greater yeomen presence. You're tasked with law enforcement in the city. If my Representative, Defender and Chief Advisor can't get home safely, the traditional course of action is resignation."

"Your Majesty—"

"Instead, I want to know who attacked Lord Landis, why they attacked him and that you have the main thoroughfares adequately patrolled; therefore, I want sight of your operational plans, an investigation into the attack and I need you to hand over the would-be assassin's body to Captain Wynfeld."

Aldhouse swallowed. "Sire, the man died. There's very little that we can do—"

"I don't believe I asked for excuses, Aldhouse. Nor will I tell you how to do your job. I will tell you what your job is and your job is to do as I request. Is that understood?"

"Yes, Sire," replied Aldhouse, cursing in his head. The would-be assassin had given the King an opening to examine the structure of the yeomen.

"Good. Then that's all for now."

The investigation would be difficult, but Adeone was determined there would be one. Was it wishful thinking to suppose there couldn't be many would-be assassins and that the chance Landis' attacker was one of the men Hillbeck had met was high? It was worth investigating. He'd get Hillbeck to view the corpse and if he was right, Wynfeld could investigate; it would be parallel and separate from the Chief Yeoman's. Aldhouse wouldn't have to know about it. There was the possibility that nothing would ever be found but it would be a test for the quality of information being received by the intelligence regiment and the yeomen.


The door had barely closed on the retreating Chief Yeoman when it opened again and Richardson was announcing General Paturn and Captain Wynfeld. They entered and saluted smartly. Wynfeld a careful step behind the General.

"General, how did my Representative end up attacked in broad daylight in the middle of Oedran?"

Paturn said, "It's under investigation, Sire. Wynfeld."

"Sir. Sire, I've had men on the street since I discovered what happened yesterday. We've located a couple of people who saw what happened. The man *was* following Lord Landis. We're sure about that. As the crowds slowed His Lordship down, he dismounted, as he's prone to do. The attacker wove his way close to His Lordship before drawing the dagger and slashing him in the side. We think he intended to slit His Lordship's throat when he was down but Lord Landis is too good a fighter. He collapsed to his knees but managed to draw his dagger and a couple of well-placed blows sliced the man's arteries. The would-be assassin dropped, and Lord Landis made sure he was dead with a couple more blows. Lord Landis then pulled himself up but started to pass out. Corporal Leech caught him, put him on Skit and escorted him home with a couple of the yeomen."

"General, any thoughts?" enquired Adeone.

Having worked his way up from one of hundreds of captains to the unique post of General, Paturn didn't delegate responsibility and didn't hide truths. "As far as I'm concerned, Sire, the fact Lord Landis was attacked is unacceptable but unsurprising. He's a target as your friend, as your Chief Advisor and certainly as Your Majesty's Defender. This attack came a bit too close. He won't thank you for having guards assigned and that would rather detract from the fact that he's your Defender. So, I suggest, we use his route home for training purposes. That'll always mean more of my men on those streets. It should hopefully protect him and give my men valuable skills."

"Quite. Organise it. I'm reassured by what you've already done. Wynfeld, I've told the Chief Yeomen to release the body of the would-be assassin to you, so learn what you can from that. We need to know if the man was working alone. His Lordship is incapacitated but do go and get his side of the story. Right, that's all for now. No, actually, Wynfeld, stay a moment, please. As you're here I'd like to talk to you about the men in your regiment who wish to accept promotion. Thank you, General." Once Paturn had left, Adeone turned to Wynfeld. "Never mind the men. Have you come to any conclusions about Landis being a scryer yet?"

"It's likely that your hunch was right, sir."

"I thought it might be. I wonder why he hasn't told me."

"Probably because he doesn't want the situation to be complicated. You're friends and this could conceivably get in the way – not knowingly, not intentionally but there might be more pressure if you officially know he can scry. I'm not saying there would be, sir, but I can see how there might be," said Wynfeld carefully.

"I know what you mean. I just wish I knew what he uses the hue for."

"I expect he uses it to collect information, Sire. There are a couple of enigmatic comments he's made to me that would be explained by this. I'm just sorry I can't be certain, Your Majesty."

Adeone raised an eyebrow. "I think perhaps you are certain but you have no evidence. Thank you, Wynfeld. Continue keeping a discreet eye on Lord Landis, if only for his safety. Just make sure you're not caught doing it too obviously. You might also be interested to know that Corporal Leech appeared to have consumed a large amount of alcohol but was coherent and able to walk in a straight line. Quite impressive I thought and so did Chapa. I'm sure you could shuffle men around to accommodate him. If the General continues with his plans, I might suggest you redeploy a sergeant into the training regiment and promote a corporal to make room."

Once Wynfeld left, Adeone examined the view across the gardens. He had long ago discovered he possessed the skills of a medium. He could sense aspects of people that they never knew were there. It was the hue that was a lesser form of the Ullian Spirit of sensor. He couldn't see magic, he couldn't know instinctively what other people possessed but he could sometimes know that people held them. When he'd sensed that Landis had one, he'd been too wrapped up in Ira's illness to concern himself with it. In all conscience, he couldn't berate Lord Landis, as a friend, for not having told him about being a scryer because he'd never mentioned being a medium. To berate him as the King would be highly unfair and very badly timed, as Lord Landis had been attacked for simply agreeing to sign the odd document. The King decided that he'd keep the knowledge, of what Landis was, private, and pretend, as he had before, that he had no inkling about the hue. There would be time to tell each other the truth one day, one day when it mattered, and that day wasn't now.

* * *

Four days later, Adeone glanced up from his desk as Richardson announced Wynfeld. The captain appeared drained but determined.

"I presume you have news, Captain?"

"Yes, Sire," replied Wynfeld. "It's mixed and my men are still hunting. Sergeant Hillbeck has verified that the would-be assassin is one of the men whom he met at the Teran Arms. The head gardener, Blackwood, has identified him as his cousin: Eric Adson, known as Adson. Hillbeck did confirm that Blackwood isn't the second man. Given the descriptions we have, we're now certain that the second man who attacked your life was a man called George Adson, known as Gad. He's short, stocky, mid-brown hair, ambidextrous and missing a little finger he likes to hide with gloves. My impression from Blackwood was that the nickname 'Gad' isn't just a shortening of George Adson but because he's a perpetual nuisance, rather like a gadfly. Blackwood also revealed Gad and Adson used to be in the army and their records don't read well, sir. They joined together, officially served in the Anaparian Legions, though they never got further than the

187

Lornford training fort. Adson could have been a corporal but he and Gad didn't settle to army discipline. Soon they were fighting others in their unit and regiment. They faced a court martial for wounding another man over a gambling debt – witnesses said Gad just flipped. He's unstable and deadly with a knife. Both he and Adson spent time in the military prison here and then entered the underworld of Oedran. I'm not sure how, but Judge Tancred got to hear about all of this. His Honour came to see me and, after I mentioned the names, he thinks the men might have been through the civilian courts as well. I've asked the Keeper to check—"

"I told Judge Tancred about the attack when I visited him for dinner."

"Thank you, Sire." Wynfeld filed the information that the King dined privately with a long-standing, highly respected judge as 'intriguing'. "I'm not sure Adson was as proficient with a knife, which makes me wonder why he, and not Gad, attacked Lord Landis. We are doing everything we can to locate Gad, but it may take a while."

"I would like him found sooner rather than later," said Adeone levelly. "Did you find out any more about what happened on the Maclan?"

"Not much, Sire. As Lord Landis was slipping into unconsciousness, he apparently muttered a curse and then something else. When Leech reached him, he heard the word or name 'Tolse', or possibly it was 'to see'. No-one knows what it means. His Lordship wasn't particularly forthcoming when I asked him—"

"What did he say?"

"With very studied blankness, 'That's odd. I can't think why I'd have said that'. I obviously don't know Lord Landis very well, Sire, but I'd say he wanted to end the conversation."

"Then what, as Captain of Intelligence, are you going to do?"

"Well, if Your Majesty doesn't order me otherwise, I was going to continue the conversation with the scriveners and see if Tolse is an inherited name in the tax records. If it isn't then His Lordship probably said 'to see' or something else."

"Did Lord Landis tell you to leave it alone?"

"No, sir."

"Then I have no objection. Richardson can probably furnish you with the name of a discreet treasury scrivener but don't tell anyone why you're asking. If that's all for now, you'd better carry on with the investigation."

Once alone, Adeone considered everything that Wynfeld had revealed. Most of all, he considered that Landis was keeping secrets and, after an attack on his life, that was worrying. He considered what to do. He could order Landis to reveal whatever it was he was keeping private – because it seemed to be more than the fact that he was a scryer – or he could use

Wynfeld's regiment to uncover the issue. As a friend, the second option might be more underhanded, but it would risk the friendship less than pulling rank. He decided to see what Wynfeld could discover about Tolse.

* * *

A fortnight later, Adeone once more listened to Wynfeld's report. It was both reassuring and concerning.

"Apologies for the delay with this, Sire. We've had to go slowly for some of it and other parts were out of our hands. Mintley, the treasury scrivener, eventually managed to find one Becka Tolse in the Landis Lordship. He had to go through the Treasurer to get access to further information and he had to wait for a pretext. I sent a man to Seeping Close to nose around. There wasn't much of interest, just your normal alley with overcrowding. He did, however, spot the mark for a black scryer. Apparently, she's not taking on work. The man was careful and went to a house we're renting off the Macarian Lordship, where he stayed for a couple of nights. We managed to get a woman through a city facilitator to play the part of a cheating wife and our scryer has said that Becka stopped following him after a short time. He reported what he'd discovered after that. She's certainly a scryer, sir, and someone is paying her so well that she doesn't need extra work."

"Which in itself is suspicious," observed Adeone. "Right. What do you make of it all?"

"I think His Lordship has been a target for quite a while, Sire. It's likely Becka Tolse followed him until she knew his movements and that His Lordship realised. Possibly because Becka was watching him more. I believe that she and her associates worked out that Skit dislikes crowds and that a crowded street was a reasonable ambush opportunity. It's more difficult for an assailant to get away but Lord Landis couldn't draw his sword, and wouldn't be as watchful about people being near him."

It made sense to Adeone. "What do you suggest?"

"Well, I'm not sure, sir. It's clear His Lordship is trying to remove her without arousing suspicion. My informants tell me that he's already had a map made of where trade symbols occur in his lordship. He's more recently also asked for a record check for all his tenants. If he can remove her as a threat without suspicion it might be best."

"Lord Landis will be able to resume most of his duties in a week. I suggest we see what he does with that time. If Becka Tolse is still a threat when he's here, I'll take thought again but an obvious arrest will raise questions. It would suggest that Landis, or someone close to him, is a scryer and as neither of us knows that officially I don't want to give my brother a chance to suspect it."

"Very good, Sire. I'll keep a watching brief on the situation."

189

# Chapter 42

# CLARITY OF PURPOSE


LANDIS NODDED when William asked if he'd see Merchant Chapa. The King's cousin entered with easy familiarity. Not a tenant seeing his landlord, not a merchant visiting a lord, just a man greeting his acquaintance. Once the door closed, Landis raised an eyebrow.

"Who or what are you hunting for, my lord? We'd help if we knew."

"You would, others might hinder or ask 'why'." He considered how far Merchant Chapa was in Adeone's confidence. "All right, Henry, I'll admit I am hunting for a way of verifying that someone in this lordship is a black-scryer working for Lord Scanlon. I think that information helped to get me attacked and I'd rather it didn't happen again."

Merchant Chapa eased himself into a chair. "What makes you so certain they're here, my lord?"

"I've had information come my way, but I need to find out by accident else Lord Scanlon would start to try to find my informant. That will not help."

"Hmm. Tell me, do you truly know who they are and where they are?" After Landis nodded, Merchant Chapa considered carefully before saying, "I'm of a different generation from you: a harsher generation. Obviously, these tactics of softly-softly are not producing results. Might I advise that you scrap them? Then wait a couple of months. Have your bailiffs find the black-scryer by pointing them in the right direction. If they're working against the empire, I'm sure Your Lordship has men on your payroll who know how to deal with them. If not, I'm certain I could find a couple of likely lads."

"Thank you. This is where I say the black-scryer in question is a lady."

"Quite frankly it makes no difference. She is still a traitor. As a Defender and as a King's Representative, you were a King's Advocate twice over when attacked. To attack you *was* and *is* treason. Maybe those responsible should be expected to take the consequences whatever their sex."

"I would not become a cold-blooded killer," remarked Landis.

"My lord, it might well be 'kill or be killed'. There is also the small fact of the number of times you are in His Majesty's company. It is a small step from watching and harming you to turning that focus onto the King. If you dislike the idea, then either turn her to your side or tell me her name and location. I'm willing to take the risk to protect the empire because your checks aren't doing much good for trade."

Intrigued, Landis glanced at Merchant Chapa. His guest's strong loyalty to the empire was well known but such a manifestation of it was unexpected.

He said, "Thank you, but I think not. I'll stop the double-checks – they're not turning up much anyway. You're right about the King; I hadn't thought of it in that light, and will have to do something more definite now. I just don't like the thought of ending someone's life… especially a woman who is unable to defend herself."

Merchant Chapa snorted. "I wouldn't go that far. Most women in Oedran can handle themselves. There are multiple uses for a rolling pin and a carving knife. There is another option open to you, my lord: inform the militia. Let them make the decision. Either way, you need to stop the woman."

"I realise that. Thank you, Henry. I needed that talk to clear my head. I have little choice, and I do have a couple of men on my payroll who might suffice, one of whom was following me more openly a few months ago before seeing the error of his ways."

"Maybe it's time to test his loyalty. Though there is one thing I hope you've considered, my lord…" said Master Chapa thoughtfully. "That the man, new on your payroll, is the second one who attacked the King's life. He must have been following you for a reason. It seems a huge coincidence to me that the man who attacked you was one of those men."

"Time will tell. Thank you again, Merchant Chapa."

The Chief Merchant took the hint and left. Once the door had closed, Landis swore. He'd not considered the possibility, but since Merchant Chapa had voiced it in well-reasoned tones, it became plausible. The man fitted the description. Cursing, he asked Clodach to check that the man was still under observation. He hadn't heard anything from him or his minder for a few weeks. Clodach returned distressed. His cousin was dead and the man had disappeared. Landis swore roundly and loudly.

Clodach eyed him. "Dunna fret. I wilna let this pass. We'll find 'im."

"You'd better! Because I've got to go and inform the King."

"Why, m'lord? The King ain't goin' t' care about my cousin's murder."

Landis didn't answer. He wasn't getting into that discussion. He didn't like losing men through stupidity and this had to rank as one of his more impressive mistakes.

* * *

Once Clodach left, Landis compiled a report, just the briefest of facts that skated over the sources of his information. Satisfied it was vague enough to obscure details but not to raise questions, made his way to the barracks and Wynfeld's office.

The captain accepted the report, intrigued that Landis had prepared it. "Thank you for the information, my lord. We were waiting to see what you did about Becka Tolse."

More impressed than he'd admit, Landis said, "I think it is time we remove the threat, don't you?"

"Yes, my lord. I'll see to it. Would you prefer an accident or a more obvious targeting? It's your lordship and will send a message," observed Wynfeld, still intrigued that Landis had trusted him.

"Your choice. There is also the matter of the man…"

"We'll hunt him out. The yeomen are investigating the murder but we'll keep an eye on it… It's none of my business, my lord, but will you be informing our King of these developments?"

"Would you suggest I do?" enquired Landis.

"It might be an idea, sir. Nothing really gets by our King. As I know to my cost."

Impressed by how far Wynfeld had come, Landis admitted, "I am going to tell His Majesty. How is the regiment developing?"

"Very nicely. I've just gained Leech, though I still need to talk to him. Jones is remaining in Garth, much to the relief of the Exarch. We've promoted two more of my sergeants, one for Serpent Isle and one for Gerymor. Escott has transferred to the training regiment to keep an eye out for new men. I'll see if there are any lads to replace them all during summer recruitment or if any experienced men want to sign on for longer when they're demobbed at the end of their service."

"Good luck with it. I'll leave you to get on," replied Landis, thinking, *'I need to readjust my thinking over you and it might take some time.'*

* * *

Leaving the barracks, Landis went straight to see Adeone and admitted everything that had happened.

When his friend had finished, Adeone cursed, but nothing in the situation could be changed. "I've been telling you you're mortal for years. This just proves you're fallible as well. I'm glad you've shared it with Wynfeld. We'll find the man. He doesn't seem to be the type to hide. If he is Gad, you killed his cousin. He'll want revenge."

"He's killed one of my best men already. Maybe the feeling is mutual."

"Quite. Oh, I ought to warn you, I've decided the children can come to Oedran for the Munewid. Tain's been pestering me for a while and it's Arkyn's cisan-age birthday the following week."

"The children are certainly growing quickly," observed Landis. "Prince Arkyn will soon be undertaking the provincial reviews for you. Any luck on finding him an administrator?"

"Edward is shaping up well. I've got to talk to Richardson about him again at some point."

* * *

In the meantime, Wynfeld spoke to a couple of the hardened men in his regiment: the ones who had morals and scruples but who were soldiers. Becka Tolse would be 'mugged' one night. It wasn't pleasant but it had to happen. It was more certain to succeed than a trip into the river or a heavy weight falling from the top of a building. The yeomen would be told after a fortnight to stop hunting for the muggers. Lord Landis would get his staff to sort out her lodgings for the next person and anything interesting would be bagged. Not that Wynfeld's men had found much last time apart from the obsidian mirror. Wynfeld suspected Lord Landis would decide to 'destroy' that himself.

# Chapter 43
## PRINCE'S ADMINISTRATOR
### Tretaldai, Week 45 – 3rd Lufial, 17th Geryis 1209
### Outer Office

AFTER TWO ALUNA-MONTHS of working in the Outer Office, Edward had mastered filing and archiving, shorthand and his disbelief. Having settled into an easy routine, he was surprised when the King called him into the office one evening with Richardson.

Adeone smiled at him. "Edward, Richardson seems to think you'll make an excellent confidential clerk. Would you be willing to take the oath?"

The last eight weeks hadn't prepared him for that question. Only the closest staff took the oath, those who dealt with the personal papers of the FitzAlcis, or those who dealt with confidential documents. It had far-reaching consequences. Swallowing his amazement, Edward nodded.

After taking the oath, Adeone continued, "Thank you, Edward. I'm afraid to say there was an ulterior motive in all this. Would you be willing to work as Prince Arkyn's *Administrator* when you have completed your training to Richardson's satisfaction?"

Shocked, Edward glanced at Richardson, whose steady face and eye told him he'd known what the King had had in mind. It also told Edward that Richardson wholeheartedly agreed with the proposition. That calmed him down. Even though he might not believe it himself, if Richardson did, then it must be right.

"I would be honoured to, Sire." Then curiosity got the better of him. "But why me, sir? Especially for such a high position."

The King glanced at Richardson before answering. "There are several reasons. First and foremost is that you have shown yourself to be trustworthy. From what Richardson has told me, you are a natural secretary and highly organised. You are young, and, in this case, I think that is an advantage. There is another reason, for which you'll have to forgive me. You are an orphan. In our society many see it as a disadvantage, but, for me, nothing could be further from the truth. Without family you can have no torn loyalties, nobody to be threatened if a traitor wishes to suborn you. There is in that one facet of your life the protection and security that we both need. All the people closest to my family's personal staff and households have been approached. If there is anyone you are particularly close to, you might wish to warn them. If they are approached, you *must* inform Richardson, or my guard – even Captain Wynfeld. I don't wish anyone to get hurt by working for my family. The last reason, Richardson is training you. He has worked in this office for almost as long as I can remember and he will retire when my son becomes king, if he hasn't before. I need to be certain, and so does he, that my son's administrator is more than competent. You've already shown yourself to be capable. I hope that my reasons are understandable to you."

"Perfectly, thank you, Sire. I hope I never do anything to make you regret your trust in me."

"I hope so too, Edward. For now, that's all."

Unsure what to make of the events, Edward bowed and left. He returned to the filing he had been doing, glad of a steady job to keep his hands occupied whilst his brain fathomed whether he was dreaming. He'd expected to end up with the clerks in another office, rather than become Prince Arkyn's Administrator. He hadn't given the possibility a thought. Edward glanced at the file in his hands and shook his head, trying to focus on where it belonged. Richardson lifted it out of his hands and put it in its place. Edward turned, bemused.

Richardson smiled at his charge, thirty years his junior. "Come on, Edward. I think we're done for the day. Let's find a tankard of something to celebrate."

They walked through the quietening Palace and into Upper Hall.

A server hurried over. "Administrator, lovely to see you. Who's this?"

"This is Edward, Denny, and, no, he doesn't have the right tokens, but you're not going to worry about that this evening because I'm telling you not to."

"Are you browbeating me, Administrator?"

"Yes. You'll cope. I'm aware of who can use this refectory and you're not going to tell me I'm not, are you?"

"Wouldn't dream of it, wouldn't dream of it, Administrator," pattered Denny. "What would you like to drink? I'll be eating the humble pie later."

Amused, Richardson said, "Two beers, please, and stop your insolence or I'll have a word with your grandmother."

"Two beers it is. She'd like to see you, so maybe the clip round the ear would be worth it." He waved to a table. "Can I get you anything else?"

"Peace and quiet?" suggested Richardson lightly.

Denny chuckled and left to fetch the beers. Richardson led the way to a table whilst the few others in the refectory showed unabashed interest. Edward could recognise and name most of them from his time in the runners and couriers and he'd been wary of every one of them because of their standing in the Palace or the King's Household.

Richardson winked at Edward. "Nosy, aren't they?"

"Not surprisingly, sir."

Once Denny had delivered the drinks and left again, Richardson looked at Edward. "How are you feeling?"

"Erm, shocked, confused – I ought to say pleased. I never expected anything like this."

"I expect not. I remember how I felt when I moved into the Outer Office as one of King Altarius' junior secretaries. I'd been a clerk for a long time and thought that was what I would remain. Anyway, they needed another secretary and, for whatever reason, I was chosen. I didn't mind hard work and I had shown I was reliable, I suppose – part of me still wonders though. Then King Adeone, or Prince Adeone as he was then, needed an administrator and King Altarius told me I was it. When the old King told you something you did it, accepted it or remembered it. King Adeone's more relaxed way of working came as something of a challenge at times."

"What like, sir?"

"Small things. We announced everyone to King Altarius. King Adeone doesn't insist on that if they hold a King's Token or are family. It was a different way of working. I'm sure Prince Arkyn will have his own as well."

A courier entered with a message for the Palace Chamberlain. Edward shrank down, relieved he hadn't been noticed.

"I take it there are still words being said within your old colleagues about your change of job then," remarked Richardson.

"I cope, sir. I've had worse in my life."

"I'm sure you have and admire your persistence to try to deal with it yourself, but it's time it stopped. Especially now that you know what I'm training you for. It would be better, by the way, for you not to mention that you know you are to be an administrator, at least for the moment. As you have taken the oath of loyalty, alternative accommodation ought to be arranged. If you're no longer sharing the same space as your former colleagues, your life will become easier."

"Thank you, sir, but I don't want to be singled out…"

"The King's confidence in you has done that. There is nothing you can do about it. I must speak to the Steward at some point tonight anyway." Richardson glanced at Edward caringly. "It's all a bit overwhelming at first, I know, but it does get easier."

A few minutes later, the Steward disturbed them by saying, "What's the lad doing here, Richardson?"

"If you join us, I might get a chance to explain," replied Richardson.

As the Steward sat down, Denny asked him what he wanted to drink and Richardson simply kept quiet until they were alone again.

"Steward, the King has just taken Master Edward's oath of loyalty in anticipation of him soon becoming Prince Arkyn's administrator."

The Steward glanced at Edward disparagingly. "I would have thought you're a bit young."

Richardson intervened. "Steward, I would remind you that the King has made this decision so your comments and prejudices aren't needed. Master Edward has already been invaluable in the time he's been working in the Outer Office."

"I get the hint. Congratulations on your appointment, Master Edward."

Richardson remarked, "Myself, the King's Secretaries, His Highness and, I suspect, Lord Landis will be the only ones to know. I'm only telling you because I need a room for Master Edward. The simple fact he's taken the oath should be enough for you to manage it without too much speculation. I'm thinking of somewhere near the King's Secretaries' rooms"

"I'll see what can be managed. Most of the rooms are full but I think there might be a spare on Secretaries' Corridor. If it were a case of him being known as Prince Arkyn's Administrator it would be easier – there are rooms set aside for that eventuality."

"Then this is forewarning. Edward will need the same tokens as Kenton and Jacobs when it comes to living arrangements for the moment."

"I'll see they're in the room when he takes it over. What time will you need waking, Master Edward?"

Edward glanced at Richardson, who said, "Six by the Court Clock, Steward. Master Edward will be following my working day. After all, the Prince's will probably mirror the King's. When will the room be ready?"

"Tomorrow evening."

Richardson watched the Steward leave. When he'd gone, Edward was surprised to see a brief grin flit across Richardson's features.

"It is all too easy to wind that man up; however, young Edward, you, at least for the time being, won't be following my example in that."

"I don't think I'd dare to anyway."

"You'll learn; you'll have to deal with them all in the end – everyone, from the Lords of Oedran to the captain of the Palace Guard and from the Chief Merchant to the Justiciar. You'll be the doorkeeper and they have to get past you. They'll try every trick there is to gain favour. Remember that."

Edward swallowed uncomfortably and finished his drink

Six minutes later, Richardson said, "You're looking tired, Edward. It might be better if you went to bed."

"I think I will, if you don't mind, sir."

"I'll be heading for mine soon. I'll see you at seven in the Outer Office."

Richardson watched the youth leave. A moment later, the Herald had joined him and was informed to stop the speculation regarding Edward's new position. When Richardson wouldn't explain why, the Herald left feeling cheated but having agreed to do what he could.

# Chapter 44
## CROPPED

Imperadai, Week 48 – 25th Lufial, 18th Lufis 1209
Anapara – Raven Hills– Black Hills House

LORD SCANLON RETURNED from the Macian Isles during the final week of 1209. Eyes darting, searching for answers where there couldn't be any, he dismounted in the stableyard of Black Hills House. Striding into his home, he ignored the gathered household and slammed his way into his study.

The man got languidly to his feet, giving a pointed bow.

"You better have a good explanation!" railed Scanlon.

"For anything in particular?" enquired his companion silkily.

"You can start with the failed attack on Landis."

The man smiled. "Ah, that. He needed dealing with, Greatness. He was laid up for weeks and the King, well, he didn't get the rest he so obviously needs. Such a shame."

"Who decided to use Adson?"

"Syri. He's been running them. I've been at Misol."

Scanlon threw his riding crop onto his desk, tearing off his gloves. "Adson was never intended to be the knife man. You knew that! He was there to calm his cousin. Keep Gad out of Oedran until autumn. He's now hunted twice over. Put him to work at Brant again. As far as Oedran is concerned, Gad has vanished. When the intelligence regiment fails to find him, we might get rid of Wynfeld's interference. Which nicely brings me on to who sent Meyer and Blunt in? They were doing good work in Lufia,

I didn't need them dead in Oedran!"

"They became too obvious. Adri thought they'd done all they could."

"I doubt it. Letting them go to Oedran isn't the sort of mistake I pay for. Next time, you ask! No-one takes unilateral decisions where to send my best men. Sicla, next you'll tell me that Becka Tolse was the victim of a chance mugging. Who worked that one out?"

His companion shrugged. "Landis has been digging into his tenants' lives. Becka thought someone had found her. She stupidly had the mark on her door. Wouldn't be surprised if Landis or Wynfeld didn't get wind of it. We offered to move her but she said that would be worse."

"You don't *offer*. You move her! Do you know how long it took me to find and convince her? I had to coerce her former landlord for a start. Do you know how much it takes to bribe a Lord of Anapara?"

"My vaults do. I pay the bribes," muttered the man pointedly.

"Your vaults will be far emptier if this carries on," observed Scanlon. "You have lost me three good men and one exceptional woman. I've lost one of the hues on my side and gained absolutely nothing from it. Have you found any others?"

"No. Not that's worth the candle," replied the man. "Syri hasn't heard of any either. I'm limited by when I can visit. Oedran is closing off to us, Greatness. Oh, you've still friends at Court but there are more rumours circulating now. Especially since the Triniculum Plan."

Scanlon's eyes narrowed. "You wasted two years' work there as well."

"No, sir, we were unlucky. If the King hadn't ridden for Ceardlann we'd have succeeded. Haster is no loss. Sergeant Hillbeck was an unfortunate complication. We had no inkling he'd be compelled to act on his suspicions."

Scanlon snorted. "As soon as you ran into him, you should have stopped the plan. *You* don't mess with valley-born. What's this about the new guard for the Exarch?"

"He is your second cousin once removed; maybe the King is paranoid?"

Scanlon shook his head. "No. He'd have done it years ago if that was the reason. I overheard the commander and Fencible in Macia talking. The commander was saying he didn't have anyone suitable and the Fencible saying the King wants it. They saw me and stopped talking. Something is happening! Find out what."

"Could it be that the King is getting wise to you, Greatness? He's going to protect his Representatives. Maybe you've been too obvious. All these failed plans—"

"These failed plans?" spluttered Scanlon, outraged. "*Your* failed plans! Yours and Syri's mess! Sicla, death and damnation. You have almost destroyed my network in Oedran. Are you double-crossing me?"

"Oh, come now, that's too paranoid even for you, Greatness. I like the glint of gold and the King doesn't hold with buying men's loyalty. He might outwardly be a weakling, but if I went to him with what I know, how long do you think I'd live? Syri saw Haster before he left. He said there were scars on his hands—"

"So what? He's a guard! There's scars on your hands too."

"Yes, but then the King's hands weren't bandaged when I got my scars. I would lay your money on the fact he life-bound Haster, which doesn't say 'weakling' that says playing a much longer game than you expected, Greatness. He's charming people, then letting them know where the line is. If he life-bound me, I'd be dead within moments, so, if it's all the same to you, *sir*, I'll pass on double-crossing you to him."

"That wasn't what I meant. Are you playing your own game?"

"Me? What would I gain from it? This year has been an unfortunate series of mishaps. Starting with the King, or Queen Ira, discovering Wynfeld. Yes, we're working to remove him, but, so far, the King has been unusually lenient. Do you know why?"

"He's not going to tell me, is he?" Scanlon replied waspishly, evading the question.

"Well, we're getting close to infiltrating the barracks. We've several hopefuls, but they may not make this year's recruitment."

"Fine! We've a lot to replace now. We need far more spies at Court. No-one just turns up in future. They're either there by right or proper introduction. Landis invited Faran, they were quite open about that, but they didn't warn the King. It suggests they didn't want word to escape, which means it wasn't accidental. Faran didn't tell Eames he was leaving Lufian, he didn't tell Adeone he was visiting Oedran. That breaks every rule. Landis knew about Meyer and Blunt, I'm sure. Who told him?"

"Take your pick from the grooms who saw Meyer and Blunt arrive—"

"Come in," snapped Scanlon in response to a knock on the door.

Administrator Dyer entered. "The King would like to know if you plan to be in Oedran for the Munewid and Prince Arkyn's birthday, sir?"

"And that couldn't wait?" demanded Scanlon.

"They are finalising preparations, sir," replied Dyer nervously.

"Fine. I won't make the Munewid Banquet. I'll advise about the other feast later. Get out."

Once the door closed, Scanlon's companion said, "You could at least see Syri if you go."

"The way I'm feeling, I'm likely to murder him. Talking of which, if the Princes and King are together, it may be a good time for an attack. Are we sure the Lords of Oedran and Representatives would support me?"

"You can never be sure when it comes to that bunch. Of course, you could try life-binding, I'd be interested to see how that would mix with a truth-bind to the King. You need them to commit to treason and then hold it over them before they'll do anything. I don't trust any of them. Oh, they say they support you but given the chance, until you prove more than a figurehead, they'd argue amongst themselves then work against you. Don't forget, if you are the only choice, killing you could mean one of them becomes king. They'll work that out, eventually. You don't have universal support from them. I reckon there's two who support you wholeheartedly, but the King has the same number, possibly more. We're working on others but, if the King and Princes died next week, no, I don't think we're ready. You need far more than the Court. In fact, you need the people running the cities, the palaces, the law houses; you need the infrastructure, the army – admittedly, the last might be difficult."

"And how long will that take?" asked Scanlon sarcastically.

"At least a year," replied his companion. "Instead of reacting like a petulant child, build your power over the men you need."

"Petulant," sputtered Scanlon. "How dare you?"

"Do continue to prove my point, Greatness. Your power comes from the King's inability to disown you. What are you planning to do when you have the crown? Sit basking in its ardour? It won't last. You don't have a son; you don't have a plan, beyond some half-hearted revenge for what? What did the King do that irks you so much? Other than being the older brother, more carefree, more likeable—"

"GET OUT!"

The man left, whistling. Fuming, Scanlon picked up his riding crop and whacked the table. Its unyielding surface gave him no pleasure. He called his administrator and worked off his rage with crop and fists. Dyer should have known better than to disturb him. It was his fault he was suffering this beating. When the administrator passed out, Scanlon stormed from the room, his companion's words resounding in his head. He didn't have a son, didn't have the spies, didn't have the declarations of loyalty, didn't have everything in place. He wouldn't visit Oedran for Arkyn's cisan-age birthday it would be intolerable. Success gleamed tantalisingly beyond reach amongst the fronds of failed plans. If Gad was the card he had left, he would change the deck but the man still had skills to use. He could make another attempt either winter or spring next year. If Adeone died, Arkyn would need a protector. The Lords of Oedran and the empire couldn't quibble that the Justiciar was the right person. That could legitimately secure his power. Until then, he would target more strategically, he would build on everything he needed. He had some resources his companion didn't know about, stashes of coin, friends in provincial capitals. Gad could have one last chance in late 1210. If he didn't succeed then, he'd be of no further use. Too many eyes would be hunting for him, and he'd know too much if he was caught. For the moment, he had other things to concern him in the attics and cellars of Black Hills.

PART 3

Chapter 45
# STORMS AND CALM
Cisadai, Week 12 – 23rd Lowal, 16th Lowis 1210
Inner Office

THE ANNIVERSARY of Queen Ira's death dawned with storms. His heart heavy, Adeone dressed remembering the ride, the fear, the laughter and the devastation of that sunny day a year ago. The storms were somehow more appropriate. It wasn't that everyone was tiptoeing around him but he knew they were intrigued by his decision not to visit Ceardlann. As the storms lashed the windows of the Palace, changing his mind wasn't appealing.

Richardson had asked if he could leave Edward in charge of the Outer Office for the day as part of his training. Disinterestedly, Adeone agreed. It wasn't like his day consisted of anything critical, Richardson had seen to that with the quiet competence that others often missed.

The morning dragged. Slipping into memories, Adeone wondered what Ira would make of their sons now. Tain, ten, lively and mischievous. Arkyn, fifteen, at Court, getting to grips with new duties and responsibilities. She'd have been proud, but Adeone couldn't hear what she'd say. The link with her was fading, the loss burning brighter for it and the rain wept, drenching the grounds with the tears of the heavens.

From the Outer Office came the murmur of voices, Edward's quietly reiterating that someone needed an appointment or must wait.

Moments later, Lord Anguis entered. "Your Majesty, about Imperadai—"

"I don't believe you have an audience, Anguis!"

"Well, the pipsqueak courier outside—"

Adeone pursed his lips. "If you barge into my office again then, Lord of Oedran or not, there will be consequences. If you dare to disparage the men whom I have working for me, maybe you'd like to consider where such disparagement may land you. If my administrator or secretaries inform you that I am unavailable, then I am!"

Anguis reddened. "Refusing to see—"

Something snapped in Adeone. "If you need an audience, organise it properly! Edward was doing his duty, something that seems beyond your comprehension. I don't want to see you at Court until the Munpyram. Get out!"

Anguis didn't move. "I am a Lord of Oedran, Sire—"

"If you continue, you won't be for much longer! No-one has automatic right of audience unless I've given them a token." He pushed himself to his feet. "Do I need to call my guards to remove you to a cell for defying me?"

Anguis wrenched the door open and strode away.

"Edward!" The secretary entered hesitantly, but Adeone ignored the nerves. "You did the right thing. Thank you for trying. Cancel my meeting with Wynfeld, please."

Once he was alone again, Adeone sank into his chair and rested his head on his hands. He felt the ghost of Ira's hand on his shoulder and choked back his emotion. He wished she was there, beside him, with him, supporting him, calming him. He shouldn't be here today; he should be with their sons but the rain was relentless and he hadn't the heart to put others through the ride.

Simkins served his lunch without comment, brought in tea and biscuits, removed the detritus and lit the fire. Nothing shifted the memories and Adeone cursed himself.

Richardson entered the office late in the afternoon and saw how little the King had read. He crossed to collect the documents.

Seated in front of the fire, Adeone said, "Make sure I'm not this bloody stupid again. I should have been at Ceardlann! Presumably, as you're here, you've heard about the incident earlier."

Unsure what Adeone thought about it, Richardson said, "Edward did his best in difficult circumstances, sir. I can't say that I'd have been much more successful."

Adeone waved to a chair. "You think he's worth all the trouble in the world, don't you?"

"Yes, sir, I do. I don't think there is much more I could teach him if we had ten years together." replied Richardson, sitting down. "I'd say he's ready, but it's not my opinion that matters."

"Hmm. He's a good secretary now. What about the other aspects?"

Richardson hesitated. "The scriveners say his mathematical ability is perfectly sound. The servers say he's not going to be breaking the best glassware. He can ride, and he's been taught how to care for horses. Your lawyers are happy he understands the treason laws. He's grasped the finer points of King's Tokens for communicating standing and favour, and for limiting automatic right of entry. Though I may also have told him that Chapa and Lady Amara get to walk over our best intentions."

Adeone snorted. "Yes, sorry about that. I feel there is a 'but' coming in all of this."

"But," said Richardson with a small smile, "he's pretty hopeless with a sword. He's more likely to injure himself than an enemy."

"Ah." Adeone considered. His staff all needed to be able to protect themselves. "How's his fist work?"

"Better than his sword skills," replied Richardson dryly. "He did grow up in an orphanage."

"Then, that's fine. For what it is worth, I've been impressed with him over the last couple of days. This Pentadai, I'm going to see the Princes. He can come with me. Ensure I remember to add him to the Rex Dallin Scroll—" He broke off as the door opened.

"Not still here, Sire?" asked Landis entering without herald. "If there's no rest for the wicked then there seems little point to you working."

"That must have lost something in the translation," muttered Adeone.

"You're one of the good, sir. You need a break. I'm surprised at Richardson keeping you working this late."

"My lord, I shall leave the King, with his permission, to your tender care," replied the administrator.

King Adeone laughed for the first time that day. "All right, Richardson, you seem to have won. We're done for the day. Enjoy your evening."

Once Richardson had left, Adeone led the way into his private sitting room. He collapsed into a chair, and Landis followed suit.

Smiling slightly, Adeone asked, "How's Cornelia?"

"Pregnancy suits her. There'll soon be another Landis to give you a headache. You will stand as nearfather again?"

"Of course, if you and Cornelia wish it. Have you chosen a name yet?"

Landis said calmly, "We were wondering about Ira, if it's a girl and you don't mind."

His voice only just in his control, Adeone said, "I don't mind, Festus. I… Thank you, but what if it's a boy?"

"We have some in mind, but Adeone is top of the list."

Adeone got up and faced the windows, distracting himself but not seeing the sodden view. He took a deep breath and turned back to his friend. "You do me too much honour. Why?"

"We're running out of ideas?" suggested Landis with bright eyes. He became serious. "You're the best friend I've got, sir. The last five have had family names. This time I want to name the child for people I care deeply about, Cornelia also. We started thinking and realised the people for whom we care that deeply are Your Majesty and your family."

Sitting down, Adeone studied his friend for a moment. "I don't quite know what to say. Thank you both. I'll try to get to see them all at some point soon. I promise."

"I know you will. I'll sort out a dinner invitation and pass it through Richardson so no clashes occur."

Adeone nodded. "Avoid Pentadai. I'm going to Ceardlann. Come with me. I'm sure Arkyn and Tain would like to see you. If not, I'm sure young Calumiel will be too polite to say anything."

Landis chuckled and, for the rest of the evening, their talk was about their families, interspersed with speculation on Court gossip.

# Chapter 46
## REX DALLIN
### Pentadai, Week 12 – 26th Lowal, 19th Lowis 1210
### Rex Dallin

ON PENTADAI, the Comptroller appeared slightly frazzled as he said, "Your Highness, maybe if we view it another way—" He turned to put some papers on the Comptroller's Chest and bowed as he registered the King had entered. Arkyn whipped round and gave a short bow.

Adeone assessed the situation. He sighed. "Arkyn, are you wearing the Comptroller out again?"

"Not intentionally, sir. Hill Beck Farm, is having a hard year. We're trying to work out how to help, but it can wait."

"Good. I've brought *you* some help, by the way. Edward, come on in. Edward has agreed to take on the arduous task of being your administrator. I hope that you can both cope with the idea."

Arkyn nodded. "Of course, father. Welcome to Ceardlann, Edward."

"Thank you, Your Highness," replied his new administrator self-consciously.

The Comptroller took advantage of a pause. "Well, Sire, Your Highness, if you'll excuse us, I'll go and introduce Edward to Kadeem and show him his room."

As they left, Tain tore into the office. Nearly bowled over as his son careered into him, Adeone gave him a much-needed hug. They perched in the Comptroller's office talking for six minutes before Adeone persuaded Tain to spend time annoying his nearfather.

Once they'd gone, Adeone asked, "What's the problem with the farm?"

"The farmer caught a chill and died," explained Arkyn. "His son is only twelve. Too young to manage the farm on his own but it seems unfair for the sake of a couple of seasons to remove it from the family. There aren't any cousins to help. There's an uncle to the boy in Oedran, but he's settled, from what I can gather. They don't want to disturb his work there."

Adeone groaned. "I've been blind, or just dumb. The 'uncle' who's in Oedran, it's Sergeant Hillbeck, I'd bet my life on it. He requested a couple of day's leave to attend his brother's funeral not long ago. I remember the widow from years ago. I used to get on her nerves. Have you asked her what they want? It's pretty pointless going over all this if they'd rather not keep the farm. We could take a ride this afternoon?"

Arkyn smiled. "I'd enjoy that, father."

"Good. We'll leave Tain and Landis here as we'll be conducting business."

"I'm sure Uncle Festus will appreciate the thought."

Adeone snorted. "He'll cope."

* * *

Two hours later, Adeone and Arkyn rode into the farmyard. Dismounting, they handed the horses' bridles to the guards, and Adeone led the way to the kitchen door. A lady answered their knock with a cheery yell of 'Come in'.

Adeone stepped into the kitchen, saying, "How are you, Susan?"

The fresh-faced lady whipped around and curtsied. "Erm... startled, Sire; though I don't know why; you do turn up in unexpected places."

"Less often than I did. Have you met my eldest before?"

"Once. Come on in, Your Highness, and sit yourself down. You too, Sire."

As he sat, Adeone's eyes met the room's final occupant. "So, this is where you hide on your days off, Hillbeck."

The sergeant grinned slightly. "Apparently, Sire. I came to give a hand."

Adeone wasn't surprised. "Yes, Prince Arkyn has been explaining the situation to me. I came to see what you wanted, Susan. If you want to keep the farm, I'm sure something could be arranged, but if you don't, we won't abandon you."

Disconcerted, Susan said, "I'm not sure, sir. My son's been rather quiet since his father died. It should be his decision. It's his inheritance after all. Help yourself to biscuits; the kettle is on."

"You always did do me proud, Susan."

"Boys need feeding up. Some more than others."

"Su!" exclaimed Hillbeck, shocked.

Laughing, Adeone caught Susan's eye. "Relax, Sergeant. Your wed-sister used to deal with me when I was Prince Tain's age. Susan, I know you never wanted to go to Oedran but—"

"I still don't but my son has a hankering to see the city, thanks to his uncle putting ideas in his head."

Feeling mischievous, Adeone said, "Hillbeck has a lot to answer for."

"So I've heard, Sire. Saving your life just isn't on, is it?"

Arkyn was sitting and listening in mounting perplexity that his father was allowing Susan to speak to him in such a way.

Adeone caught the expression on his son's face and winked at him as he replied, "No, it's dreadful; however, I am grateful. Now, come on, Susan,

209

be serious. Could you return to Ceardlann?"

Susan pouring boiling water into a teapot chewed at her lip. She replaced the kettle and sat down thoughtfully.

"I don't know, Sire, and that is the truth. I'm not sure I could return to my former position. My son wouldn't fit there either. He's too lively, for the Comptroller's sensibilities." Adeone went to say something but Susan was continuing, "The problem is, we *can't* manage the farm on our own and, much as I appreciate my wed-brother's help, he can't always be here."

Adeone sighed. "No, he can't. Your off-duty time, though, Hillbeck, is your own so I shouldn't be commenting. Have you any ideas, Sergeant?"

"Only one, sir. I have the lad to live with me in Oedran and see if the Herald has a spot for him. He's a hard worker, trustworthy, normally full of energy. You could do worse."

Adeone turned to Susan. "What do you say to that idea?"

"I… Letting him go will be hard but he needs to spread his wings a bit. That just leaves me. I'll muddle along somehow."

Adeone caught her eye. "When I offered you a post at Ceardlann; it wasn't your previous one. I was thinking of a supervisory post – such as *housekeeper*. You've always been the sort of woman who can see what needs doing and doesn't scrimp when it comes to getting it done. You shouldn't be wasted out here… Come and supervise the young maids there – the Comptroller will welcome not having to. Come and tease Cook, make me a spiced pudding or two—"

Susan swallowed. "I… Will the Comptroller have me back?"

"Of course. Come on, Susan, you've either got to keep the farm going or move away. I don't like the thought of you and your son being split but this way—"

The door opened and a lad around twelve summers entered looking drained. He hardly noticed anyone else, walking straight through the kitchen and through the opposite door.

Susan watched him sadly. "Will you excuse me, Sire?"

Once she'd gone, Adeone wrapped his hands around his mug of tea. "How are they really, Hillbeck? And tell me the truth."

Hillbeck considered for a moment. "They're exhausted, Sire. Radley's illness had already taken it out of Su. Coping with the farm as well has made it more difficult. It might be better to decide for them. Not pleasant, but Su will work herself into the ground for Caswal, and he for her."

"I was getting that impression. She did a lot for me when my mother passed on. I'd like to make sure she's all right."

"I never realised how well she knows you, sir."

"It's been a few years since I've seen her. Oh, and you've not heard this very unconventional meeting."

"Of course I haven't, sir. This is the valley, not real life. If you'll excuse me, Sire. I really ought to go and carry on. I'm on duty at six."

"Of course. I'm leaving Ceardlann at seven. Contact Oedran and return with me. It should give you a couple of hours more with your family."

"Thank you, Sire. It's much appreciated." He saluted and left the kitchen thinking he'd seen another unknown side of the King.

Adeone and Arkyn sat talking over their tea for some time. Just when they were beginning to wonder where Susan was the door opened and she entered the kitchen obviously troubled.

"I'm sorry to have kept you, sir."

Adeone shook his head slightly. "Don't be. What did Caswal say?"

"He doesn't know. He feels like he's abandoning his father if we move away from here, but he can't cope…" She slumped onto the bench.

Adeone moved around the table and, sitting with his back against it, put a hand on her shoulder and squeezed it in sympathy. He waited for a moment before saying, "I can't let you continue like this, Susan. I'm taking the decision out of your hands. We'll find someone else to take on the farm. You're coming to Ceardlann to start with and then, when Caswal's feeling stronger, if he wants to, he can go and live with his uncle and we'll find him a job at the Palace. Prince Arkyn will see that whoever takes over here does so on the understanding that if your son wishes to return when he's older, he can. I'm sure some younger sons of the valley would like the chance to flex their wings. Will you agree to all that?"

Trying to regain composure, Susan said, "We can hardly refuse if *the King* orders it."

Adeone squeezed her shoulder again. "I have my uses, so I'm told. You know you shocked your wed-brother, don't you?"

She glanced sideways at him. "I shock myself too. Why do you put up with me, sir?"

"I don't forget the year my mother died. You, the Comptroller, Laioril and Judge Tancred all pulled me through that time. I *don't* forget, Susan." Adeone rose. "We'd better get back to Ceardlann before they send out search parties."

Susan rose. "Thank you for everything, Sire. I feel as though a weight has been lifted from me."

He gave her a warm hug. "Look after yourself until Prince Arkyn or the Comptroller have humoured me and worked out the small details."

Two weeks later, the Hillbeck family were once more settled, Susan at Ceardlann and her son working as a runner in Oedran.

# Chapter 47

# BAYAN AND BANDITS

Alunadai, Week 16 – 22nd Macial, 1st Easis 1210

Garth

JONES CONSIDERED Lord Scanlon's visit to Bayan as an opportunity. Protecting the King's acknowledged cousin from the King's murderous brother couldn't be too difficult, could it? Lord Scanlon wouldn't be in Garth for long, though his retinue suggested otherwise: a hundred guards, ten lawyers, three advisors, a manservant, four footmen, two houseboys, his administrator, six scribes and various grooms, draymen, coach drivers and miscellaneous persons that seemed to carry a lot of muscle and nothing else. Keeping an eye on all of them was going to be difficult, Jones had to admit *that*.

He went to see the Commander of Bayan – a much more reasonable man than Captain Sharparu – and had three units seconded to him. Their captain wasn't overjoyed but Jones didn't see it as his job to placate his peers. The men weren't bothered; it saved them having to be involved with making the city look nice for the Justiciar. Jones wouldn't have believed how much trouble the provinces went to if he hadn't witnessed it. The city was sparkling. The main streets to the Citadel had been swept and would continue to be throughout Lord Scanlon's visit. Windows were washed, the Citadel was inspected, and any repairs made, the rooms decorated where necessary, new furniture commissioned and old refinished. Garth would gleam by the time Scanlon entered where the Great Gates had hung before the Bayan Rebellion.

The Exarch briefed Jones on what was expected. Lord Scanlon still maintained the accoutrements of a prince and expected the same level of respect and service. Jones was to ensure the Exarch's safety but officially Lord Scanlon's came first. His guards took priority. Jones was also to be careful of Scanlon's entourage. There were men in it who wouldn't think twice about cutting his throat. If the captain discovered anything about the dealings of Scanlon's men, unless it threatened the lives of the King's family in Garth, or was treason, he wasn't to interfere. He was to send the information to Oedran. It was an open secret that Lord Scanlon's men were more than domestic servants. Some were there to make sure that Lord Scanlon was satisfied by whatever means possible. Jones was intrigued the Exarch would permit that.

"Sometimes, in power, you must wait before striking, Jones. If a snake strikes at a rolling rock, it may not strike at a predator later, for its teeth are broken. We bide our time. His facilitators are a nuisance, but if they're caught, we don't have to deal with them for long. They die in mysterious circumstances, and Lord Scanlon finds others in the courts. He leads a privileged existence in the full meaning of the word. As the King's brother, His Lordship has the right for us not to question his methods. He is careful never to break the law himself."

"Your Excellency, I do know of his actions—"

"No, you don't, Jones! You know of rumour and speculation. Whilst His Lordship is here, you don't even know that. Am I making myself plain?"

"Yes, Your Excellency."

"Good, because you'll be in our company a lot and you can't show you know anything. His Lordship isn't renowned for sitting for hours on the courts when he does a law review. He waits for his lawyers and advisors to compile the reports before adding his thoughts. During that period of compilation, I'll be riding with him, dining with him, and keeping him occupied. The public will see an affable young man, you'll probably witness a different side. I will be at his beck and call, allowing others to get on with their jobs. You will be at my side. My grandmother may decide to visit, or she may not. If she does, your priority will be her safety. She is much more valuable to peace in the empire than I am."

"It will be an honour to guard Princess Lilith, Your Excellency."

Tyler Galwood didn't detect any sarcasm. "Thank you. She is a pivotal reason why we kept so many freedoms after the 1169 rebellion and she was instrumental in maintaining peace, with my grandfather, following it. I won't let that peace shatter now. I've enough trouble with the bandits on the ridge."

"They're being rooted out, Your Excellency," said Jones. "We've captured some."

"Yes, but they were found on Heritor Fullerton's land. He died recently and his son was unable to secure the estate or deal with the formalities due to illness. Not that he'll be titled heritor, but it was still his family's land and he was still culpable for bandits on it. His trial's next week. He's already lost his land. It's a mess. It's within the Anaparian Marches as well."

Jones didn't need to be told what that meant: strategic importance along a once disputed border. Instead, he waited until the Exarch dismissed him before returning to the fort and putting his new units through some tougher training, constantly watching them to find men he could trust.

* * *

Two days later, Adeone closed the messenger link with the Exarch and swore roundly. Two of the bandits had escaped, their guards likely bribed by Scanlon's men. The reasons for Scanlon being behind malcontents weren't clear, but they obviously had some worth to him.

213

The King had the regiment posted elsewhere and replaced with one that he was certain his brother hadn't infiltrated. Other regiments in the area redoubled their efforts but to little effect. The bandits had disappeared. It later transpired they'd moved north and onto the Anaparian side of the ridge, closer to the city of Paras. Adeone simply gave orders they were to be eliminated as quickly as possible – amongst other things he had Merchant Chapa constantly pointing out the disadvantages of having bandits operating in the empire's first province. Half teasingly, after the tenth rendition of the lecture, Adeone had enquired when his cousin planned to retire. All Merchant Chapa replied was that the King might find out one day. Adeone had merely laughed; both of them knew that the question was a jest. Merchant Chapa would never be pushed out for simply telling the truth.

# Chapter 48
## GLIMPSING HOPE
Hexadai, Week 20 – 27th Meithal, 13th Meithis 1210
Palace – Prince Arkyn's Office

FOUR WEEKS LATER, Arkyn rode into Oedran, unsure if he was glad that his duties required him to visit more frequently. He had to be visible, seen, build his reputation but not slip up. His uncle would use any chance to undermine him. His visits were irregular, helping to protect him. If no-one knew when or for how long he would be in the city, attacks were harder to plan.

When he'd taken over his formal chambers, he'd felt strange. Memories ambushed him in every room. Used by the eldest prince for centuries, his father had occupied them before his accession. He remembered running around them as a young child, his mother chasing him. Now, though, with his own items strewn around or arranged neatly, they were losing the tugs on his heart. His bedchamber, bathroom, dressing room, small library, triniculum and servants' areas were Kadeem's domain. The inner and outer office with archive space was Edward's.

Almost as soon as they'd arrived, Edward had to deal with a close colleague from his time as a courier.

Craig Ganon entered Edward's office with a scroll from Richardson. "How're you finding your new job then, *Administrator* Edward?"

"It's busy and rewarding. Why the questions, Craig?"

"It doesn't matter."

"Obviously it does." Edward broke the seal, read the top line, flicked open a diary and made a note before furling the scroll and grinning at Craig. "There's no reply. So, why are you so curious?"

"You seem so much more at home here. Like you've finally found where you're meant to be. I wish I could. Everyone's been wondering how you're getting on. Even a couple of strangers have asked if we've heard anything."

Edward stilled. "Really? What are they asking?"

Craig shrugged. "Just whether you're settled, I suppose. A man asked me the other day. I said I thought you were enjoying it. Seemed quite curious, one way or another. Not surprising really."

"Have you told anyone else this?"

"Didn't see the point. There's lots of curiosity."

"Who was the man who approached you?" enquired Edward.

"Not sure. I vaguely recognised him. He might well work here but it's no-one who uses the couriers. I suppose you could call him stocky. Sounded a bit like he was from outside of Oedran. Not too sure really. The same nosy gossip as most, I suspect."

"Yes, just be careful what you say about me... please. I don't want to be the subject of gossip. The speculation should have stopped. I've got a new job, that's all."

"I know. I try to shut them up. Tell you the truth, I think some of them are jealous that you've succeeded in becoming an administrator. Orphan Edward bettered them – if you know what I mean."

"Yes. Some days I pinch myself to see if I'm awake," admitted Edward.

"Not surprising when you consider where you were this time last year."

"You're the first person in a while who's even treated me normally."

Craig smiled. "You're still you. I suppose I ought to let you get on."

"If you must. Actually, can you wait whilst I write a note to one of the captains at the barracks and run over with it?"

"No skin off my nose."

As he wrote the note, Edward wasn't so sure. He handed it over. "Just one thing, be truthful and, believe me, I have good reasons. You need to see Captain Wynfeld. Password is 'fey'."

Once Craig had gone, Edward tried to forget that he'd asked Wynfeld to interrogate a person as close to a friend as he'd ever had.

* * *

Wynfeld read the note, told Craig to sit down and sent for Beaver and a clerk. Then, seemingly to pass the time, Wynfeld said, "So how long have you known our Prince's administrator?"

"We started working at the Palace on the same day, Captain," replied Craig, wondering why he hadn't been dismissed.

"What's he like?"

"I get on with him. He's always been hardworking and, although quite serious, is up for some fun."

"It must be strange for you?"

"I suppose it is a bit, Captain."

Wynfeld asked, "Do you see much of him anymore?"

Craig got the feeling Wynfeld was testing him. "Not at all unless our paths cross professionally, as might be expected, sir."

As the door opened, Wynfeld smiled. "I'm impressed, Craig. Most wouldn't have noticed anything amiss in my questions. Ah, Beaver, meet Craig Ganon – a courier and former colleague of Administrator Edward."

Beaver glanced at Craig, who simply wanted to get out of the office, finally understanding Edward's enigmatic comments.

Seeing the uncertainty forming, Beaver said, "Don't worry, Ganon, I'm sure there's an explanation somewhere for why you're currently seated in here. Captain?"

Wynfeld replied gravely, "There is. Our stocky friend has been asking him questions about our Prince's administrator."

Beaver stilled. "Ah. We've not heard from him in a while, sir. He must be getting lonely after his cousin was killed."

"Why am I here?" blurted out Craig.

"Because you've been approached by someone we know attempts to coerce officials."

"You mean a traitor, sir?"

Beaver said, "That's exactly what we mean, Craig. How much do you remember of the man who approached you?"

Craig told them what he'd told Edward.

"You're a good witness. Would you recognise our stocky friend again?" asked Wynfeld.

"Yes, sir. I'm good with faces. It's just matching them to names I have problems with."

"Ever thought of joining the army?" enquired Beaver. "Names and faces don't matter so much when they're at the end of a sword."

Wynfeld said, "Leave the lad alone, Beaver. He's got more information for us yet, I'll warrant."

Craig looked fearfully at Wynfeld. "I've told you all I know, Captain."

"About that individual, yes. Have any of the other couriers been approached?"

"I don't know, sir. I expect so. The Herald might know."

Beaver muttered, "Or maybe he's going round in a daze as usual."

Wynfeld frowned at him, "Sergeant, don't talk disparagingly of the

King's appointees. I might get paranoid. We'll have to talk to the Herald. There is one other thing, Craig… When we were talking, before Beaver arrived, you had already given me quite a lot of information without knowing it. Through the information that you gave, I could find out things about Edward whilst enquiring about you. A traitor might even harm you to get to Edward. You *were* quicker than most at shutting me out, but you must be careful. If anyone asks you if you know anything of Edward again, say that you've 'lost touch', or words to that effect. Finally, don't blame Edward for this interrogation. He had to inform us… Beaver here might well be in contact again. That's all. You can escape now." Once Craig had left with a word of thanks, Wynfeld turned to the clerk who had been silent and unnoticed through the whole thing. "Could you make that up into a file and attach it to the others? Also, make a file for our friend Craig. I might well use his eyes again."

Once they were alone, Beaver said, "One more for the books, sir. He's a good witness. Do you think it was Gad who approached him?"

"Yes. It's interesting he's been inside the Palace again. Craig vaguely recognised him, which means he might be there regularly. Though that might have been from last year, I suppose. At least he hasn't been in contact with the head gardener, that we do know and Hillbeck hasn't seen him."

"Will you inform the King, sir?" asked Beaver.

"Yes. I must. Gad isn't quite as inactive as we supposed. I wonder what's driving him now."

"Probably a desire to see his cousin avenged; he didn't die well."

"Most likely. Thank you, Beaver."

* * *

Wynfeld made his way over to the Palace to inform Adeone, who accepted assurances that the matter was under investigation. Once he left his King's office, he made his way to Prince Arkyn's.

Wynfeld smiled. "Making yourself at home, I see, Administrator."

Edward hesitated. "I'm sorry, Captain, I thought it might be better if you knew—"

"Oh, I'm not rebuking you, far from it. I needed to know everything that Craig could tell me. He's going to keep an eye out and I've told him to say that you've lost touch if anyone approaches him again. If he comes for a natter make sure he has a scroll to make it believable. Is His Highness free for a word?"

Once the door had closed behind his administrator, Prince Arkyn said, "What can I do for you, Captain?"

The last year had changed his Prince dramatically. He still had a fresh-faced appearance, but the worry lines had gone and there was a more definite edge of authority forming. The child had all but disappeared.

Answering the question he said, "Nothing too calamitous, Your Highness. I thought I ought to inform you we're investigating a situation after Edward told us the couriers are being approached concerning him. We're not sure it's general curiosity. We'll keep an eye on him and make sure he's safe."

"Thank you. Was there anything else?"

Two minutes later, Wynfeld once more saluted and left. He winked at Edward and the administrator felt better about any perceived betrayal of friendship.

* * *

Arkyn detested walking into Court alone, the feeling of being evaluated was always worse until he was talking to someone. That evening, as the presiding lord, Landis greeted his nearson formally and they spent several minutes talking before Arkyn spotted Lord Irvin Iris and excused himself.

He and Irvin found an unobtrusive spot and stood talking about their common interest in history. Soon people's gaze turned elsewhere and Arkyn relaxed. A short time later, his skin tingled. Someone was watching him. He glanced around, but everyone was engrossed in their conversations. No-one was standing alone, no-one was gazing around the room, no-one was staring fixedly at anything, let alone him. There were distinct groups of people and nobody was looking in his direction. He rubbed the back of his neck, shivering. He glanced up at the dome. A roof garden surrounded it, but no-one was watching him from there either.

"Is there anything I can help with, sir?" asked Irvin.

Arkyn shook his head. "No, thank you, my lord. I was distracted for a moment. You were saying…"

Six minutes later, Arkyn still felt jittery. "Shall we take a walk, my lord? I should spend time in the other rooms."

"Of course, sir. My apologies for monopolising Your Highness."

"I'll cope," replied Arkyn dryly.

They walked through several rooms before settling in the Terasian Room, with its stormy murals and snug atmosphere. There weren't many people and Arkyn watched the merchants with interest. Where the lords vied for attention or arrogantly presumed they didn't need it, the merchants talked business or family. Merchant Chapa bowed slightly when Arkyn entered and after a few moments excused himself to his companions and made his way over to the Prince.

"Your Highness, I hope you don't mind an interruption."

Arkyn's lips twitched. "Are you going to tell me anything I won't want to hear, Merchant Chapa?"

"Not at all, sir. At least, I hope not."

"Then join us. I expect you know Lord Irvin Iris already."

Merchant Chapa nodded. "Aye, sir. Nice to see you, Lord Irvin. My regards to your grandfather."

Arkyn murmured, "So any reason for disturbing me, Cousin Henry?"

"Just to keep everyone else guessing mostly, Your Highness. Though I would be honoured if you'd come to dinner one evening…"

A few minutes later, Merchant Chapa left with a wink. Watching him join his merchant friends, Arkyn rubbed at his neck again. He scanned the room; no-one was looking in his direction.

Half an hour later, he and Irvin had walked through Court again, spent time in the Lufian Room and Macian Room, but the feeling of being observed was insidious and seeped into Arkyn's bones. The hairs on the back of his neck and arms stood on end. It got to the point where he felt almost panicky. He half wished his father was present. They were back in the FitzAlcis Chamber glad for once that it was busy when a voice made him jump.

"Your Highness."

Arkyn turned. "Lord Landis, how may I help?"

Landis glanced at Irvin, who tactfully moved off. "I was wondering about the supper, Your Highness…" As people turned away, he added quietly, "What's concerning you, sir?"

"It's nothing, my lord."

He murmured, "I shouldn't be saying this, especially not at Court, but you seem highly unsettled."

Arkyn commented wryly, "Since when has saying something that you're not supposed to bothered you, Lord Landis?"

"Habits can be broken, sir, as much as traditions may be changed… Shall we find somewhere more private, sir?"

"If you think it would be a wise idea, my lord," replied Arkyn.

Two minutes later, they were both seated in a small room containing three couches arranged around a fireplace, a sideboard holding jugs and goblets and a server to see they had everything they needed.

Landis waved the server out. Once alone, he said, "Would you like to tell me what's bothering Your Highness?"

Arkyn held his gaze. "What would you say if I thought I'm being watched at Court when no-one is looking my way?"

"Honestly, sir, I'd say '*Sicla!*' Closely followed by '*Not again!*' My next question would be, do you think that there is a substantial watcher? That is, do you think it is a person in the room?"

"Who else would it be? And what do you mean by '*not again*'?"

Landis said, "I was being followed by a scryer before I was attacked, sir, but I thought we'd dealt with them. I had the feeling I was being watched for weeks. It was like an itch in my mind."

"That's meant to reassure me, I suppose," observed Arkyn dryly. "I'd say it's by someone in the room watching me intently. When I move rooms, it takes a few minutes for the feeling to reappear. Almost as though the watcher must find their way there."

"Right, sir, I'm not going to tell you it's all in your head because that would be both annoying and insulting, and probably incorrect. What I will do, if you'll permit me, is to stay within the same room as Your Highness for the rest of the evening. I'll keep an eye out."

"Thank you, Uncle Festus. Father will think I'm a fool."

"Do we tell him?" asked Landis.

Surprised, Arkyn said, "I'd have thought you would have done."

"Prince Arkyn, you're now fifteen; if you request that I don't tell your father then that is an order I must follow. Anyway, everyone has secrets sooner or later. What's a nearfather good for if I can't keep the odd one or two for my nearson?"

Arkyn grinned. "Thank you. Maybe it would be better not to worry him."

"He'll never stop worrying about you, you know; it's part of being a father. So, let's concern him in other ways; how about I set you up with a couple of dancing partners for later this evening, Your Highness?"

"You do, Uncle Festus, and I might inform Lady Amara that you're missing her company."

"Your Highness has certainly mastered the lesson for just rewards."

Arkyn merely smiled as he walked into the public Court rooms. "I'm so pleased that we understand each other, Lord Landis. That's all."

Landis laughed. "Of course, sir."

Arkyn made his way through the Court talking to different people but never staying still for long at a time. Keeping moving kept his feeling of paranoia mostly at bay. Landis shadowed Arkyn discreetly and also had the strange sensation that there were more people in the smaller rooms than could be counted, similar to a scryer being present but also different. He spent some time glancing out the corners of his eyes and once, with his blood running cold, he thought he glimpsed someone who wasn't there.

# Chapter 49
# SHARING THE LOAD

Septadai, Week 20 – 28th Meithal, 14th Meithis 1210
Wynfeld's Office

THE FOLLOWING DAY, Captain Wynfeld found Lord Landis sitting in his office waiting patiently for him, but there was a tensing of the muscles and a stillness Wynfeld had come to associate with a cat stalking its prey.

Sitting down, he said, "Good morning, my lord."

"Morning, Wynfeld. Interesting report yesterday. Is there any more news about our stocky friend?"

"We've been investigating but without success, my lord." In his head, Wynfeld muttered, *'Give us a day at least!'*

Guessing what Wynfeld was thinking, Landis tried to mollify the situation. "I'm not criticising you, Captain. I am about to hand you some useful information. Tell me how much you know of the Ullian Legacy."

"Not much, sir: never had much time for stories as a child. Work got in the way."

Landis raised an eyebrow. "Then I suggest you start reading now, Captain. Ullian Spirits are pure forms of magic – the purest that exist on Erinna. They are complete skills, but they are scarce. Each spirit has hues, lesser forms of a particular skill: you know and have dealt with scryers; they are a hue of a seer and are quite numerous. The point, however, is that each spirit has different hues; you do know that much?"

"Yes, my lord," replied Wynfeld, thinking, *'I'm not stupid!'*

"Good. Those who possessed hues were always more numerous than those with spirits, for what reason even Laioril doesn't know – trust me, that's rare. Anyway, one of the spirits was that of an espien – from which we get our word 'spy'. They could vanish from people's sight: simply fade into the background. Only another espien would be able to see them. A corresponding hue was a 'vigilant'. These had nowhere near as many facets to their skill as the true espien but one thing they could do was fade out of sight. Well, that is almost true. They couldn't be truly unseen, that is part of the spirit of the espien. They could be unnoticed. They would be unseen if you looked at them directly, face on, but they couldn't hide from your peripheral vision. They couldn't become invisible, like the espien, but, unlike the espien, they can still be sensed by normal people. That is, you might feel them watching you."

Wynfeld said, "Have I got this right, my lord? You are trying to suggest that Gad possesses either the hue of a vigilant or the spirit of an espien?"

Landis smiled grimly. "Much as my confidence in you has increased,

221

Captain, I wouldn't be here treating you to a lecture if I had only suspicions. You have to believe me. There is little doubt left in my mind as to the fact we are dealing with a person of Ullian predisposition. The information came my way by chance last night – a feeling of paranoia and a figure in my peripheral vision. As I can see him from the corner of my eye, it tells us we're dealing with a vigilant rather than an espien."

"I may regret asking this question, sir, but where were you when you had this feeling?" enquired Wynfeld. *'Sicla! You really are serious, aren't you? Now I'm worried as well.'*

Landis conveniently forgot to mention it wasn't he who had had the feeling. "I was at Court when all this occurred. The feeling, or gentleman, if you will, followed me through several rooms, always just out of reach."

"At Court! Why is it always where you can't do anything without the world knowing that these things occur?"

Landis smirked. "Because, where would be the challenge in that, Wynfeld? There is another advantage with all this: we know our man is still in Oedran. Admittedly, last being seen in the Palace or at Court is slightly problematic. Even I, as a Defender, can't keep the King away from Court forever, nor Prince Arkyn now, of course, but we can get more people watching for Gad. He can't hide in the shadows forever."

"He's certainly doing a good enough job of it at the moment, my lord!"

"He'll slip up, one of these days, Captain. Now, I must leave you."

Landis left, a grave expression on his face, matched only by Wynfeld's in the room behind him.

* * *

Landis made his way to the Palace thinking hard. Gad had to show himself for long enough to be seized. He wouldn't be able to fade if someone had hold of him. Landis made his way through the Palace, trying to devise a plan that wouldn't involve danger for anyone but guards. He ambled into the King's Chambers still thoughtful and six minutes later was sitting in a meeting with Adeone and others. He remained focused for nearly all of the meeting but as the King was concluding, without consciously realising, he returned to pondering on the problem of the vigilant. As Adeone rose, to signal the meeting's end, it took Landis a couple of seconds to realise. He hurriedly got to his feet, and the King held his gaze. That glance kept Landis behind as everyone else left.

"What's got you thinking?" enquired Adeone once they were alone.

"It's nothing, Your Majesty."

Adeone sat behind his desk. "Stop prevaricating. Last time you were this preoccupied I disregarded it. I named you Representative and then Adson attacked you. Don't expect me to make the same mistake again!

222

What's concerning you?"

"It is a personal matter, sir," replied Landis.

"Right, stop lying, Lord Landis. You've never let personal matters interfere in meetings. Why should today be any different? I want to know what is concerning you."

Landis tensed. "Your Majesty, I cannot tell you because I don't know completely myself."

"Not good enough, Landis. You could tell me what you do know."

Cornered, he started to say, "If I did that, I'd be breaking faith with…" He trailed off. If he even said his name, he'd have broken Arkyn's faith.

Adeone snapped, "You might remember that if you don't answer me, Landis, you're breaking my faith also! Somehow that might be the more important."

Equally annoyed by Adeone ordering him to break a confidence, Landis demanded, "Yet I must break faith with someone neither of us would ever want to?" In a resolute voice that was meant to end the discussion, he said, "The situation is being taken care of, sir." Before Adeone could reply, Landis bowed and opened the door.

"I never gave you leave to go, Landis."

Landis paused momentarily before continuing. He got as far as the door to the Audience Chamber before he felt a hand on his arm.

Richardson whispered, "My lord, it would be better if you went back to the King. If you don't *today*, I'm not sure your friendship will survive it."

Furious, Landis said, "How dare you presume, Richardson!"

"Because today was Queen Ira's birthday, my lord; the King doesn't forget Her Grace and he's tearing himself apart at the moment."

With gritted teeth, Landis turned back. "You just *had* to remind me!"

The administrator moved aside. "I didn't know what else to do, sir."

Landis glared at him before re-entering the Inner Office. Adeone eyes burned through him and, now he had let go of his preoccupation, Landis saw the pain in them. He let the door close and then, as tradition dictated he should, he knelt.

"Pass me your King's Token!" commanded the King.

Richardson had been right. If he'd walked away, he'd never have walked back. He located the token and, still kneeling, passed it to Adeone, who had moved round to collect it.

Adeone put it on his desk. "Must I ask you *again* what concerns you?"

Landis tried to refuse one last time. "I beg you, don't make me—"

"Don't demean yourself; you never beg," spat Adeone. "I need to know and if it will help salve your conscience, you will have no choice but to tell me. Pass me your hands."

For the first time, Landis shrank from the power in Adeone's face. Compelled to do so, he raised his hands, palms upward, fearing what the King was about to do. Adeone placed his hands palm down on top.

"In truth, Lord Landis, what concerns you so deeply?"

The words left Landis' lips without freewill. "In truth, my liege, Prince Arkyn is being followed by a vigilant; whom we believe is Gad."

Shocked, Adeone nearly broke the contact but he had to know one more thing. "In truth, why didn't you just tell me?"

"In truth, my liege, because I told Prince Arkyn I would not."

Adeone felt sick. He nearly said *'Forget I asked'* to wipe the memory from Landis' mind, but he couldn't do it, couldn't add insult to injury. He lifted his hands, turned, picked up the token, placed it back in Landis' hands and, shaking, left for his private quarters.

Once the door closed, Landis swore roundly. Not because he'd been forced to tell Adeone but because of the way his friend had looked when he'd realised he'd made Landis break Arkyn's confidence. Landis stood in the office for a moment before thinking that convention didn't have a place at such a time.

Entering the sitting room, he crossed to the sideboard, pouring his friend a whiskey.

Even as he took it, Adeone said, "Thank you but just leave me alone."

"Not a chance of that."

"Leave me, Landis!" ordered Adeone.

"I'm not going anywhere. Rant and rave at me as much as you want to. Just do what you need to but don't expect me to walk away when you're obviously in need of support. That's not what a friend is. Especially when I'm the reason you're in this mood."

Adeone continued staring at nothing. "Why are you pushing me today?"

"Because I'm a bloody fool! What else do you expect?"

"You certainly are." Adeone shrank down, and Landis knew that he was relaxing for the first time that day. "I'm—"

"You don't need to apologise. I was being mulish."

Adeone finally turned to him. "No, I was being too… autocratic. I should have realised that you— Alcis, there are times I hate myself. Festus, let me just say this… I'm sorry."

"Thank you, Adeone – so am I. Now, are you going to hide in here for the rest of the day?"

The King downed his drink. "No. I'm going to spread my stress around. What's more, you're going to help – if only to stop me going too far again."

"Very well, Sire," replied Landis carefully.

"You don't want to be there, do you?"

"I'd rather Prince Arkyn didn't know I betrayed his confidence, sir."

"You didn't. There is no choice when I ask you as I did. I forced it from you. He'll… understand."

"I only hope you're right, sir, because I feel as though I've let him down."

Adeone said, "I've been letting him down ever since Ira died."

Landis shook his head. "You know that's not true. You've never let the boys down. Trust me on that."

Adeone looked at his friend with unspoken thanks. Landis saw some of the guilt and pain leaving the familiar features, and he was glad of it. Adeone felt things deeply; over the years, he'd learned to deal with such feelings, but Ira's death had knocked down the walls he'd built in his mind and it was taking a long time to sift through the rubble to rebuild them.

* * *

Once in the Inner Office, Adeone summoned Richardson and asked to speak to Arkyn, Edward, Paturn, Wynfeld and Pixney. Twelve minutes later, a very puzzled Arkyn and Edward were admitted.

"Prince Arkyn, you're returning to the Rex Dallin as soon as possible. Edward, please go and arrange that. Anything His Highness was meant to be doing, see Richardson knows about it and I'll send his apologies."

As Edward left, Arkyn eyed his father and nearfather uncertainly. Once the door closed, he asked why.

Hating himself, Adeone said, "Because I say so, Arkyn. For the moment, please just accept that I need you safe."

"This hasn't anything to do with last night, has it, Lord Landis?" enquired Arkyn accusingly.

Adeone cut in. "Your nearfather held out until I forced a fealty reading."

Arkyn read the truth in Landis' face. "I'm sorry, Uncle Festus. I still think, though, that I—"

"You can think what you want, Arkyn, as long as you are in the Rex Dallin," retorted his father. "I'm not having you threatened like this."

"It was paranoia, father. Nothing more—"

Landis broke in, "I'm afraid it was a bit more than that, sir."

Arkyn whipped around. "There was no-one there, Uncle Festus. It was just me being stupid. You *know* that!"

"It wasn't, Your Highness. Honestly, it wasn't paranoia. There was a vigilant in the Court. I glimpsed him from the corner of my eye."

Arkyn turned back to his father. "Then I can help catch them, father. They're obviously interested in me."

"You're *not* bait and I'm not having a discussion," snapped Adeone. "You're leaving for the Rex Dallin. No argument."

Arkyn's face set. "What do I tell the Comptroller, Tain and Elantha?"

"You can tell the Comptroller the truth. As for your brother and cousin, tell them that you became bored. Arkyn, enough! You're leaving for the Rex Dallin. I'm sorry but—"

"Mother would never have let you do this!"

Adeone's face twitched.

Landis broke in. "Your Highness, your mother would only ever have wanted your safety as your father does. She loved you deeply and would never have wanted you in danger. This decision isn't easy for your father, but he's trying to ensure you're safe. Your mother would have understood."

Gripping the edge of his desk, Adeone pleaded, "Don't make this harder for me. I don't want you in the Rex Dallin. I wish you could always be here, but you've got to at least accept that I'm trying to protect you in the best way I can. She'd want that."

Arkyn said, grudgingly, "I know, but I'm old enough to make my own choices."

"I never doubt that, my son, and your choices will always be sensible and certainly more apt than mine ever were at your age, but sometimes I must be everything I hate. I have to order you."

Arkyn looked at his father. "I'm sorry, sir."

"Don't be sorry for putting your opinions across, Arkyn. Just come and give your father a hug." Adeone held him in that hug for longer than normal, taking strength and comfort from it. When they broke apart, he tousled his son's hair. Half choked with emotion, he said, "Just remember, that your mother would be proud of you and I am proud of you beyond what I can declare."

"Come to Ceardlann with me."

"I'll think about it, Arkyn. Now, disappear and leave your beleaguered father to drown under responsibility."

The Prince left, knowing what '*I'll think about it*' meant.

Adeone watched the door close. "He puts me to shame sometimes."

"No, sir, he's your son – every inch of him. Will you go to Ceardlann tonight? It might mend a bridge or two."

Adeone sighed. "I know. I'll see how things go with everyone else."

Landis said, "Shall I see if they're here, sir?"

A few moments later, General Paturn, Captain Wynfeld and Captain Pixney had entered and saluted. After a significant glance from the King, Landis moved directly behind him. The very presence of Landis in that position told the others that this meeting concerned the protection of the King.

"Right, I'm not going to trouble to be diplomatic about this," said Adeone. "I want Gad caught and yesterday wasn't soon enough. You've had over a year and I'm *not* happy, gentleman. He's managed to infiltrate the Palace again and has even turned his attention on Prince Arkyn. My life I can accept being under threat but my sons' I will not. You've got a fortnight to show me some improvement in locating him. We know he's in Oedran and we know he's visiting the Palace. Get checking people. My patience is running out! That's all." After the three men had saluted and left, Adeone eyed Landis. "You'd better go and invite yourself into the crisis meeting that Paturn will have just set up. I meant the fortnight deadline. I can't keep Arkyn out of Oedran for long, not anymore."

Landis said, "I know. Is there anything you want me to point out?"

"I want resignations if that man isn't found by the end of the winter. I'm not a tyrant but no-one – wanted as much as that man is – should be able to hide for this long – vigilant or no."

# Chapter 50
## CRISIS MEETING
### Late Morning
### Barracks – General Paturn's Office

LANDIS RETURNED TO THE BARRACKS in a grim mood. Adeone should never have been put in the position of losing his composure to such a degree.

He didn't blame his friend for the fealty reading or the consequences, but he wanted to make sure there weren't further repercussions. Adeone had been understanding until Arkyn was targeted and that said everything anyone needed to know about the King.

He gave the day's password to the men on the gates, who didn't even bother listening before they'd saluted. His quick eyes missed nothing as he strode through the barracks, acknowledging the salutes of officers and soldiers.

He glanced at the General's corporal-clerk and simply received a nod. The man either considered stopping Landis beyond his remit, or the General expected him, conceivably both.

He entered Paturn's office with the briefest of courtesy knocks. The office itself was large enough to contain the General's work-a-day desk, a simple chair, a set of shelves and a large table for laying out plans, or meeting with his officers. It contained no ornamentation, nothing that stamped General Paturn's personality on it until one realised that the lack of ornamentation was part of Paturn's personality as much as an ornament might reflect someone else's.

The General was poring over a map of Oedran. "Checking up on us,

Defender?"

"It's in all our interests to see that we catch Gad, General. I'm here to remind you of that fact. Also, I want him caught. It's been over a year and the only reason we're not hunting two men is because I killed Adson. Strangely, I have no wish to see the King or Prince Arkyn suffering what I did. So, we *are* going to find this man."

The General straightening up gave a belated salute. "I hope so, sir. You know, I saw something of the old king in King Adeone's manner today."

"You're not the only one, General. Did it concern you?"

"A bit. King Altarius got what he wanted or people paid the price. King Adeone gets what he needs without having to resort to such measures. I wouldn't like to see that change."

"Yes, and we both know there are far worse methods than the King's; however, he's not pleased with the lack of progress. What time did you order the meeting for?"

Paturn never considered how Landis knew about it. "About twelve minutes. Did His Majesty ask you to attend? The rest of them don't have to know, but I'd like to."

"Yes, he did, but I'd have come anyway," said Landis honestly.


Twelve minutes later, they were joined by Wynfeld and Pixney. The Major of Oedran had also been invited and one of Wynfeld's clerks was there to make notes.

Landis deferred to the General for chairing the meeting, even though as King's Defender he could have taken over.

The General said, "No damned excuses, Wynfeld, why haven't you caught Gad before now? You have a decent description. You know his name and where he's from. It's about time you widened your net."

Wynfeld tried to remain calm. "We're doing everything we can, sir. We're just no closer to locating him. I can even tell you what his favourite foods are, but it still doesn't help in finding him."

Landis snorted. "You simply have to make sure you have people talking to every purveyor of his favourite foods until you find the one selling him them."

Wynfeld said, "If only it were that simple, my lord."

"It shouldn't be much harder," remarked Paturn. "You have a thick file on the man already. Surely there are things in there which could be used to entrap him."

"I'm sure there are, sir, but, equally, if we don't know exactly where his haunts are, then we have a problem. He's never returned to the Teran Arms, that much we do know. We have located the prostitute and pimp whom

Hillbeck informed us were there on one occasion and, do what we may, they haven't a clue who the men were. The prostitute admits that she was paid to distract Hillbeck but that's all she knew. On the positive side, she is now working for us. A regular income was enough to buy her loyalty."

The Major said, "I'm pleased that you are increasing the informers on your books Wynfeld, but your work still needs to be improved. The King wants this man caught and we've got to make sure he is. He must be living somewhere. Are we certain that he isn't in touch with the head gardener?"

"As certain as I can be, Major. I've got Blackwood so closely watched he's beginning to be paranoid."

Landis interrupted, "Back off a couple of paces and see if he will lead us to his cousin. He'll be no help to us if he knows he's watched."

"Very good, sir. I'll pull back, but I am not going to leave him unobserved."

The General said, "Pixney, what can be done about the fact that Gad has been noticed at Court?"

"Not much, unless we're alerted when he's there."

"Not good enough," remarked Paturn. "We've just had an ultimatum. Saying there's nothing you can do is obstructive. Have you got the plans of the Palace?"

Pixney unrolled them, saying, "This shows all entrances to the Court and the layout of it. It also shows the servants' routes as well. The guards' positions are shown with crosses and the servers with dots."

"Defender, where was the man when you spotted him?" asked Paturn.

Landis got up and tried to orientate himself. "About here, General. Prince Arkyn was here."

"I'll give our man this much credit," said Paturn. "He can choose his spot. He'd be out of the peripheral vision of all the guards and servers. Most of the Court don't pay attention to what's around them."

Studying the plan, Wynfeld remarked, "Maybe then we ought to think about moving the guards' and servers' positions…"

Pixney shrugged. "I can move the guards' positions only so far and we'd need to consult the Steward to move the servers—"

"As Defender, I can simply tell him to move them, or the King can," chipped in Landis dismissively. "Do we know who all the servers are?"

Pixney replied, "I'm afraid the Steward was being rather protective about the lists of staff in the Palace, my lord. He wouldn't let them out of the building."

Landis frowned. "We'll have to have another meeting in the Palace as well – that is, if we want to sort this out today. If it can wait until tomorrow, I will get the clerks to copy the list. I won't have the Steward obstruct us."

Wynfeld said, "Both might be more useful, my lord."

"Why?" asked the General.

"We can sort out today's problems and then I can go through the lists and predict tomorrow's, sir. I could do with a complete list of the guards as well, Pixney."

Landis crooked an eyebrow. "Are you thinking about being anticipatory and not reactionary, Wynfeld?"

"I'm trying to carry on the traditions that made this city great, my lord, and also stop our King being killed," replied Wynfeld, inwardly enjoying surprising Landis.

"We all are. Let's work out the best placing for everyone so that the corners of the rooms are covered. If we keep the Court secure, we have done something."

General Paturn said, "Aye, Defender, but will we have made any progress in catching the man we're after? I'd say not. And, before you say 'one step at a time', we've been taking things one step at a time for the last year and it's got us nowhere."

"You don't need to remind me of that fact, General," replied Landis. "The problem is you can only take one thing at a time. It's the speed at which we react and therefore cause something else to occur that matters. The King is a tolerant man, but his tolerance is becoming strained and requests for resignations are likely. I'd say the best way forward is to make the Court secure, back off from Blackwood and re-interview all Gad's known acquaintances. See if we can't get a likeness drawn by an artist, and then show it to the runners and couriers; there are no better eyes and ears in the Palace. Wynfeld, get spies in the inns and taverns nearest the Palace radiating outwards. He must be living and sleeping somewhere. Pixney, get your men to search the entire Palace. Make sure that he's not using an unfrequented room – attics, cellars and under-crofts included. Send multiple shifts round to help eliminate mistakes."

The General said, "That's given us all plenty to do. What about you, Defender?"

"I'll make sure the King sees reason for the next fortnight. Just keep me updated."

Wynfeld said, "I'll send you a report as soon as I have enough information, my lord. Shall we look at Captain Pixney's plans and get things started?"

No-one except Pixney thought there were enough guards at Court: for prestige or practical reasons. He pointed out that his men were stretched to the limit already. Landis simply told him to recruit more but Wynfeld's men were to check out the new recruits. He didn't want Gad getting another job at the Palace. They worked out the minimum number of men needed to ensure there was no corner unwatched. The servers they left mostly untouched.

Their positions tended to change depending on courtiers' needs. Landis suggested that the pages and ushers could stand in the corners of the rooms, instead of being near the doors. No vigilant could then utilise them. By the end of the meeting, they were confident the new layout meant that no vigilant could infiltrate the Court in such a way again.

A short time later, Landis and Pixney entered the King's Chambers together. Pixney waited in the Outer Office whilst Landis consulted the King. Two minutes later, Landis returned. Adeone had agreed to their suggestions.

Re-entering the Inner Office, Landis asked, "Are you planning to go to Ceardlann, Sire?"

"You *are* keen to get rid of me, Festus."

"Obviously, sir; however, it might—" started Landis.

"If you say 'do you some good', I'm likely to throw something at you."

"I was going to say it might please the Princes and Lady Elantha."

"All right, I'll go to Ceardlann this evening on one condition; you come as well," said Adeone. "They like to see their Uncle Festus occasionally."

"I'd be glad to, sir. Shall I let Richardson and Simkins know?"

"Definitely up to something, I'd say; however, yes, if you'd be so kind. Also, tell your long-suffering wife I'll have you home by midnight."

Landis laughed. "Cornelia will appreciate it, sir, but she'll probably be napping herself. She's due any day now."

"Then you'd better leave instructions that if she needs you, you are to be contacted. Can't have you miss the birth."

Landis left to inform Richardson that the King would be spending the evening and possibly the night at Ceardlann and would ride there with the Prince. A courier entered with a note for the King from Arkyn. Landis simply took it in himself. He wondered what it meant.

King Adeone read it. "He's already left for the Rex Dallin, without coming to say goodbye. Maybe it would be better to let him simmer down in peace…"

"The ride might well calm him down, sir. Go anyway. He can rant at you in the Rex Dallin as he can't here. It might clear the air. He's hurting as much as Your Majesty is. I've not heard him mention Ira in months. The way he dropped her into the conversation today shows she's as much in the forefront of his mind as she is in yours, sir."

Adeone swallowed. "Tain's probably having a hard time of it as well. I'll leave in a couple of hours. Let the Comptroller know we'll be there for dinner, will you?"

## Chapter 51
# GRIEF
Evening
Ceardlann

ADEONE AND LANDIS entered Ceardlann to discover Tain and Cal engaged in a game of marbles. Adeone smiled as he almost got flattened.

"Arkyn's being boring, father; he's gone and shut himself in his room."

Adeone said, "Then I'd better let him know that I'm here before someone else does. Why don't you show your Uncle Festus what you're doing?"

Tain sagged but took his nearfather's hand, dragging him along.

"I appreciate the thought, Adeone," murmured Landis.

Adeone simply chuckled, winked at Cal, then left, striding through Ceardlann to his elder son's room.

His gaze took in the occupants. Arkyn sitting on the bed, his knees drawn up, angry and upset. The Comptroller perched next to him listening then endeavouring to be the voice of reason. Kadeem off to one side. Adeone caught the Comptroller's eye.

"Thank you; we won't keep you."

As the Comptroller and Kadeem left, Arkyn got up, eyeing his father uncertainly. The manner of dismissal said he was in trouble.

Adeone waited until the door closed. "Why did you leave without saying goodbye, Arkyn?"

"Because—" He stopped. Head suddenly held erect, he said, "I was a fool, sir. I'm sorry."

Adeone sank onto the edge of the bed, his head in his hands. "Be mad at me. I should have been more tactful in telling you to return here and I'm sorry. I forced a friend to betray a confidence, to betray *your* confidence. Never make that mistake, Arkyn. It burns your heart. Your mother would have been ashamed of me."

Arkyn didn't know what to say. He simply looked at his father and smiled sadly. Then he bit his lip and turned away.

Ignoring the resistance, Adeone pulled him into a hug. "It seems we both need more support today than we've admitted to."

Arkyn said, "I'm sorry, father. I should have said goodbye. I shouldn't have simply left. If I were a lord, I'd be receiving a dressing down."

"Yes, but, as my son, you're more than entitled to get annoyed with me and to go off in a huff. What's more, you need your freedoms and I'm denying you them. If it were me, I'd be highly annoyed. I'm just trying to make sure you're safe. You're the future this empire needs and that requires protecting."

"I'm not sure I'll make a good king."

"I and a hundred others are. You're far more sensible than I am. Far kinder than your Uncle Scanlon would be, he loves power too much. You seem to respect power without it being all-consuming."

"I try to, but there are days I wish we could be a normal family."

"So do I, Arkyn, but it's not our fate. We have to lead. There are decisions that must be made that make you hate yourself and that cause others to hate you. Yet they'd soon complain if they weren't made. I've tried to be more relaxed than any other king and people still criticise me. It sometimes feels like I can't do anything right. Your mother would tell me I was being a fool at this point. She'd be right as well, but is Scanlon's way any better? He causes people to fear him and authority. He thinks I'm too relaxed, I know that much, but I'm trying to do the best I can."

Arkyn realised that his father needed to talk to someone who didn't *have* to listen. He sat down at the head of his bed, curling his feet under him. "Complainers are always louder than supporters, father."

"I just wish I could be told that I'm right occasionally and trust it. I can never trust anyone's word."

"At least there are no rebellions."

"Nevertheless, there are times I wish there was something more."

Arkyn said, "Where would be the mystery in that, father?"

"I don't want mysteries. I want life to be simple." He sighed. "You don't need to listen to my troubles..."

"It doesn't bother me."

Adeone gazed at him. "I don't know what I'd do if anything happened to you."

"I hope you never have to find out, father."

"What time did the Comptroller persuade you to order dinner for?"

"Half-past seven, sir. His manipulations are becoming slightly obvious."

"Yes, I thought you didn't seem surprised to see me. You've your Uncle Festus to thank for my visit though. He said something about mending bridges..."

"I wonder what he meant."

Adeone glanced at his son and in that one sentence realised that Arkyn had forgiven him. "I can't imagine. I left your brother annoying him. It'll do him good."

Arkyn laughed. "I suddenly feel sorry for Uncle Festus. Can we rescue him?"

When they located Lord Landis, he was listening to Tain's monologue.

Arkyn smiled at his nearfather and clipped his brother round the head. "Have you got a word in, Uncle Festus?"

"One or two. Tain must be feeling tired."

Arkyn dodged aside as Tain went to thump him. "I'm impressed. It's more than I've managed in days."

Tain grumbled, "You haven't been here. So, that's hardly fair, is it?"

Adeone laughed. "Your logic is certainly improving, Tain. Don't tell me you've been studying?"

"Why would I want to do that, father?"

"It's traditional, you know."

Landis murmured, "Traditions can be changed."

Adeone turned to him. "Whose side are you on, Festus?"

A grin filled Tain's voice as he said, "Mine it would seem."

"Whatever gave you that idea?" asked Landis. "I'm impartial. No doubt about that. Totally impartial. Certainly impartial. Why would I be partisan?"

"Who are you trying to persuade, us or yourself?" enquired Adeone.

Landis laughed. "Both. It's never a wise idea to disagree with kings or princes, and I would appear to be in a hopeless situation on that front."

Three hours later, after they'd all dined and Elantha was in bed, Doctor Chapa's griffin messenger popped up, asking for a link with Landis. A few hours later, just after midnight, Landis contacted Adeone to tell him Cornelia had borne a girl and that they'd named her Ira. She'd been born on the cusp of midnight and so Landis said, if Adeone didn't mind, they'd make her birthday the same as Queen Ira's had been. Adeone didn't mind. As he drifted into sleep, he almost heard and felt Queen Ira saying in his ear, *"Sometimes my cousin Festus is an enigma, at others he's simply mischievous but he has a warm heart."*

## Chapter 52
# PONDERINGS
Alunadai, Week 21 – 1st Seral, 15th Meithis 1210
Wynfeld's Office

THEY COULDN'T GIVE UP HUNTING GAD, but there were times, Alcis there were times, when Wynfeld wished they could. Making the Court secure might be important, but it wouldn't catch the man. How were they meant to apprehend a vigilant? They could hardly sidle up to him.

He opened the file in front of him, hunting for something they hadn't investigated. They knew Gad's old haunts, they knew his friends and they also, as Wynfeld had said to Landis, knew his favourite foods. None of that mattered, however, as they didn't know the man's current haunts, acquaintances or if his tastes had changed.

He wondered how many of the landlords from Gad's old haunts would be willing to tell him if they'd seen the man in the last year. If not, they had to work out what had changed the man's habits. Only something major would make the man completely lose his past. Well, trying to poison their King *was* something major… It was ground they'd gone over a hundred times to no avail.

A knock at the door heralded Beaver. "Erm, there's been an unconfirmed sighting of our old friend, Gad, sir."

Heart quickening, he asked, "Where?"

"Bar of an inn last night. Leech was worried. He's tailing that merchant, Hob Fullerton, from Garth, the one who the courts have stung. Gad heard Fullerton muttering about it and started trying to tell him it wasn't the Justiciar's fault but the King's. He had him convinced in the end."

"What did Leech do when the men split up?"

"This is where it gets interesting, sir. They've agreed to meet up again. Same bar tonight."

"Good, get a squad together."

Beaver grimaced. "I'm not sure that will be successful, Captain."

"Do it. Our King has ordered movement on catching Gad and if we don't manage it soon, we can all retire extremely early. Do you want to see myself, the General and Captain Pixney having to resign?"

"No, Captain. I'd prefer us to catch Gad but he's prejudiced a perfectly harmless merchant. We can't simply let that fester. Currently, we haven't a clue who Gad is working for. We just know what his work has been. We could use the merchant to our advantage. If we can get Fullerton to work for us – I'm sure we can find what he wants – we can use him to interrogate Gad. He must know at least one other name. He'll lead us to someone else and then we might even get to Scanlon."

"*Lord* Scanlon! I'm still uneasy. I'd rather catch Gad immediately. If we did it your way, what do you think the merchant would accept?"

Beaver said, "You're aware of the bandits from the Gardian Ridge who were caught and then escaped; they were caught on Hob Fullerton's land. He was arrested and tried for harbouring bandits. The only thing that saved him was that he'd been ill. Too ill as it turned out to declare his recent inheritance formally to the Exarch. Which meant that he wasn't the landlord when they were captured because the Eschervin had already confiscated the land. I don't pretend to understand it all. The land is now Lord Rathgar's and there's little doubt in Fullerton's mind that no matter what happened he'd have been hounded until that land was His Lordship's. Our friend persuaded him that since Rathgar has acquired the land, the King must have told Scanlon to get it for him. When you think of the way favours have worked in the past, it isn't so unbelievable to a person from the provinces and Hob Fullerton isn't in a rational frame of mind."

"Sicla, Beaver, how many more times? *Lord* Scanlon and *Lord* Rathgar!" Wynfeld swore softly. "Fullerton is still under observation, isn't he?" (Beaver nodded.) "Keep it so and don't move in yet. I need time to think. Just don't lose him and if he and Gad split company for good, drop the merchant and follow Gad. I'm not losing him again and if you do, you'll face a court martial. Next, we need to know where Gad lives. Get our scryer onto it. When he's with the merchant, he can begin to follow him. No normal tracker will manage. Just trust me on that. That's all for now."

A moment later, Wynfeld swore. He'd forgotten to ask which tavern and they weren't even sure it was Gad. Should he send a report to the Palace when they were uncertain or should he wait and see if this was a false dawn? He needed advice. Could he go to Rayburn or the General? Beaver was right; they could use the merchant to find out who Gad answered to. With his King's current frame of mind, though, would he accept that the man could lead them to bigger fish? Normally Wynfeld would have said yes, but something had happened yesterday and he knew it was a side of his King he hadn't seen before. What he didn't know was if it was a temporary change or permanent.

He suddenly saw the answer as clear as day. He had to tell his King. Not doing so because they'd all had a roasting was stupid. Whatever they did, their King could say they their choice was wrong. He had to know, had to agree with and, in fact, make the decision. That way no-one could suffer if things went wrong. So Wynfeld went to tell the General what had happened and the fact he was planning on reporting to their King in person.

General Paturn said, "I hope you know what you're doing, Wynfeld. A king shouldn't be told anything he doesn't need to know about."

"Yes, sir, but I think, for all our sakes, he needs to know about this."

The General watched his subordinate officer for a long moment. In a neutral voice he remarked, "Then, Wynfeld, you'd better tell His Majesty. Just one thing, Captain... Make sure you realise the consequences if the King doesn't want to hear what you're telling him."

* * *

When Wynfeld entered the Inner Office and saluted, the King said, "I hope this is quick, Captain. I have to visit my new neardaughter."

"I'll be as fast as I can, Your Majesty. Congratulations—"

"The Landises need those. I'll pass them on. What can I do for you?"

Wynfeld took a deep breath. "We've had an unconfirmed sighting of Gad with a merchant from Garth."

236

"Why tell me if it's unconfirmed?"

"We've a dilemma on our hands, Sire. We're pretty sure it's Gad; however, Sergeant Beaver has seen that there might be an opportunity here…" Wynfeld carried on explaining.

At the end of the explanation, the King shouted for Richardson and told him to let Lord Landis know he'd be delayed. He rose and pointed at the table. "Let's have a look at your file then. I can see your issue. Whatever you do, you think I could disagree with it?"

"Yes, sir. Frankly, anything we do I can disagree with. I reasoned that even if I asked the General for orders, we'd be left with the same problem."

"Normally, I'd have said go to Paturn but, I think, in this case, you were right. I needed to know about this. How reliable do you think Merchant Fullerton could be?"

"His father didn't turn traitor in 1169, so we think he's likely sensible."

"Good. What information have you managed to unearth about Gad?"

Wynfeld took a breath. "Briefly, sir: after he and Adson ended up in the underworld of Oedran, they killed a few men in the heat of the moment, but one day their luck ran out. Judge Tancred's memory was accurate. The yeomen arrested them and put them on trial. Again, they escaped the worst and even prison. Various key statements, which I am reliably informed were given, were 'lost'. It's at this point that we're not quite sure what happened next. The men left the court and went for a drink and then the trail goes cold until they appear a fortnight or so later at the Palace and obtain jobs as under-gardeners. Their references were untraceable forgeries, Sire. They seemed to have kept their heads down, then they received a promotion when two other under-gardeners had the unfortunate experience of being killed at the hand of an unknown knifeman. This promotion meant they had rights to be inside the Palace delivering produce to the kitchens mainly. I strongly suspect that they killed the other gardeners. If they did, it was at that point that things changed. They'd never killed in cold blood before. Suddenly, they knew they could. They took advantage of the fact Blackwood was a relative and played on that. They managed to get another promotion and we suspect they started to abuse the small amount of power they now had. There were several men of standing threatened with the disclosure of affairs they were conducting in parts of the Palace grounds and we're almost certain that Gad and Adson were responsible. They basically began to enjoy themselves, Sire. They enjoyed frightening people. Then it stopped and they turned up to work bruised. I think their employers discovered what had been happening. They'd been keeping the backhanders. One of their former colleagues who stumbled on the information was paid to keep his mouth shut. Then we think they were told to target Your Majesty.

We know what happened there: the captain was visited, a guard's tabard obtained and poison was provided. They were still working at the Palace at that point but to plan the attack they'd been into the city drinking, more often than the head gardener thought seemly. Then word reached him that they'd been overstepping other marks and he sacked them. Now a second attack would be harder. We lost track of them before we even discovered who they were. Once we got names, we used everything we had to find them. We knew where they had been drinking and where they had been lodging whilst working at the Palace but nothing helped. They had vanished and we seemed to be chasing shadows on an Alcis Day. I think they even left the city for a bit. They returned, and it has since transpired that they had a new target: Lord Landis. Gad was spotted drinking in the Administrative Quarter talking of revenge for his cousin's death but by the time we got there he'd gone. We've kept an eye on the tavern in question but he's never returned. That was the last news we had of him until he approached Craig Ganon. Then Leech was keeping an eye on Fullerton last night and he, Fullerton, happened to be accosted by Gad."

"Are you certain that Gad is answering to someone?" enquired Adeone.

"Yes, sir. For three reasons: he was picked up by someone when he escaped prison, he'd never killed in cold blood and then he did and, finally, he's changed targets twice but, without laying our hands on Gad or following him, we haven't got a clue who his paymasters are."

Adeone snorted. "I expect my brother is ultimately responsible."

Wynfeld said, "It's the proving of it that's the problem, Sire. If Gad could lead us to one, then we can lift Gad and follow the other and so on."

"If you lifted Gad, he might tell you."

"He might, sir, but I think he's a puppet. Someone has him well and truly bridled. He might seem to be free, but the beating we know about probably wasn't the only one. I'd guess that it's the same man who made sure they escaped the courts. He effectively would have saved their lives. There's always a debt to that, but this time I think they were snared. In the Age of Tyranny, if a man saved another's life – and if the saviour was of higher standing – then the beneficiary was tied to them and their life could be dictated by their saviour. He owned them effectively. Some people still believe that is the right way of doing things."

Adeone said, "Yes, my brother does, for a start. He has always loved the power he holds instead of respecting it. That's all beside the point now. You want to know what I wish to be done with this situation?"

"Yes, sir."

"Congratulations. Now there're two of us in a quandary. Is there a chance you could lose Gad again?"

Wynfeld said, "Yes, Sire. There is always that chance. We've located him by accident, if indeed it is him; however, we'll do everything we can to keep him in our sights. Scrying included."

"He might know if he's being scried, Wynfeld. As Lord Landis proved."

"Yes, sir, but he can't do anything about it."

Adeone sat thinking for a moment. "Right, Alcis knows if this is the right decision; I'm going to say keep him under observation. If you're convinced he's being given orders then that's good enough for me. Do we know what will persuade the merchant to work with us?"

"No, sir, not know. I suspect that he wants his land back. He could hardly declare it when he was in a fever. His father died of the same illness; it wasn't just a mild cold he's using as an excuse. He left Garth directly after his trial and came here. We're not completely sure why, but it could be to avoid the speculation there."

Knowing the danger of false promises and, without certainty as to Fullerton's motivations, Adeone didn't want to commit himself. "Get Jones investigating everything surrounding this. *Everything*, Wynfeld. The illness, the confiscation of land, the bandits. I want a detailed report on it. As for Fullerton, for now, I'm not making promises, but if he takes an oath of loyalty and sticks to it, I will forget the events of the last few days. I will certainly forget them if he continues to help us from Garth. If not, his next court appearance may not go in his favour."

"Thank you, Your Majesty. I hope it all pays off."

"It had better. How was the crisis meeting yesterday?"

Unsurprised, Wynfeld said, "Went well, Sire. The Court will be secure within a week."

"That's something. You didn't even try to deny that it happened."

"The General, I've found, has predictable methods, Sire."

"He has found methods that work for him, Wynfeld."

Wynfeld smiled slightly. "Yes, Sire. I hope we all have."

"I would say some have found rather controversial methods that work. How is the regiment progressing?"

"Very well, Sire. Thank you. Our new acquisitions are hardworking. The only thing is that, at the rate we're going, we'll need more clerks."

"I'm sure that could be managed. Are you at the stage of needing a whole building yet?"

Wynfeld answered truthfully but dryly, "Not quite, Sire. Give us a couple of years."

Adeone laughed. "I could almost believe you mean that."

# Chapter 53
## LIGHT RELIEF
Late Morning
Landis House Study

ONCE WYNFELD HAD GONE, Adeone visited his youngest neardaughter. She was a red-faced bundle who opened her blue-grey eyes to all the new wonders. Cradling her, Adeone ponderingly asked her what she planned in life and how many hearts she planned to break. He never heard Landis telling him to stop being a bad influence. He was taken back to holding Ella in his arms just after she'd been born; remembering Ira telling him he was too soft-hearted. Blinking back the brimming tears, he gathered the shawl around her.

It was a good half hour before young Ira started whimpering. Landis rang for Nursie, who'd overseen his nursery since the twins had been born. She smiled as the King said matter-of-factly,

"I think she's hungry. Not surprising really, such a lot to take in."

"No different to the rest then, Sire. It's good to have a healthy appetite."

Adeone grinned. "Well, I hope young Ira gives you less trouble than her siblings."

"Ah, I'd rather have the trouble than a peaceful life, sir. Let me take her. Come on, little one, let's get you fed and changed."

Once they were alone, Landis grinned at his friend. "You do still like to be mischievous, don't you?"

Adeone looked supremely innocent. "I can't imagine what you mean. She's beautiful."

"Thank you, sir. I'm just thinking what the future holds for me with four daughters to find husbands for…"

"Let them chose their own. A lot less headache for you. There's fourteen years between young Ira and Julia. Plenty of time for marriages to happen without conflict. How are all the rest of your brood?"

"Hopefully studying, but I shan't hold my breath."

"Why don't we go and give them an excuse to stop? I'm sure their tutor and governess would like an afternoon off."

"Would you like me to send any warning?" asked Landis innocently.

Adeone's eyes sparkled. "Oh, I think not. Where would be the fun?"

Landis chuckled. "I thought we were meant to get more sensible as we got older?"

"No everyone just hoped we would. Two completely different things when you consider them."

The children's tutor hurriedly rose as they entered the schoolroom. Adeone nodded to him and winked at his nearchildren, who were overjoyed as their father told the tutor to take the afternoon off.

Once he'd gone, Adeone said, "Isn't anyone going to give me a hug?"

Landis chuckled as all five children ran over and buried their nearfather in hugs.

Adeone laughed. "That's better, though what it's going to feel like when your new sister joins in, I hate to imagine."

Julia shrugged. "Then don't, sir – just wait and see."

"Very practical. So, what are you all having to put up with being taught?"

"Julia and I are currently being told how to behave in front of the King," said Julius gravely.

"Why behave? He doesn't. According to your father, he's a dreadful influence."

Julius looked uncertain and Julia said, "But the King can't be wrong, so people should just alter their perceptions."

Landis coughed slightly. "Julia…"

Adeone laughed. "Festus, go and bury your head in a scroll. You might even want to contact Wynfeld."

"I can tell when I'm not wanted," muttered Landis amiably. "Will you stay for a meal?"

"I'd be glad to."

Once their father had left, the children deluged Adeone with questions. He happily answered them and quizzed them in return. They managed to waste an hour before Landis reappeared to say lunch would soon be ready.

Walking to the dining room, Landis said quietly to Adeone, "You're right, I had an interesting chat with Wynfeld. I think you made the right decision."

"Good. I thought it might be more worthwhile than simply picking our man up. I just hope that Wynfeld knows what he's doing."

"Oh, I think he does, Sire. In fact, I think he needs a wider area to flex his wings. There's a sergeant of his who could take over the Oedranian end of things more than competently. If there's chance, I'd say promote Wynfeld to commander."

Adeone raised his eyebrows slightly as they reached the dining room. "I shall keep it in mind but he still messes up."

"Don't we all, Sire? I know I do. He lets you know when he's gone wrong, but not when he's succeeding at his job. You do realise that?"

"He is perfectly competent. I'll never disagree with that. If he wasn't, he wouldn't still be in post; however, we're talking work again, my lord."

"I'm sorry, Sire. Wouldn't you say it's a beautiful day…?"

Adeone simply glared at him as he took his seat. Landis raised an amused eyebrow in return.

* * *

An hour later, Adeone and Landis were ensconced in the study. It *was* a nice day and the sun streamed in through the window, warming the room as it couldn't warm the world outside due to the autumn winds. Adeone seated himself in a patch of sunlight, like a cat basking in the sun.

Landis passed him a whiskey. "You know, you should get out more."

Languidly, Adeone said, "If you're not careful, Festus Landis, I might throw something at you."

"You'd have to expend energy for that. All right, all right, I'll be good." He caught the small paperweight and replaced it.

"I doubt you know the meaning of the word."

Sonorously, Landis replied, "I follow the example of my King, as all good vassals should."

"If you carry on like that, Festus, I will throw something else at you."

"A biscuit would be best… Then we can both say I take the biscuit!"

"If it wasn't your study I'd say 'get out!' As it is, if Cookie has any ginger biscuits going, I wouldn't say no."

Twelve minutes later, they were both munching away and talking about affairs the empire over before returning to Oedranian matters.

Landis asked, "What are you going to do about Merchant Fullerton?"

"I'm going to get the facts of his case before I even contemplate doing anything," said Adeone. "I don't have enough detail, but his lands were in the Anaparian Marches. Officially, I don't know anything yet; therefore, Jones will be looking into it."

"Do you think Fullerton's right? That he was always destined to lose it?"

Adeone considered. "Anaparian Marches. Close to Shinglis? Why would that ever be of strategic importance? I mean, there's no fort, town or major mail route junction there at all. It's not the main route between Garth and Oedran either."

"I can recognise sarcasm," grouched Landis. "Do you think Fullerton had any hope of keeping the land?"

"Yes, but he could have lost his life shortly afterwards for harbouring bandits. A nasty conundrum and if I find my brother is behind it, I will have to do something for Fullerton. I'm sick of Scanlon messing around with people's lives as though they don't matter."

Landis tactfully changed the subject.

# Chapter 54
## STAKE OUT
Afternoon
Wynfeld's Office

FORTUNATELY FOR WYNFELD there weren't any merchants in the Woolsack Inn who knew him. He had one leisurely tankard of beer before leaving. The brief interlude told him all he needed to know about the inn. They'd be lucky to get anyone in there who didn't stick out like a sore thumb just after the hammer had hit it.

He swore. Leech would have to be there that evening, come what may, but they ideally needed someone else as well, someone known there. If they couldn't find anyone then Leech would have to manage on his own.

The inn sat on the wide, open square of the Guildhall Plaza in the Administrative Quarter. Through the day the plaza bustled with merchants and their wares but at night it became quiet with few places to observe from and no narrow alleys for men to lurk in. The buildings surrounding the square were either shops or merchants' residences with no handy porticos either. At first glance, the impressive Guildhall – with its long, buttressed hall – seemed perfect until one realised that far from creating shadows the moonlight would chase them away.

Two roads led off the square: The Pike – a tree-lined ceremonial avenue that led from the Palace to the King's Gate – and the Giltwynd. The trees on the first might offer some cover but his men would still be noticeable and were likely to be accosted by yeomen or working girls.

The Giltwynd curved away to the north on the opposite side of the Guildhall Plaza; its name gained because of the financiers who kept premises there. There would be shadows to hide in there and as long as they picked the right ones, there was some hope.

They might be able to follow Gad once he left the inn, as long as he didn't resort to his Ullian skills. The Administrative Quarter wasn't a ghost town at night, far from it, but people did tend to move around rather than stand in one place. It was all basic stuff but, somehow, the basics hadn't worked before, and Wynfeld had the feeling that they wouldn't here. There'd have to be more than a couple of people on this man's trail at various distances so that they could notice if anyone else was following them.

On top of that, they had to get to Fullerton and see if he'd be willing to help their cause. He then had to keep up an attentive but discreet watch on Gad. The man's paymasters wouldn't leave him unobserved, no matter how high he had risen in their esteem. Somehow, they had coerced him into doing what they wanted. Gad might have been lowlife, but he hadn't shown the personality of a traitor even when kicked out of the army. Someone had known he had a skill with the knife and, more importantly, that he was a vigilant and had gradually turned him until nothing seemed too difficult and nothing was beyond his reach, even treason.

Wynfeld decided to coordinate the evening's work. He wanted to know what was happening as he was responsible if things went wrong and their King found out. So, he called Beaver and Leech into a meeting along with several other men whom he trusted. They decided to leave it with Leech in the bar. They had men who would observe both the front and back entrances to the Woolsack Inn, as best they could, and they had two others who would follow Fullerton. One would linger long enough to judge if anyone was following the merchant. Their scryer would be watching the bar and not just Gad. Lord Landis' experience had shown that it was possible to tell if one was being scried and, as Gad was a vigilant, he *might* be able to sense scryers with more certainty; therefore, the military scryer would be watching the bar not staring at the man in question. Idly, Wynfeld wondered if Lord Landis would be watching as well. If he were it might feel claustrophobic. The scryer would pursue Gad home just in case he was lost by the three others tailing him. Leech would stay in the bar for long enough to ascertain if anyone else in there was an acquaintance of Gad. That should cover the most conceivable possibilities.

The evening arrived quickly. They were all at their allotted posts and were all on a knife-edge of expectation. So much could go wrong. They had to track Gad this time. This time? It was the first time they'd had him in their sights. After a year of searching, they were finally able to start trapping him. Were they right to wait and see? Were they right to leave him free for a little longer? Alcis knew that they needed to catch the people above him but was this the right way?

As it turned out, Leech couldn't hear anything said and he cursed himself for it. The bar was one open room with a few tables littered around and walls to lean against. Leech picked a spot of wall not too far from the bar and not too far from the merchant Hob Fullerton and Gad. Between him and the pair came two older merchants, who shouted at each other. Leech watched for an appropriate moment to move without it being too obvious, but Fullerton's meeting with Gad was brief. They were deep in discussion for around eighteen minutes. Leech for the first time wished that he was able to lip read. Frustration didn't cover it. Gad left without obvious warning. That also surprised Leech. The night before it had been Fullerton who had left first. He just had to hope that the men outside weren't fazed. Fullerton stayed in the bar for some time. The only person who spoke to him was a well-known Oedranian merchant, who seemed to want to commiserate with him because of the deaf merchants. Leech did pick up on one interesting piece of information from their talk, but it didn't have any impact on the more pressing matter in hand.

Outside, the men had picked up Gad's trail and were surprised to find later that they, themselves, hadn't been followed. They'd been expecting something to happen, whether on the way to Gad's lodgings or when they got there, but nothing had. Two men stayed to keep an eye on the building once they had ascertained that there was only one way in and out. Despite all speculation, he was living in a normal lodging house in the city. The scryer pulled out of the observation.

They trailed Hob Fullerton to a house in the Administrative Quarter. No-one else followed him. That discomforted Wynfeld's men. Surely Gad's paymasters would have made sure that anyone he'd been in contact with was followed to make sure he wasn't in the pay of someone else. Or were his paymasters so certain of his loyalty to them and his abilities to hide that they had overlooked this simple precaution? Wynfeld, when he was told, accepted that they had. He posted two men to keep a watch on Fullerton.

Wynfeld finally rolled into bed knowing that there was nothing more they could do. They knew where Gad was living, they knew where Fullerton had lodgings and both men were under constant surveillance. He finally felt like they were getting somewhere.

# Chapter 55
## DIFFERENT PERSPECTIVES
Cisadai, Week 21 – 2nd Seral, 16th Meithis 1210
Inner Office

HAVING WRITTEN UP the previous evening's work, Wynfeld took the report with the usual morning briefing to the Palace. He wasn't surprised when Richardson informed him that his King wanted a word.

Feeling the tingle of anticipation, he entered the Inner Office. It was knowing he was in that room. He had never dreamed he'd ever see it. His King's gaze scrutinised him and he acknowledged that some of the tingle might be fear.

"I'm hoping your gamble paid off, Captain."

"It seems to have done so, Sire. We know where Gad is staying…"

As Wynfeld explained, he watched his King's face and later couldn't say exactly when it changed to annoyance. The change was subtle but, by the end of his recitation, Wynfeld knew he wasn't going to receive a polite thank you.

"Why was Leech alone in the bar?"

"Pure necessity, Sire. The innkeeper is sharp and he can spot men of the militia. He thinks we cause trouble."

Adeone steepled his fingers. "I don't care if *he* doesn't like it. I gave you permission to make sure your men don't look and act like men of the militia. Are you telling me that was for nothing?"

"No, sir. I'm saying that the innkeeper kicking up a fuss, had he spotted more of my men, would have scared Gad off and we'd have lost him. My priority was finding out where Gad's living—"

"Quite; however, by only having one man in the inn, you lost a valuable amount of information. Had you had more than one, then there's a chance that something could have been overheard. Do you know who the merchants are who prevented Leech from listening? Do you know if they were specifically there so you *didn't* hear anything? Do you have anyone in your regiment who is skilled in lip-reading?"

Wynfeld considered. "I'll make it a priority to find someone if we haven't, Sire."

"Good. I am glad you know where Gad is; however, Captain, I did expect more from your men. It's one thing to know where a traitor is, a far different thing to know what he's plotting."

"We will find out, Sire."

"You had better do so before I or someone I love is attacked again. You have made sweeping changes but I want to see more results. Last night wasn't as successful as I anticipated."

Wynfeld's heart plummeted. "If I or my men have failed Your Majesty, I can but apologise, my king."

Adeone regarded him levelly. "Is that all you can do, Wynfeld?"

"If you require it, sir, I will also resign."

"Not today. That's all."

* * *

Wynfeld left the Inner Office understanding his King's opinion and feeling a failure. He walked through the Audience Chamber not noticing the details he'd delighted in before. The King's Corridor, with its painted columns, stained glass and gilding, did nothing for his mood and he still felt drained walking down the Golden Stairs with their elaborate, gilded tracery. He passed the entrances to the Court, and the opulence began to break into his contemplation. He appreciated how different the building was from the utilitarian barracks.

He'd just passed the last door to Court when it opened and a voice said, "Captain, how are you?"

He turned back, distracted. "Fine, Advisor Rayburn—"

"Come and talk for six minutes."

Wynfeld glanced at the door to Court. "Probably best not to, Advisor, but thank you."

Rayburn chuckled. "Not there." He led the way to his office and waved to a chair, passing Wynfeld a drink. "From all I've heard, you've been busy since you were last here. What's caught your thoughts today?"

Wynfeld put his drink on the edge of the desk. He started explaining trying not to let his emotions come into play, for he wanted Rayburn's honest view of the situation.

The advisor listened carefully, considered for a few moments before saying, "The King *hasn't* asked for your resignation, Wynfeld. If he wanted it, he would tell you; therefore, he wants something else from you. What?"

Perplexed, Wynfeld said, "I keep messing up, Advisor. Not small catastrophes either."

"Not massive ones. The guards of King Alvern had a *catastrophic* failure – mind you, they were also bribed but hindsight is wonderful. You've not been bribed, have you?"

"Not that I've noticed, sir."

Rayburn chuckled. "Good. Think, Captain, what could the King want, given your record?"

Wynfeld leant forward, hands clasped. After a time, he groaned. "I don't know, Advisor. The only thing I can think is he wants me to stop making mistakes, but that's far too obvious."

"Maybe not as obvious as you think. Certainly not in Oedran. Mistakes and accidents happen, it's not that they happen that's important. In King Adeone's service, it's how one reacts to them that is crucial. Yes, in King Altarius' day you'd have been better resigning. King Adeone sees something in you, Captain. I suggest you catch Gad, continue doing your best and then see what happens."

"Last night wasn't my best, was it?"

Rayburn shrugged. "You weren't to know that two deaf merchants would cause havoc. Have you learned from it?"

"Bit hard not to, in the circumstances."

"Then, I doubt you'll make that mistake again and, if there's one thing for certain, it's that the King doesn't forgive the same mistake made more than once. Whatever it feels like now, no-one died. As mistakes go, there were worse available. Just pick up the pieces with the competence we've all come to respect in you." He noticed Wynfeld's surprise and chuckled.

"Did the General ever haul you over the coals about your reforms?"

"Erm, no, sir."

"Did the Major ever pull you up?"

Wynfeld considered. "He told me not to get too used to officer fare."

"He tells that to all new officers. Your talents for seeing through situations, for taking appropriate action are noted, Captain. You've handled yourself diplomatically at Court; Ryson still chuckles about the fact you need orders to cause trouble. Just pick up the pieces from last night and continue to the best of your ability. Don't let the doubts destroy the successes. You've found Gad. Now catch him."

* * *

By the time he left the Palace at Stable Gate, Wynfeld was formulating plans to find lip readers and deciding who would go and talk to the deaf merchants – to determine whether it was chance that they'd been at the Woolsack Inn. His gut instinct said that it was, but it was clear his King wanted more certainty than that.

He acknowledged the salutes of the guards on the barracks' gates and walked along the flagged paths. The buildings in the barracks were all stone built with ashlar and their uses carved into the door lintels. What did that say about military ways? They were set in stone and couldn't change?

On entering his office in the administrative block, he closed the door carefully and saluted. "Lord Landis. I hope Corporal Drave has offered you refreshment."

"Yes. Sit down."

Landis didn't have the set of a man about to heap praise on someone. Rayburn's reassurance was a faded memory just seeing him.

Landis didn't mince words. "You're a bloody fool, Captain. You're damned lucky that the two men you put onto Gad aren't dead. They've been attacked, knocked out from behind."

Wynfeld whitened. "I've told His Majesty we have that man under observation! Sicla, death and damnation! What in Sicla's Cavern were they doing? Looking in the other direction?" His thought spiralled out of control, *'You just had to tell me yourself! Rayburn... Did Rayburn warn... No, there wasn't time but how...'*

Landis replied calmly, "They'd hardly have stared someone in the face as they were knocked out from behind."

"Bollocks to being facetious, my lord. Alcis, what kind of fools are in this regiment? No, never mind what fools they are, they can wait. How do *you* know this before my men have informed me?" *'No, don't tell me – you scried it.'*

"I had my men follow yours and then had them keep so far back they

248

might as well not have been there. It's bloody lucky I did, Wynfeld. Never get two men who are so obviously military casing the house of a known traitor. Our friend spotted them at dawn and has changed lodgings. Luckily, he accepted the help of two street sweepers when they saw him struggling with a box and, in case he should be suspicious when they start sweeping his new street, I've got other men watching him. You might be glad to know I do not plan to bring all this to the attention of His Majesty." *'Mainly as my men are completely fictitious in the first instance, although not anymore.'*

Wynfeld collapse into his chair. "Thank you, my lord. Are my men all right?" *'And now I owe you a debt. How will you call it in?'*

"They should be back on their very military feet soon. I suggest you use them as heavies and not observers. Hob Fullerton and Gad are meeting again tonight, same place. I'd suggest you trust Beaver in person. In fact, let him take charge this evening."

"Anything else, my lord?" asked Wynfeld, his thoughts still spiralling. *'Why Beaver? Are you going to suggest I'm replaced? Or are you merely going to replace me when you know there's someone who can take over?'*

"Just remember, this problem could have happened on any job, it is merely unfortunate that it happened on this one."

Wynfeld sighed. "Thank you, my lord. I'll try to pick up the pieces."

"Someone's got to. It wasn't too big a mess anyway. Beaver should do a good job. Here's Gad's new address." Landis left thinking, *'If I have my way, you won't always be in charge of this regiment.'*

# Chapter 56
## BEAVER
Late Morning
Wynfeld's Office

THE GRIT OF DESPAIR rolled with Wynfeld's emotions in a mill, grinding hope and optimism to dust in the wind. Landis' visit, after his King's displeasure, had crushed any confidence that Rayburn had given him. It was only a matter of time before he was posted or demoted. One blunder and he'd be out. They'd almost lost Gad when they'd finally found him, and his King had been unhappy with him before that. He oversaw the regiment, the effectiveness of his men and they were failing. He must take responsibility. Around him were only ruins of Fitz's hard-won success. His King needed someone more competent to protect him. He called the duty sergeants together and handed over command for the evening's operation to Beaver, trying to hide his despondency and the fact he noticed the raised eyebrows. The whole barracks must have noted Landis' visit and know he was doomed.

Beaver told his fellow sergeants to be ready for a briefing in half an hour. When alone with Wynfeld, he said, "I don't feel confident enough for this, sir."

"Doesn't matter. You're in charge," replied Wynfeld tiredly. "Get on with the job. We can't afford another failure. I won't attend the briefing."

Worried, Beaver left. Landis' visits normally created focus in the captain, not despondency.

* * *

At the briefing later that day, Beaver said, "Right, if you think Gad is going to tamely sit there and talk treason all night, you can rethink your bloody positions in this regiment. He's not going to be that grass green, and neither are you. I don't want any excuses if things go wrong tonight like they did this morning. I want to hear that Gad doesn't know we exist. What's more, lads, the captain won't stand for twaddle either. We want to prove to the King that he's taught us tricks we didn't know before he got here. Otherwise, our next few years mightn't be so comfortable and sure of promotion. Got that? We're doing this for the captain as much as the King."

There was a chorus of affirmatives, but one voice had to ask, "Captain being sacked then?"

Beaver glared at the enquirer. "Not to my knowledge, but can any of us be sure that if we fail, he won't resign?"

Even the enquirer glumly admitted that they couldn't. They left the barracks in ones and twos with a new determination.

* * *

Beaver entered the inn and glanced around. Gad wasn't there, but his own merchant contact was and had struck up a conversation with another of his kind. He walked over to the table and greeted his contact. Merchant Reddy introduced him, luckily by a pseudonym, to, of all people, Hob Fullerton from Garth. A merchant in the finer things of life: silks to spices, gems to goblets and beyond. Feigning disinterest Beaver, with half his face averted, nodded to Fullerton and then caught the eye of the barman.

Banging a half-full jug of ale and a tankard down on the table, he snapped, "You pay now here. If you don't like it, you can skedaddle. I cater for merchants, not your sort."

Seeing Beaver didn't want to talk to his new acquaintance Merchant Reddy excused himself to Fullerton, as soon as the barman left, and turned to the sergeant. "What's upset you?"

250

"One of those days. How was your trip to Garth?"

Merchant Reddy shrugged. "Good enough, as I was just telling Fullerton here. He's from there. It's a beautiful city. You should visit it at some point. Stop living your life in Oedran."

"Oedran's been fine for me and mine for many a year. You know what you're getting here. Can't stand foreign parts."

The merchant merely raised an eyebrow. "One day you might find yourself elsewhere other than in our beautiful, if contradictory, city."

"However, until then, I'll buy you a drink and listen to your stories. Get robbed by bandits?"

"You know not everywhere outside these walls is inhospitable. Even the army knows that, surely? Bandits had disappeared by the time I came back. Tell you one thing, though, with Lord Scanlon there I'm not surprised they went to ground. I would have done, had I been of the criminal fraternity. He's not a man to cross; I'll say that much for him. Could do with him in Oedran more. Crime would be down. Can't walk the streets at night, these days."

"Could we ever? It was only Prince Lachlan who set up the yeomen."

"Yes, but they were doing a good job when he set them up. They've got slack. So, what news have you for me?" enquired Reddy.

"Not much. Oedran is as ever Oedran. I was expecting to be happily sitting here for hours listening to you."

"I can oblige if you're not going to offer the entertainment."

Beaver grinned and topped up the merchant's tankard as Gad approached Fullerton and greeted him with whispered words, which stayed private. Suddenly, there was a slight scuffle and the beginnings of a fight by someone who didn't know how to. A knife blade flashed. Beaver's companion glanced at the disturbance, jumping up.

In a furious voice, he said, "That's what I'm on about. That! There! The fact a decent man can't have a quiet evening drink in this city without some bloody fool deciding he wants to disturb everyone's peace. Great Alcis what on Erinna do you think you're doing? Yes, you there…" he demanded in a peremptory voice of Gad.

Beaver had to make a split-second decision; it would be suspicious if he didn't respond; it would also be odd if he looked up too withdrawn and incurious; so he plumped for the half-frightened stance. "Leave 'em to it, Red. It's only a dispute. Don't get involved."

The merchant glared at him. "Fat lot of good you are as a soldier; I can see why they left you in Oedran."

Gad glanced at Beaver and barged across the tavern and out the door.

Beaver tried to salvage the situation. If he lost a contact, he lost a contact.

"I tell you what, mister perfect merchant, why don't you keep your ample overblown opinions to yourself? I don't stick my nose into your business so keep your nose out of mine!"

"Don't stick your nose into it? Really? That's a new one on me—" snarled Reddy.

"Everything is new to you. Gallivanting off all over the empire leaving others to do your work here. At least I've never shirked my responsibilities like that—"

"Oi, you two cretins, take it outside!" yelled the barman. "I ain't having my regulars disturbed by the likes of you! OUTSIDE NOW!"

Beaver threw a disdainful glance around the bar. "If you call this being hospitable, I hate to see your definition of inhospitable. Goodnight all, I'm taking myself off as you see! Enjoy your drinks. He charges you over the odds for them."


He'd barely leant against the wall outside when the knife tickled his ribs.

A voice said, "Who are you?"

"A pissed off, fed up soldier with a dagger at my ribs. What more do you need to know?"

"Your name?" came the sarcastic reply.

"Oh, that. I'm known as Cogin."

The blade was withdrawn, leaving only shifting shadows in the gloom.

Beaver ambled away. Unsure whether he was being followed, he did what any annoyed soldier would do, found the nearest tavern and appeared to drown his sorrows, before taking a circuitous route back to the barracks. When the guards wanted the password, he simply said,

"Pass… Pathwordy… Pissword… Tell youse later, just don't tell me captain or I'll do something, anything you don't like. Fat-tig…Fatigues wud be good… or stop…ping your leave, you don't *need* leave, do you? Sush, better not tell the captain else he'll want me guts. Need to find me guts to… to give 'em to t'cap'in. Which way? This way. Will tell you pisswordy later… password… pisswordy, like that one… no… Which way? Gate's too small… Ah… Do you know… no… never mind… Fatigues… pisswordy…"

A few minutes later, he entered Wynfeld's office, dropped the pose of being drunk and related what had happened.

"Did the merchant know who you are?" asked Wynfeld concerned.

"No, thank Alcis. Nor that I was there to watch Gad. is Leech back?"

"No, not yet, but the men on Gad are still in place. What do you think we should do with regards to Fullerton?"

Beaver shrugged. "Lift him. Gad almost had a knife in his ribs – he thinks he was betrayed by Fullerton."

"Damn! Our one way in and we've lost it. I might as well resign now."

"No, you don't, Captain! We can pull this one back; we've got a handle on Gad at last. Fullerton's done the empire that much of a favour. His lodgings are in the Administrative Quarter. If you want to lift him, we should be able to do it in the small hours. Or we could wait until tomorrow, when there's more chance we won't be noticed."

"Up to you, Beaver. You're in charge."

Beaver sighed. "Aye, Captain, but I feel out of my depth and would appreciate your advice."

"Tomorrow is less conspicuous. If we're sure he'll not run for it."

"I don't think he will. Where's he going to run to anyway?"

Wynfeld said, "True. Then wait for the other reports and debrief me in the morning. I'm going to begin the report for our King."

"I'll give you a hand, sir. Two heads'll make light work of it."

They worked in near silence for much of the time. The reports didn't have to be brief, but they needed to be concise. As Wynfeld pointed out to Beaver, their King didn't have all day to read a report. The important things should be at the beginning but, equally, their King wouldn't accept any excuses for missing essential details. It was unwise to try to hide things from him. That knowledge made Wynfeld wonder if Lord Landis was right to keep the information that they'd nearly lost Gad from their King; however, he followed Landis' underlying instruction and didn't mention it.

Slightly merry, Leech returned to say that Fullerton had sat brooding with a full tankard for most of the night. It was the brooding of a man who could see his road was coming to an end.

# Chapter 57
# FULLERTON

Tretaldai, Week 21 – 3rd Seral, 17th Meithis 1210
Oedran – Administrative Quarter

FULLERTON CONSIDERED THE EVENTS of the previous evening as he dressed. Remembering Gad's violence, his hand shook as he did up his doublet. The knife glinting in the candles, Merchant Reddy yelling. He'd be dead if it hadn't been for that. The soldier not caring; in Garth they always cared. He fought down the rising bile. Why hadn't that soldier cared, cared that someone was attacking him? Why had he just sat there? Was he being watched here? Was it coincidence? He glanced out of his window, but the street looked the same. Should he leave via the backyard? No, he didn't want to suffer the stink of the rotting piles of who-knew-what in the alley. His lodgings had a respectable air, a cheaper than expected bill and clean sheets. It would be odd if he left via the back.

He needed to exchange a guild note for cash at the Guildhall and visit the library to hunt out more contacts, either for importing or exporting, or just to visit their workshops and shops for new ideas. That was more important than paranoia, though he'd keep an eye out for Gad.

He was most of the way to the Guildhall when someone took his elbow.

"Merchant Hob Fullerton, for the King's peace, you are under military arrest."

* * *

Once inside the barracks, contrary to what he expected, the soldiers gripped his elbows even harder, marched him to the far end of the compound and deposited him in a cell. He didn't bother to object; it was clear they wouldn't answer questions.

His mind whirled. Military arrest horrified him. He'd expected the yeomen. In Garth, the militia did arrests but rarely were detainees taken to the fort. His incarceration here, in this place, spoke of something else. He tried not to think about his conversations with Gad. After everything he'd suffered, after everything he'd gone through, after everything he'd lost, he didn't want more trouble. He'd been talking to Gad to get his mind straight. Were there ears *everywhere* in Oedran? Could it be about something else? His mind eventually shut down. The cell was dark, only the smallest opening high on the wall gave any light. As he grew accustomed to the dimness, he wished he hadn't. It was dank and damp. He just wanted out.

Taken from the cell, a sack serving as a blindfold, he was disorientated and led to a room, pushed onto a chair and his limbs secured to it. Only then was the blindfold removed. A table, chairs and several instruments he didn't want to find out the uses for faced him. He closed his eyes, shutting them out, but scrapes and bangs behind him made him open them. They wanted him to see, to imagine, to fear. Against his will, he obliged and dread ate at him.

"You are Hob Fullerton of Garth?" a voice behind him demanded.

Startled, he couldn't reply.

"An answer would be wise!"

"Yes, I am Hob Fullerton."

Something screeched across the flagged floor, well out of his sight.

The voice asked, "You were accused of felony there and before the courts?"

254

"How…?"

"We ask the questions. You answer them, willingly or not."

Unable to see his questioner, he continued staring at the instruments. 'Willingly or not' resounded in his head. In a more furious voice than he intended, words escaped him, "Yes, I was! It was rigged!" He shrank, expecting a blow.

"It's possible."

Astonished, he tried to turn.

The voice said mildly, "You'll not succeed – accept that I am anonymous. Otherwise, you'll do yourself an injury. It's amazing how self-inflicted injuries happen in here."

He shivered. "What do you want to know?"

"Who do you blame for your misfortune?"

After a moment, he said, "The King."

"Why do you blame our King for something that isn't his remit?"

The smell of a brazier stirred to life reached him. Could he smell hot metal or was it his mind playing tricks?

"Because Lord Rathgar – one of his *friends* – got my land. It was arranged. Those bandits even escaped!"

"Does our King have to be a friend of all his lords?"

Anger burned hotter than any brazier. Couldn't they see it? Couldn't they understand? "He needs their loyalty and land buys loyalty!"

"In an ideal world," commented the voice.

A rush of cooler air, a click of a door, the tramp of boots, how many? He couldn't tell. The snap of someone coming to attention? Who had entered? Why had they entered?

A second voice asked, "What did the man who met you last night want from you?"

He tried to ignore the question but two men walked forward – two men who looked as if they had the strength to lift an ox – they rummaged amongst the instruments, bringing out a rusty serrated knife. If he didn't bleed to death, the infection would kill him.

"He wanted to find out if I was annoyed enough to turn traitor," he half-whimpered.

*The second voice from behind him said, "Blindfold the merchant."*

As the blindfold went around his head, the first voice enquired, "Are you annoyed enough?"

"I don't know what I was two days ago, but I'm not now."

"No, because now you're terrified and in a room kept especially for traitors. Were you planning anything?" asked the first voice.

*"How about the one on the left? It might have a better edge," instructed*

*the second voice.*

Clanking metal, flints striking, panic began to overwhelm him. Deep breaths, deep breaths to regain control. Surely, they wouldn't… A leather strap went round his throat, not taut enough to strangle him, though that was a very real option. A second strap forced his head back.

Deep breaths. "I wasn't planning *anything!*"

"Was your friend?"

"I think *he* was." The breaths were working. "He wouldn't say much. Just how the courts were still ultimately the King's responsibility. That he was the reason I'd lost the land my forefathers owned. That the King didn't care for the provinces, that he wasn't worthy of the title…"

More clanking of metal.

The second voice enquired, "Did you believe him?"

"I was drunk!"

"Wrong answer!" snapped the first voice. "He asked if you believed him, not your state of sobriety!"

The smell of hot metal stung his nostrils. A grinding stone whirred and hot sparks seared his arms. Whatever he said, he was doomed. He told the truth.

"Yes. I did believe him. I might be a fool and that might have led me into treachery but in the sober light of day I'd never harm the King. I was going to tell him that last night but he pulled a knife on me before I could!"

*The second voice said, "Remove the blindfold."*

The first added, "That's enough of a demonstration on how to sharpen a knife, blacksmith. You can go."

"Oh, right. Thank you, sir. If you ever need another…"

Fullerton blinked as the blindfold was removed, squinting at the light until his eyes became accustomed to it once more.

The first voice asked, "Why did he pull a knife on you?"

"I guess, he thought I'd betrayed him to you lot," he said despondently.

"In a manner of speaking, you had. We've been watching you since you arrived in Oedran. We had no idea where your new acquaintance was until you bumped into him. The man you don't need to worry about – yet. We've moved your lodgings by the way. He's not a man to cross. Now, what was his plan?"

"All I know, sir, is that it involved the death of the King and possibly Prince Arkyn – or the Prince and possibly the King. I don't know when, where or how but I got the feeling that it would be towards the end of this year rather than imminently. He wanted to know if I'd been at Court and if I could introduce him to someone there. It was almost like he'd lost a contact."

The second voice asked, "Anything else he wanted?"

"Erm… any gossip I had on any of the merchants of Oedran. I told him I was an outsider, hardly here long enough to pick any up."

"Was he satisfied with that?"

"No. He wanted to find out if the rumour about Merchant Chapa retiring was true."

"What did you say to that?" asked the second man.

"I told him all I knew was that the merchant seemed to have been wrapping up acquaintances in Garth or, at least, the impression there was that he might retire. That's been the same for years though. Probably as Merchant Chapa is the only Oedranian merchant we care for. He's done us a lot of good—"

"Eloquent now, aren't you?" interposed the first voice, adding, "Now we're away from the subject of your treachery, that is. Did your new friend ask you anything else?"

He swallowed his queasiness. "Yes, sir. The layout of the Guildhall. I told him what I knew, which isn't much: just how to get from the door to the Library of Merchants."

"Would you be willing to see your friend again to gather more information for us?"

That came out of the blue. Without thinking, he said, "After the knife at my ribs, I'd rather prefer not to."

"How do you fancy dancing a hangman's jape instead?" threatened the second voice.

"Tell you truth, sir, I think I'd prefer certain death to meeting Gad again."

There was a pause. Why had no-one moved towards him? Had he given the right answer or the wrong one? He desperately wanted to get out of the room intact.

After a few moments, the first man said, "I think you can release the merchant's head, then leave."

Duly released, Fullerton rolled his neck from side to side. Were there only his questioners left now? Footsteps. A captain and a sergeant moved in front of him, at home with their jobs and their uniforms. His brows knitted. The sergeant seemed familiar, but he couldn't place him.

The first voice turned out to be the captain. "Right, let's get this straight. You're the only hope we have of catching Gad red-handed. So much so, that we've negotiated a potential pardon for your more recent activities."

He glanced between them. "You mean I'd get to *live*?"

"You'll be made to swear an oath of loyalty to both our King and the empire before you leave but, yes, you get to live, whatever else you decide. We don't make false promises; so, I'm not going to say that you'll never hear from me or my men again, but I will say that you will be free to live your life."

"Really? Why?" he asked, blinking hard.

"Our King's instructions."

"He knows?"

The sergeant snorted. "Of course he knows. Well, he knows there are traitors around and he states as long as no actual physical treason has been committed, if they swear an oath of loyalty, they can live their lives—"

"You might as well tell him the colour of our King's tunic, as well, Sergeant!" snapped the captain.

"Sorry, sir. That could be easily guessed though – scarlet and gold with a touch of emerald green. I was going to add that he only gives people one second chance."

Fullerton looked between them. What was happening? They had him tied up and were arguing about inconsequential details. Why? What?

The captain took pity on him. "You swear an oath of loyalty, your record is wiped clean. You break that oath, you're not only arrested but will die – quite horribly by Bayan's laws. You must now decide. Will you aid the capture of traitors or not?"

He glanced into the corners of the room and decided he didn't want to know what the table with straps was for. The captain put a hand on the sergeant's arm to stop him interrupting. Did they mean the offer? Walking out of the barracks would be good enough for him after the day's terrors. If this truly was the King's mercy – and, as he was in the barracks, it seemed it was – then maybe he had got his assumptions of everything else wrong as well. Why would the King hound him to lose his land if he would pardon treachery? Was it because he had got what he wanted? No. There was something honest in the captain's eyes. He *could* have used the implements spread out around them, but he *hadn't*. He had *chosen* not to if he didn't have to. That was new. That was unheard of. If that's what the King ordered, then maybe he could find a different way of raising his grievance. Would a man who pardoned others be so unreasonable if he was petitioned over an injustice? He hadn't intended to, but could he petition the King about his lands? If he helped capture traitors, it would create a debt, or create something anyway. Help capture Gad? He shivered, but the thought that helping these men could help him was intriguing. He looked again at the captain and sergeant and finally recognised the sergeant. He'd been the one in the Woolsack Inn. That made sense.

Finally, he said, "Can I opt for the middle ground? I'd like to help but Gad won't ever trust me now." He glanced at Beaver. "Your merchant friend made sure of that. I will help you catch other traitors though. If

Gad approaches me again, I'll do my best to get him to confide but please don't make me openly go hunting for him. Please."

The captain said, "That seem fair to you, Sergeant Big Mouth?"

"Yes, sir."

The captain turned to him. "Then we'll accept your gracious offer. Someone will release you presently and take your oath as well as telling you whom to inform when you have any information. Goodbye, Fullerton."

He sighed with relief as they left. Honesty, an oath and a mutually beneficial outcome. He definitely hadn't expected *that*.

# Chapter 58
## OF CAPTAINS
### Early Afternoon
### Inner Office

LANDIS REGARDED ADEONE LEVELLY. "All I'm saying, Sire, is that Captain Wynfeld is a fantastic officer but he's done all he can in the intelligence regiment. He could run it for years; the network would grow but the rest of the army would lose out. He's transformed information gathering. Before him, I'd be surprised if they had more than fifteen informers passing information back on a regular basis. Now he has a couple of hundred or more. His men are working harder than they ever did under Fitz—"

"Fitz is a good captain!" snapped Adeone, making Advisor Rayburn jump.

"Yes, I don't doubt that," replied Landis. "I wish we had twenty of him in your army, but his skill is in personal protection for Your Majesty and Their Highnesses. It always has been his strong point. Your father made him Captain of Intelligence because he trusted him. He had his own network and not all trusted Wynfeld the same way. I'm not criticising Fitz—"

"Good." Adeone was brusque.

"I am, however, saying it might be time that the regiment gets a captain whose expertise is collecting information. Someone who isn't Wynfeld."

Adeone frowned. "Why are you so determined? What has happened?"

"Nothing, sir. I just think his talents are wasted. On average, your captains make more mistakes than can be counted on your fingers and toes in a year. So far Wynfeld has made fewer than the fingers on one hand and, what's more, he's *admitted* to them—"

"Have you discussed this with Wynfeld?"

"No, Your Majesty. I think though he might be worried about his future. I did suggest that he let Beaver take over an operation. I think he thought it was criticism."

"If you've made one of my best captains paranoid, I'll not be happy!" declared Adeone.

"I'm not out to destroy Wynfeld, Sire, just to try to get him promoted for the good of the empire."

Adeone ignored the wry note in his friend's voice. "Rayburn, you've been very quiet about all of this. Is it because you can't get a word in or because you have no thoughts on the matter?"

Rayburn said, "Certainly not the latter, Sire. From what I can see, Wynfeld is an officer with potential. He will act when required, and he's loyal to the point where his career is a secondary consideration. Given history, that's rather rare and a trait that should be encouraged. I don't believe his senior officers have any complaints either, not now they grasp how he works. If you were to ask me if Wynfeld is the type of man to promote, I would advise that he has much to recommend him and little to condemn him. Your Majesty could promote him but leave the intelligence regiment in his purview; it would be unusual but not unheard of."

"How much time have you spent with him?"

"A reasonable amount, sir. I've let him get his head straight on a couple of occasions and spent time talking with him at Court. He's handling that experience very well."

"Talking to you at Court can be a challenge, Rayburn," said Landis with a quiet smirk. "Faran always warned me about that."

Adeone chuckled. "I should remember you were all contemporaries at the Advisors' School."

"I was ahead of them, Sire," said Landis smugly.

"From what I heard, only in years," replied Adeone innocently. "Wynfeld is having Fullerton picked up today, isn't he?"

Landis could hardly fail to notice that Adeone's mind was firmly rooted on one problem. "Yes, Sire. He informed me that he intended to and I agreed with the action. Somehow Gad realised that we were watching him, and attacked the merchant last night."

Adeone asked, mildly, "How did he realise?"

In a conciliatory voice, Landis said, "It was bound to happen eventually. Military men tend to look like military men even when not in uniform."

"When *exactly* did Gad twig that he was being observed?" demanded Adeone. On hearing the reply, he said, "I want Gad lifted now, before he slips through our fingers again."

"I can understand why but, as your Defender, I considered it better that Gad is free to lead us to others, Sire. If anything happens to Your Majesty due to my actions, I won't be hiding. Others might be because every fibre and moment of my life from then on would be devoted to hunting down those responsible."

Adeone smiled despite himself. "He says he's a courtier, Rayburn."

"I'm not. That was the truth, Sire," interjected Landis.

Adeone looked him in the eye. "I'll hold you to that thought. You are saying to leave Gad alone is our best option?"

"Yes, Sire. I truly believe it is."

"Rayburn?"

The advisor considered carefully. "It's not exactly my area of expertise, Sire, but if you need knowledge, you don't kill your tutor."

"Quite. All right, I'll compromise. Leave him be for two aluna-months. Get every possible person watching him. If you think there's a chance that you'll lose him then you *must* arrest him. I will not accept anything else. I might change my mind on timescales after I hear Wynfeld's report on his dealings with Fullerton."

Landis said courteously, "That, of course, Sire, is your prerogative."

"You're right, it is. What's more, no smooth-talking will change my mind so stop being obsequious."

"Whatever my King demands."

Entering after a brief knock, Richardson found Rayburn chuckling to himself and the King glaring at an innocent-looking Lord Landis.

Adeone said, "Would you mind just leaving again, Richardson? I'd prefer to throttle Lord Landis in peace."

Taking the comment as it was meant, the administrator crossed to the desk, handing over a sheaf of documents. "Captain Wynfeld's report on the interrogation of Merchant Hob Fullerton, Your Majesty. Might I suggest poison rather than throttling? It's a lot easier."

"Thank you, Richardson. I'll remember your concern another day," muttered Landis.

"If you live so long," grumbled Adeone by way of reply.

Richardson merely bowed slightly and left.

"How come your administrator gives the impression of solidarity and yet comes out with ideas like that?" asked Landis.

"Too many years working for me. Rayburn, are you still laughing?"

"Sorry, sir. I have always admired your administrator's sense of humour."

Adeone grinned. "So've I. That's all for now." Once alone with Landis, he remarked, "He rates Wynfeld."

"Yes, he certainly seems to, sir," replied Landis. "I'm sorry I ordered Wynfeld not to tell you about Gad's change of lodgings, but I didn't do it to trip him up."

"Hmm. I accept that you didn't lose Gad. If you had, it would be a very different outcome."

"I wouldn't expect anything else, Your Majesty." Landis' eyes slipped to the report Richardson had left.

Adeone noticed. "Shall we see what Wynfeld has to say?"

Landis nodded, hiding his apprehension. He poured two drinks, placing one by his friend's hand before going to peruse the view. All the leaves had left the trees and gardeners were removing the last of them to compost. He watched them at their work, pondering on Blackwood's relationship to Gad and speculating if there were any more such relationships in the Palace. Not the blood tie, there were enough of those, but rather the fact that one relative was a traitor. Was there any way of finding out before they found themselves in the same situation again?

Adeone finished reading the report and handed it over to Landis, who flicked through the transcript of the conversation.

He glanced up when he reached the end. "For once Wynfeld leaves out his feelings on the matter. Would it be worth talking to him, Your Majesty?"

"I was wondering why he'd done that myself. It could mean one of two things. One, he has no feelings and is simply relating fact. Two, you've made him think that his feelings don't matter!"

Landis swallowed. "I hope it's the former. Otherwise, I've done unintentional damage."

"Let me send for him. I'd like to know why at this crucial point he's sent an incomplete report. Then I'll decide how to proceed."

Adeone wasn't surprised to find that the captain had brought the report himself and waited to see if he was needed.

Wynfeld entered, saluted and noticed Lord Landis. Uncertainty clouded his eyes.

Adeone glanced between them. "Make yourself scarce for half an hour, my lord."

Once he'd gone, Adeone got up and pointed to the more comfortable seating around the fire, asking the captain if he'd like a drink. Wynfeld accepted gladly.

"I believe you think Lord Landis has doubts about your command of the regiment?" observed Adeone sitting down, waving at the seat opposite.

"Yes, Sire," replied Wynfeld, inwardly acknowledging he believed his King had doubts too.

"What is your opinion? Are the concerns justified?"

Wynfeld swallowed. "I don't know, Your Majesty. I've made mistakes since I took over, I shan't hide that. Two years ago, I'd have said that I was the wrong choice, but I would now hope I've not disgraced myself."

Adeone regarded him solemnly. "I'd say you've not disgraced yourself. You've worked hard to correct mistakes. You just need to stop doubting yourself and your abilities. That is the only qualm I hold." He turned the talk to other matters, outside of their professional spheres, and soon Wynfeld had relaxed. Adeone was pleased. He didn't like seeing the captain nervous or uncertain. Once Wynfeld had accepted that every mistake wouldn't mean he was sacked the captain would be one of the best officers in the army.

Landis knocked and re-entered half an hour later. He took in the scene and when Adeone motioned for him to join them said, "I see you've taken to a more comfortable working arrangement, Sire. As I'm still standing, would anyone like a refill?"

Adeone said, "I'll have a whiskey. Wynfeld?"

Wynfeld was thinking, *'Is the show for me, I wonder?'* He came out of his reverie to say that he didn't need a drink.

Landis said, "Are you sure? Alcohol works wonders, I understand."

Wynfeld smiled but didn't get time to reply before Adeone interrupted.

"Get on with pouring the drinks, my lord, and then sit down." Once Landis was seated, Adeone said, "We've read your report of your interrogation of Hob Fullerton, Wynfeld. Do you normally conduct them using trickery?"

"If it works, Sire. We were fortunate in this case that it did."

"Then what are your unwritten concerns?"

"Sir?"

Placing his drink on an occasional table with deliberate care, Landis stated, "You left out personal views on the information gleaned. That has troubled the King."

Wynfeld thought, *'Or has it worried you?'* He said, "I didn't write any because it was a factual report, Sire. It is sometimes hard to judge if a man in Hob Fullerton's position is being honest. I would say he was. He was certainly scared."

"Do you have any concerns, Wynfeld?" enquired Adeone, rolling the whisky in his glass.

"My only real fear is if Gad discovers we've questioned the merchant and attempts to harm him. It was sheer luck he didn't knife him last night. Beaver was annoyed at his contact for getting involved but if he hadn't, I believe Merchant Fullerton would be dead this morning. For that reason, I plan to keep the merchant always in sight. I also believe Jones might find him of use as a spy, Sire. Fullerton owes his current health to the fact Your Majesty is merciful, he has a debt to pay."

Adeone said, "Flattery, Wynfeld, gets you nowhere—"

"He threatened to throttle me earlier when I tried it," added Landis, conversationally.

"It's still an option. Make sure your debt management doesn't make him feel too pressured, Wynfeld. He might turn against us for that reason."

"That thought had crossed my mind as well, Your Majesty," replied Wynfeld. "We shall try not to be too heavy-handed."

"Good. What did you think about the rumour that Merchant Chapa is planning to retire?"

"It isn't the first time that that rumour has been passed our way, Sire. It would be helpful to know if it were true."

"It would indeed. Maybe you could discreetly find out."

Landis asked, "Merchant Chapa's not told you, sir?"

"No, but my mother's cousin was always a slippery customer. The same traits are put to equal effect by Doctor Chapa. It keeps it in the family."

Landis smiled slightly, saying to Wynfeld, "We just have to recall that the King's mother, may she shine in the heavens always, was a Chapa."

Adeone said, "Wynfeld, Landis is in a mischievous mood— Come in."

Richardson entered. "My apologies, but the Chief Merchant wondered if you had a moment, Sire."

"How opportune. If you think I have, Richardson, I have. Wynfeld, I'll allow you to monitor Gad for two aluna-months longer. Then we'll review the situation again. That's all. You can escape as well, Festus. I doubt you can add anything but inanities to my next conversation."

"Traditions can be changed, Sire," said Landis. "All right, I'm going."

## Chapter 59
# OF MERCHANTS
Mid-Afternoon
Inner Office

MERCHANT CHAPA returned the King's greeting cheerfully. "I shouldn't be troubling you for long, Sire."

"That's a shame. A bit of rest with congenial companions helps the day along. What can I do for you?"

"I've just heard some of our merchant guests are being targeted by your intelligence regiment, Sire."

Adeone waved to a chair. "They are. Well, to be exact, one is. How did you get to hear about it?"

"Hob Fullerton came to see me this morning, Sire. He asked my advice as to what he should do if he thought he was being followed."

Adeone frowned, picked up Wynfeld's report and read the front page. He called for Richardson and told him to get Landis and Wynfeld back and to tell Wynfeld not to let Fullerton go if they hadn't already. Surprised, Richardson left.

Merchant Chapa looked at the King's grave face and was even more perplexed when Adeone didn't explain but just deluged him with questions.

The King discovered that the man who had visited Merchant Chapa had left an hour before and bore a striking resemblance to Gad. Having asked what had been discussed, Adeone discovered his cousin hadn't said anything that might compromise the empire, and hadn't invited the man to Court.

"Is the man a traitor, Sire?" asked Merchant Chapa.

"It's likely," replied Adeone. "Ah, Wynfeld, come in."

Wynfeld saluted. "We've a couple of problems, Sire. Firstly, we'd already released Fullerton. Secondly, Gad was seen entering the Guildhall and my men didn't have all exits covered. I've confined them to barracks. Several other men are on Gad's known lodgings. We'll pick him up again but he's currently on the loose, sir."

Adeone got up. "Sicla! Right, we'll wait for Landis. What's keeping him?"

Six minutes later Landis hurried into the office, barely stopping to bow. "We've picked Gad up. He returned to his new lodgings. He's also paid for some months in advance. Or someone has for him. One of my men got the name. I'm having my chief bailiff trawl through my tenancy lists to see if it occurs in my books. If it does then we know there are houses or rooms all over the city being used by whoever Gad is working for."

"We've nearly lost him twice now," fumed Adeone.

"No, we haven't, sir. The army has. That's not a criticism, Wynfeld, but it is the truth. He can spot soldiers. It's probably in their bearing as much as their uniform. I have several tenants currently unable to pursue the career of their choice who don't look like soldiers. They owe me for not turning them out onto the street. I've told them to report to Beaver for some light work they can manage. They'll not lose Gad."

"Unless you can guarantee that, Landis, I want Gad lifted."

"All I can do, Your Majesty, is tell you we will do everything we can."

"Might I suggest you spook Gad a bit?" mused Merchant Chapa. "Leave obviously military men watching him, ones who lose him. He'll know he lost them at the Guildhall. That's why he talked to me for so long. He wanted them to get bored and slack. He'll lead you a merry dance but it will pay dividends, I'm certain of that. If he approaches me again, I'll tell you."

Landis looked to the King for a decision.

Adeone hesitated. "I'm uneasy if he's on the loose. I can't hide that. He's already been within a hairsbreadth of killing me once. His cousin nearly killed you, Landis. I can see the advantage of collecting more information but he's turned his attention on Prince Arkyn, Edward and you, Cousin Henry. Who can say where his attention will turn tomorrow?"

Landis shrugged, "Prince Arkyn is safe in the Rex Dallin. We can get Merchant Chapa protection. I honestly think to step in now might be unwise. As has been said, Gad can lead us to so much more."

"Wynfeld, it's your men involved. What is your opinion?"

"I'm uncertain," admitted Wynfeld. "I can see what both Your Majesty and Lord Landis are saying, and I also tend to agree with both of you. If we lift him, we remove the immediate threat to Your Majesty but we might find more about future threats or other threats if we leave him for a time. All I can say is that if Your Majesty decides to learn what we can from Gad, I will try to ensure that all possible protections are in place for yourself, Prince Arkyn, Merchant Chapa and anyone else who requires them. If he hadn't already attacked Your Majesty, I'd say leave him and find out what he's planning."

"Landis?"

"I'd agree, Your Majesty. We don't know what is planned and there is always the chance that Gad's immediate employers will simply find another operative and carry out the plan that way. We don't even know if Gad will execute the next plan."

"Are we certain there is one?"

Wynfeld answered, "I think so, but I haven't got a clue what, sir. Hob Fullerton certainly thought there is one. We might be lucky and find out some other way, but Gad keeps plans close to his chest. We know that from Hillbeck's experience."

Adeone made the decision. "Right, then I think, at least for today, we'll leave him free; however, if you find he's giving you nothing at all he *is to be arrested*. Is that understood, gentlemen? I'm not leaving him free unless he is giving us something."

Wynfeld and Landis both agreed, and Merchant Chapa raised an eyebrow slightly. Adeone signalled dismissal to Wynfeld and Landis, and when they'd gone, turned back to the Chief Merchant.

"You know, cousin, I have the feeling that decision wasn't the wisest."

"If it's any consolation, I think your father would have made the same one, Sire. He was all for removing threats, but he did like to get information from them first."

"I know. I'm sorry Gad came to you though."

Merchant Chapa shrugged. "It's not a problem, sir. If he'd gone elsewhere, we'd never have known he was impersonating Fullerton."

"That's true I suppose. Thank you for informing me."

"I didn't intend to, Your Majesty. I intended to ask why observation had been started on visiting merchants. That was all."

Adeone regarded him shrewdly. "They have been following the real Hob Fullerton since he entered Oedran because Jones in Garth alerted Wynfeld to the fact that he was feeling aggrieved…" Adeone carried on explaining before saying "We only watch people we're concerned about. Ninety-nine per cent of merchants in Oedran remain unmolested. Fullerton was a bit of an exception to the rule. Gad was probably trying to find out how much you knew."

"Nothing. That would have come across plainly enough."

"Good. Right, was that all, cousin?"

"As I'm here, Sire…"

Adeone inwardly sighed. He liked his mother's cousin, he really did, but he wished that once, just *once*, the answer to his question would be *'yes'*.

The Chief Merchant finally left and Adeone put the list he'd made to one side. He'd consider the suggestions when he had a couple of days to spare. Ones like setting up a yearly trading fair, like the Frander of Byfa, would take that long on their own.

# Chapter 60
## UNCERTAIN PLANS
Imperadai, Week 25 – 4th Ralal, 4th Ralis 1210
Inner Office

AN ALUNA-MONTH LATER, Adeone called everyone back together. No-one had been idle in those four weeks. Gad had stopped looking over his shoulder so regularly. He had led them to several houses of apparently law-abiding citizens with dual personalities. Given time, Wynfeld would investigate them. Merchant Chapa had been left alone, as had his family. Adeone was relieved; he didn't need his cousins targeted.

He asked, "Do we know *what* Gad is planning yet?"

Wynfeld answered honestly, "No, Sire. We'll find out though."

"What about Hob Fullerton? Has he been of any use?"

"Some, sir. Gad hasn't approached him again, but he has been watching him. He hasn't heard we pulled the merchant in for questioning. He, himself, was attempting to deceive the Chief Merchant at the time, but he hasn't found out subsequently. We think if he had, he'd have killed Merchant Fullerton and gone to ground."

"As an aside, do we know if the Chief Merchant is planning to retire?"

Wynfeld said, "From what we can find out, it is certainly on the cards. I think his eldest son might be able to tell Your Majesty."

"Then I'll talk to Nicholas. I need to know, but I'd also like to know why he hasn't told me himself."

"I doubt it's for any nefarious reason, Sire," replied Landis. "I expect he doesn't want a fuss. He's been Chief Merchant for many years."

"Quite. Right, how long will you request I leave Gad free for this time?"

"I'd say until the middle of spring, Sire. He might lead us elsewhere."

"Wynfeld?"

The captain replied levelly, "That's about what I thought, Sire. Then review the situation again. He's not slipped through our fingers for weeks now. I've our scryer keeping an eye on him at times as well."

"Good. All right, Captain, keep me updated. That's all for now."

Wynfeld saluted and left, leaving Landis and Adeone eyeing each other.

"He's still doing a good job," remarked Landis.

"I know. Which is why I'm leaving him there for the moment. *Without* discussion on the matter, Festus."

"I can take a hint."

"So, it's true, there is a first time for everything." Adeone got up and passed his friend a drink before easing himself into a comfortable chair, looking into a low fire.

"Won't it seem a bit odd if you speak to Nicholas Chapa?" asked Landis. "You always deal with his father these days."

Adeone said, "I suppose I do. Do you have any reason for sending for Nicholas yourself? He is one of your tenants."

"I'm sure I could find something, Sire. If I let you know when, would you *unexpectedly* drop round to see your nearchildren?"

"I'll take a headache cure first. How is everyone?"

"They're fine. The twins are counting down to their fifteenth birthday and young Ira is proving she's voluble. I can hardly wait until she learns to talk."

"I'm sure it will be sooner than you think possible."

"You might be right there. Where are the years going?"

"Into the past but at least we're living them."

Landis laughed. "Pragmatist."

Adeone smiled smugly. "I'll take that as a compliment."

"One should always compliment the King. Apparently, it's the way favours work."

"Then whoever says that needs a quick lesson in my perceptions. I can spot smooth-talking a mile off. Talking of 'a mile off'… Don't you have things you need to be doing?"

"There's always things I need to be doing. It's why I appreciate your company, Sire. It gives me an excellent excuse for not doing the things which need doing."

A week later, Backery showed Nicholas Chapa into Lord Landis' more-than-comfortable study and he inclined his head to his landlord. Landis could see puzzlement clear in the merchant's eyes. He smiled in welcome and dismissed Backery with a glance.

"Come on in, Master Chapa. I'll apologise for this very unconventional meeting in advance, but there are good reasons for it—"

There was a knock at the door and William announced Adeone and Richardson. Landis rose and Nicholas turned around, surprised.

Adeone entered, saying lightly, "Festus, you'll have to forgive me. I didn't want to be late, but I do still have a couple of urgent documents to deal with, so you'll have to talk to me as I read and sign them. Nicholas! How are you?"

"Erm, perfectly well, Your Majesty. I hope you are also?"

"Well enough, cousin. Landis, shall I make myself scarce?"

Inwardly appreciative of the King's acting, Landis said, "No, Sire. I don't think that will be necessary. I'm sure I can trust your discretion."

Adeone crooked an eyebrow at Nicholas. "You have a jester for a landlord, cousin."

"I've known that for years, sir. We simply smile out of kindness."

Adeone laughed. "I'm not the only one then. Right, I shouldn't disturb your meeting. Richardson, have you got that information from the Chief Yeoman?"

Landis avoided the administrator's eyes. "Nicholas, what is the truth of the rumour that your father plans to retire?"

Nicholas grasped that the King's presence *wasn't* a coincidence. "There have been rumours for years, my lord." He glanced at the King who seemed to be absorbed by the report he was reading.

"Yes. Is there any truth in them?" enquired Landis.

"My father seems to be a law unto himself, sir. I wouldn't like to say."

From behind him, Adeone glanced at Landis and the glance clearly said, *'Don't accept that.'*

"Master Chapa, obviously your father would have told you if he planned to retire. I'm asking you to tell me if he has," explained Landis.

"I don't know if I can, sir," replied Nicholas.

Adeone looked over his shoulder at his administrator and Richardson left. The click of the door made Nicholas turn slightly.

Adeone regarded him shrewdly. "Cousin, you're stonewalling. Your landlord asked you a question. It is normally polite to answer it without such tactics."

Nicholas swallowed. "My loyalties are torn, Sire. If my father's asked that

I don't mention matters of business, who am I to break that confidence?"

Adeone's gaze didn't change. "Am I to understand by that explanation that Merchant Chapa is retiring?"

"Your Majesty should, I'm afraid, draw your own conclusions…"

Adeone watched him for a moment then glanced at Landis, who simply left. Adeone smiled, unnerving his cousin. "Right, forget I'm King and deal with the fact I am also blood-kin. Does my first cousin once removed plan to retire? I wouldn't be asking if I didn't need to know."

Nicholas sighed, defeated: as soon as the King pulled the family card, he'd lost. He tried one last time. "Why hasn't Your Majesty asked him, sir?"

Adeone's expression spoke a thousand words, including, *'Do you really think that would work?'*

Nicholas wrestled with his conscience for a short time before giving in to the inevitable. "Yes, my father does plan to retire. He doesn't want *anyone* to make a fuss."

Adeone motioned to a chair. Nicholas sank onto it, hardly reassured.

"That is an admirable Chapa trait," observed Adeone. "If I said I didn't mean to make a fuss, would you believe me?" Incredulity blazed across his cousin's face. "Then I won't bother. I won't hide from you that I wish to honour your father's work, but I have yet to determine what could be of use to him or a fitting reward for that work."

"He would say it was his job and his duty to the empire, Your Majesty."

"Does it follow that duty shouldn't be rewarded?"

"Erm… I'm not sure he'd quite agree, sir."

Adeone laughed. "I expect not. When does he plan to announce to the merchants that they have to elect another chief?"

"Sorry, sir, it might be one step too far. To change the subject, it is a few years since we saw you at the Guild Banquet."

Adeone's eyes narrowed. "Thank you. Should your father ever ask me how I discovered every detail, I shall never mention your name."

"Thank you, sir. I do quite enjoy the thought of being his heir."

Adeone chuckled. "The Chapa sense of humour has a lot to answer for. Now, everything before aside, how are things?"

"Perfectly fine, sir. Life seems to be progressing as ever. My eldest has decided not to set up on his own and is carrying on helping me."

"Are you pleased?"

"Yes, I think so. His mother is anyway and if she's happy…"

Adeone smiled sadly. "I remember that feeling well."

"I can imagine, sir. Memories keep people alive, or so they say."

"That's true, I suppose. Time makes fools of all our memories though."

Nicholas said, "Only of some, sir. How are your brood?"

A knock heralded Lord Landis. "Sire, I'm sorry to disturb you…"

Adeone looked at Nicholas. "But… There's always a 'but'…" he whispered conspiratorially.

"…but Richardson's fretting about that information reaching the Chief Yeoman…"

"They like to keep me in my place, Nicholas. I suppose I'd better continue working. I'll see you soon. You'll have to come to dinner."

Nicholas turned back to Landis as Adeone picked up the report he did have to read.

Landis shrugged. "Sorry for the subterfuge. I didn't need to see you about anything. I am but the puppet of my King."

Without looking up, Adeone remarked, "Yes, it's just a shame most of the strings have a mind of their own. Never believe your landlord, cousin."

Nicholas grinned. "I shall remember that, sir. I have a feeling it might come in useful. When he says he's put the rent up, for example."

Lord Landis shook his head, disbelievingly. "Now you have conspired with the King, I shouldn't keep you any longer, Master Chapa."

As Nicholas left, Richardson slipped back into the room.

Adeone looked at him. "Tell the Chief Yeoman I don't want excuses then clear the rest of this lot away. I'll see you in the morning and pencil in a dinner with Nicholas for me. I hardly had time to exchange news."

Once Richardson had left, Landis raised a questioning eyebrow.

Adeone said, "He's going to announce it at the Guild Banquet at the end of this year. All credit to Nicholas, he didn't tell me straight out."

"I doubt Henry will appreciate the subtlety."

"I'm sure he *will* because he's not going to find out from us that his son told me, is he?"

Landis grinned. "Well, Wynfeld's intelligence network does such a good job, sir, it was bound to reach your ears that he was retiring and the banquet is the obvious place to announce his intentions and Nicholas would never get cornered into revealing anything during a private dinner, would he?"

Adeone said, "Pity my mother's cousin is shrewder than to believe any of that."

"Now, Sire, your nearchildren are all currently awake, in one case screaming…"

"All right, I'll submit myself to torture."

Adeone entered the night nursery smiling, winked at Nursie and confidently picked up his screaming neardaughter. "Now, little one, what's all the noise for? Eh? Why the crying? Are you too hot, too cold, hungry, thirsty? Or are you simply trying out those Landis lungs of yours? You're certainly growing…"

She was watching his face and had all but stopped crying. Clear eyes met penetrating ones and were content to look at each other. Cats might look at kings, but young Ira didn't know that she shouldn't gaze at him quite that openly. Adeone never even noticed when Landis and Nursie left; he was still talking softly to young Ira, talking to her as though he was talking once more to Queen Ira, talking out the grief he'd hidden for so long.

Young Ira watched his face. Tiny fingers flexed and Adeone put his finger next to them. She took it in her hand and held it, content. Gradually, she fell to sleep.

After six minutes, to compose his face, Adeone got up and put her down into her cradle. He watched her for another couple of minutes – thinking of her future and his lost daughter – before walking out of the room, careful not to disturb her slumber.

Landis noticed his mellow mood. He simply nodded for Nursie to go back to her charge. Once alone, he asked, "How do you think your ears will stand up to the other five?"

Appreciating the tact, Adeone said, "Reasonably well. Then I really must greet Cornelia. I've hardly seen her since the birth."

Together they entered the main nursery where the other five Landis children were annoying each other with an aplomb that showed they'd inherited traits from their father.

## Chapter 61
# GADDING ABOUT
### Pentadai, Week 34 – 12th Bayal, 5th Bayis 1210
### Oedran – Medlars Close

GAD SMILED TO HIMSELF as he looked around his room. Adson would have liked it, but that knowledge brought back the way his cousin had died. They'd tossed for the chance to attack Landis. Gad had lost, but he had begun to wonder if his cousin had cheated. Still, there would be revenge. He'd make sure of that.

Three years since he'd first been captured and he knew the rules: don't try to escape, don't get caught, don't displease the overseer. They were simple. Brant had been unexpected but he was glad to be back in the city with its opportunities. He had as much freedom as anyone else if he was available to the overseer.

He glanced through the grimy shutter's slats, taking stock of the faces in Medlars Close. It wasn't a bustling thoroughfare, new faces were rare and yet, for the second time that day, a different beggar was sitting on a step at the mouth of the alley. Did they think he was stupid? True, there weren't many things the watchers could do that wouldn't draw attention. Begging was obvious, but real beggars tended to have poorer clothes and stick to the same spot, not the same step becoming home to multiple beggars with clothes just a bit too cared for. Oh, there'd been the sweeper – sweeping an alley that Lord Teran never cared about. That had been rather revealing, especially when his landlady had demanded to know what the man was doing. Maybe it was time to lead them another merry dance.

Being a vigilant was handy. He couldn't be truly unseen or know he was being talked about, he couldn't draw a map, or understand languages but he could know he was being followed if he concentrated. Almost like seeing threads in cloth, he could picture the lines tethering the watchers to him.

There was a burning flame of enjoyment as he concocted places to go. He had been told to avoid any Lord of Oedran or their families. That was fine. He didn't want to get noticed by them because, after a failed attack on the King and Lord Landis, he didn't know what they had been told or if they'd been asked to watch for a man of his description.

It was almost a shame he'd had to kill Vince. He'd been a very useful contact but, unfortunately, he had caught him passing information to his cousin. Still, there might be opportunities from what he'd learned. Other people who could be useful. He'd passed the details on rather than keep them to himself. The overseer knew more than he let on; when Gad hadn't admitted to his hue, Adson's sister had been beaten. They'd given up keeping secrets after that.

Gad whistled to himself as he dressed. He had to avoid the Palace now, and the events at the Woolsack meant he couldn't go there for a drink but an amble through Guildhall Plaza picking up the gossip couldn't go amiss. He'd then meander towards the wharves. He always liked taking his watchers there. They were so obviously on edge. He'd pick up one of the ghost packages whilst he was there and deliver it... Where? Well, a mail lodge to some lord elsewhere in the empire would cost him, so that was out of the question. He could try Master Galdwin's but that was a little too near Landis House and would tempt fate too much. He couldn't risk leaving it for an official as that would rouse suspicions and stories about empty packages would reach Captain Wynfeld's ears and then he'd know that he was being led a dance. He'd drop it at an inn to be called for in a couple of days. He'd then collect it and move it elsewhere when different men were watching him.

He made sure of the knife in his boot and his wrist knife before leaving the room and locking it. He was sure *they* hadn't searched it *yet*. He idly wondered why he hadn't been arrested. *They* knew who he was and where he was. He wasn't complaining. He had plans still to make and the only reason he could think of was that they thought he was giving them important information. If only they knew.

He dropped a coin into the beggar's bowl out of mischief and then sauntered to Alcium Plaza – the large City Alcium at its centre, smug and proud of itself set apart from the other buildings. He decided against entering it for the fun of losing his tail in the dim interior and instead eyed the people milling around. He spied a trader who appeared more than usually confused, slightly awed even, and deduced that he was a foreigner. His belt pouch was tantalisingly visible. Gad hummed to himself and started hurrying in his direction, feigning tripping as he bumped into the merchant, a swift cut with his wrist knife, a sincere apology, and he was off again. He was out of sight around the side of the Alcium by the time the trader knew what had happened. He concentrated for a moment and then smirked. They were still tailing him but hadn't interfered. He didn't fool himself that they hadn't seen. He emptied the pouch into his own. Counting the contents could wait. He might pawn the ring or maybe drop it in at the Merchants' Guild and claim a reward. It would give him a chance to explore. As he left the shelter of the wall, the trader was talking with the guards on the King's Gate. Walking brazenly past them was pushing his luck a bit too far. He grinned and returned to the edge of the lordships, dodging through the streets and alleys of the Macarian Lordship, picking up a pie from a bake-square stall and a fresh loaf from another. There was nothing like fresh bread. The pie he ate in all of three bites, but the bread he lingered over. By the time he reached the Ratharia between the Macarian and Rathgar Lordships, he hoped he was making the people tailing him hungry. He crossed the busy street and darted through the Rathgar Lordship until he crossed the Dallin Road and entered the Ryson Lordship where he sauntered to the wharves. They were always bustling and thriving with barges bringing goods from the port. Leaning against a warehouse wall, enjoying the melee, he watched the stevedores offloading barrels of goods, foremen shouting where to put it, traders haggling before it reached the warehouse, carts laden making their way through the confused jumble of people and goods. He clipped a cutpurse around the head as he tried to remove his belt pouch and then, deciding he'd seen enough, wove his way to the Anchor's Rest and got the landlord's attention.

The landlord passed over an unremarkable package, wrapped in a dirty piece of sacking. Gad took it, winked and left again. He purloined a wineskin a dockhand had left unattended whilst answering a call of nature, grinned at a boy who'd also been eyeing it and tossed it to him before shouting *'Oi, he's nicked your drink,'* and watching the mayhem ensue, picking up a small barrel of whiskey whilst everyone was distracted. He hoped he was giving *them* a lot to report about. He would have hated wasting their efforts. By the time he was back on The Strait, the barrel and package were getting heavy so he called in at the Pass Inn – somebody's idea of a joke, obviously – and sold the barrel on the understanding that he had nine more. Gad insisted on a deposit and the landlord – ever one for a bargain – agreed to pay for half the cost of one barrel as that deposit. Gad agreed, walked out with a nice profit and the false promise he'd bring the cart round with the others in six minutes.

He slipped into the alleys of the Teran Lordship and chuckled to himself. So far, it had been a good day for him. He dropped the package off at the Cup Bearer and whistling made his way home, where he counted and hid most of his ill-gotten gains in the chimney of his room on the salt shelf. He then pocketed enough for an evening of enjoyment and glanced through the shutter slats again. Another new face. The last must have got bored or tired. Well, this one could watch him visiting Madam Little's and imagine what he was getting up to there. He was sure the man wouldn't mind. He chuckled to himself again and went and ate a bowl of his landlady's remarkably good soup before doing another round of the streets before ending up, almost accidentally at the Golden Hare, where Madam Little welcomed him as the good customer he was and passed on a message that the overseer wanted a chat about his plans. Gad went to the back room, which had the feel of a storeroom with odd sacks lying around, and hooks on the ceiling, presumably for hanging things out of the way of rats.

"Whiskey? Where are the proceeds?"

"Safe, sir," muttered Gad, cursing. He'd thought it was only the idiots from the intelligence regiment on his tail.

"And the trader's purse?"

"Also safe, sir," grouched Gad. "I don't see what harm it does. I didn't kill him."

"No, but I can't let you run around with your own funds. You're known to get a little too lax about 'not killing' when you see gold. Did you find out anything today?"

"No, but then neither did *they.*"

"True. Except that you're an opportunist. That lad you threw the wineskin to will be up before the courts. What progress have you made?"

"Can't get in," muttered Gad.

"Can't get in? Why not?" asked the overseer coolly. "I thought your skills were honed just for this."

"They keep the doors closed at this time of year and you told me I'd been rumbled when I posed as Fullerton."

"You were. It was a foolish mistake. You're nothing like Fullerton. Foolish mistakes will get us all killed."

"Not you. No-one knows your name."

"I intend to keep it that way as well," said the overseer mildly. "Do you even have a plan, Gaddy Gad Gad?"

"Yes," said Gad mulishly. "Would have been easier with my cousin, but you got him killed."

"His stupidity got him killed. I did tell you Landis was a good fighter. So, your plan, what is it?"

Gad explained and pretended not to notice the four men who had entered.

"That only works if everything falls into place, doesn't it? If the Chief Merchant is retiring, if the King accepts the invitation, if introductions are made… There's a lot of ifs in there, Gaddy Gad Gad."

Gad swallowed. "But *if* I'm in the hall, I might have other opportunities, *sir*. I can't go to Court now. They've changed everything. There's nowhere for me to hide. It's *not* my fault, sir. Lord Landis has been interfering since the attack failed."

The overseer leered viciously. "It was the day after you attended that the changes started to happen. It is your fault. I don't know how exactly but it is because you were there and that can only mean that they know you were there. Now, you need to learn to be more careful. Please strip."

Gad glared. "No."

"Oh dear. You came to a brothel. You wanted to be comfortable. I'll not ask twice."

Gad crossed his arms defiantly. A large sack was thrown over his head and tied off below his arms. Panicking, he struggled and fell against someone, who pushed him into another's arms. The blow caught him low. As he doubled up, he was thrown sideways into the wall. They all had their *fun* before the overseer said,

"That money, I know how much there was. You will give it to Madam Little tomorrow or suffer much worse than this. You are drawing far too much attention to yourself for no benefit! How many lessons is it now?"

Gad felt four slashes with a sharp blade and knew he wouldn't be sitting down for a while. The light tread of the overseer left the room and he lay still. He thought the others remained and he was right. One tied his feet together. The heftiest hoisted him aloft and hung him up by his ankles from a hook in the ceiling. He struggled to no avail. The men were talking options, turning him around, poking at him. He was their toy, but he now knew he was too valuable to the overseer for them to kill him; however, that didn't end his torment. The overseer thought it kept him afraid and obedient, and he wasn't wrong. It seemed an eternity before they left, but it was probably only a few minutes. It wasn't many more before he heard another tread in the room and Madam Little's laughter. Several of her girls were with her and they made comparisons about his manhood before letting him down. If torture and torment from men weren't enough, prostitutes were tormenting him as well. However low he was, he was better than them. When he snarled that at them, they simply laughed, pointing out that they had freedoms and got to keep a good proportion of their earnings. Madam Little watched with a grin as her girls belittled him. The overseer paid her to gather information, and she was quite happy, therefore, to do what he bid.

Dawn was breaking as he limped home, exhausted. Stumbling into his room, he collapsed onto his bed wishing for the oblivion of sleep, for some way of revenge, for something, anything that wasn't this life. He was half asleep when a hand slipped over his mouth and the ordeal continued. All he'd done was rob traders and he was being tortured for it. Another cut was made. When he jumped up to challenge the man, there was nothing to challenge but thin air. He shivered, terrified. Someone with far greater Ullian skill than his was watching him. He would never know if he was alone again.

Chapter 62

# REPORTS

Alunadai, Week 35 – 15th Bayal, 8th Bayis 1210<br>Wynfeld's Office

WYNFELD SCRUTINISED the scruffy individual. He even had a limp which stayed on the same side. "You're not one of mine, are you?"

"Name's Wharfsratter, sir."

"Seriously?" asked Wynfeld. "You need a word with your ancestors. So, who sent you?"

"Lord Landis, sir. I'm a Meddling."

Wynfeld nodded. It had seemed an appropriate name for those watching Gad, given the location of his lodgings.

"Go on then. What's your report?"

"Not interesting, sir. I've been begging at the alley for a few days. Don't think 'e realises 'cause he dropped a bit in me bowl t'other morning instead of slitting me throat. Yon corporal should be able to tell you where he's been a going but from what I've seen, he ain't acting oddly, well not for low life. No visitors, stays out late some nights; I had t'sleep on the step t'other

277

evening. Seemed a bit beaten that night. Ah, here's your men…"

Corporal Dunson and Soldier Lennox saluted smartly and waited.

"Dunson, Lennox, anything of interest?"

Dunson shrugged. "I don't think he knows we're following 'im, sir. Over the last few days, he's robbed several men, some very openly – sliced a merchant's belt pouch off him in the middle of the Alcium Plaza. He's been walking to the wharves a lot and watching the boats arriving. Not sure if he's waiting for something. He did cause a distraction the other day by pinching a wineskin and then accusing a young boy of it. Lad's name's Bradach. Not sure if we can do anything for him in the circumstances. We didn't interfere…"

As he carried on explaining, Wynfeld's frustration rose. They should be discovering more than they were. It all amounted to Gad wandering around the city, exploiting opportunities without revealing motive. Muggings, strange parcels and distractions weren't going to prove anything. They were making note of the places visited and Wynfeld was despatching men to them, but they weren't hearing anything interesting afterwards.

They needed something definite. Something they could move on after they arrested Gad because once his employers realised that he'd been arrested tracks would be covered and evidence destroyed. Nothing seemed to be helping in the larger picture of proving Lord Scanlon guilty of treason.

Wharfsratter, Dunson and Lennox left, unaware of the extent of Wynfeld's frustration. The only silver lining was they were proving that the army and civilians could work together.

He consulted Beaver, suggesting they searched Gad's lodgings but, even as he said it, they both realised that one thing out of place would alert Gad to the fact he was being watched. He seemed to believe he wasn't under observation. No-one who was would rob people. Then Wynfeld realised that they might if they wanted to see if they were being followed. Only sharp eyes would have spotted the muggings. If anyone raised the alarm then Gad swiftly disappeared and – hopefully unbeknownst to him – his follower followed.

A few days later, they thought they had a breakthrough. Gad visited the yeomen. Did that mean someone there was working for Lord Scanlon? Wynfeld reported it to Adeone who simply told him to do some digging, which turned up nothing of significance. Was Gad planning *anything*? All his actions seemed normal for a piece of the city's lowlife. It was the fact he called once more on the yeomen that kept Wynfeld following him throughout the winter and early spring.

# Chapter 63
## A MAN OF LAW, A FRIEND
Tretaldai, Week 35 – 17th Bayal, 10th Bayis 1210
Inner Office

READING THE CONFIDENTIAL REPORT from Jones, Adeone tapped his fingers thoughtfully on his desk. The information left him in a dilemma; should he talk with the Exarch about it or not? He was just concluding that he'd have to when Richardson entered.

"Judge Tancred has called by, Sire, and wondered if you have a moment."

Adeone furled the report and crooked an eyebrow expressively.

"There's nothing that can't be rearranged, Sire," replied his administrator.

"Then what are you doing blocking the doorway?"

A lean man in his sixties, whose eyes spoke of a kind nature and whose smile spoke of reassurance, entered. He bowed with an easy familiarity.

Once Richardson had left, Adeone pushed himself to his feet. "Brandy?"

"That would be very nice, Sire. Thank you. I hope I am not disturbing Your Majesty."

"I very much doubt you know how to, James. Did you call by for any reason in particular?"

"To deliver a dinner invitation, only, sir. Bets is insisting on a meal to mark my birthday. I would very much be honoured if you could make it."

"It is I who would be honoured. Do I have to be on my best behaviour?"

Glass in hand, Tancred chuckled, waiting for Adeone to sit before taking his place. "I am sure none of my guests would say anything if you were not, Sire. It will be a small gathering. My son, the Keeper and a couple of lawyers whom I think you might remember from Prince Lachlan's office: Widders and Melling."

Adeone sighed. "Sounds like just the dinner I need. Thank you."

Tancred looked caringly at the King. "How are you, Sire?"

"Frustrated currently. It comes with the seal," he added wryly.

"Is there anything I can help with, sir?"

"You already give me far too much help, James."

"Then might I ask how my Princes are, sir?"

Adeone smiled. "Arkyn seems to be taking his new responsibilities well, as we all expected."

"I am glad, sir. I know you were worried about him."

"It's a father's duty, isn't it? I have never been worried about the way he will face his duties but... Do you remember the first days we spent any real time together?"

"Of course, sir," said Tancred, recalling the weeks after Queen Eliza's death.

"I had a form of collapse. No, James, I did. We both know it. You listened when I was ready to talk and I have never forgotten and never will. You, the Comptroller and Chief, Susan, you all helped me through those weeks. When Ira died, Wynfeld listened to Arkyn and since then he's been far easier in himself. I don't know what Wynfeld and he talked about – Wynfeld won't tell me and I haven't asked Arkyn – but I no longer fear that he will suffer the depressions I did."

"I am glad, sir. Apparently, Wynfeld is a most remarkable officer."

Adeone crooked an eyebrow. "What have you heard?"

"That he shuns traditional methods for his own, that he acts to solve issues rather than adapting to them and that his dedication to his work is rare. When I met him, he seemed straightforward. Apparently, Your Majesty is also being very forbearing of his mistakes. I may now understand why."

"Am I so easy to read?" asked the King sadly.

"No, sir, not at all. I have the honour of having known Your Majesty for many years and you have mentioned the captain prevented your son from having a breakdown. There is nothing wrong in recognising that debt."

"As long as the debt doesn't outweigh the service," replied Adeone, as though reading a long-memorised text.

Tancred chuckled. "Aye, there is that. Your uncle had a lot to answer for."

"And I still miss him for all of that. I've become very staid since he died. Far too enmeshed in what I should be. There are days when I want to escape."

"Then do. Ceardlann is still close. Visit your sons and walk by the river. Let the Lord and Lady take your cares away," said Tancred with a smile.

"Unfortunately, mythological personifications of an ideal can't solve my problems."

"No, but I rather suspect Prince Tain could help chase them away – the problems, that is, not the Lord and Lady of Encilla."

Adeone laughed. "You never know. Oh, one of these days, James, you really will have to spend some time with him. He would keep you smiling if nothing else. Uncle Lachlan would encourage him to such mischief, and Tain would relish it. He is very like I was but without the burden of expectation."

"Only because you have not placed it on him yet, Sire," said Tancred.

Adeone sighed. "Yes, that is coming." He went to look out of the window. "I wish I could keep him in ignorance, but it's not possible, is it?"

"No, sir, sadly, it is not. His Highness will have hard years ahead. Especially if your fears are well-founded."

Adeone swallowed. "I think we both know that they are…"

Tancred crossed over to him and squeezed his shoulder. "If you were at fault, sir, your brother would have far more supporters than he has."

Adeone flashed him a wry glance. "I'm not sure that's how you should reassure me, James." He made up his mind. Tancred's visit was too well timed for him to ignore. He crossed to his desk, picked up Jones' report and passed it over. "I'd be interested in your thoughts on the legalities of that, Your Honour."

Tancred took the report and tilted it to the light from the windows before absentmindedly perching on the window sill to read it.

Adeone watched him for a couple of minutes. His uncle's closest friend had become his own confidant many years ago. He'd known him longer than Landis. He hadn't had a nearfather and he'd often visited his uncle's chambers; Tancred had been there many times. Both adults had treated him as an intellectual equal, even when he'd been young. They'd enjoyed many debates; Tancred always respectful but never sycophantic and Adeone had learned the difference between those two manners of behaviour in those chambers. He had a lot to thank his uncle and Tancred for. Watching the judge read the report, he wondered if their friendship would endanger Tancred. He knew if he suggested it, the judge would say it didn't matter if it did; he had been a target of contempt in his youth, of snobbery when he became the first cisan-born judge and of resentment when he had become friends with the FitzAlcis considering his history.

Tancred rolled the report up and handed it back thoughtfully. "Bayan law is not my speciality, sir."

"No, but I'd bet you know more of it than I do. Just get on with your conclusions, James."

Tancred inclined his head slightly. "Very well, sir. Heritor Fullerton's death was unfortunate and it seems, if not suspicious, curiously timed. The confiscation of the land was swiftly enacted by the Eschervin. From your man's report, Merchant Fullerton was incapacitated, delirious and confined to bed unable to write for a fortnight at least after his father's death. The facts as I know them are that a heritor's heir must travel to Garth and declare the inheritance in person to the Exarch – I believe the wording is something like 'before the moons are full'. This has kept lawyers in pay over the centuries, but nothing has been done about the wording. Merchant Fullerton fell ill at Fullers Hall. His journey to Garth would have been impossible in his condition. He had only a few days to reach Garth before the Alcis Day when he came out of the fever. He set out but by the time he arrived – three days after the Alcis Day – the Eschervin seems to have unilaterally decided to confiscate the land. As it was a matter of law – as Chief Judge of Bayan – he has that right but it would be courteous and more usual for His Honour to have talked with the Exarch—"

"Can I do anything?"

"Your Majesty gives power to your Justiciar, who appoints the Eschervin. Theoretically, you could ask for an investigation as to whether it was reasonable for the land to be confiscated whilst Merchant Fullerton was ill."

"Do you recommend I do?" enquired Adeone, knowing Tancred would advise without meaning it as a recommendation.

Tancred considered carefully. "I believe that a formal investigation may cause more damage than might be intended. It would be unusual in Bayan for the King to interfere in a matter of law. Especially when it is a case that would not normally merit Your Majesty's attention."

Adeone snorted. "Yes, there is that. Anything else?"

"On the acquisition of the piece of borderland by Lord Rathgar, Sire: His Lordship placed the highest bid for it. That is all legal. Captain Jones' report is certainly curious as to the tactics used so that very few could bid on the land. Those tactics are more questionable in law, though not in themselves illegal. The fact His Lordship has failed to declare the land without ramifications is intriguing. As a lord, and a Lord of Oedran, the position of law may be different. The other reason the Eschervin may not have acted is that with Lord Scanlon currently in the province, the legalities will be presented to His Lordship. It is worth noting, however, that the decisions of the Bayan courts do not negate the necessity for His Lordship, that is Lord Rathgar, to also declare the acquisition of land to Your Majesty, as it would now fall under his dues to Your Majesty, and would count as part of his estate, whatever he plans to do with it in the future. He has, in many ways, returned the land to the FitzAlcis and must pay tribute on it."

Adeone considered that. "So, basically, my brother's friend is exploiting the connection and has potentially landed himself in trouble and me in the political mire? Sicla. Any suggestions?" He saw Tancred's hesitation. "I won't tell my advisors if you don't."

Tancred chuckled. "My general advice in any situation involving controversy, sir, has not changed: do not act in haste, assemble the facts, take advice from your lawyers and act only when there is certainty. If this case was before me in court, I would be considering the value of the land, the circumstances of the confiscation and, also, the manner of declarations or lack thereof. Given the delicate nature of the source of Your Majesty's information, it may be prudent to wait for the Munewid Lists, which should detail the transfer of land. I am also intrigued that Merchant Fullerton has travelled to Oedran in the wake of this matter. It suggests to me that he might be wanting to bring it to Your Majesty's notice during the Petitionals. If that is the case, then it would give Your Majesty a legitimate reason for investigating the potential issues at hand."

"Yes. What about this business with the bandits?"

"Ah. That. The court has judged him innocent, Sire; therefore, he is innocent. You could say the Eschervin's actions saved Fullerton. I am not convinced that he would have been convicted but the fact that the land had already been confiscated when the bandits were captured was fortunate because the law is very specific. At least, the normal interpretation of it is. It states that, to be guilty of harbouring bandits, the landowner must have had evidence they were operating on his land and not acted to apprehend them. That to harbour bandits, the landowner must therefore be protecting them, offering them shelter and safety from reprisals or similar. The Fullertons had reported the bandits to the fort; therefore, they had acted to help apprehend them. The fact the army was dilatory and lost the record of the report complicated matters but, in finding Merchant Fullerton innocent, the court set that record straight."

Adeone absorbed that. "I now don't know if Fullerton was lucky or unlucky that he fell ill. What would the case be if I, for the sake of argument, returned the land to Fullerton, or a portion of it? Would the issue of the bandits being on his land be resurrected?"

Tancred considered. "No, sir. I do not believe so. A court found him innocent, and the land wasn't in his possession when they were captured. If anyone were to be tried for it now, it would have to be the Eschervin or Exarch as they were guardians of the land until Lord Rathgar acquired it. If anything were to be said to Fullerton about it, I would suggest he points that out and watch the accusations fall away."

"If ever you need lessons in being crafty, talk to a man of law," muttered Adeone sagely.

Tancred's eyes creased with merriment. "We all have our skills, Sire."

* * *

Half an hour after Tancred left, Landis entered the Inner Office and was passed Jones' report to read.

When he finished it, he said, "What did Judge Tancred make of it?" He saw the resigned look on Adeone's face. "Hillbeck mentioned he'd been by."

Adeone explained Tancred's thoughts carefully.

"We could do with more judges like him. I agree with his advice as well."

"You don't think it's underhanded to know this and not act to prevent Rathgar and my brother being involved in controversy?"

"I think, sir, that, whatever you do, the controversy is already with us; therefore, revealing your spy network is improving is probably more damaging in the long term. When you do find out officially, it might be worth asking Lord Scanlon to check why the Eschervin acted so promptly. It was well known that both Heritor Fullerton and Merchant Fullerton

283

were ill. Personally, I'd be more worried that Scanlon will be leaving Garth soon. It means he'll be heading this way."

"Landis, you aren't meant to disparage my Justiciar like that."

"No, and he's not meant to plan to murder you, Sire. As your Defender, I believe honesty is important in private."

"Your honesty is always an example of something," muttered Adeone.

# Chapter 64
## VISITING
Alunadai, Week 37 – 1st Teral, 1st Teris 1210
Ceardlann

ON THE FIRST DAY OF SPRING, Ceardlann gave off its normal atmosphere of peace and contentment. Dismounting in the stableyard, Adeone passed Pursuit's reins to Alfred, scooped up one of the stable cats who was weaving between his legs purring and grinned at the Comptroller.

"I know, I know, you like warning."

"I do, Sire. I like to know that everything will be ready for your visit and that Cook has the meals planned."

"Cook always cooks as though we're entertaining the army and has a definite sense of premonition where I'm concerned. So, I don't see that that's a problem. Anyway, it's proof I have confidence in your management," he added with a grin. He looked down at the purring cat in his arms. "I don't think the Comptroller is convinced, Speckles. I think he wants me to behave as I should..."

The Comptroller chuckled. "Sire, that would just worry me more. It's good to see you. Are you staying tonight?"

"Why not? I'll leave after breakfast. Dare I ask where the terrors are?"

"In the Great Hall, Sire. Well, Prince Tain and Master Calumiel are. Prince Arkyn is with Advisor Spellen. Shall I send someone for him?"

"Might as well," replied Adeone, scratching Speckles' head. "I like to cheer up my children."

He entered the Great Hall of Ceardlann smiling. The hall was the oldest room in the house and, although not vast, was airy and bright. A tall arched window behind the dais overlooked a small courtyard garden. There was little call to use the hall for feasting or sleeping these days so there were no lower tables, just cabinets and upholstered chairs set around the half-panelled half-whitewashed walls. The flagged stones were bare but well swept and maintained. Around the walls hung tapestries and weapons and he wasn't surprised to see Tain and Cal were looking at the Skifta's Sword, a pattern-welded weapon that seemed to be full of twisting fire. It was a relic of the Cearcall surrounded by myths and legends. Tain had clearly decided they should lift it down from above the door to the small antechamber. He was in the process of climbing on an old, black-lacquered, spindly-legged cabinet as Adeone entered. The crash as it gave way, tumbling Tain to the ground and shattering the cabinet, was all the louder for the stone flagged floor.

For a moment Adeone's heart stopped, then anger hit him as Tain laughed. He strode over to the mess of son and cabinet, lifting Tain clear.

Frightened when he saw his father's face, Tain bit his lip, waiting.

"It is not a laughing matter, Tain! That cabinet was as old as the house and it, and the items in it, all deserved more respect. You do not climb on furniture, understood?"

"Yes, sir," mumbled Tain with a sniff, inspecting the flagged floor.

"Are you hurt?"

"I… No, sir, not really," he whispered.

Cal said quietly, "The back of your leg is bleeding, Your Highness."

Adeone roughly turned his son around and examined the cut. "It's not bad. Maria can salve it for you. Anything else?"

Tain looked beyond his father and shrugged. "Maybe bruises."

"Well, they'll remind you not to be silly next time. Why were you trying to lift down the Skifta's Sword?"

"That *was* my idea, Sire," admitted Cal. "I'm sorry. I haven't seen anything like it before and I wanted to look at the patterns."

"Many people have found it fascinating and one day I'll tell you the legends surrounding it but for today – and until you're tall enough to reach it down without climbing on furniture – it stays where it is. Is that clear? Both of you?" (The boys both nodded.) "Good. You must start to restrain yourselves and all your mad ideas. Start to think about what you're doing and don't act on impulse. Now, go and let Maria clean you up," he finished in a slightly kinder voice.

The boys left as Arkyn entered. His gaze took in his father, crouched over the mess of cabinet and curiosities. "What happened?"

"Your brother happened. How are you?"

Arkyn snorted, crossed over to the mess and retrieved a small model of Ceardlann, putting it on the trestle table on the dais before bending to retrieve an inlaid box and brass bowl.

"I'm better than this cabinet, father. How are you?"

"I was happy to be here before your brother destroyed this."

"The pieces have survived well enough, and one of the carpenters might be able to mend the cabinet. Or at least incorporate some of the panels into a new frame. What was Tain trying to do?"

"Reach the Skifta's Sword. It's staying on the wall until he and Cal are tall enough to take it down with proper care."

"Understood. At least he didn't fall holding the sword, sir."

Twelve minutes later, Maria entered the Great Hall and gave a brief curtsy. She saw more ordered destruction and caught the King's eye, asking for a word in private.

Adeone watched Arkyn leave. "How is the rascal?"

"Contrite and upset, sir. Even the offer of lemon cake hasn't worked."

Adeone snorted. "You're far too soft on my children."

Maria's lips twitched. "Yes, Sire, of course I am."

* * *

He found Tain curled up sobbing in the night nursery. Picking him up gently, Adeone sat hugging him. Arkyn's words about how much worse the accident could have been put everything into perspective and – although he wasn't about to undermine the lesson – he was glad to have been taught one himself. Tain's tears eventually stopped, but he carried on hugging his father and his father carried on hugging him. Neither of them noticed the door open a crack and Speckles sneak in. Adeone jumped as the cat wove itself around his ankles purring before jumping onto Tain's bed and then across onto Tain's lap, headbutting him and continuing to purr. Tain chuckled and Adeone knew the worst was over.

A few minutes later, Adeone whispered, "Are you all right?"

"I'm sorry, father, truly. I don't know why I laughed."

"Thank you for apologising. There wasn't much damage done to the contents of the cabinet and Arkyn has suggested that some of the panels could be made into a new cabinet. Do you want to help the carpenters design it?"

Tain agreed, putting his head back on his father's shoulder.

"Good. Now, Maria told me you've refused lemon cake. You're not running a fever, are you?"

"I don't think so, sir. Why?"

"Only reason I can think of why anyone would refuse lemon cake."

Tain laughed. "Cook could make us one. If you're going to be here… I mean…"

"It's a valid point," said Adeone, not getting riled. "Let's see if we can persuade him."

They wandered down to the kitchen, where Cook glanced over from near

286

the fire with his hands on his hips.

"Warning, I'm sure there's something about warning, Sire."

Adeone chuckled. "You cope, Cook. We've been talking about your excellent lemon cakes and wondering if we can prevail on you for one."

"Or two," said Tain cheekily.

"Two?" enquired his father. "I don't doubt you could eat them but why two?"

Tain shrugged. "You can take one to Oedran with you."

"Fair point." Adeone looked at Cook hopefully.

"Hmm," said Cook. "Do you exist just to cause me work?"

Adeone grinned. "Yes, I suppose I do. Go on, Cook. Humour your Prince."

"My Prince, Sire?" said Cook, struggling to keep up the act.

"He asked for two, so it can't possibly be my fault," replied Adeone.

There was a small chuckle from Susan who was blatantly watching the drama unfold with a grin. As soon as she laughed, there was a general susurration of amusement from the kitchen staff.

"Hmm," muttered Cook again. "Two lemon cakes, was it? You hear that, you lot. The King wants *two* lemon cakes."

There was something in the way he said it that made Adeone suspicious. "What are you up to, Cook?"

"Well, what are we meant to do with the third?"

Adeone laughed. "You made three cakes before you knew I was coming. Why?"

"As you said, Sire, Prince Tain can eat two on his own," replied Cook with a wink at Tain. He glared at his staff. "Right, you nosy lot, get on with your cooking. How are you, Sire?"

"Feeling cheated I didn't manage to catch you out," admitted Adeone with a grin. "What's for lunch and dinner?"

"Food if you let the kitchen be mine," grumbled Cook.

Adeone chuckled. "I'll see you later. Come on, Tain, let's go and annoy everyone else."


They entered the nursery companionably. Arkyn was curled up reading with Speckles asleep beside him. Cal was writing to his parents but broke off as the door opened. Spotting the King he rose and gave a very correct bow. Adeone sighed inwardly; he would prefer it if Cal wouldn't be quite so correct but, from everything his sons had told him, Cal wouldn't relax formalities. Elantha was sketching, oblivious of everything else. He crossed to her, touched her shoulder lightly. She turned. Dropping her pencil, she flung her arms around her uncle.

Adeone said, "I can always tell when you're pleased to see me, can't

I, little flower? What are you drawing? Ah. It's very good… I'm not sure Cal will appreciate it, though."

Elantha laughed. "I hadn't anything else to draw."

"Let's see," demanded Tain.

Elantha shook her head. "No. You'll only laugh."

"Would you laugh, Tain?" enquired Adeone.

"He always does," murmured Elantha.

Adeone raised an eyebrow at Tain. His son had the grace to look uncomfortable. He waited until Tain said,

"Probably, sir."

"Then don't show him, little flower. Only show people you want to. If they ask to mock you, they aren't worth the consideration, no matter who they are."

Elantha and her uncle exchanged a meaningful look and she nodded. Tain shuffled his feet. His father didn't need to emphasise the point and Tain wasn't foolish enough to comment himself. As Elantha showed Adeone other drawings she'd done, Cal glanced at his half-finished letter.

Arkyn said, "You might as well carry on, Cal. No-one will mind."

"Thank you, Your Highness."

Subdued from the rebuke, Tain looked at Arkyn. Feeling mean for considering it deserved, Arkyn winked at him and instead of joining his father and cousin started talking to him.

With his back to his sons, Adeone listened to them as much as to his niece. He didn't like telling them off but knew he had to. They had to be good men, and it was difficult for power not to be overwhelming and all-consuming. Scanlon had fallen into that trap and it hadn't been helped by his father. Adeone was determined not to make the same mistake with his sons.

A couple of hours later, they returned to Ceardlann after a walk. El wanted to finish her drawing and Cal asked to be excused to finish his letters. So Adeone entered the snug with his sons and smiled at the sight. A fire burnt brightly in the grate, a pot of tea was keeping warm on the hearth, and a lemon cake cut into segments sat on the table with a note.

*Don't spoil my lunch, Sire.*

Adeone chuckled and passed the message on to his sons. "It's a shame I have a meeting with the Chief Merchant tomorrow. I need more of this."

"Has he told you he's retiring yet, sir?" asked Arkyn.

"No. I have the feeling he won't warn me. Technically, he doesn't have to. Oh, it is polite and I'm sure I shall receive copious apologies, but it's a matter for the merchants of Oedran, not the King. Normally, chief merchants change every six years or so. He's been Oedran's for twenty. The last time he was elected, they granted him the post until he decided to leave. That is unique in our history."

Arkyn said, "I wonder who will replace him."

"Hopefully someone as erudite. The rumours will have ensured that others are asking. We'll have to see. I expect a lot will ride on Merchant Chapa. His opinions will still be important even after he's retired. I'll still invite him for dinner. He's good company. I'll be interested to see if I receive my normal invitation to the Guild Banquet this year. I've missed attending since father died. Would you feel up to presiding at Court for me on Munewid Eve, Arkyn?"

Arkyn shrank into himself. "If needs be, sir."

Adeone smiled reassuringly. "You'd be fine. It might not happen anyway. Now, I've had enough of talking about Oedran. I half expected to see Laioril here."

Arkyn shrugged. "He's not been all year."

"Then he'll be here nearer the Munewid. Every so often, he likes to be here as the year changes. Probably has some significance for him. No-one knows what though."

There was a knock on the door and the Comptroller entered just as Tain asked,

"Is Laioril always mysterious, father?"

Adeone winked at the Comptroller. "Are you always mischievous, Tain?"

Tain pouted then grinned. "Yes."

"Then, yes, the Chief is always mysterious, but I'd trust your lives with him as no-one else. Sometimes the mystery is a good thing."

"Does that mean that sometimes mischief is as well, father?"

Adeone groaned at himself for a fool. "I never said that, Tain… but now you mention it…" Adeone grinned as the Comptroller gave a slight cough. "I don't think the Comptroller wants me to say 'yes'."

Tain smirked. "But you're the King. You can do what you want."

"I only wish I could," admitted Adeone. "Sometimes it's more prudent to do what you should, my son, not what you want."

The Comptroller said quietly, "Lunch is ready, Sire."

* * *

That evening, once peace had descended on the chaos of the kitchen, Adeone entered it armed with a decanter of good whiskey and two sparkling glasses. Cook was sitting warming his feet by the cooling fire with two other chairs pulled close.

"You look far too comfortable, Cook."

289

"Join me then, Sire. You look like you need some comfort. How's the youngster? The cabinet was a mess."

"The scars will heal," replied Adeone, handing over a glass of whiskey. "Thank you for the cake and laughter."

"All part of the service," replied Cook placidly. "I was going to make lemon meringue, but it still feels too raw."

"It does a bit. I'll never eat it without thinking of Ira."

"How are you anyway?"

"Still here, which has to be an achievement."

"Especially without me to watch over you, sir," said Fitz, entering.

Adeone shared an amused glance with Cook, who shrugged slightly. "Join us, Fitz. We're having a relaxed conversation."

"Oh dear," replied Fitz, easing himself into the third chair by the fire. "I'll be ready for the hangover tomorrow."

"I only supply the whiskey. I'm not responsible for how much you drink."

Cook chuckled. "There's a truth there right enough, Sire."

Fitz studied Adeone. "You said 'still here'. What's happened?"

Adeone explained about finding Gad and the decisions since. That everyone believed he was planning something for around the Munewid. "…I just don't feel comfortable leaving him free. Oh, Wynfeld's right he's leading us to some very interesting places, but I'm worried it might be a wild goose chase."

"When you're ready to cook his goose, we've some nice root veg to go with it."

Adeone groaned. "That was an atrocious line, Cook."

"I know," said Cook placidly, "but what's good for the goose is good for the gander."

"Why do I employ you again?" asked Adeone rhetorically.

"You like his cooking more than his jokes," answered Fitz anyway. "If you're sure whatever Gad is planning is around the Munewid, just have him arrested on Munewid Eve. It's before the Petitionals start, before the banquet, before everyone knows exactly where you'll be. What's more, Sire, don't tell anyone that's what you plan. That way they don't get chance to change your mind but you can change it if necessary."

Cook chuckled. "Kings change their minds all the time to frustrate underlings."

"He's speaking from experience," retorted Adeone with a grin.

Fitz laughed. "Ah, we've all had experiences like that. So, what's this I hear about your young rascal destroying the old lacquered cabinet?"

# Chapter 65
## INVITATION


**A** COUPLE OF DAYS LATER, Adeone glanced up as Landis entered his office. A subtle grin lit his friend's face.

"Sire, I've just had an interesting letter from Chief Merchant Chapa. He's organising their banquet at the Guildhall."

"Mm?" Adeone was smiling.

"Let me read you what he put... *My lord, as always I would be honoured if you could join us for the Guild Banquet. As I've never been a good courtier, I shall get straight to the point. We've invited His Majesty and would really like him to join us. It's a few years since he did and we are quite missing the lively atmosphere that is created when he dines with us. We've moved the banquet to the evening before to try and avoid conflict with his other duties. Maybe you could twist his arm up his back and prevail upon His Majesty to join us?* He goes on for a couple of paragraphs, sir, but that is the gist of his letter."

Adeone shook his head slightly. "You know, Landis, something tells me that Cousin Henry would be mortified if he knew you'd read me that. Ask Richardson if he's seen my invitation."

Two moments later, Adeone read a very formal invitation. He flicked the card over and grinned – in Merchant Chapa's handwriting was the caption:

*Come and cause mayhem, Sire. I've invited the Princes as well.*

"What reason could I give for going this year and it not seeming odd?" asked Adeone.

"The sheer fact that they've changed the eve to accommodate you. Do you need another? We know it'll be the last banquet he presides at."

"Get Richardson." As his administrator entered, Adeone said, "I'm attending the Guild Banquet." He saw Richardson's face. "Whatever clashes, rearrange. I've sent enough apologies to my cousin over recent years."

"Very good, Your Majesty. Shall I inform the Chief Merchant?"

"No, I'll do that. Thank you, Richardson." The administrator left and Adeone turned to Landis. "You can help me write the reply. How do you think I should begin? *Lord Landis having twisted my arm up my back...* What do you think, Festus?"

"I'm sure Merchant Chapa would appreciate the result, Sire, but I'm not sure I'd ever receive another invitation, which would be a pity; I enjoy their meals."

Adeone laughed. "All right, I'll be kind and simply tell him when I see him. I'll also tell him that my mayhem days are sadly over but give it a couple of years and Prince Tain can happily oblige."

"I'll suggest they invite Julius and Tain together if they want to see mayhem. That should keep them all on their toes."

"For some, that would be like reliving the past. No, I think Merchant Chapa's successor won't be so appreciative of the sense of humour we have engendered in our sons. Now, did you merely come to twist my arm up my back?"

"Yes, Sire. Shall I leave you to continue running the empire?"

"Please, I have a meeting in about twelve minutes with the General."

* * *

Far away in Garth, in a very private room, Advisor Bantling was listening to Scanlon saying, "This time next year, Bantling, things will be different. We'll reap the benefits of this year. All the hard work. All the bribes. There will be rewards. I just wish I knew who the spies were here. Information has been reaching Oedran. I can't believe that the intelligence regiment, so-called, has become worthwhile. Meyer and Blunt's deaths still rankle. They could have been useful here. Faran should have been in Lufian. I ought to find some reward for him. Have we had any news of him recently?"

Bantling said, "The only information is that his wife gave him a son."

Scanlon sat thinking. "Make sure the boy dies before the Munewid, Bantling. That should be reward enough."

Mindful of his own life, Bantling said, "Very good, Greatness."

Scanlon looked at him, openly sneering. "Fear is good, Bantling. It makes people obedient. That is all that matters."

Bantling merely bowed slightly – wanting to leave the room. Scanlon saw it, so kept him there for over an hour, enjoying tormenting him.

Chapter 66

# CHIEF OR CAPTAIN

Late Spring

Rex Dallin – Wanda Camp

LAIORIL ARRIVED IN the Rex Dallin during the final weeks of spring. Arkyn was in Oedran on the day they arrived but once he was back Tain dragged him, Cal and Elantha along to see the Chief.

They walked into the Wanda camp as though it had never left the year before. Greetings were shouted at them from every angle. They shouted them back, Arkyn slightly more reserved than the previous year.

"Might 'ave known it'd be you that the fuss was for," said Laioril. "You're a bad influence on them, lads and lass. Come on into my tent. Expected you all sooner, I did. Some of 'em started telling me my age was showing. I told 'em that it showed itself a long time ago and hasn't been hiding since."

"You're not that old, Chief," observed Tain impishly.

Laioril winked at him. "I'm as old as my tongue and a little older than my teeth. It's a hard age to judge."

The tribe's healer entered the tent with a tray of food and drink. "There you go, sirs, my lady. If you need anything else, ignore the Chief and come and find me."

"Tell me why I put up with you, Miranda?" grumbled Laioril good-humouredly.

"Because you like my wine and I dose everyone up when they're ill. What other reason do you need?" With that, she left the tent.

"That woman has an answer for everything. I ought to tell her rhetorical questions don't require one. Not that it would work. Now, don't tell me you came to talk to an old man?"

"We came to hear a story but talking to an old man is almost as good," explained Tain.

Arkyn clipped his brother round the head. "Sorry, Chief. Subtlety has never been his strong point."

"I dunna mind, lad. He might need his head on his shoulders at one point or another though."

Cal said, "Don't know why, Chief. He doesn't use what's inside it."

Tain turned to him. "You're just jealous because I have something there."

"Do you?" asked Elantha, grinning.

A couple of moments later, the Chief interrupted their jibbing. "Hey, youngsters, remember you're guests around here. Tch, what will the world come to with you all in charge? Now, who wants to hear Uil's Story?"

Time passed, and the Wanda stayed in the valley. All the children spent hours in Laioril's tent listening to his vivid stories or just talking and Arkyn realised that Laioril only expected them to be themselves, whether they were bickering or laughing. He never delved but would listen, encourage and support without being obvious about it.

* * *

On the day of the Guild Banquet, the Comptroller – worried when Fitz hadn't returned from a day's leave in Oedran – tried to contact Adeone or Richardson. Unable to obtain a link with either, he contacted the only other person he could think might know what had happened; General Paturn said he'd find out.

A couple of hours later, the General's messenger appeared. "Fitz has been taken ill, Comptroller. He started throwing up last night. My doctor won't let him out of bed, but he should be back on his feet tomorrow."

"However, today Their Highnesses, Her Ladyship and Master Calumiel are meant to return to Oedran. Is there another captain you can trust?"

Paturn snorted. "Not without the King's word and His Majesty's in a meeting with Lords Teran and Para. Then Jacobs informs me the King will be changing and leaving for the Guildhall. By which time it'll be too late to get Their Highnesses here."

"His Majesty will want to know why Their Highnesses aren't at the banquet."

"I will inform Richardson as soon as I can, Comptroller, but I am not disturbing His Majesty whilst he's talking with two of Lord Scanlon's closest supporters. Certainly not for something so trivial and I wouldn't advise that you do so either."

The Comptroller bit back that to the Princes it wouldn't be trivial but knew what the General was saying. Forcing links meant something disastrous had happened. Even if Adeone subsequently explained, the rumours that he was playing down the situation would be rife.


When the children reached the house, they had Laioril and Miranda with them. The Comptroller greeted everyone but even the Chief, with his aptitude for ignoring the obvious, couldn't miss that something was wrong.

"I'm afraid, Your Highnesses, Captain Fitz was taken ill yesterday and the General says there isn't another captain who can come to escort you to Oedran."

Arkyn asked, "Seriously ill?"

"I'm not sure, sir. The General just said ill. I think he was a bit busy."

"But surely there must be one captain—" pleaded Tain.

"Obviously not," chided Arkyn softly. "There's nothing we can do. Father wouldn't want us to go to Oedran without someone he trusts."

"Why doesn't he come here? His guards—"

"Because he's in meetings all day and it's the Guild Banquet tonight. We won't be making that; I'll need to let Merchant Chapa know."

Downcast, Cal asked, "Comptroller, could you let my parents know? They'll be expecting me, you see."

"Certainly, Master Calumiel. Prince Tain, I am sorry, sir, but there's nothing to be done."

Tain sagged. "It's just so unfair."

Arkyn said, "I expect the Comptroller was hoping for some peace as well, Tain."

Tain apologised, and, kicking stones, went indoors. Cal and Elantha followed him.

The Comptroller looked at Arkyn. "Thank you, sir."

Arkyn shook his head slightly. "He'll get over it. Not sure I will…" He also went inside.

Laioril said, "Let the lads go, Comptroller. What harm can it do?"

"Chief, it isn't my choice. We can't disturb His Majesty and he's been certain Their Highnesses don't leave the valley without trustworthy guards who know Oedran."

"Would you think me a good enough guard for Their Highnesses?"

"You, Chief? Aren't you a bit old in your joints these days?"

"Aren't we all, Comptroller? I can keep guards in line as well as the next man. Have done many in my time."

"Yes, it's the guards who'll need protection, isn't it, Chief?" observed Miranda.

Bright-eyed, Laioril glanced at her. "Can't imagine what you mean, lass. The offer's there, Comptroller. Now, if you'll excuse me, I'll go and raid your amply stocked kitchens—"

"You're not joking, are you?" said the Comptroller.

"I never joke about pinching from the King."

"No. I know. Look, Chief, thank you for your offer, but I think they best stay here. If it were the whole tribe then that might be a different matter. The lads could hide in your melee without a problem but—"

"You'd let the lads and lass go with me if it were the whole tribe?"

"Erm, I suppose so, Chief," replied the Comptroller.

Laioril turned to Miranda. "You heard the man. Come on, let's get the others. We're going to Oedran. You'd better take your kit in case… Can't see those kids disappointed. Don't know what's got into me."

"I doubt it's called sentimentality," muttered the Comptroller. "That would change the habit of a lifetime. Chief, there's no need…"

"I'll ignore that. We'll take a few of your resident guards with us. Guess we'll need a cart too for the young lass and Maria. No, not a coach, far too obvious, wouldn't you say? Tell them that a solution has been found."

Later, the Comptroller didn't know why he'd done it. Normally so careful of his charges' safety, he had let them blindly go to Oedran with no more guard than a tribe of the Wanda and a handful of the resident guards of Ceardlann. The only thing that consoled him was remembering the King saying he trusted Laioril when it came to his sons' lives.

# Chapter 67
# TROUBLE!
### Hexadai, Week 48 – 27th Lufial, 20th Lufis 1210
### Oedran – Medlars Close

IN OEDRAN, the streets were cooling down after the heat of the day. The men watching Gad were bored of the vigil; he'd given them nothing new for a fortnight. Wharfsratter, half-hidden by a stall in front of a shop, watched as Gad turned, caught his eye and gave a four-fingered wave, fading out of sight. Wharfsratter turned so the spot was in his peripheral vision. Nothing. Gad had disappeared. There wasn't any sign of him. He swore so loudly that passers-by looked around and a voice admonished him from above.

Then Gad whispered in his ear, "Tut, tut, tut… you should be more careful," as a dagger plunged between his ribs.

Blood poured from the wound and ran along the pavements into the gutter. With the last breath he held, Wharfsratter croaked, "Tell Lord Landis, now…" to a lady passing, as, with the last of his sight, he saw his companion, yards away, fall as well.

The passer-by screamed. People flocked to the spot. A yeoman calmed the hysterical woman. When she was in control of herself, he asked her if the dead man had said anything. When he heard the message, he glanced around. What was a street vagabond doing waving the name of a King's Defender around like it was normal? His mind jumped to conclusions he never dreamed it could, more quickly than he liked to recall later.

He spotted a colleague walking towards the crowd and said, "Sort this out. Send the body to Lord Landis', I think."

He didn't reply to his colleague's confusion but simply hared off. They were on the opposite side of the city from the Landis House, and he had to somehow talk his way in and get to see the Lord of Oedran.

* * *

A footman answered his hurried ringing of the bell. Seeing the yeoman he said, "You should have gone round the back."

The yeoman, panting, his hands on his knees, ignored the rebuke. "I must see Lord Landis. I've got a message from a dead man." Even to his ears it sounded mad.

The footman reacted as though it was completely normal and stood aside. "Wait in the hall, please. I'll see if His Lordship is busy. Your name?"

Rushton took it that he was invited in. He half stumbled into the entrance hall, unsure if he was glad to get the chance for a breather. A minute later, he was shown into the lord's study.

Landis was obviously busy. "What's the message, Rushton?"

"Tell you truth, sir, I'm uncertain. A dying man, stabbed through the ribs, said to a witness 'Tell Lord Landis, now'. That's as much as I know."

Landis' concern was easy to read. "When and where was this?"

"Quarter of an hour ago or more, in the Teran lordship, in the mouth of an alley called Medlars Close, m'lord."

"Shit! Right, catch…" Landis tossed the man two darl. "Keep your mouth shut about this. *Really shut.* My servants will show you out and thank you for your promptitude."

Perplexed by the abrupt dismissal, Rushton said, "Right, m'lord. Erm… thank you."

Before the man had even left the room, Landis was in a link with Wynfeld.

The captain said, "Mine was killed too. We've lost him and I'd bet we've been led a dance for weeks."

"I'll inform the King."

Wynfeld swallowed. "We should have anticipated this. Tell His Majesty I'll resign my commission."

"No, you bloody well won't, Wynfeld, and that's an order. Stop being melodramatic and get every man you possibly can onto finding Gad. There're more major events in the next week than the rest of the year put together. Sicla! Their Highnesses are due to arrive from Ceardlann any time now."

Wynfeld said, "Fitz is ill, here in Oedran. Last night he started throwing up; our doctor won't let him out of bed."

"Thank Alcis for that. The Comptroller won't let them out of the valley without him. It's the Guild Banquet. I'm going to be there, as is His Majesty. I'll tell him there. He's in a meeting with two of Scanlon's supporters. There's no way I'm barging into that and letting them know we've lost one of Scanlon's men. Just make sure that His Majesty's route is safe."

Breaking the link, he saw a timepiece and swore again. He had thirty minutes to get to the Guildhall. Racing up to his private rooms, he ignored everyone he met en route. He flung on his official tunic and mantle with more haste than was normal. Even William ended up flustered. On second thoughts, Landis decided to warn Adeone before he left the Palace. Fully dressed, he contacted Richardson, who answered the messenger.

Landis was brusque. "We've lost Gad. Warn His Majesty."

Richardson said calmly, "His Majesty left for the Guildhall early, my lord. He should have reached there half an hour ago."

"Send a damned runner to his sergeant, go yourself or messenger him. Just make sure they know. I'm still at home. I'm about to set off for the

Guildhall… Are Their Highnesses staying in the Rex Dallin?"

"As far as I knew they were coming here—"

"Fitz is ill. Check and get the Comptroller to keep them in the valley."

Startled, Richardson nodded and Landis broke the link. He had quarter of an hour to reach the Guildhall. It was half the city away. He flung on his sword and raced to where Clodach was holding his horse. He ended up galloping most of the way, for once ignoring the fact Skit didn't like crowds and urging him on as never before.

* * *

Landis reached the Guildhall at the same point as a runner from the Palace was leaving. He acknowledged the lad and later realised it was Sergeant Hillbeck's nephew; the sergeant met him, looking grave.

Hillbeck said, "I've told them to check all invitations. That won't help if the man's already here or uses some other method to gain entry, but, with the King's presence, there are palace guards here this evening. Merchant Chapa insisted on them."

Landis blanched. "That's no guarantee of anything, Hillbeck. Think back. The man has a guard's tabard! Damn it. I should have issued a new one. Alcis, I'm a fool! He could be here and we wouldn't know."

"*I would,* sir. I've not spotted him yet. Trust me, I'll be watching carefully, from all areas of my sight as well. I'll tell the lads too. Everything will be fine, my lord."

"I wish I could believe that, Hillbeck, but my gut is telling me something else entirely. I'll inform the King. Where is he?"

"Talking with Merchant Chapa, my lord."

Landis was gone. He knocked on the Chief Merchant's door, walked in and bowed. Carefully, he said, "I've just seen Hillbeck, Sire…"

"How pleasant for both of you. Sit down and stop being official. I gave Hillbeck orders to be elsewhere. I'm hardly in danger here." Adeone saw his face. "Well?"

"We've lost Gad, sir. He faded from sight and then killed two men watching him."

"Great Alcis! Your timing couldn't be worse!"

"Trust me, Sire, we're doing everything we possibly can to find that man." He inwardly prayed that Wynfeld was doing that. "I'm having every measure possible put around the building here tonight. Gad was lost about an hour and a quarter ago in the east of the city. I expect he disappeared to give himself time to plan whatever it is he's planning."

"Do what you can then think over what I'm likely to be saying to you all in the morning. That's all." Adeone sighed and turned back to the Chief Merchant. "Sorry about that, cousin."

"I can cope, Your Majesty. There's good men working on the problem you might say. Shall we go down to hall?"

# Chapter 68
## INTRODUCTIONS
Evening
Guildhall

FULLERTON DRESSED WITH CARE. It was one of his last evenings in Oedran. He'd stayed to hand the King a petition about his lands in a last-ditch attempt to retrieve them. The King would be at the Guild Banquet; he hoped he would have a chance at least to meet him. Meeting someone amongst hundreds, in the Petitionals, would mean the King could forget him, but meeting him at a banquet, he hoped that meant there was less chance of being lost in a sea of faces.

At the Guildhall, his invitation was checked. "Merchant Fullerton, there was a guard here with a message for you earlier. Someone inside should have it. Well, he went inside to hunt for you, so I'm assuming they will have."

Directed straight into the Hall of Merchants, Fullerton was confused when no-one told him what the message had been, but he'd soon forgotten that there was even meant to be one.

As an usher announced the King, Fullerton turned and bowed. Merchant Chapa was presenting merchants but slowly because Adeone wanted to talk to the people who were being introduced, though some he seemed to know anyway.

"I didn't expect to see you here, Chapa."

"Likewise, Sire, but my cousin remembered I exist. Nice of him that. Personally, I wonder what the ulterior motive was."

"That makes two of us. Does it make us cynics?"

"It keeps things in perspective, sir," replied Chapa, amused.

"Yes, I'm just concerned about the vanishing point. Merchant Figgis, how nice to see you..."

The King was getting closer and closer to him. Maybe this *was* the opportunity he'd been waiting in Oedran for. The King was moving towards him and he was bowing as the Chief Merchant introduced him. A flash in his periphery vision. He flung up his left arm, grabbed at cloth, pulling down as he rose from his bow. Suddenly, there was another figure with them, struggling to make a backhanded swipe. The King turning, stepping back.

299

Fullerton, his fingers burning from coarse cloth being ripped from them. He grabbed the wrist, twisting it, barging the man aside. The dagger clanged on the flagstones. The King still turning, missing his footing, stumbling, falling away from him. Fullerton grabbed at the man again, holding him, determined not to let go. No-one else existed. Guards laid hold of the man. Fullerton released and finally recognised him.

He blanched. "You!"

Sound came back, shouted orders… *"Get irons on him now! Even when they're on him don't let go…"* A child's voice wailing the mayhem… *"Father—"* Another voice… *"Lad, calm down…"* Another voice… *"Let me take care…"*

He spun on the spot, unable to focus on anything, new faces, everything spinning blurring into distorted shapes.

Then the voice ordering people about said, "Hillbeck, don't let Fullerton go. He's not under arrest but he's not to leave this room."

That brought him back to reality. He looked down at the floor to focus on one thing. The King was lying on it unconscious, a gash from right to left across his chest, his tunic blood soaked.

* * *

"At least that secures him," muttered Landis as Fullerton fainted. "Your Highnesses, go with Nicholas, please. Hillbeck, get this place secure. Doc?"

"I've nothing with me…"

"Damn it! Let's see the damage. At least Fullerton stopped his throat being slit."

"Here, doc, use this. Just hand it back to the Chief when you're done." Miranda put her medical roll down and disappeared into the crowd.

Without even glancing up, Doctor Chapa said, "Thank you," undid the straps and unrolled the kit.

Landis undid the King's mantle. He put pressure on the skin surrounding the gash as the doctor sewed it up and put healing ointment on the wound. They could only hope.

As Landis took in everything else happening, he tried not to smile. Laioril was *helping* Hillbeck and ordering the merchants around for good measure. Sayre of the Wanda even had merchants clearing one of the trestle tables. He glanced at Fullerton. The merchant was conscious but unsurprisingly glum and fearful.

# Chapter 69
## FEARS AND FEASTING
Late Evening
Guildhall

SEEING HIS FATHER FALL, a horrible realisation swept over Arkyn: change could come swiftly. He shielded Tain from the chaos of the hall, glad Elantha had gone straight to the Palace.

He helped shepherd his brother to the library, where Nicholas Chapa managed to distract Tain with an ease that Arkyn liked. Nicholas seemed unfazed by what was happening; only a set of the head giving away that he was listening for hints of what was transpiring. The fact their near-father trusted Nicholas reassured Arkyn. He slipped quietly out of the room when he knew Tain would be all right and discovered Carlon Silversley guarding the door.

"What's happening?"

"Not sure. Do you want me to find out, sir?"

"No, thank you. I wouldn't want to… Well, I'd be in the way." He glanced along the corridor and, spotting his administrator talking to another of the guards, called him over. "I think it would be as well to know who was here and where they were when everything happened, Edward. Can you see if there's a…? Ah…" Arkyn saw a portly merchant lumbering up the stairs. "Merchant Figgis, are there any clerks here tonight?"

"Watkins was around here somewhere. I'll send someone to find him for you, sir."

"Thank you." After the merchant left, he continued, "Include *everyone*, the cooks and servers too."

"Very good, sir. Is there anything else I can do?"

Distracted by guards carrying his father up the stairs on a board from one of the trestle tables, Arkyn didn't reply. He stepped forward then stopped. Landis noticed.

Crossing to his nearson, Landis dismissed Edward and drew Arkyn along the passage a few paces away from Carlon, turning so he was shielding Arkyn from the gazes of those behind them.

Very quietly, he said, "He'll mend. He's knocked himself unconscious but the doc's optimistic—"

"Aren't all King's Physicians?"

Landis chuckled. "Aye, they might be, but when has the doc played by that rule book? I'd tell you if it were serious, sir."

Arkyn tried to pull himself together. "So I should hope, Lord Landis. I've asked Edward to make a list of everyone who was here and where they were. Do you want it?"

Landis was intrigued that Arkyn had taken that initiative amidst his concern. "I'd be grateful for a copy, sir, as would Wynfeld, I expect."

"Will father sack him?"

"I don't know and that's the truth of it, sir."

"Oh... I ought not to keep you, my lord. If you could let me know when we can see father..."

Landis squeezed his shoulder. "I'll make sure of it." He walked away, aware that Arkyn was watching him go. As he passed Carlon, he said, "If Captain Wynfeld turns up, send him to wherever the King is."

Arkyn watched Landis enter a room further up the long corridor and slowly walked back to where Carlon was standing. "Do you know who Wynfeld is, Silversley?"

The guard gave a small snort. "No, sir, but I'm sure I'll find out."

Arkyn chuckled. "I do. I'll pass on the message. How's your grandfather?"

"He's well, sir. Young Iestyn is keeping him on his toes now he's toddling..." As Carlon talked, Arkyn gazed between the head of the stairs and the door of the room where his father was. Two moments later he saw Landis exit and walk towards him.

"He's awake, Your Highness, but has asked to see the merchant who saved his life. Once that formality is out of the way, I'll tell him you're here. You'll get more time with him then."

Disappointed, Arkyn watched Landis escorting Fullerton to the room with a hand under the merchant's elbow. He wanted to run to his father, explain the dread he'd felt, the sudden knowledge of how little he knew but he didn't move. He heard a commotion at the bottom of the stairs and moved until he saw Wynfeld arriving with several men.

"Captain."

Wynfeld glanced up the stairs, stopped momentarily, saluted and then hurriedly ascended.

"What's happened, sir? Our scryer spotted Gad here."

"His Majesty has been attacked. Lord Landis has asked that you join them." Arkyn pointed along the corridor. "You'll spot the guards." Watching Wynfeld hurry away, Arkyn sighed. "Silversley, just knock twice on the door when it looks like the right time for us to see His Majesty."

* * *

Wynfeld entered the Chief Merchant's office at Landis' command and tripped straight over Fullerton kneeling just inside the door.

"I've heard of falling at the King's feet when things go wrong, Wynfeld, but I don't think you're meant to do it quite like that," remarked Adeone. "Nor knock over the man who saved my life." As Wynfeld righted himself

302

and saluted, the King's voice hardened. "Gad is now under arrest, Captain, and is being handed into your care. Be less careless this time. Remove him immediately to the barracks for questioning and accompany him yourself. I shall speak to you tomorrow."

Wynfeld's gaze took in the blood-soaked tunic and the King's pallor. His stomach dropped. The blame would fall on him and it was his to bear. He saluted and left without a word. Everyone could keep their advice. He knew what he had to do.

Adeone turned to the immediate matter. "Pass me your hands, Fullerton."

Fullerton couldn't mistake what it meant and was oddly relieved not to be facing Wynfeld again. He held his hands up, palms upward. Adeone placed his on top and had the merchant swore a truth-binding fealty.

A moment later Adeone was asking, "In truth, did you know what was planned this evening?"

"In truth, my liege, I did not."

"In truth, have you communicated with Gad since you were arrested?"

"In truth, my liege, I have not."

Adeone released his hands. "Thank Alcis for that. Festus, is there a chair? No, make that two." A moment later, he said, "Sit down, Merchant Fullerton. Thank you, for saving my life."

"I reacted instinctively, sir," replied Fullerton, surprised by the invitation to sit. Even Lord Landis was still standing.

"Still, you did save my life and I thank you for it. Now, I know you plan to lodge a petition with me. It is unnecessary and, this aside, it always was. I know of your case and am working to resolve it; however, because of this event, you will reclaim your family's land in full or I will grant you the title for land of equal or greater worth next year on the same terms. Also, all debts accrued by your extended stay in Oedran will be paid in full for you."

"Sire, I can't accept—"

"Merchant Fullerton, it's not a matter for discussion! I'll also inform the Exarch of events. If ever you're in trouble in Garth, you can use my name to help. Though I think a merchant such as yourself rarely gets into the kind of mess you've found yourself in…" He winced.

The doctor said, "Sire, save your strength—"

"I'll do this, Chapa! Just go and lose yourself."

The doctor left, grumbling. He stayed in the corridor and, two minutes later, Fullerton joined him.

Chapa said, "Let me guess, you're not to go back to hall yet?"

"Yes, but why?"

"Looks better if the King walks in. Get ready to bow because I see the next generation of FitzAlcis approaching." In his head, he amended

'FitzAlcis' to 'trouble'.

* * *

In the room Adeone was saying, "The children *are* here and you never told me... What did they see?"

Landis ignored the question. "Nicholas sorted them out, Sire. Though Arkyn took it on himself to establish who was present."

"Even so... Where are they?"

A voice said hesitantly, "We're here, father."

Adeone turned to find Tain regarding him solemnly. He glanced beyond his younger son to his elder, then for his niece.

"Elantha went straight to the Palace," explained Arkyn. "She was tired, father... She never entered the Hall."

"That's something. Come here and greet your father carefully. That is, don't knock the bandages."

Tain gave his father a restrained hug. He wouldn't let go and Adeone motioned for Landis to leave.

* * *

A few minutes later, at a word from Landis, the newly-arrived General joined the group waiting in the corridor saying, "The whole Guildhall is surrounded by my men. Wynfeld is dealing with Gad. Do you have any instructions on that front, Defender?"

"Only one: postpone his execution. He thinks he'll die before dawn. Unnerve him if he's still alive as the sun reaches the clear sky."

Ignoring everyone else Paturn said, "Right, Defender. I just hope you know what you're doing. Who's with the King?"

"The Princes. Give it six minutes."

Merchant Chapa joined the party. "We're ready for the banquet again. At least it's a different type of mayhem he's caused this year."

From behind them, Adeone said, "No, this year you can truly say I am a bloody nuisance, cousin."

A general smile rippled along the group, followed moments later with inclined heads and salutes as the King passed through their midst. On their way to the hall, the King turned to the Chief Merchant.

"I apologise. Maybe it would have been better if I hadn't come."

"Your Majesty, all that matters is that you're alive. I'm sure we can cope with a little liveliness. It will stop all the elderly merchants falling asleep in their soup for starters—"

"Meat and sweet?"

Merchant Chapa grinned. "They'd still be asleep when everyone else has left."

304

Adeone walked into the hall and cheers erupted, filling the Guildhall to its rafters. He walked carefully to the middle of the dais and motioned for silence before saying, "Thank you. It's nice to know you appreciate me but, I believe, we're about to be treated to a speech by the Chief Merchant."

Adeone, waiting for everyone else to be seated, took a sip of wine and then laughed, fishing out a carved wooden bug. He turned to the Chief Merchant, "Whose idea?"

"Erm, mine actually, Sire."

"Then you are to be congratulated on your audacity; now how many more tricks are up your sleeve for the banquet?"

"There were one or two, Sire. Lord Landis made a few suggestions."

"Oh, did he now!"

From the other side of him, Landis grumbled, "I really must do something about my tenant's obligations to their lord. Not dropping him in it would be my favourite."

The Chief Merchant chuckled. "Aye, my lord, it would be. I shall apologise to His Majesty forthwith and take all the credit myself."

Adeone smiled wanly. "I'm not sure that I would believe you with Landis also here tonight, cousin. Anyway, my apologies, Merchant Chapa, we're preventing you from opening the banquet."

The Chief Merchant inclined his head slightly in thanks. "Your Majesty, Highnesses, Lord Landis, Merchants of the Oedranian Empire and our unexpected guests, welcome to the Guild Banquet. Before we all start enjoying ourselves too much, I have an announcement to make: some of you here already know that I have been considering retirement for some time but have never got around to doing it. Well, as a very dear cousin used to say to me, all good things end one day. Tonight is my last official engagement. I am pleased that you are all here to share it. I've enjoyed my time guarding your interests and can only hope that you've benefited from what I've tried to achieve. With that said, we've a feast to enjoy."

As Chapa sat, Adeone rose, quelling the susurration of surprise.

"Your Highnesses, Lord Landis, Chief Merchant Chapa, Merchants of the Oedranian Empire and unexpected guests, I am saddened to hear that Merchant Chapa has decided to retire. He has, perhaps, done more than many of you are aware. He is responsible for many of the relaxed laws when it comes to trading beyond Anapara and I, for one, must thank him for that. Without his foresight, the empire would not be the thriving place it is today. He'll deny he's ever done anything, as is his wont. I, however, am not fooled and I hope that no-one else is either. Merchant Chapa, I did know, before tonight, you were planning on retiring. I've taken thought for how I can repay all the hard work you've done over the years and made me do. I've asked your colleagues, but they couldn't think of anything you'd want. I asked Doctor Chapa, as a mutual cousin; he was very unhelpful suggesting only that, as age-defying medicine hadn't been found, you'd have to live with the wrinkles…" Laughter resounded and Adeone glanced at an unnerved Chief Merchant. "I even asked Lord Landis, but he said he'd still require your rent. I twisted his arm up his back – it is a technique you advocate, I believe…"

Merchant Chapa glanced at Landis resignedly and Landis simply smiled back innocently.

"…Anyway, as I was saying, I tried to find something that would make a difference to your life as you have made to many merchants in this city…" Adeone took a scroll from one of his guards – a wince well hidden. "…Merchant Chapa, I have here two documents. Jesting and jousting aside, Lord Landis did come up with the goods. One is the freehold of your house, for the duration of your life and that of your family. The second, from myself, is free trading rights throughout the empire and freedom of the cities of that empire. So, I think all that is left, is to apologise for this more sensible mischief and to thank you, formally, for all you've ever done."

As he sat down, clapping and cheering erupted. Then there was slight laughter as the Chief Merchant, obviously in shock, rose once more.

"Erm… Thank you, Sire, my lord. I think I'll ask Doctor Chapa if he knows the elusive cure for mischief yet. Thank you again. I thought I'd kept the secret well enough… Obviously, Your Majesty is omniscient. Now, let the banquet begin – before His Majesty gets any more ideas!"

The servers moved forward and Adeone turned to his mother's cousin. "Have a drink and calm your shock, cousin. Now, when you've retired as Chief Merchant, you're not going to shun the Palace are you?"

"No, Sire. I still need to remind the Court who runs the city."

"Have they got the message yet?"

"I don't think they have, sir. We keep trying."

"Good. You must dine with me as well. I shall miss our discussions."

"Thank you, Your Majesty, I'd like to."


For all the laughter, no-one could forget the King had been attacked – the blood-stained tunic barely tacked together was a testament to that. Adeone was quiet throughout the banquet and more than one person noticed the King drank more wine than usual. Doctor Chapa kept a careful watch on his charge. When the main banquet ended and people were once more milling around, he informed the King a carriage was waiting to take him back to the Palace. Adeone didn't make a murmur of protest. He simply

rose, thanked and apologised to Merchant Chapa, and made his way out
of the hall with his sons. The merchants started cheering and clapping.
Adeone left the hall, glad that the moons were covered by clouds, hiding
his face where emotions were clearly written. He was touched and surprised
by the merchants' reaction to the attempt on his life.

* * *

Jack greeted them at the Palace. He helped the King alight, waving other
grooms and footmen away.

"I'm all right, Jack."

"Yes, Sire. Never said you weren't; however, several people have been
busy. There's a chair if…"

Adeone sighed. "Did Chapa have a hand in that one?"

"Lady Amara did, sir. Her Ladyship also said a lot of things I won't
be repeating."

"I'm not going…" He swayed and suddenly Ira seemed to be in front
of him.

*"My dear, you'll only tire yourself out and our sons don't need to see
their father a broken man."*

She held out a hand to him and he was walking, following her without
knowing where he was going. He found he was sitting in the chair.

*"That's right. Just remember whom you live for… Give them a hug
from me."*

She shimmered out of existence as the pole-bearers took up their
burden. He woke up when he reached his chambers, remembering he'd
given Simkins the evening off but someone had indeed been busy. Simkins
helped him to remove his tunic. The doctor checked the bandaging and
mixed a pain killer. He handed it to the King who drank it without even
asking what it was. A moment later, Doctor Chapa handed him another cup.

This time Adeone asked, "What is it?"

"Sedative, sir. You asked me not to trick you, remember?"

"I'm not taking it. I'll be asleep soon enough."

A voice said, "Stop arguing, Sire. You'll do less damage to yourself
if you drink it."

He closed his eyes, defeated. "Pass it here, Chapa. Then you can all go.
Lady Amara will make me sensible." Once alone with his aunt, he said,
"Where are the boys?"

"Hopefully in bed. Arkyn shepherded Tain away." She pulled the
covers straight over him, holding his hand. "I'll stay until you're asleep."

* * *

When she left, she found Landis sitting dejectedly in the Inner Office and

307

crooked a finger.

Dreading the interview, he followed her to her chambers on the floor below. She didn't have the air of someone about to thank him.

She sat, carefully arranging her skirts. "Are you going to tell me what happened freely? I don't just mean tonight's little event. I mean *everything*."

Landis concisely explained the events.

Amara hissed, "A vigilant can know if they're followed! *You* risked the King's life because *you* wanted bigger fish. *You* left a man at large who knows how to kill and didn't research what he could *do*. That *doesn't* happen again. The King is *not bait!* Understand?"

"Gad could have—"

"No, he couldn't. He won't know who employed him. He won't know names. They're not stupid. You remove such men. Yes, they'll find more, but that takes time. Your first duty is to the King's immediate safety."

Landis swallowed. "How is he?"

"Asleep." She took in his appearance: drained, blood spattered, shaking. "We work together in the future, young Festus. Oh, stop looking at me like that. I'm not that bad. Come on, there's a coach to take you home. Cornelia's expecting you and knows what's happened. I've also ordered a hot bath for you." She smiled at the look on his face. "William's very good at saying 'Yes, my lady,' isn't he?"

"Not to me." Landis sighed. "Thank you."

She squeezed his shoulder. "Adeone needs you, Festus, as much as you need him."

# Chapter 70
## REPERCUSSIONS
### Septadai, Week 48 – 28th Lufial, 21st Lufis 1210
### King's Chambers – Bedchamber

THE KING WOKE to his younger son bouncing onto his bed. He opened his eyes, glanced sideways at Tain and then at Simkins.

"Lose yourself for six minutes."

Tain simply looked at his father. "I thought you'd left us as well."

Adeone pushed himself up, gathering his son to him as carefully as he could. "Not a hope of that. You'll have to put up with me still. Anyway, your mother would berate me if I left the mortal world too soon. Just remember, never get on the wrong side of your wife."

Tears ran down Tain's face. Adeone simply held him reassuringly. Eventually, tears spent, Tain fell asleep against his father. Adeone watched him, protectively.

His manservant re-entered the room and assessed the situation. The King raised an amused eyebrow at him. Simkins tiptoed over and helped Adeone carefully disentangle himself.

"Just tuck him up. I don't think he's slept at all," whispered Adeone.

Six minutes later, he struggled into a tunic. Walking back through his bedchamber, he noticed Tain stirring so sat on the edge of his bed as his son woke once more.

"Are you all right?" asked Adeone and his son nodded. "Stay here and sleep for a bit if you want."

"No, father… You can't shout at people if I'm here."

Adeone smiled. "Here's a hint, when people expect you to shout, it makes them feel worse when you don't. Useful trick." He winked at his son and ruffled his hair as he rose and left for his office.

Tain pushed himself up, hugging his knees. "Is that true, Simkins?"

"For some people, yes, Your Highness." There was a pause. "His Majesty is just sending for a couple of people and then I'm to take him breakfast. Would you like some as well, sir?"

Half an hour later, Adeone watched Tain leave and wryly thought that the time spent with him had softened his anger. It was still there but it was glowing embers instead of flames.

* * *

He'd sent for the obvious suspects: Landis, Paturn and Wynfeld. Whilst he waited, he riffled through several documents on his desk. One didn't make him any happier than he had been the night before.

Fingers steepled against his mouth, he watched as the three men made their way into the Inner Office with some trepidation. He motioned for Richardson to stay.

"Explain, Defender."

"What we know, sir, is that Gad realised he was being followed – when exactly we don't know – last night he must have disappeared in front of his observers, doubled back and stabbed them. One used his dying breath to get a message to me. I alerted Wynfeld, who had just discovered his man had been killed…" Landis carried on for some minutes, piecing together the puzzle for the King.

At the end of the explanation, Adeone said, "General, I hold Wynfeld's resignation. Do you suggest I accept it?"

Landis swore under his breath. He glared at Wynfeld. The General was a traditionalist: when things went this wrong resignation was the best solution. Adeone waited. He knew what the General's feelings were when it came to mistakes amongst his officers and whatever else had happened last night, Wynfeld had been in charge of keeping an eye on Gad.

Paturn held the King's gaze. "That, of course, Sire, is your choice, but I would be extremely sorry to see Wynfeld leave the army and my command."

Adeone thanked the General and then turned to Landis. "Defender?"

Stunned, Landis said, "Erm, you know my thoughts, Sire."

"Yes, but now tell Wynfeld exactly what you think of him."

Wynfeld glanced between the King and Lord Landis uncertainly.

Landis took a breath. "Wynfeld, for the last few aluna-months, I've been trying to get His Majesty to promote you to commander, working with the regular army somewhere in the empire."

Astounded, Wynfeld turned back to the King, unable to speak.

Adeone made a small gesture which clearly said, *'There you are then.'* What he said aloud was, "Do we pretend this resignation never landed on my desk, Wynfeld? Because I certainly don't want or require it."

Wynfeld swallowed. "I failed, Your Majesty. Badly."

"Not just you, Captain: there are more at fault than you. I should have followed my own instinct which was to lift Gad in the autumn. I cannot resign my post, so I don't think it's fair, in this case, that you must; however, to help with your dilemma, I'll decide for you. Richardson, burn this letter and remove any record of it from the office scrolls." He rose. "Right. I'm not going to pretend I'm not angry at what happened. I am. Very. What I will say is it's no good crying over spilt milk. My chest will hopefully heal. I'll do no good whatsoever by yelling at you all. Let's start picking up the pieces."

They moved to sit around a table and Richardson put paper, pens and ink in front of them all.

Adeone said, "I presume Gad was executed."

The General said, "No, sir. We've kept him alive in case you wanted to question him yourself."

"I don't. Has he given your more skilled men any information?"

"No. He claims he's in bondage for his life and that he has no idea who his master is. He's lost a finger trying to escape the serfdom—"

"Do you believe him?"

"There are marks to suggest torture at another point in his life, sir."

Adeone said, "If he's not giving you anything useful execute him. Check though as to when he realised that he was still being followed. There might be places he's led us that aren't as smoke in the wind…"


When the debriefing finished, Adeone asked Landis to stay behind. He looked at his friend. "I saw Ira last night. It was her. Standing before me and telling me to live, for our sons' sake."

"She'd always have wanted that, sir."

"I know, Festus. It just made me think. I knew that something would happen around now. I was going to order Gad's arrest today. A day late, it seems. Maybe my powers of a medium aren't so strong after all."

Landis stood stock-still. "Pardon?"

Adeone looked his friend in the eye. "Are you suddenly afraid that I might know your secret, Festus?"

"What secret's that then, Adeone?"

The King grinned at him. "Oh, I think we'll just have to wait and *see*, don't you, my lord?"

Landis relaxed. "I'll keep that in *mind*, Sire."

The friends watched each other. Without saying anything they'd said it all.

* * *

Adeone's chest healed remarkably well and Doctor Chapa was rumoured to be pestering Laioril for the recipe for the salve that he'd smothered the wound with. The Petitionals for 1211 were uneventful. Scanlon arrived in a flurry of officialdom for a fortnight. Faced with the evidence that 'persons unknown' had manipulated Fullerton's situation for Lord Rathgar's advantage, he played along and the land was handed back to Fullerton.

Adeone puzzled over Scanlon's motives. Two years ago, he'd have said all his brother wanted was absolute power. Now he wasn't so certain. He abused the powers the post of Justiciar gave him but never actively used them to gain more. If his brother did become king, would he just watch the empire destroy itself? If he did, why? Whenever Adeone tried to work out the threads, the starting points, the reasons, he couldn't catch them.

# Chapter 71

## TERASIA

Septadai, Week 5 – 7th Tradal, 14th Middis 1211
Oedran

A FEW WEEKS AFTER THE MUNEWID, Adeone walked into the Outer Office, said '*Good morning*' to Richardson and then repeated himself. His administrator came out of a trance as he apologised and returned the greeting.

Adeone crooked a finger at him. Once in the Inner Office with the door closed on the other secretaries, he asked, "What's got you worried?"

Richardson sagged slightly. "It's nothing really, sir. It's just that my youngest decided to study law. I couldn't persuade him otherwise and even after the first few weeks, he's not changed his mind."

Adeone considered his administrator steadily. It did explain the preoccupation and was certainly a disturbing proposition for someone as loyal as Richardson.

"If you can't, Richardson, I don't know who could."

"Thank you, sir. I just feel we've somehow betrayed you."

"Don't be a fool. You could never do that. If it puts your mind at rest Prince Tain will need good men in the judiciary in the coming years. I have no doubt that young Tristan will be amongst them. Now, I've decided to send Prince Arkyn as my Representative for the Terasian Provincial Review. We need to start planning his trip."

Richardson hesitated. "I don't mean to criticise, Your Majesty, but isn't His Highness a bit young to be undertaking a review somewhere as distant as Terasia."

"Probably, but my sons need to be prepared. Oh, don't look like that; you know that my brother will succeed in killing me one day. Back to Terasia: I wish I could give Prince Arkyn a couple more years' freedom but I can't, so… Can you prepare a briefing and talk to Edward about procedures? The usual things. I'll talk to Prince Arkyn and Lord Portur. I'd also better see Lord Teran. I'll need to talk to him today if possible."

Once the door closed behind Richardson, Adeone watched the gardens and spotted Arkyn and Tain on one of the areas of lawn. Even from this distance, he could tell Arkyn was teasing his younger brother. He sighed softly, wishing he could join them in the sunshine. He was never quite certain how long he'd been standing watching them when Richardson announced Lord Teran.

Lord Teran, charged with representing Terasia's interests in Oedran, was a sharp-featured, sly-looking gentleman, whom Adeone heartily disliked. He was one of Scanlon's confederates and even if he hadn't been Adeone would still have found it difficult to like him. As he entered, Adeone turned and made his way back to his desk. Teran certainly wasn't high enough in favour to be seated comfortably.

* * *

When Teran had left, Adeone went in search of his sons. He found them still wrangling on the lawn. Grinning, he waved the guards further off.

"What's the dispute about then?"

Arkyn and Tain whipped around, jumped up and gave short bows before Adeone hugged them. Arkyn answered first.

"Nothing calamitous, sir. We were betting on whether you would be sending me to Terasia or not."

Adeone was impressed. He had mentioned the idea to no-one before that morning. He lay on the lawn, watching the scudding clouds, enjoying

312

the sun on his face. Tain lay on his front, his legs kicking the air, whilst he picked at the grass, Arkyn settled himself cross-legged and also picked at the grass.

Adeone said, "You two never cease to amaze me. Do you want to go?"

Arkyn thought for a long moment. "Yes, in a way I do, but I'd be slightly—"

"Scared." Tain completed the sentence for him with his normal aplomb.

"I don't blame you. I know I was during the first review I undertook. The odd thing is that this morning I decided you would be going. I was impressed with how you handled events at the Guildhall. I just came to tell you."

Tain sat up. "Can I go as well?"

Adeone looked at his son's excited face. "Not this time, maybe another. Your brother will have more than enough on, without wondering what *you're* getting up to. Carry on destroying Ceardlann for a couple more years."

Tain grinned sheepishly but went back to picking at the grass, disappointment ill hidden on his face.

Arkyn poked him. "Just think of all the boring meetings I'll have to endure. At least you'll be able to be out and about."

"Suppose. When will you be going?"

Adeone heard the note of disappointment ease as uncertainty took its place. He sat up. "Oh, not until the autumn. Lord Teran has a report to write. It'll take him that long to find a pen!"

His sons laughed. They all spent a pleasant quarter of an hour before Adeone spotted Richardson.

"Oh no, I've been found. Could you hide me?"

Grinning, Tain and Arkyn jumped up, shielding their father from view.

Richardson came over grinning. "I don't suppose Your Highnesses have seen His Majesty?"

Arkyn said seriously, "Not for a while, I'm afraid, Richardson."

"If you do happen to see him, sir, could you tell him General Paturn requires a word? Regarding Terasia of all places."

Adeone, behind his sons, groaned and rose. Richardson, pretending to be surprised, glanced at Arkyn.

The Prince shrugged. "I never said in how long a while."

Ruffling his sons' hair, the King left.

Once in the Inner Office, Adeone motioned for General Paturn to explain. Half an hour later, Wynfeld was confirmed as Commander of Terasia, allowing the current incumbent his requested retirement and Adeone peace of mind.

Over the next few days and weeks, Adeone completed the preparations for Arkyn's trip. He chose Fitz as Captain, a reliable clerk was found to act as Edward's deputy and Kadeem located someone to act as his, along with footmen, clerks, grooms and guards they made up a sizable entourage. It would take over three weeks to reach Tera. Not wanting to leave anything to chance, Adeone planned out the route with Fitz and Arkyn. They would use the main highway, skirt the Rex Dallin, then stay at Amphi Palace for a couple of nights before riding south through Areal until they reached Terasia. The route left little to the imagination, but the stops had to be carefully orchestrated so there was enough contingency time. Some were at the Arealian forts, some at lords' manors.

The day Arkyn left for Terasia, the King found a note on his desk. He opened it expecting to see Richardson's or Simkins' writing. The note, however, was in neither and Adeone's blood ran cold.

*Day soon turns to night.*

# CHARACTERS

# FAMILIES

| | | |
|---|---|---|
| **FITZALCIS** | KING ALTARIUS APOLINAR | King of the Oedranian Empire |
| | PRINCE ADEONE ALTARIUS | Heir to the Oedranian Empire |
| | PRINCESS IRA | Adeone's wife |
| | PRINCE ARKYN ADEONE | Adeone's eldest son |
| | PRINCE TAIN LACHLAN | Adeone's younger son |
| | PRINCESS ELIZA (ELLA) | Adeone's daughter |
| | PRINCE LACHLAN | Altarius' brother |
| | LADY AMARA | Altarius' sister |
| | LORD SCANLON | Justiciar of the Empire |
| | LADY AELIA | Scanlon's wife |
| | LADY ELANTHA | Scanlon's daughter |
| **LANDIS** | LORD FESTUS LANDIS | Lord of Oedran, Defender of the King's Life, Chief Advisor, nearfather to Adeone's children |
| | LADY CORNELIA LANDIS | Long-suffering, hardworking Lady of Oedran |
| | JULIUS AND JULIA | Eldest children, twins |
| | MARCELEA, ANTONIA, LUCIUS | Younger children |
| **GALDWIN** | MASTER GALDWIN | Cloth Merchant, Cal's father |
| | MADAM GALDWIN | Cal's mother |
| | CALUMIEL GALDWIN (CAL) | Eldest son |
| | HALTERN, LOUISA, CRISPIN, TABITHA | Younger children |
| **WANDA** | LAIORIL | A chief of the Wanda |
| | MIRANDA | Wise woman of the Wanda |
| | SAYRE | Man of the Wanda |

# KING'S RETINUE

| | |
|---|---|
| RICHARDSON | King's Administrator |
| SIMKINS | King's manservant |
| DOCTOR CHAPA | King's Physician and cousin |
| MARIA WYNFELD | Nurse to the Princes |
| CAPTAIN FITZ | Officer of the FitzAlcis |
| CAPTAIN HASTER | Captain of the Palace Guard |
| SERGEANT MARSH | Head of the King's Guard |
| KENTON | King's Secretary |
| ADVISOR RAYBURN | King's Military Advisor |
| ADVISOR VANVAL | King's Court Advisor |
| KADEEM | Footman |

# SCANLON'S RETINUE

| | |
|---|---|
| BANTLING | Advisor |
| DYER | Administrator |

# CEARDLANN

| | |
|---|---|
| COMPTROLLER | Gentleman in charge of Ceardlann |
| COOK | Cook |
| ALFRED | Chief groom |

# LANDIS HOUSE

| | |
|---|---|
| WILLIAM KADEEM | Lord Landis' manservant |
| CLODACH | Chief groom |
| COOKIE | Cook |
| NURSIE | Children's nurse |
| BACKERY | Footman |
| SANDBINE | Warden |
| GIBB | Chief Bailiff |

<table>
<tr><th colspan="3">IN OEDRAN</th></tr>
<tr><td rowspan="5">COURT</td><td>LORD ELIDIR RYSON</td><td>Lord of Oedran for Gerymor</td></tr>
<tr><td>LORD ANGUIS</td><td>Lord of Oedran for Serpent Isle</td></tr>
<tr><td>LORD IRVIN IRIS</td><td>Young lord of the Court, grandson of Lord Iris</td></tr>
<tr><td>ADVISOR MEYER</td><td>An advisor</td></tr>
<tr><td>ADVISOR BLUNT</td><td>An advisor</td></tr>
<tr><td rowspan="7">PALACE</td><td>STEWARD</td><td>Gentleman in charge of day-to-day running of the Palace</td></tr>
<tr><td>CHAMBERLAIN</td><td>Gentleman in charge of the individual rooms in the Palace</td></tr>
<tr><td>HERALD</td><td>Gentleman in charge of the mail routes, runners and couriers</td></tr>
<tr><td>HILLBECK</td><td>Palace Guard</td></tr>
<tr><td>JACK</td><td>Chief Groom</td></tr>
<tr><td>BLACKWOOD</td><td>Head Gardener</td></tr>
<tr><td>DENNY</td><td>Chief Server of Upper Hall</td></tr>
<tr><td rowspan="4">CITY</td><td>MERCHANT CHAPA</td><td>Chief Merchant of Oedran and King Adeone's cousin</td></tr>
<tr><td>ALDHOUSE</td><td>Chief Yeoman of Oedran, head of law enforcement</td></tr>
<tr><td>JUDGE JAMES TANCRED</td><td>Judge of Oedran, Friend of King Adeone</td></tr>
<tr><td>KEEPER OF THE JUSTICE HALL</td><td>Superintendent of the Courthouse of Oedran</td></tr>
<tr><td rowspan="4">ARMY</td><td>GENERAL PATURN</td><td>Head of the King's Army</td></tr>
<tr><td>CAPTAIN SHARPARU</td><td>Captain in Garth</td></tr>
<tr><td>SERGEANT WYNFELD</td><td>Sergeant</td></tr>
<tr><td>SERGEANT BEAVER</td><td>Sergeant of Intelligence</td></tr>
<tr><th colspan="3">IN THE EMPIRE</th></tr>
<tr><td rowspan="3">BAYAN AND GARTH</td><td>LORD TYLER GALWOOD</td><td>Exarch, King's Representative and second cousin once removed</td></tr>
<tr><td>HERITOR FULLERTON</td><td>Last Heritor of Bayan</td></tr>
<tr><td>MERCHANT FULLERTON</td><td>Son of Heritor Fullerton</td></tr>
</table>

# DELVINGS

# Lexicon

## OF THE MOONS

| | |
|---|---|
| ALUNA | The larger of the two Erinnan moons |
| ALUNA-MONTH | Four weeks |
| ALUNAN | The higher section of society |
| ALUNAN-AGE | Twenty years old. Alunan become adults in law |
| CISLUNA | The smaller of the two Erinnan moons |
| CISLUNA-MONTH | Three weeks |
| CISAN | The lower section of society |
| CISAN-AGE | Fifteen years old. Cisan become adults in law |

## FOR THE ANCESTORS

| | |
|---|---|
| ALCIA | A guardian of the ancestor's memory |
| ALCIUM | A place to remember the ancestors, for blessing new life, for contemplation and for funerals. |

## ON RELATIONSHIPS

| | |
|---|---|
| NEAR* | Named when a child is born, *nearparents* act as mentors for a child and would act as guardians should the child be left orphaned. Nearparents' children are *nearcousins*, unless the child lives in the same house, then they're *nearsiblings* |
| WED* | This prefix denotes relatives married into the family, rather like the suffix *in-law* |

## IN OEDRAN

| | |
|---|---|
| KING'S ADVOCATES | A group consisting of the King's Defenders, heir and Representatives in the empire |
| TRINICULUM | A formal dining room at the Palace. |
| AULNAGER | Chief cloth merchant |
| YEOMEN | Law enforcers |

# HONOURIFICS

| | |
|---|---|
| SIRE, MAJESTY | The King |
| GRACE | The Queen |
| HIGHNESS | Princes |
| ELEGANCE | Princesses |
| EXCELLENCY | King's Representatives |
| GREATNESS | Scanlon |
| MY LORD | Lords |
| MY LADY | Nobel Ladies |

# FEALTIES

| | |
|---|---|
| FEALTY | A declaration of loyalty from one person to another: a declaration to take up the fight for the liege by the vassal |
| TRUTH- BINDING | In addition to fealty, the vassal swears to speak to the truth to the liege when required. |
| SPEECH- BINDING | In addition to truth-binding, the vassal swears never to reveal anything confidential, never to say anything to annoy the liege, to speak only for them not against them. |
| HONOUR-BINDING | In addition to truth-binding, the vassal swears only to work for the honour of the liege, not against them. |
| LIFE-BINDING | Melding all aspects of truth, speech and honour bindings, the vassal ties their life force to the wishes of the liege. If they annoy their liege, they feel pain. If they commit treason, the vassal will die immediately. |
| VALLEY-BINDING | Specific to the Rex Dallin, this binding is said to be life-binding but may stop short of death. |
| OTHER BINDINGS | There are oaths which fall short of the recognised fealties, that are sworn when taking on specific duties or when an employer requires it. |

# ON MONEY

| | |
|---|---|
| DARL | Gold coins |
| TALENCE | Silver coins, twenty to a darl |
| CRESCENTS | Bronze coins, twelve to a talence |

# The Cearcall and Ull's Legacy

At the beginning of the reckoning of years, the Majistar Ull brought magic to Erinna. Twelve star sapphires controlled the creation of the magic. Ull gifted the star stones to twelve individuals, each with a magical spirit. For six hundred years they, and their successors, controlled magic on Erinna, formed laws around it and maintained peace. In the year 600, they died, blown to the winds when magic, wielded by the Tribility who held three spirits, destroyed the Cearcall Tower in Denshire. Since 600 magic has been weaker, almost dormant. Some stones were lost, their location hidden by history, along with some items related to the members of the Cearcall.

| Title | Spirit | Stone Colour | Item |
| --- | --- | --- | --- |
| AMSER | TIMER | TURQUOISE | AMSER'S WATCH |
| BERAN | BEARER | BLACK | BERAN'S PENDANT |
| ESPIER | ESPIEN | YELLOW | ESPIER'S GLASS |
| JECI | ILLUSIONIST | BLUE | JECI'S RING |
| MEITHRIN | HEALER | PINK | MEITHRIN'S VIAL |
| MEMINI | MEMOR | GREY | MEMINI'S MANUSCRIPT |
| RHEOL | BALANCER | WHITE | RHEOL'S NEEDLE |
| SENNACHIE | SEER | GREEN | SENNACHIE'S BOWL |
| SENTIRE | SENSOR | RED | SENTIRE'S KNIFE |
| SKIFTA | SHIFTER | PURPLE | SKIFTA'S SWORD |
| SUNDRIAN | SPLITTER | ORANGE | SUNDRIAN'S WHISTLE |
| WRIGHT | MANIPULATOR | BROWN | WRIGHT'S BOX |

Each magical spirit manifests differently from healing hurts to splitting the mind, from creating illusions to manipulating objects.

More than one person at any one time can hold a spirit, but only one spirit wielder can possess the star stone and unlock its full power.

Each spirit has a collection of *hues*, lesser forms of the spirit, which may manifest in anyone.

People who wield magic are said to be affected by Ull's Legacy.

# Provincial Information

| Province | Capital City | Lord of Oedran |
| --- | --- | --- |
| ANAPARA | OEDRAN | PARA |
| AREAL | AMPHI | RALE |
| BAYAN | GARTH | RATHGAR |
| DENSHIRE | CEARDEN | CEARIS |
| GERYMOR | RY | RYSON |
| LOW PLAINS | EYLLYN | IRIS |
| LUFIAN | LUFIA | LUX |
| MACIAN ISLES | MACIA | MACARIA |
| PALE LANDS | MEITH | LANDIS |
| SERPENT ISLE | ANGUIN | ANGUIS |
| TERASIA | TERA | TERAN |
| TRADERE | BYFA | FAIRSON |

| Province | King's Representative | Chief Judge |
| --- | --- | --- |
| ANAPARA | DOMINI OF PARAS | CHIEF JUDGE (PARAS) |
| AREAL | GOVERNOR | KENNER |
| BAYAN | EXARCH | ESCHERVIN |
| DENSHIRE | VISIR | HAKIM |
| GERYMOR | DEY | BORSHOLDER |
| LOW PLAINS | TUCHLIN | DOMESMAN |
| LUFIAN | SAGAMORE | DEEMSTER |
| MACIAN ISLES | FENCIBLE | DOMARE |
| PALE LANDS | JARL | LAGHMAN |
| SERPENT ISLE | PASHA | TUOMARI |
| TERASIA | MARGRAVE | TERAZI |
| TRADERE | SATRAP | ARCHON |

| Province | Symbol | Colour |
| --- | --- | --- |
| ANAPARA | THREE CROSSED ARROWS | PURPLE |
| AREAL | A KEY | SILVER |
| BAYAN | A BIRD IN FLIGHT | ORANGE |
| DENSHIRE | A TWELVE-POINT MYSTIC ROSE | BROWN |
| GERYMOR | A SET OF SCALES | WHITE |
| LOW PLAINS | AN EYE | GREEN |
| LUFIAN | A FLOWER AND SNOWFLAKE | BLUE |
| MACIAN ISLES | A TRISKELE OF THREE SPIRALS | RED |
| PALE LANDS | A VIAL | PINK |
| SERPENT ISLE | A CURLED SNAKE | YELLOW |
| TERASIA | A BEAR'S PAW PRINT | BLACK |
| TRADERE | AN HOURGLASS | TURQUOISE |

# Notes on Time

<table>
<tr><td rowspan="7">WEEKDAYS</td><td>ALUNADAI</td><td rowspan="7">FESTIVALS</td><td rowspan="2">MUNEWID</td><td>FIRST DAY OF SUMMER</td></tr>
<tr><td>CISADAI</td><td>FIRST DAY OF THE YEAR</td></tr>
<tr><td>TRETALDAI</td><td>MUNPYRAM</td><td>FIRST DAY OF AUTUMN</td></tr>
<tr><td>IMPERADAI</td><td>MUNDIMRI</td><td>FIRST DAY OF WINTER</td></tr>
<tr><td>PENTADAI</td><td>MUNLUMEN</td><td>FIRST DAY OF SPRING</td></tr>
<tr><td>HEXADAI</td><td colspan="2" rowspan="2">These festivals are known as Alcis Days and are marked by both moons being full</td></tr>
<tr><td>SEPTADAI</td></tr>
</table>

## ON TIME

| | | |
|---|---|---|
| 1 MINUTE | = | 60 SECONDS |
| 1 HOUR | = | 72 MINUTES (12 X 6 MINUTES) |
| 1 DAY | = | 24 HOURS |
| 1 WEEK | = | 7 DAYS |
| COURT CYCLE | = | 12 DAYS |
| 1 FORTNIGHT | = | 2 WEEKS |

| Season | Aluna-month | Week | Cisluna-month | Season | Aluna-month | Week | Cisluna-month |
|---|---|---|---|---|---|---|---|
| SUMMER | CEARAL | 1 | CEARCIS | WINTER | RALAL | 25 | RALIS |
| | | 2 | | | | 26 | |
| | | 3 | | | | 27 | |
| | TRADAL | 4 | MIDDIS | | ANAPAL | 28 | NORIS |
| | | 5 | | | | 29 | |
| | | 6 | | | | 30 | |
| | | 7 | TRADIS | | | 31 | ANAPCIS |
| | | 8 | | | | 32 | |
| | LOWAL | 9 | LOWIS | | BAYAL | 33 | BAYIS |
| | | 10 | | | | 34 | |
| | | 11 | | | | 35 | |
| | | 12 | | | | 36 | |
| AUTUMN | MACIAL | 13 | MACIS | SPRING | TERAL | 37 | TERIS |
| | | 14 | | | | 38 | |
| | | 15 | | | | 39 | |
| | MEITHAL | 16 | EASIS | | GERYAL | 40 | SOUIS |
| | | 17 | | | | 41 | |
| | | 18 | | | | 42 | |
| | | 19 | MEITHIS | | | 43 | GERYIS |
| | | 20 | | | | 44 | |
| | SERAL | 21 | SERIS | | LUFIAL | 45 | LUFIS |
| | | 22 | | | | 46 | |
| | | 23 | | | | 47 | |
| | | 24 | | | | 48 | |

# POSTSCRIPT

# To you, my reader…

Thank you.

I hope you enjoyed *Treason*, the first book in the *Treason and Truth* series.

Please consider leaving an honest review of this book wherever you feel most comfortable. Reviews really help readers find their next book and help authors find their next reader.

# Acknowledgements

Authors rarely get to publication without help and support. They sit and write in snatched hours or minutes. Sometimes stories flow unceasingly from their fingers, clamouring to be heard amongst the din of everyday life. When the last scratch of the pen and click of the keyboard is done, then comes the editing, the interior design, the cover…

My journey has not been solo. From my friends and family who have read, re-read and given me honest feedback to you, the reader that got this far, I say thank you.

This book is dedicated to Chris. From first giving me a love of reading to a belief in myself, this series, as much as this book, is dedicated to her. Having read more versions than we can recall, from book 1 to book 12, and a few between, her support, patience and honesty has been a cornerstone of my life and journey.

# Explore Erinna

Please visit https://erinna.co.uk for more about the Erinnan Legacy or sign up to The Court Newsletter